P9-BJN-604

NO LONGER PROPERTY OF
SEATTLE PUBLIC LIBRARY

PRAISE FOR YASMIN ANGOE

Her Name Is Knight

An Amazon Best Book of the Month: Mystery, Thriller & Suspense

"This stunning debut . . . deftly balances action, interpersonal relationships, issues of trauma, and profound human questions in an unforgettable novel."

—*Library Journal* (starred review)

"A parable of reclaiming personal and tribal identity by seizing power at all costs."

—*Kirkus Reviews*

"Angoe expertly builds tension by shifting between her lead's past and present lives. Thriller fans will cheer Aninyeh every step of the way."

—*Publishers Weekly*

"An action-packed thriller you can lose yourself in."

—*PopSugar*

"Memorable characters, drama, heart-pounding danger . . . this suspenseful novel has it all."

—*Woman's World*

"A crackerjack story with truly memorable characters. I can't wait to see what Yasmin Angoe comes up with next."

—David Baldacci, #1 *New York Times* bestselling author

"Yasmin Angoe's debut novel, *Her Name Is Knight*, is an amazing action-packed international thriller full of suspense, danger, and even romance. It's like a *John Wick* prequel except John is a beautiful African woman with a particular set of skills."

—S. A. Cosby, award-winning author of *Blacktop Wasteland*

"It's hard to believe that *Her Name Is Knight* is Yasmin Angoe's debut novel. This dual timeline story about a highly trained Miami-based assassin who learns to reclaim her power after having her entire life ripped from her as a teenager in Ghana is equal parts love story, social commentary, and action thriller. Nena Knight will stay with you long after you've read the last word, and this is a must-read for fans of Lee Child and S. A. Cosby. I found myself crying in one chapter and cheering in the next. I couldn't put it down!"

—Kellye Garrett, Anthony, Agatha, and Lefty Award–winning author

"This was a book I couldn't put down. Yasmin Angoe does a brilliant job of inviting you into a world of espionage and revenge while giving her characters depth and backstory that pull the reader in even more. This story has depth, excitement, and heartbreaking loss all intertwined into an awesome debut. The spy-thriller genre has a new name to look out for!"

—Matthew Farrell, bestselling author of *Don't Ever Forget*

"This brave and profoundly gorgeous thriller takes readers to places they've never been, to challenges they've never faced, and to judgments that leave the strongest in tears. *Her Name Is Knight* is a stunning and important debut, and Yasmin Angoe is a fantastic new talent."

—Hank Phillippi Ryan, *USA Today* bestselling author of
Her Perfect Life

"*Her Name Is Knight* is a roundhouse kick of a novel—intense, evocative, and loaded with character and international intrigue. Nena Knight is a protagonist for the ages and one readers will not soon forget. *Her Name Is Knight* isn't just thrills and action, either—the book lingers with you long after you've finished. More, please."

—Alex Segura, acclaimed author of *Star Wars Poe Dameron: Free Fall*, *Secret Identity*, and *Blackout*

THEY
COME
AT
KNIGHT

OTHER TITLES BY YASMIN ANGOE

Her Name Is Knight

THEY COME AT KNIGHT

YASMIN ANGOE

This is a work of fiction. Names, characters, organizations, places, events, and incidents are either products of the author's imagination or are used fictitiously. Any resemblance to actual persons, living or dead, or actual events is purely coincidental.

Text copyright © 2022 by Yasmin Angoe
All rights reserved.

No part of this book may be reproduced, or stored in a retrieval system, or transmitted in any form or by any means, electronic, mechanical, photocopying, recording, or otherwise, without express written permission of the publisher.

Published by Thomas & Mercer, Seattle

www.apub.com

Amazon, the Amazon logo, and Thomas & Mercer are trademarks of Amazon.com, Inc., or its affiliates.

ISBN-13: 9781662500077 (hardcover)
ISBN-10: 1662500076 (hardcover)

ISBN-13: 9781662500060 (paperback)
ISBN-10: 1662500068 (paperback)

Front cover design by Anna Laytham
Back cover design by Ray Lundgren
Cover images: © Regina Wamba of MaeIDesign.com; © Txema Yeste/Trunk Archive

Printed in the United States of America

First edition

To my mom, Evelyn, who walked so that I could run

Heroes are made in the hour of defeat. Success is, therefore, well described as a series of glorious defeats.
—Mahatma Gandhi

1

Right off Lowcountry Highway in South Carolina sat an antiquated white home nestled behind the expanse of lush, green lawn and white picket fences. The all-white house reminded Nena of a smaller plantation home. It was more modern, but here anything even slightly resembling those picturesque, ancient homes still elicited uneasy feelings for what they'd once represented.

Nena looked around at the pockets of pond water blanketed with green algae and the aged, gnarled-limb oak trees draped in low-hanging gray Spanish moss. It all made her imagine how things used to be here. She wondered what stories these centuries-old trees had to tell. What secrets hung on those twisted limbs that stretched out like long brown talons. Stretched out to here.

Nena chuckled. Shaking her head for letting her mind wander there, to places that scared even her, the supposedly unflappable assassin. The wudini, here on a mission, sitting quietly on the white wooden porch swing, her arms resting on her knees as one hand held a .45 and the other settled the gun's silencer atop the barrel, her fingers deftly attaching the two pieces together.

There were no neighbors nearby. Probably didn't need the silencer. Still, she remained cautious on the off chance that someone was in the woods or elsewhere on the grounds. Regardless of its history, Nena could understand the allure of this place. It *was* beautiful. This whole area was beautiful; she wouldn't deny it that. Its lushness reminded her of home.

Home home. On Aburi Mountain. One of the two places she'd felt at peace. She closed her eyes and listened, the inability to see sharpening her hearing. There was nothing but birds and nature and stillness. Too still. Solitude was what she'd thought she enjoyed the most, but she'd come to realize she only enjoyed it amid commotion and life, like her home in Miami brought. Even on Aburi, in the home cut into the mountain, there'd been sounds of Africa. Here, there was nothing. She didn't care for that very much.

It was time. And once again, Nena felt the barely perceptible change come over her as her wandering thoughts focused, her emotions melted away into the stifling heat, and she slipped into her other half.

Echo stood, letting the swing bump against the backs of her knees and still. She walked over to the front door, put her gloved hand on the ornate handle, and pushed the door in. She appreciated that the fall weather was cooler, not so "famously hot" like South Carolina was known for. Whoever had coined that had never been to Ghana in the summer, obviously.

Air-conditioning greeted her, even if it was November. The house was stuffy and in desperate need of airing out. If the wife and kids had been home, perhaps it would have happened. But they weren't, having left the man of the house home alone while they went away on holiday.

His muffled cries restarted the moment Echo stepped inside. She knew the house, having walked its floors from top to bottom while she'd waited for its owner to return, hand in hand with a redhead who looked nothing like the wife in the family photos decorating the walls. They'd been pawing each other, barely through the door before he'd been on the woman, groping her as if he were some adolescent experiencing his first time.

Echo had glanced again at the staggered portraits of his three children, who he'd dishonored by bringing the woman here. She'd tutted softly, preferring not to watch but watching anyway as they'd made their way to the parlor and to the couch, where he'd plopped himself down. The woman had quickly gone to work on his belt, then his pants, lowering them to his knees. As she had, Echo had pulled out the dark dish towel she'd borrowed from the kitchen. *Borrowed* was the wrong word. She wasn't going to return it.

She'd taken out her small bottle of chloroform, and while sitting on the stairs, allowing the two to get really into each other, she'd doused the towel with the liquid, holding her breath so the smell wouldn't mess with her sensibilities. Then she'd followed the sounds of pleasure until she'd been standing behind the woman, who'd been on her knees, face in his ample lap, servicing his less-than-ample groin. That last bit was a guess. Echo couldn't confirm this because she couldn't see it, thank God.

The man's head had been lolled back against the couch, eyes closed, mouth open and moaning. His hand had been on the woman's head, helping her along, though she hadn't seemed to need any assistance. She was a pro. Like Echo. Doing what she needed to do. Like Echo, and Echo had no qualms with the woman's hustle.

Echo had bent down, grabbed the woman by her forehead, and yanked her back hard. The man had yelped, a high-pitched thing, likely from the hard pull. And maybe from some teeth too. His eyes had flown open, but Echo had already had the woman in her arms, towel clamped firmly over her nose and mouth.

The moment she'd begun to struggle less, Echo had reached to pull her gun from the back of her belt and swung it around, aiming at the man, who'd scrambled up in his seat as if a mouse were at his feet. He hadn't put himself back in his pants. What was it Elin had said once? *It's not the size that counts. It's the motion of the ocean.* Whatever motion this man had must have been earthshaking.

The woman was deadweight. Echo had dropped her where they'd stood.

"Please," he'd begged, his Algerian accent thickening as his fear and panic had increased. "Please, whatever you want. I will give."

But he hadn't given. "Anything but that," he'd said when she'd told him what she wanted. "Please. He will kill me."

Torture was not Echo's preference—she'd been there, experienced that, and had no appetite for it. But a dispatch was a dispatch. She'd cut him, just a little bit. Money people had no tolerance for pain. And after all, he was the one who'd chosen to make this hard by bargaining.

He had passed out. His behavior was a bit overdramatic and the reason why she was still there, walking back in from the porch after giving him time to recover, think about his predicament, and ready himself to provide answers when she asked for the final time. Because there would only be a final time.

Now she stood in front of him again, bending until she was eye level. He was crying, his words muffled through the tape and a pair of his wife's panties, which she'd stuffed in his mouth for a touch of poetic justice.

She slapped him. The sound ricocheted throughout the high-ceilinged room, stunning him into silence. She needed him focused long enough to give her the information she required. She peeled the tape partially from his mouth.

"Was it my wife? Did she send you?" he asked through puffs of vile breath.

Echo considered letting that be the thought he died with, that his wife, knowing of his treachery, had gotten the final word. But it would be a lie. And Echo was not a liar when she didn't have to be.

"Last time," she said. "The location of General Konate's outpost."

"Allow me to live?"

Bargaining as if he had anything worth trading. Information, she supposed, but Nena would extract that from him regardless.

4

His eyes were those of a man with no more chances. In the end, they all looked the same right before. "Let me live if I tell? I have a wife. Children."

She glanced down at the woman lying prone on the floor, hopefully dreaming the dreams of queens. Then she looked at him. "Seriously?"

Now he was blubbering, mouth moving like a puffer fish. "Please!" He let loose a string of words in his native language, and Nena briefly considered learning Arabic. Could be useful.

"No."

"Then why should I tell if you're going to kill me anyway?" Panic flooded his eyes like a feral animal.

"Because if you don't, you will suffer immensely. Your choice. Go easy." She stared at him dispassionately. "Or go hard."

He chose to go easy.

He confessed as if he and Echo were on either side of a confessional, disclosing the whereabouts of the employer for whom he cooked the books, a maniac who called himself military and claimed he worked for "the people." However, General Konate was the epitome of the corruption and rot the Tribe worked tirelessly to fight against. He was nothing more than a gluttonous pig, stealing from villages of whatever African country he selected to defile. He looted and pillaged, lining his pockets and terrorizing all who fell into his path.

Echo put the muzzle of her .45 ACP flush against his temple and ended the philandering accountant's life.

Her next work was to wrap him, head in the plastic sheeting he hadn't even noticed was there when his girlfriend had begun pleasuring him. She secured him with the same industrial tape that had covered his mouth. The Cleaners would take care of his remains and her kill site.

Echo took a final look at the red-haired woman's still form. She would wake, freak out, and run far away if she was smart. Echo guessed she would.

"Dispatch was successful?" The question popped into her ear as if she'd thought it.

"Yes," she told the Network operative, always there, always reliable, always watching.

"The Cleaners are en route."

Echo stepped around the woman, sweeping the house and porch for any remaining trace of her she might have forgotten. She locked the front door of the house, then started around back to where her car was parked, listening to the sounds of wind rustling through the tree branches along the way.

2

"Bloody hell, I'm uncomfortable," Elin grumbled as she squirmed in the passenger seat of Nena's Jeep to find a better position. "I hate being pregnant. It's like my body isn't mine." She tugged at the seat belt.

"Apparently, you're growing a baby," Nena answered, used to Elin's complaints. Pregnancy had not been in Elin's five-year plan.

"I'm sorry, Nena," Elin sighed, now pulling the material of her dress away from her stomach. "I get so salty that I forget my manners."

"That's a first for you?" Nena returned a tiny smile in a lame attempt to keep her sister happy and not thinking about the past.

Elin hit her lightly on the shoulder, ignoring Nena's protest that she was driving. "You got a little bit of cheek in you today, sis. I'm rather proud. Think I might be rubbing off on you, yeah?"

"Not in the least."

Nena focused on the road as Elin composed herself.

"How'd it go last week?" Elin asked. "Your first solo in a while."

Elin wasn't asking if Nena had gotten the job done. Network was already working the intel from the accountant and planning to dispatch General Konate in the coming month. Elin knew all about that already.

"If you mean was I rusty, the answer is no."

Elin rolled her eyes. "I'm asking how you feel after it. After all of it."

How did she feel . . . Nena had spent the three months since returning to Miami from Ghana—five months since she'd gone against Council decree and dispatched one of their own—trying not only to adjust to the revelations about her brother but to ensure her actions didn't blow back on the people she cared for and the Tribe to which she was beholden. She was the reason Elin was going through this pregnancy alone; for the friction between her parents and the Tribal Council. She was the reason Cort Baxter wanted her nowhere near him and his daughter.

"About business," Nena said, changing the subject.

Elin threw her arm across her eyes in protest. "I'm not in the mood."

"But there are things to be done, and you don't want Dad on your case. Or Mum."

"Nena, I just want to chill and not think about bloody work for a change. I just want you and me to drive around town for lunch and be regular bloody people for a change. Isn't it possible? To be regular?"

Unlike Nena, Elin had never been given the choice to grow in this life. To be the child of Noble and Delphine Knight.

Nena felt horrible. It could be possible, but they were Knights. They had the Tribe. There was always something.

"But you know our work is never done."

"Right, not until we're toes up in the ground. That is our lot in life." Elin gazed out her window, chin in hand.

That wasn't what they should be discussing on the way to Elin's ob-gyn visit. Nena chanced another look at her sister. She looked worn. Nena noticed the bags under her eyes and remembered that the baby was active at night. As Elin had been, which Mum never failed to remind them whenever Elin complained.

It was the first time Elin had ever mentioned tiring of her duties for the Tribe. Maybe it was the pregnancy talking. Nena's stomach tightened. Maybe it was grief over Ofori—Oliver, as Elin had known him. She'd always assumed Elin was satisfied with her responsibilities. Had always thought Elin wanted the responsibility given to her as the child of Noble and Delphine Knight. But unlike Nena, Elin hadn't chosen this life; she'd been born into it. Nena wasn't sure of anything.

"Do you need a break?" Nena asked.

"I love what we do; don't get me wrong." Elin turned to her. "It's just that now that I'm to be a mother, I'm seeing things through a different set of eyes. I need to think about my work and my son. I'm tired right now, but I'm more resolved than ever to ensure our family remains strong, and the Tribe."

Elin straightened herself, brushing back her new bangs, which dusted her sculpted brows, and asked, "Right, then, what about the business?"

"There are the preparations for the charity dinner and dedication happening in Ghana during the Council meeting in January. Confirming our travel and security. The house is ready and fully staffed. Witt is rechecking the security plan and the assigned guards."

At the mention of the charity dinner, Elin broke into a smile. Discussing the African Tribal Council's acts, like the charity dinner and dedication of the women's and children's medical facility they were building in Ghana, always made the two of them feel it was worth the lengths the Tribe went to for those victories. It was the goal their father had long worked to accomplish: the advancement of all Africans and all people of the diaspora—to make Africa a continent truly for the people, by the people. A One Africa movement. When the Tribe doled out death decrees, they were a necessary punishment to those who sought to undermine the advancement of Africans as a whole. The Tribe spent far more energy giving back to their people, doing charitable acts, and ensuring their people had food, medicine, water, and a good way of living. It made up for the lives Nena took every time she went out on a dispatch.

"Mum has run lead on the planning. I like to attend parties, not plan them," Elin said, "but it's coming along well. Donations are pouring in from our member countries, Dad's been working on his speech, and the groundbreaking dedication at the site will be monumental."

Nena felt her sister's eyes on her as she pulled to a stop at a stoplight.

Elin didn't have to say anything more. *Monumental* was an understatement. Dad's suggestion that they build near the Compound, which had been a living hell for Nena and so many other girls, meant more than Nena could express. She was still processing it all, didn't know what it would feel like to return to one of the places of her nightmares, because when Nena had taken Ofori's ashes to their village, N'nkakuwe, she had not gone *there*. Maybe when they broke ground for the medical center, maybe then Nena would begin to see the change no longer as an end to what she'd once known but as a beginning for so many others.

Nena cleared her throat. "And while there, we'll have our meeting with the Gabonese reps."

Elin groaned. "Don't remind me."

"As a show of good faith. With Paul and Oliver gone, you inherit the role of Council rep for Gabon."

"One other thing to piss the Council members off. They already think I'm compromised, that all I do is give Dad an additional vote. We haven't even voted on anything worthwhile."

"Yes, but you should understand where they are coming from. And that is why you need to meet with them while we're over there and determine who will sit in your seat, so you can serve the Tribe as you've been doing."

Elin dismissed Nena with a wave of one ring-adorned hand while simultaneously rubbing her bulging belly with the other. Elin could bemoan pregnancy all she wanted, but she loved this baby. It was evident in every move she made.

She pointed to a McDonald's coming up on the right.

"Seriously?" Nena said. "You hate fast food. Can it wait until after the appointment? Then we can go to a proper restaurant."

"The baby loves Big Macs, and I'll not deny him."

Elin waited until Nena finished placing the order, plus a Coke for herself, before asking, "Have you heard from Cort?" She added, "Georgia?" As if Nena needed further reference.

Answering was the path of least resistance. "She texts occasionally."

"How long are you going to keep ignoring the kid? Can't be good for her psyche, you know." Elin waved her fingers in the air in a swirly motion whose meaning Nena couldn't decipher. "Kids are a sensitive lot. And teens . . . whew. I couldn't . . ."

Nena couldn't either. Reach out to Georgia, that was. Before learning the true nature of what Nena did for the Tribe, Cort had been attacked and shot. Had lost his best friend, Mack. His daughter had been kidnapped. All by Nena's brother.

Even though Nena had saved Georgia, brought her back with barely a scratch—perhaps some PTSD or some nightmares, nothing Georgia couldn't get over with some good TLC or a therapist—Cort had ended their relationship. The ex–police officer and federal district attorney couldn't ignore the work she did for the African Tribal Council. So Nena had resigned herself to living a life without Georgia and Cort. Just when she'd become comfortable with the idea of having the Baxters in it.

Eyes on the road, Nena said, "You realize the baby will eventually become a teen?"

Elin's middle finger sprang up. Yeah, Elin was back to her usual. "I'll have, like, fourteen years before it happens. That's a load of time for us to prepare."

"Us?"

Elin gave her a pointed look. "What? You think I'm going at this alone? Bloody hell I'm not. The whole family is involved. Dad's changing nappies. The whole bit."

Nena doubled back to her sister's earlier comment. "I should go against her father's wishes?"

"You should let her know you're not mad at her."

"She knows." Right? Georgia was intuitive enough to know none of this was her fault.

"But does she? I know Cort said to give him time, but our family is a lot. What we do, it's a lot, especially for a person who toes the line."

"What are you, Dr. Phil now?"

Elin snorted. "Anyway. Call the damn kid."

Her lecture was forgotten the moment Nena handed her the brown bag of piping-hot food. Elin attacked the fries, breathing out as the hot oil burned her mouth. She moaned in pleasure, then offered Nena a fry.

"I'll pass."

"Your loss." Elin shrugged, pulling the bag back to her body and offering no more.

3

The team moved in a synchronized dance, the six of them, one behind another, automatic rifles drawn and engaged. Nena, team lead, was first through the door. Alpha was next, with Sierra behind Kilo. Then Charlie, with Yankee rounding them out and watching their rear.

Nena's muzzle swept left, right, as she entered the room. Alpha trailed her, following suit, then came around her to take the lead, just as they'd planned. The six moved efficiently and with little said among them except to call out when they came across a target, which they shot, or a friendly, who they'd better not.

Nena's first target popped up to her right, and she fired. Single shot. Her bullet found its mark in the target's chest. The team continued in their lined formation, creeping down the hall awash in natural light that filtered through large factory windows. It was a beautiful day. They snaked past several dark-green-painted doors, all closed. They paired off. Nena and Alpha headed toward the farthest room while the two other pairs took their places at the remaining doors.

Everyone paused, waiting for Nena's signal. She raised a fist, indicating they were go for entry. In sync, each pair burst into the rooms, Nena sweeping their left as Alpha swept right. There was nothing; the room looked empty. But a second later a target popped up against the wall, and Alpha launched two shots, one to the chest, the second a head shot. They moved in farther, and Nena twisted around the open door to check for a target hiding behind it. She hesitated a fraction of a second when she realized there was an innocent being held as a shield in front of the armed target. She recalibrated in that fraction, aiming the muzzle higher, just above the innocent's ear.

There was no time to think. She took the shot, putting a bullet between the target's brows, all the while hoping his finger wouldn't jerk.

"Clear," Alpha said. He was across the room, but the comms made him sound like he was in her head.

"Clear." She was disappointed in her handiwork. Should have aimed for the arm holding the gun. What if the target's trigger finger had flexed and the hostage he was using as cover had become collateral damage? That would be unacceptable.

"How are we in two and three?" she asked, switching her safety on before casting a quick look at Alpha.

There was a beat before the response came through. "All but one was taken out," came Network over the comms.

"Shit," Alpha groused. His blue eyes flashed annoyance. The son of South African parents who'd emigrated to Australia, Alpha was the cockiest of the team, fancying himself the resident *GQ* model as well. Today, he was irritated because one target left meant—

"My bad," Sierra admitted, appearing at the doorway. "I missed one in the closet."

Alpha slid his headset down so it sat on his collarbone. "Now you're dead and our mission failed."

Sierra looked at her feet, biting her bottom lip. Frustration was written across her face, an emotion shared all around. Alpha might be a prick, but he was right. A missed target meant a dead Sierra and a failed mission, even if during practice.

"Come on now, Sierra." Alpha continued to chastise her in the condescending tone they heard often. "We've run this same play ten times already. If you don't nail it, we don't leave General Konate's outpost alive."

The rest of the team congregated just outside the door, and while they kept no secrets from one another when it came to team matters, Nena wasn't about to let anyone be embarrassed in front of others, either, especially not by her second.

"Alpha." Her tone was curt. Her silencing look finished it.

Granted, he was right. Sierra kept missing her marks. She either hadn't memorized the building's layout or was too distracted by something. Or maybe she didn't want to do it. Maybe she was burned out. It happened to the best of them. It happened to them young, and Nena's team was one of the best Dispatch teams in the Tribe. They had always been called on for the heavy jobs, but since the Paul mess earlier, the team had been relegated to second string, its members lent out to other teams for extra support or for solo jobs. Nena had let them go too long without coming back as a unit, training and working together, and today's practice was the result of her lapse.

It was Nena who was the failure. Off her game and distracted with life. Cort's rejection had devastated her more than she'd thought possible. Hurt her in ways she hadn't imagined, a deep, cavernous, consuming thing. Nena had thought she'd suffered the worst when she was young. She had. But she hadn't been prepared for the whiplash, the quickness with which she'd obtained and lost her chance at something real with Cort. Returning her brother's ashes to Aburi Mountain had helped her begin to sort it out. She'd come back to Miami ready to dive full-on into the daily dealings of the Tribe, take on a more active role as a Knight daughter, be a better team lead for now, and eventually become the lead for Dispatch.

Presently, Nena had been slipping her duties, not following up with her team and ensuring they were physically—and, most of all, mentally—prepared to take on a dispatch as big as General Konate. Nena needed to get her head back in the game, do better. It was time to work.

"Enough," she said.

Alpha threw his hands up, done with the whole team.

"He's right, though," Sierra mumbled, suddenly finding the floor at her feet interesting.

"Even so." Nena looked pointedly at her second-in-command, who wasn't acting like one at the moment, until he finally broke eye contact. She returned to Sierra. "There is a time and place to discuss failings and successes. You took down the target in the main room, the one who looked like a friendly, right before we entered the hall. Alpha missed it."

"Hey, now didn't you just say it wasn't the time to talk about failings?" Alpha whined.

He was right, but it felt good to stick it to him just the same. Nena instantly regretted the nasty thought. She shouldn't find pleasure in making her subordinates feel less-than, even if they were being jerks.

"Besides, I didn't miss it. I left it for Yankee. You know he never gets any play being last one in."

"Fuck you, Al," Yankee said from the hall. "I get in plenty because there is always fire on our tail. I lay them out, pretty boy."

"Don't hate my prettiness," Alpha joked. "You can't help that your talent and your name both come last."

They bickered back and forth until Nena told them to stop. What the team didn't need was dissension. Not when they were to travel to Kenya the following week for their mission.

"Alpha's dick measuring again," Kilo said, laughing. "It's always little, those Napoleon type of dudes."

Alpha shoved past the group clustered at the door, grumbling about amateurs and wasting his time and not having to take any more of this shit. He chest bumped Kilo on his way through the doorway, and Kilo responded with a shove. When Alpha made a move like he was about to strike back, Nena got in between them, placing a calming hand on Kilo and telling Alpha to walk it off. She made a mental note to speak with him later. This behavior was unacceptable.

This was her fault too. She needed to keep a pulse on Alpha. But she knew what he was upset about. They all did. He wanted to lead his own team, and she had yet to recommend him. He wasn't ready, and the behavior he currently displayed was testament to the fact. She followed him, retracing their steps back down the hall and through the outer room, which had been designed to look like the general's Kenyan outpost.

"Can you reset the room, please?" Nena said to Network, as she and her team spilled outside into the sweltering Miami heat. "Take a minute," she told the team. Alpha was in the distance, having a smoke break. Yeah, they'd have to talk. But first things first. "Sierra, have a chat?"

Nena didn't get out the first line before Sierra was apologizing for her screwup. Nena wondered what Witt would do if he were here right now. She didn't remember her first team bickering like this when he'd been training them. And Goon, who was the cockiest of them all back then, had never been maliciously so, not like Alpha. But again, Goon hadn't had Nena standing in his way, like Alpha did. Maybe Nena was being too harsh and holding Alpha to an unfair standard. Maybe she should just tell Witt to give him a team.

"You're going to kick me off the team, aren't you?" Sierra's eyes grew round. "Retire me?" It came out a whisper, the cursed word that it was. Retirement, in the Tribe, was permanent.

They weren't even close to that outcome—but Nena was confounded at how a person who'd been so spot on during big-ticket missions in the past could be falling to pieces like this. She was beginning to second-guess her team member, and that didn't bode well for either of them. Maybe she *should* bench Sierra. Make her invest in some self-care because Sierra's head wasn't fully in the game. If they were to dispatch the general successfully, every member of the team would have to be on point.

"Enough, Sierra." Nena squinted against the sunlight bleaching the anonymous factory, located at one of Miami's many shipyards. She looked at the rest of the team: Alpha and Kilo were at it again. Charlie was trying to referee. Yankee was checking his gear and smartly ignoring them all. As the newest member of the group, he had no skin in the game.

"What is the problem?" Nena asked calmly.

Sierra dropped her eyes. "Distracted, I guess. I don't know . . ."

"We can't be distracted when we're working."

"I know, E."

"It's life or death for us if we are. What we do affects the whole organization."

Sierra agreed.

"But I get it," Nena sighed. "We all have our moments. Even me."

Sierra snorted, her look dubious.

Nena eased her gun strap over her shoulder. "It's true. But then I look at the rest of our team, and I see why I must have my moment and then get back to focusing. Do you know why that is?"

Sierra followed Nena's gaze, her lips twisting in an unimpressed position. "Because we're women and they're guys."

"And we're in a man's world. In a man's business, where guys like Alpha want to be the alpha in every way possible. We have to work ten times as hard and be twenty times as smart to prove we belong here, that we've always belonged."

"That's really screwed up," Sierra said. "Unfair."

"Agreed. But that's the way of the world, yeah? Especially so because we're women of color. A triple threat." Nena nudged her subordinate with an elbow. "Turns out you and I are triple threats."

The last part elicited a snort. "Thanks, E," Sierra said, her Jamaican accent soft and introspective. "Was a way better pep talk than what Witt probably would have given me."

Nena raised an eyebrow.

Sierra put on a stern face and lowered her voice several octaves. She slipped into Witt's Rwandan accent with ease. "Suck it up and shoot your damn gun."

Nena gave a nod, ushering Sierra back to the group as Network informed her the reset was complete. Sounded about right.

"All right, y'all. If we can run through this without any mistakes or any arguments"—her silent message to Kilo and Alpha was clear—"then we can call it for the day."

"And go bowling?" Sierra asked.

Nena paused on that one. She didn't bowl. And their team didn't hang out.

"Team building," Sierra added, grinning now, knowing there was no way Nena could say no to building a team even though Nena didn't know how bowling could build anything.

Alpha rolled his eyes. Kilo and Yankee shrugged. Charlie announced he held the title for best bowler in his village back in Congo.

"We didn't have an alley either. We bowled down dirt ruts we'd dig out in between chores. I'm a warrior!" he boasted, beating a closed fist to his chest as if channeling Tarzan.

"Get in line, then, warrior," Alpha returned, a trace of humor lacing his words. He sauntered into position, oozing his usual swagger. "Sooner we finish this, the sooner I can take that title too."

Turned out Alpha's bowling title would need a rain check. Because when the team had completed all their run-throughs, a text was waiting on Nena's cell. It was from Georgia Baxter, and it made Nena drop everything and run.

4

The only words in Georgia's text were that she was back at Jake's, and they were all it took to make Nena drive like she was on the Grand Prix back to the restaurant where the story had started for her and the Baxters. Georgia had been under strict instructions not to return there alone, not after what had nearly happened to her there. Yet according to her text, that was where she was, and Nena was livid.

The kid's only save was that it wasn't late enough in the day to be dangerous, Nena thought, as she parallel parked her Audi across from the red-and-white-themed burger joint. She was out of the car, pressing the button on the key fob to lock it as she hurried across the street.

Her pace slowed when she noticed a familiar black Escalade parked up the street, toward the bus stop. She approached, circling the back to glimpse the license plate. Its presence here now wasn't a coincidence.

The smells of burgers on the grill and french fries in the fryer assaulted her, and her stomach responded in kind. She gave a quick wave to Jake's staff, then directed her attention to her usual booth in the back corner against the wall. Georgia was waving with unrestrained excitement.

She wasn't alone. At the end of the booth, with a chair pulled up, was the owner of the Escalade. Nena frowned at her so-called friend. Keigel knew better, knew Georgia shouldn't be there.

"Is everything okay?" Nena asked, looking back and forth between them. "What are you doing here?"

"Having lunch," Georgia replied, slipping out of her seat. She sneaked in a quick hug before Nena had a chance to react, then slid into the bench on the other side.

"Lunch," Nena repeated incredulously. "And you?" She turned. Keigel was in a border dispute with the rival gang who'd attacked Georgia before Nena had stepped in that day. He knew how dangerous it was bringing her back here.

Keigel held his hands up as if saying, *Wasn't my idea*. "I'm just the Uber."

If looks could kill, he would be more than six feet under.

"Real talk," he added. "Lil homey called me and threatened to take the city bus if I didn't bring her here. Threatened. I think you're a bad influence."

Nena was dumbstruck.

"And we all know what happens when I take the bus to parts unknown, don't we?" Georgia grinned unabashedly.

Elin would say the girl was a cheeky, blackmailing little thing, and currently, Nena could hardly disagree. Keigel wasn't being helpful, either, as he plucked a laminated diner menu from the table and began reading through the options, as if he didn't already know what he wanted. Between this place and their favorite wing spot, he and Nena were near-weekly regulars.

Still trying to figure out what to do—text Cort, pretend she wasn't happy about seeing the girl?—Nena took her seat on the bench Georgia had vacated, knowing Nena preferred her back to the wall because even when she wasn't on the clock, Nena Knight was always on duty.

"Georgia, you know what your father said. Where does he think you are right now? Because I remember you promising you wouldn't go off without his knowledge."

"I know. I'll tell him when I get home, but right now he thinks I'm with my best friend. You remember Kit from school?"

"Yes, the nice one who hung around that obnoxious racist girl. The blonde one. She's not expelled or flunked out yet?"

"We should be so lucky," Georgia deadpanned.

Keigel shook his head. "Y'all are hard core. And here I thought folks I deal with are cold blooded."

Against her better judgment, Nena ordered her usual when the server appeared, pad and pen in hand with an expectant look. No use in wasting a Jake's visit. But they needed to be quick because Keigel had to take Georgia home. Nena surely wasn't going to do it. When the server left, she launched in.

"You can't continue to lie to your dad, Georgia. You promised, and we don't break promises, even if we don't like the response."

"And I will be at Kit's. After here. Keig will drop me off." She grinned at him, and like an indulgent doofus, he grinned back.

Nena felt her face contort into a look of disbelief. Where and when had the two of them become so friendly?

As if reading her mind, Keigel offered, "When you weren't answering the kid's texts, she started texting me. We exchanged numbers back at the mansion when you and I rescued her from that crazy motherfucker."

"*I'm* the bad influence?" Nena pointed to herself.

Keigel nodded, mouthing, *Yes*. He looked on innocently.

"At least Keig answered me, since you didn't care enough to."

Georgia's tone was laced with such accusation and hurt it ripped through Nena like a tomahawk. All she could do was nod and look away, accepting the admonishment. She deserved that one.

Keigel's head was moving from one side to the other, clearly not liking where the conversation was going. "Hey, wait, now, G, hold up—"

Nena's mouth had dried like the Sahara. "You know I care."

"Some way to show it. People don't ghost people they care about."

Does your father know that? was what Nena bitterly wanted to shoot back. But his behavior was not Georgia's fault, and a kid shouldn't have to pay for what the adults in her life did.

When Nena had regained control of her words, she said, "You're absolutely right."

"Anyway," Georgia said, "I'm not lying entirely. And maybe if you answered my texts, then I wouldn't have had to resort to lies."

Nena focused her attention on Keigel, who was checking his phone and subtly monitoring the other diners. "You know Cort doesn't want her around me. We discussed this."

Keigel could not care less. "Well, sometimes dudes can have fucked-up ways of thinking and don't know what's best for them. If that motherf—look, G, he's your dad. No disrespect."

"None taken." Georgia, unbothered, sipped her soda.

They gave each other an intricate hand dap, which made Nena suspicious. When had these two found the time to create it?

"If *dude* don't know you're the best thing smoking," Keigel said to Nena, "then it's his loss. But that don't mean it's gotta be G's loss, feel me? Adults make dumbass decisions on the regular."

Keigel told no lies there.

Georgia continued, "I had to see that you were okay. Make sure you hadn't gone back to that place where you close up."

"And be all fucked up and unhappy and shit," Keigel added helpfully, though it wasn't. Nena's twisted lips were proof of that.

"I'm . . ." She swallowed. "I'm touched." She meant it. "Thank you for trying to take care of me when I haven't been there for you like I should have. I'm sorry."

Their food arrived, thankfully, and the plunging tone of their conversation began to reverse itself.

"Well," Georgia said politely, positioning her basket in the way that she liked. Burger on the right, opposite Nena. "You know . . . just don't do it again."

Keigel chuckled as he took a huge bite of his double. "The kid's all right."

Nena agreed, plucking a deep-fried onion ring from her basket and dipping it in Jake's zesty sauce. "Hmm. See how all right she is when she comes clean to her father." She pointed a finger across the table. "Which you will do, Georgia. No more lying or sneaking around. Keigel, you take her straight to her friend's. Don't let her convince you to take her anywhere else."

They happily agreed, and Nena allowed herself to relax a fraction more.

"You'll talk to my dad?" Georgia asked, becoming somber. "Try to work things out?"

She hated the hopeful look in Georgia's eye, the plea in her voice. Nena wished she could make every one of Georgia's dreams come true. But that was not the way the world worked.

"Your dad made his decision," Nena began, because she would never lie to Georgia, not even if it was something the girl wanted to hear. "If anyone makes a move toward working things out, it will have to be him first."

Nena wondered if the words were an attempt to convince herself too. So far, she'd refrained from pulling up Cort's name in her contacts to view the image saved there. From texting him or from driving through his quiet neighborhood to see if his prized SS was in the driveway. She wouldn't do that. That would be creepy. Though she'd be lying if she said she hadn't considered it. Still, she couldn't stop punishing herself for allowing the Baxters to become involved in her life, for bringing them into a world they had no place in. Though Georgia would dispute that. The fifteen-year-old loved everything about Nena's world, romanticized it, placed Nena on a pedestal. Nena liked having someone see nothing ugly about who she was or what she did. Georgia had witnessed both Echo and Nena and accepted them both. Nena had thought Cort would be the same way.

She'd been wrong about that.

5

The upcoming dispatch loomed over Nena, and she shoved aside worries about Georgia in order to keep it front and center in her mind. There was new intel to go over and old intel to revisit. There were endless trainings and refreshers she could be conducting—in hand-to-hand combat; in weapons of circumstance; in sniper targeting; in her fighting model of choice, Krav Maga; in various methods to dispatch quietly with poisons or excess medicines; or in mere strengthening and endurance.

Her first mission was to make it through bowling night.

She spent the day considering multiple ways to get out of the rain check she'd promised her team. There were no texts from Georgia asking to meet up again or family emergencies that would save her from this pastime to which she preferred not to give any time. She considered flat out saying no, but she'd already committed. She couldn't back out now.

There were too many colorful, flashing lights, too many people clashing in a cacophony of cheers, arguments, and raucous breakouts of applause. Nena would probably hear the pings of arcade games from eons ago—the *Pac-Man*s and *Donkey Kong*s—when she went to sleep. The clanging of balls traveling through mechanisms of the return was continuous rumbles of thunder, and the crash of weighted balls on the greased wooden floors set Nena's teeth on edge. The environment was unsettling. She found it distracting even though she'd trained over half her life to work in distracting environments. This noise was nothing like the noise of a mission, of a firefight, which Nena would gladly take over this.

She wouldn't talk about the rented shoes. Shoes that had housed a multitude of sweaty size seven and a half feet. Had she thought of it, she'd have purchased her own ball because the only one available in her size was bright, sparkly, and hot pink.

Her upper lip twisted as she stared at it. So very pink.

———

Nena launched her sparkly hot-pink ball down the oiled lane. She watched it go while she tried to push away thoughts of fungal spores winding their way through her porous socks to turn her feet green, make them fall off. The pink ball reached the end of the alley, knocking down ten pins out of twelve. An improvement from when the night had begun.

She sauntered back to the C-shaped bench where Yankee, Charlie, and Kilo cheered her on. She shrugged, but she kind of felt proud that she'd hit so many of the stupid pins.

"You have one more throw," Yankee said, stopping her dead in her tracks. Nena looked back down the lane at the two pins staring at her and wondered how she was supposed to knock them down without going into the gutter.

She picked up the sparkly pink ball, thinking long and hard about how she was going to make this work.

"I literally feel the grays growing on my head waiting for you to throw the damn ball." Kilo laughed from the benches.

Nena approached the stop line of her lane, letting Kilo's jabs roll off her back like shower water.

"Where'd Alpha and Sierra go?" Yankee asked.

Kilo said, "Who the fuck cares? I go next, and I'm winning this shit. Only title Alpha's winning is Asshole of the Year."

Nena tuned them out. Heard the balls dropping and gliding down the lanes. Heard the chorus of cheers and jeers. The applause and the snide comments about cheating or who was winning. She heard the group two lanes down erupt in laughter and clink bottles of beer. She planted her feet. Lifted the ball in her right hand. Positioned the ugly thing in front of her face as she focused on the two pins that were too far to the right.

As if on a string, her right arm and leg pulled back. Then she swung her arm forward, but this time only her knee moved, bending to allow the give, her toes digging into the floor as her fingers released the ball. It coasted, dropping midway down the lane, spinning like a top in a perfectly straight line. Her hands balled up in front of her and her body curved, trying to get the ball to follow suit and hit those remaining two pins.

The ball refused, and Nena remained frozen in that position, wishing death upon those pins through slit eyes. She hated when she missed her target. *Any* target.

"If you had thrown like that the last time, you would've had a strike," Kilo said, approaching from behind with his ball in hand. "Now move aside, boss, and watch a master at work."

She turned slowly to look at him, letting him know how unimpressed she was with him. In turn, she received a playful grin and a wink that knocked a bit of the frost off her. Only time he'd try to be cheeky with her was now, because on the job, Kilo would never have dared.

She shook her head, returning to where the rest of the group was adding another frame to the board.

"No more after this for me," she said. "I'm done." She waved away the protest. Then held up two fingers, front, and then flipped them back in a silent question.

"Not back yet," Charlie answered. "Said they were going outside for some air."

Yankee snickered. "If that's the new term for fucking, then okay."

Nena frowned. Sierra and Alpha? There was no way.

"Ain't nobody giving Alpha any ass," Charlie said, laughing. "That's his damn problem."

The two of them slammed hands, ending their handshake in the Tribe's loud finger snap.

"I'll be back," Nena said, although they no longer heard her as they erupted in shouts at Kilo's strike. The building was alive with a million different things going on, and no one noticed her slip out the front door, rented bowling shoes still on her feet.

She found Alpha and Sierra in the parking lot, next to his GMC truck. He was posted against it, cigarette drooping from his mouth as he motioned animatedly with his hands. He took a step toward Sierra, and she raised a hand as if to say she didn't want to hear it. She shook her head at him. *No.* He was pointing now, emphasizing words Nena couldn't decipher. She tried to read their body language. Didn't seem angry but their conversation was heated for certain.

Was Yankee right, and the two of them were dating? Nena was confused. Of all people Sierra could link up with, Alpha? He treated everyone horribly, Sierra most of all. The Tribe didn't have any decrees about team members dating, and what the two of them did wasn't any of Nena's business. Until it affected the team. And then Nena would have to deal with it. She didn't relish the thought and hoped Sierra would soon come to her senses.

Nena returned to the bowling lane. Alpha and Sierra weren't far behind. As she sat on the bench to wait until her last two turns came up, Sierra plopped down beside her while Alpha sauntered toward the others. Charlie gleefully pointed to the scoreboard. Kilo was in the lead with Sierra a close second.

"Fuck that!" was Alpha's response.

Nena leaned toward Sierra, who seemed quieter than she'd been before.

"You good?" she asked, trying to get a read on what kind of energy Sierra was putting out. It was important she knew her team.

"Yeah, E." Sierra cocked her head to the side, giving Nena a quizzical look. "Why?"

"Nothing really. It's just . . ." Should she really go there? It wasn't her business. "Yankee mentioned maybe you and Alpha were . . ." She let her interlaced fingers finish her thought.

Sierra cackled. "Please. He's an asshole, and he's not my type." She looked at Alpha's back, and Nena could have sworn she saw her lip curl. "I have a girlfriend at home."

Nena nodded. "That's good." Sierra had more to look forward to than she.

"He just talks shit and is angry at the world." Sierra reached out and tapped the back of Nena's hand. "You and me, triple threats, right?"

Nena considered Sierra, still wondering if the time had come to do something about Alpha. There was a spark smoldering behind the younger woman's eyes, a fire Alpha had put there. But Sierra was asking her to let it go. And Nena would do as she was asked.

She nodded. "Always triple threats."

6

Bowling ended with Sierra declared the winner, (mostly) lighthearted protests from the men, and Nena's relief that the team finally seemed to be gelling again ahead of next week's Kenya mission. However her relief was short lived, as a 119 came through from Elin demanding she come to the condo. Nena counted how long she'd had a semblance of *all's well with my world*. Couple of days to be exact.

Quickly, Elin texted. I found something odd. No specifics. Just dramatic, as was Elin's way. So when Nena arrived at the penthouse condo overlooking Biscayne Bay, she imagined the 119 was to beg for McDonald's and the "something odd" was to bemoan a stretch mark that had suddenly sprouted across a new part of Elin's body.

However, one look at Elin, and Nena knew there was more going on than a craving for hot fries. It was written all over Elin's face and in the way she shoved plain Lay's potato chips into her mouth while her eyes were fixated on the computer monitors mounted on the wall in her second-floor office.

Nena crossed the threshold from the hall into the room, as expertly decorated as the rest of Elin's home. Everything sang of her expensive tastes: the chandelier lighting, the pristine white glass, the ergonomic desk, and the white leather office chair that Elin was not sitting in. Currently, she was spread out across the small couch, a wireless keyboard on her lap as she gazed at spreadsheets and other overlapping windows. Nena sat in the swivel chair, white like the rest of the non-baby-friendly furniture, and waited for Elin to tell her what she was looking at.

Elin, eyes on the monitors, grumbled, "Your jeans better not stain my furniture."

Nena glanced down at her dark-rinse jeans, then twisted around to see if there was anything on the chair. There wasn't. She looked suspiciously at her sister.

"How do you know what I'm wearing? You haven't even looked my way yet. Plus, you better be nice to me." She held out the bag in her hand. "I come bearing Big Macs and fries."

The bag drew Elin's attention. She gave Nena a slow, excruciating once-over. "How do you know when someone's armed just by looking at them? I just do." She abandoned her bag of chips, stretching her arm out at Nena and wriggling her fingers.

"What happened to the manners you said you had?"

"Please and thank you." Elin pulled a face, settling the brown bag in her lap and digging in. "When are you not wearing jeans? It's your uniform. Dark jeans. Black jeans. Black trousers. Dispatch gear. Rinse and repeat, blah, blah, blah."

Nena shifted in her seat, unimpressed with Elin's hot take on her clothing. "I'm trying to understand why you're monitoring my wardrobe." She hated the bit of self-consciousness creeping into the edges of her mind. "It's comfortable."

"Bullshit," Elin said. "They hide the bloodstains." She dipped two fries in an open container of sweet-and-sour sauce and pushed them in her mouth.

Elin was being obnoxious. She also wasn't wrong, and while Nena would have liked to engage a bit more, she had to get to the issue at hand.

"You texted like we were back home in London, 119, to criticize my wardrobe?"

Elin gestured half-heartedly to the monitors and the Excel spread-sheets displayed on the screen, now more into the Big Mac than her visitor.

"What is it?"

Elin belched, and Nena rubbed her temples, begging herself to exhibit patience.

"You know how one of the philanthropic ventures the Tribe is involved in is to provide food, supplies, and health care to smaller African villages? We've been doing a heavier push in countries that aren't members of the Tribe. You know, goodwill so that the countries get to know us, learn to trust us, maybe eventually join in."

"Mm-hmm."

"Well, I was checking the books. Typically, I don't, but every now and again I like to see for myself what's going on. We track the merchandise from purchase to delivery, and we conduct the business through specific subsidiaries, so all can be easily accounted for. All aboveboard."

Elin highlighted several rows on one of the spreadsheets. "These are purchases of items that were supposed to go to villages in Congo, Tanzania, and Mozambique. When the supplies arrive at the villages, there is a point person who is supposed to confirm receipt with us and distribute to the people."

Nena indicated she should go on.

"But there haven't been confirmations of receipt on several deliveries—hundreds of thousands of dollars' worth of supplies and food. In the last couple of months, three deliveries are unaccounted for."

"Where did they go? Rebels? Local gangs or armies?"

"No." Elin said it with a pop of her lips. She began licking salt off her fingers, then begrudgingly snatched the napkins Nena wordlessly held out to her.

"If Mum saw the way you just brushed crumbs onto the floor, she'd throttle you."

Elin's shoulders lifted. "Good thing Mum's across the pond, yeah?"

Nena reminded herself to exhibit patience, releasing deep breaths before continuing. "What are the contacts at these villages saying about the drops? Or the people who loaded the shipments at the warehouses? Are villagers complaining when they don't receive anything?"

"Do you truly believe they'd complain about something they're getting as goodwill?"

Elin adjusted herself on the sofa, wincing suddenly and putting a hand to the side of her belly. "Muscle pull. I can literally feel the stretch marks forming as we speak. How the hell am I going to wear a bikini after the baby comes?"

"How indeed." Nena ducked a flying fry or two.

"Anyway, they wouldn't want to make waves with us, so they don't ask and go without. If they were expecting the shipments in the first place. Bloody crazy, right?"

"It's not crazy. Africans are loyal to those who take care of them. A couple of missed supply drops wouldn't negate the fact that they've received even one. It's honorable."

Elin snorted. But she wouldn't be able to understand. She'd been born into a life of opulence and privilege after Noble and Delphine Knight had established themselves in London. Nena might not have had a rich lifestyle when she was a child, but she knew the privilege of growing up in a good family. She also knew what it was like to have it all ripped away. To live in fear, wondering when food would next come.

Nena could understand why villagers would say nothing while they went without, because it was how she herself thought—to never complain to the people who had done so much for her, who'd changed her life entirely and given her a chance. Like those villagers, she'd remain loyal, always.

"Are you listening?"

Nena rerouted her attention to see Elin lifting herself off the couch. She stood in front of the monitors, pointing at the second one, the one reflecting the missing drop dates.

"Someone is stockpiling either supplies or money, and while these are large sums, they aren't so large that they would immediately raise flags in our systems. However, money is money, and . . . either someone is bad at maths, in which case I'll fuck 'em up, or someone is stealing, and you'll fuck 'em up."

Elin's elocution was unparalleled.

It wasn't often that Nena caught her sister in moments of true concern. Every issue, Elin believed, had a reasonable solution and was no cause for concern. But this time . . . this time Nena saw the way Elin's brows peaked on her forehead and the way she worried the lace fringes of the nightgown she'd once said she'd "never be caught dead in," but "now this blend of cotton is the only thing that doesn't irritate my skin at night or make me feel too hot when I try but fail miserably to sleep, since that's when the baby likes to kick my stomach like he's an American footballer"—Elin's words exactly.

Elin said, "Who the hell would have the balls to do either to the Tribe? That's a signed and sealed death warrant."

This cute vision of her sister wasn't enough to counter the weight of Elin's findings. The mood in the room was heavy, like Miami weather right before a sudden thunderstorm—the way the electricity crackled and the clouds rolled in, thick and ready to unleash a waterfall over the city. It was the smell of an approaching storm. It was the inkling Nena was beginning to get, though she couldn't quite put her finger on why what was probably an accounting oversight felt so pernicious.

"You'll be the one to tell Dad, yeah?" Elin asked, her voice going tiny and eyes wide. "Tell him 'bout this?"

"This is your news. I'm already on the hook for all the trouble after going against the Council and not killing Cort. Plus, you're older."

"But you're the Noble whisperer. It's common knowledge."

It wasn't. Their parents listened to the both of them equally.

"Learn from my mistakes," Nena said. "Tell Dad. And tell him sooner rather than later."

Their expressions mirrored each other. "It's like the feeling of having to throw up before it happens," Elin said, reading Nena perfectly. Nena nodded.

Stealing from the Tribe under the guise of the Tribe's philanthropy was a statement.

Question was, Who was making the statement?

And to what end?

7

A day later, as Nena sat in her backyard botanical garden beneath the wooden pergola she'd erected to shade her from the sun's intensity, she was losing the battle to study the latest intel on General Konate. All around her were reminders of home: the palm trees Florida was known for and other exotics like her rubber trees, elephant-ear plants, lilies, and a baobab tree, newly planted. She hoped it would thrive here, in a climate not so different than Ghana's, one of the many countries where the baobab was native.

Nena's thoughts began to stray from the maps laying out what Network had determined to be the general's outpost and over to her team. Despite Sierra telling her not to, she should have said something to Alpha, made sure he hadn't been coming down too hard on her. But then again, Sierra was grown and had handled herself through more than one dispatch. If she could take down armed adversaries, she could handle some ribbing from Alpha.

Nena wondered, not for the first time, if it was her own leadership she was questioning. She wasn't the same Nena, or the same Echo, from six months ago. Not after she'd sought revenge against Paul, Attah Walrus, and Kwabena for eradicating her village and her family with it. Not after she'd had no choice but to kill her own brother. The unexpected knock at her front door pulled Nena's thoughts back to the present. She opened the security-camera app on her phone to see who had the nerve, though she had her suspicions. They never failed her.

"Run something by you?" Keigel asked, his mane of newly freshened locs held back by a band at the base of his neck. He'd just returned from the hair shop and sported a perfect edge-up as well. He raised a couple of bottles of Coronas in his hand after she disengaged all the locks and opened the fortified front door to her own personal panic house. One could never be too careful in her line of work.

Keigel clinked the bottles together with one hand. Nena pulled a face. "I don't drink."

"I know that," he scoffed, entering her home when she stepped aside. "They're mine. Your present is me." He grinned widely, pleased at his quip and the way the disappointment on her face disappeared when she spied the familiar white plastic bag with the red smiley face on it. She knew exactly what was in there and whom it was for.

She waved for him to follow as she returned to the backyard, and while he got himself comfortable on one of her lounge chairs, she put away her work materials and closed her computer. Keigel placed the bag on the table and slid it toward her.

"You wouldn't have gotten past the doorway without it," she grumbled, though they both knew that wasn't true. She pulled the bag open, then popped up the top of the Styrofoam container to gaze at her cherished lemon-pepper wings.

"One day you'll have a beer with me."

"Beer is rancid." She breathed in the intoxicating lemony-pepper smell before remembering Keigel had a reason for his visit. "What's on your mind?"

Who knew what Keigel was about to lay in her lap? He was the only person she knew whose observations could make her wonder after her own sanity. He could be introspective about the plight of Black people in these American streets or throughout the world—"if they knew their place in it." To which Nena assured him that no matter how many generations removed he was from the first enslaved people brought to these lands, Black people would always have a place and history.

Then there were the times when Keigel's questions were so unexpected and out of pocket that she was rendered speechless and had to ask if he was winding her up. Most times, he was, and he'd laugh at her frustration at having taken him seriously.

Tonight was a different story. His face was unreadable. Neither serious nor playful. It was a blank slate, which was unusual for a guy who broadcast every thought like a neon billboard. He took a deep swig from his first bottle, making Nena think this visit was a serious one. She sat down and waited.

"I gotta meet up with the other neighborhood heads later, the ones I distro to. Distributions," he explained when it seemed she wasn't tracking. "The connects you hooked me up with can provide more product because we've all been killin' it with sales. Killin' the game. Thank you for that, by the way."

She nodded. Didn't know why he bothered thanking her when she hadn't done anything more than ask a Tribe associate to find better connects Keigel could work with. Keigel was the one who'd made such an impression that the associate had said he'd only deal with Keigel, not the other gang leaders. Keigel should give himself more credit for his business acumen. When she'd moved to the neighborhood and become friends with him, she'd seen he had a vision similar to her father's in wanting to grow his brand and give back to his people here. Her father's story had been similar to Keigel's when he'd first started out, running packages, and more, for the local gangs in London.

He continued, "I want them to be prepared to push more weight. But I also want them to have more of an interest in the whole thing. Like shares and all that. Less competing with each other for territory, more invested in supporting our own on a bigger level, like how the Tribe does it."

"How do you think they'll take the idea of a change in business model?" This wasn't her wheelhouse. She didn't get involved enough with Keigel's business to know these heads or if change was what they'd want.

He shrugged. "Real talk, I don't know if they're yet of the mind to be partners. They'll be uncomfortable with change, but it could fly if we work together, like we've been doing but on a higher level. I just need to know who's really one hundred in and who's just talking shit and will end up being the weak link."

"You'll have to tell them and then allow them time to digest. You can't expect them to give you their best-informed response the moment you drop this on them."

He said nothing, just downed the rest of his beer and popped the second one.

"What prompted you to want to share your position?"

He shrugged again. "Because maybe I'm tired of the daily hustle or I want something else that better fits my goals. To diversify."

"In what way?"

"I haven't figured that out yet. But I also want to make sure that in my little bit of the world, I'm working with people."

Her lips pursed as she considered his words. The air was still muggy, but the outdoor fans Nena had installed kept them relatively comfortable.

"What do you need?"

He shrugged again. "For you to tell me if I sound straight-up ridiculous."

That wasn't even her style. "It's never ridiculous to do things that you think could better yourself and your people. That doesn't mean everyone will agree with you, though."

He scratched at the back of his neck, deep in thought.

"I could accompany you," Nena suggested. "Suss out how the others react and if they seem genuine? One thing my dad has always done was to never propose new ventures to partners alone. He always has one of us with him who can read the room, offer a different perspective, because in the thick of it, he may not be able to accurately determine who's genuinely on board or who may later pose a problem."

Nena could read Keigel's feelings because his billboard was on total display, a blend of appreciation and relief. "You'd do that for me? I mean, I know you don't like to mix up in any of what I got going on. I mean, you have all your shit you deal with. And it'll take away from your downtime."

"I don't know if I'm more insulted that you'd ask me if I'd do something like that for you or that you think my downtime is more important than my friend."

Well, now she'd done it. A six-foot-plus man whose mouth ran more than a generator, one who was no less lethal than she, looked upon her with watery eyes and seemed at a loss for words. She let out a breath, annoyed.

"Seriously?" she asked, hoping he'd get himself together because she didn't feel comfortable with this kind of Keigel. What's more, she didn't like how this one was currently making her feel.

But he kept on staring at her, waiting for a response. Finally, she said, "Look, you were there for me without hesitation when I went after Paul. And you risked Cort's wrath to bring Georgia to see me. You think my family is cool. I mean, do I need to go on?"

He grinned. "Guess not."

But she did because it was finally worth saying, at least this once. "You're a true friend to me. True friends are hard to come by, and . . . I cherish our friendship."

His eyes were dry now, and he touched a hand to his chest. "I think I'm touched, Nena Knight!"

"Yeah, well, don't expect to hear that anymore, okay? When do we go?"

Keigel grimaced. "Tonight?" His body tensed as he braced for her wrath.

But the only sign she gave him was when her nostrils flared. She swallowed her annoyance at the short notice, looking wistfully at the wings she wouldn't get to eat right now.

"Let's go get it sorted, then."

8

When Keigel was done laying out his idea to the leaders of the six local gangs, he stopped talking and let his words settle. There were a good number of them inside the abandoned industrial building—representatives from a variety of cultures that created much of the racial makeup of Miami-Dade County. They were meeting outside the city, where there was more privacy and hopefully no law enforcement watching. Each had come with one or two representatives from their territories. Keigel had done the same; Omar and Boaz were standing inside, but near the door to make sure nothing happened out there while they were all in here.

Things had so far stayed on the up and up. Nena stood nearby, not fully in the group. She wasn't a part of their business but off to the side, observing their reactions. They were a jittery bunch. The building was dismal, and they all shifted on their feet as if they were more ready to flee at a moment's notice than prepared to talk big business. No one liked sudden late-night meetups. They liked change even less.

This wasn't how Noble would conduct business. There'd be a presentation of food because Africans equated refreshments to respect, fellowship, and comradery. They'd all be sitting at a table, as if relaxed. Maybe they'd ask after one another's families or the latest deal someone had made. A script of pleasantries to follow before they finally got around to the topic that had brought them to parley. Here, Keigel had just assembled the others like some basketball team huddle before game time. Maybe one day she'd suggest a different type of atmosphere, if Keigel ever asked for her input. Nena wouldn't offer it. She wasn't here to critique his presentation methods. She was here to see who was in or who was a possible out.

The other gang leaders seemed intrigued, for the most part. There was one who didn't seem on board, and that made Nena especially interested in him. She recognized the royal flush playing cards on his hat, representing his set. She didn't recognize his face, but she knew him to be the leader of the Flushes, whose members Nena had had to dispatch when they'd attacked Georgia outside Jake's. She'd let Keigel handle the fallout with the Flushes. Though he'd never shared exactly how he'd kept the peace, and Nena hadn't asked, she guessed the agreement was for Keigel to retain control over the turf but allow the Flushes to do their work on it when they needed.

But now, the head Flush, his name momentarily eluding her, kept glancing her way, looking at her through narrowed eyes as if he were trying to place her. She didn't know him. He hadn't brought the one Flush she'd let get away either. Rumor was he hadn't lived much longer after fleeing Jake's alleyway instead of defending his friends. Nena supposed the rumor was correct. At any rate, the vibes she was getting from . . . Trek, that was his name . . . weren't good ones, and Nena worried he'd cause a fuss before Keigel could get the rest of the apprehensive group on board.

"I don't know, bruh." One of them finally spoke up. "You're proposing a big change here. How do you even know it'll work?"

Keigel said, "How do we know it won't, though? What's the harm in trying?"

Another laughed. "Us killing each other if it don't. You know we all ain't cool like that. We barely have a treaty to keep peace."

46

"Shouldn't that be what we all want? Peace?" Keigel asked. "Who wants to be fighting all the damn time? Not me. I'm tired."

Trek said, "And if we don't go with your idea? This co-op shit. If we don't, then what?"

Keigel turned to him, shrugging. "Then you go your own way, that's all. No hard feelings."

"With your connect?"

Keigel shook his head. "The connect only works with me. Their stipulation. And they have the marina on lock, so . . ."

Trek said, "What you're talking 'bout sounds like blackmail. Sounds like if we don't do what you want, then we don't eat. That what you saying, Keig? That's how you get down now?"

The leader of a Latinx gang spoke up, stepping farther into the group. "Don't put words in his mouth, Trek. Ain't what he said."

"Then what's he saying?"

"If you don't want to be in the co-op, then you go with our blessing. It means you find your own connect, though," Keigel answered.

The leader of the gang of bikers, a man with more tattoos than not, who transported goods farther than any of the others, spoke. "I don't mind it. If it means more money and less running up and down Ninety-Five hustling shit, I'm down."

"All right, all right," Keigel said, pleased with how everything was turning out. "There's no use in us fighting and killing among ourselves, because we're all here to stay. We're all partners in this. Even though the connect comes through me, the cut remains the same. We all equals. Have equal share and say in how business is conducted throughout the city. We work as business folk and see a future instead of just right now, the present."

One man, big and tall with a full beard that likely had its own personality, said, "All we got is right now, man. You know that. If we don't get us, cops get us, prison gets us . . . shit, the educational system gets us."

Keigel pointed at the man. "Exactly, my dude, and as a co-op we can change that. If we ain't fightin', then we making money. Money is what makes the world go round. Money gets police off our asses. Money gets our kids in schools that give a fuck about teaching them. Or money gets the teachers we need right here to do what they need with our kids. Money gives us air to breathe, and we need to breathe. You feel me? We can be self-sufficient and survive if we do this shit together, as partners, not as enemies."

The group was quiet, feeling the weight of Keigel's words, understanding entirely what he meant. Though he talked about money, he meant providing more opportunity for them. He meant giving them a chance to get out of the hamster wheel they were on and a chance to live as people of color in a world that seemed dead set on killing them all under the guise of protecting the public.

Trek sucked his teeth. "So now we all kumbaya and shit, that's what you telling us? You roll with that African bitch, and now we all supposed to fall in line"—he snapped his fingers—"just like that?"

Nena had been waiting for him to speak. His glowering stares had only intensified each second the group sounded increasingly like they were on board with Keigel's offer. *That African bitch* was meant to be an insult, yet Nena found it a compliment given by a less-than-average man who tried to seem bigger than he was by being a walking display for every clothing brand imaginable. Next to him, Trek's second looked on uncomfortably. He muttered, "Come on, man," attempting to calm his boss down. Nena's hand moved toward her hip and stayed there.

Keigel stepped toward Trek. Gone was the easygoing business demeanor he had been serving the entire time. Trek's hostility had cooled the temperature, and everyone was throwing jittery looks around.

"What you won't do, dawg, is disrespect my fam. She's my fam, feel me? Don't disrespect her." He let that sit in the air for another second, his eyes not leaving Trek's until he was satisfied Trek understood, plainly. Keigel continued, "No, we don't ever have to be friends, you feel me?

48

Don't think I forgot how your crew nearly got law on our necks because of what they pulled on a DA's daughter, on my turf. If she had been clipped, that would have come down on my crew's heads. Remember that? You got off easy, bruh."

"Two of mine gettin' killed by your bi—" Trek checked himself, tossing a thumb in Nena's direction. "By her is gettin' off easy? Seems you owe me."

"You should thank her." Keigel's voice lowered, becoming more menacing. Gone was the playful friend who joked too much and always wore an easy smile. In his place was someone she knew well: a killer. Keigel stepped closer, and the pressure in the room ticked up two more notches. His man Mendez tensed up behind him. Trek's second, whose name Nena could not remember, put a hand on his boss, whispered in his ear. Told him to chill.

"Thank her?" Trek's eyes ran the length of Nena, his head cocked to the side while a slow, nasty smirk spread on his lips, a gold tooth glinting at her in hello. "I should kill her."

The crowd broke out in a chorus of calls for peace and to let things go. They tried to play it off as if Trek were making jokes, like his deliberate threat was just talk from a guy too high off weed and alcohol. His second pulled at his arm, attempting to make him fall back as Trek stared down Nena. She stepped to him, matched his wild gaze with a steadfast one. Her hand moved to the back of her belt, the hilt of her blade, strumming it as she calculated the distance between her and his throat.

Keigel, who'd come beside her when she'd moved, was in lockstep. Gone was the aspiring businessman, the mediator and moneymaker. The man beside her was on her team. Was no less so than Alpha, Kilo, or Sierra. She knew she could take this fool, this Trek, who was trying her, egging her on. She could slice his throat from ear to ear before his crew pulled any pieces on her. But she wouldn't because this was Keigel's show. Tonight, she was on *his* team.

"What you trying to do, Trek?" Keigel asked in a low register. His body was a massive coil of muscles ready to spring. The electricity crackled off him. It was a Keigel people rarely witnessed. But when they did . . .

"I'm just fucking with her," Trek drawled, breaking away as he slowly rubbed his hands together. He gave Nena the cockiest victory smirk.

Self-satisfied prick. She'd had her fill of them, was tired of biting her tongue when men like Alpha and Trek walked around acting like they were big men, blowing smoke and putting on airs. Perhaps, one day, she'd get a chance to show them what crossing a woman like her really meant.

Today was not the day. But she'd seen something in those moments. The sort of nuance she'd wanted to be here to watch out for. Trek was too busy leering at Nena to catch the flash of anger, the resentment, scrolling across his second's face. The embarrassment at his behavior. They were all embarrassed. A business meeting turning into a dogfight. Trek's gang was worried he'd bring them down like crabs in a barrel. They all knew it too. He didn't deserve to lead a conga line, much less a crew of people who depended on his decisions to put money in their pockets, food on their table, and a blanket of protection around their shoulders.

"We good?" Keigel said. A statement, not a question.

"We gone," Trek replied, signaling to his people they were leaving.

No one had to articulate the significance of Trek's sudden departure. He was out of the co-op. And if he was out, it meant he was rogue and could try to find a connect of his own. He wouldn't—the Tribe's associate had Miami and the southeast coast on lock—but it meant he might come after the other gangs, steal from them, wage war. Be a menace. For no good reason, because that was what little men like Trek did.

Sometimes it was better to cut out the rot before it was allowed to infiltrate and infest the rest. Nena would have to think a little longer about that one.

Trek was already on his way out when his second broke away from him and approached Keigel, who was assuring the rest they could do this without the Flushes if they had to.

Keigel stopped talking when the younger man jogged up to him, eyes begging for a second chance. "Keig, man, I'll chop it up with him. He just needs a minute to come around."

"He don't have long, Lonzo," Keigel said gravely. "Get your boy to understand what needs to happen."

Lonzo nodded, but the worry and doubt etched in his face when he left were too easily read.

Nena stepped away from the group of chatty men to ratchet herself down. She had been a second away from slitting a man's throat, in front of people she did not know. She needed a moment to make sense of her rapidly churning thoughts. Even if Trek were to change his mind, he would always be a threat to the co-op. To Keigel. Keigel would always have to watch his back because Keigel was who Trek wished he could be. And people like Trek would never learn. Would always be a malignancy that needed cutting out.

And Nena was happy to oblige.

9

They stood side by side, watching as the others melted away to their own areas of the city.

Nena turned to Keigel, scrutinizing him until he cleared his throat and shot her an unsure look.

"What?" He scratched the back of his neck. His locs were now bound in a thick, single braid. She liked that he took such great care of his hair. "What'd I do now?"

"I'd like to show you my side of the world." She didn't know why she was saying it. She just knew in this moment it was right.

He cracked a wry grin. "Why? Because you're tired of slumming with us in the lower echelons of the great Miami?"

Though he was joking, his words hurt. In his "slumming" was where Nena had found the first true friend who wasn't family. Keigel reminded her of Goon, one of her earliest teammates—the way he could switch from jokester to business in a millisecond; the way he had built himself from what he called nothingness to, in Goon's case, leading missions and, in Keigel's, to leading a legion.

Nena would never think less of Keigel. Had he not accepted her as she was without question?

And what was more . . . Keigel had no earthly idea where she had been and what she had been through. Slumming? No. Living in Keigel's world and his neighborhood was like living among kings and queens. It was her honor, and she told him so.

Keigel's head dropped in a blush, and he kicked at some nonexistent pebble. "Kings and queens? You got jokes now."

"When do I joke?"

He thought about it. Scratched inside his ear and made a motion to his guys to do a sweep for stragglers and round up.

"You have no idea where I've been and where I've lived." She paused. "What I've had to do to stay alive."

"Once in a while you throw out zingers that come from nowhere. But that's on brand for you since you do what you do. But to be honest, I've never seen you in action."

"What do you mean? You drove me to the mansion to get Georgia."

"When I see you, it's before or after shit goes down. We got the lil homey, yeah. But I didn't *actually* see anything pop off." He was grinning now, enjoying the rise he was getting out of questioning Nena's chops. "You disappear and reemerge like Clark Kent and Superman. Never the two in the same place. You could have gone in there and had some tea and crumpets while a team of operatives went in and killed up everybody and you brought Georgia back like she'd been at a playdate."

No, she'd gone in and killed the last remaining member of her family. Her brother. But now wasn't the time to say it. "She's a bit old for playdates, yeah? And I don't care for crumpets. You're stereotyping Brits."

He laughed. "Just saying."

"You'll come then? See a bit of my world?"

"To London?" he asked dubiously. "Mannnn, I don't know. It's cold there."

"Ghana, I mean. The family has a trip coming up."

"I don't have a passport. I never even been out of the States. And I got a history that would probably keep me from traveling abroad." He gave her a meaningful look.

"Have you forgotten who you're dealing with, Keigel?" She gave him a look that said, *Come on now*, making him raise his hands in mock surrender.

"All right, then."

Nena wasn't sure why, but she enjoyed hearing Keigel's southern drawl. It was like a blanket of comfort to wrap herself in.

"I'm down," he added.

———

"Make sure tomorrow's dinner at the hotel goes well with no complications," Noble Knight was saying. "Witt will be there, and I want any of our attending Council members happy and reminded of their commitment to the Tribe's interests."

"Of course, Dad," Nena said.

"Stick to the script."

Speaking of, Nena began texting Elin. Now's a good time to tell him about the money.

Elin grinned. "Don't we always?" Meanwhile, she typed, Hell no. See how wound up he already is? Not a good time. Her head gave an almost imperceptible shake to emphasize her response.

"Darling," Mum cut in sweetly when her husband's mouth opened to tell Elin how very off script his daughters had become.

Through the computer screen, Nena viewed her mother pouring hot water from the kettle into her cup. The morning after Nena had extended her invitation to Keigel, the Knights were enjoying one of their regular video calls. Five hours ahead, her parents sat at the breakfast table in the kitchen of their London home, having their afternoon tea, while Elin yawned on screen from her pillow-laden bed. Nena was in her favorite location with her own cup of tea.

She'd been looking forward to when they'd all be together in just a few short weeks for the holidays and for the Tribe's dedication and charity dinner in support of the new medical center, their latest philanthropic venture to promote regular and progressive medical care for the underserved.

This dedication was personal to Nena because it would be in memory of the girls who'd been held captive at the Compound with her, the ones who'd survived it and the ones who hadn't. It was the least the Tribe could do to make up for not stopping the abuse and slaughter sixteen years ago when they could have. In Nena's eyes, while the state-of-the-art facility to be built on the Compound's site would help thousands, if not more, it would never be enough to make up for the suffering she and countless others had endured at the hands of Paul and his men. Nothing would. But it was a start and the only reason Nena had agreed to be present for the dinner and dedication.

"Which darling?" Elin asked, yawning again, propped against a backdrop of fluffy pillows. "Hopefully not this one, because it sounds like you want something."

Mum flapped her hand at their images crowded on the screen. A while ago, Elin had suggested their parents buy a big-screen TV to mount in the kitchen, like the setup in both Mum's and Dad's offices, but Mum had nixed that idea, insisting that the kitchen was for family and eating. Not for work or looking at the television.

"Anyway, it's been a few months, and perhaps that young man Cortland has had enough time to mull things over. Perhaps give him a call, sort things out?"

Nena felt her mum's eyes drilling into her through the screen.

"I don't like seeing you like this."

"She's all out of sorts, Mum," Elin quipped, too eager to indulge in her sister's discomfort. She leaned forward, dropping her voice conspiratorially. "Our dear girl is lovesick."

Mum swooned, her hand landing on her chest. "Call him."

Nena rubbed her closed eyes and sighed, thinking of ways in which she might use her dispatch skills on Elin.

"For what?" Noble barked.

The corner of the financial pages, which had been slightly obscuring his face, snapped down. Forever old school, Noble Knight would always favor the feeling of paper between his fingers over scrolling a computer screen for the day's news. He glowered at his wife.

"The man is with the authorities. Leave him where he is and be glad he hasn't talked. That we know of."

"If he was going to say anything, he would have done so by now, Noble." Mum took a delicate sip of her tea, a smile playing at her lips. "At any rate I think his discretion is telling. Don't you, dear?"

Dad's volume ticked up a notch. "I do not, Delphine, and I'd advise you not to think his silence says anything more than he chose well by no longer involving himself with our daughter."

His words stung. Rejection didn't feel great, and everyone knowing you'd been rejected was even worse.

Nena must have been unable to mask her reaction, because her father's face crumpled into horror, realization dawning on him. "I didn't mean it that way, Nena. What I meant was—"

"It's fine, Dad." Didn't make it hurt any less.

Nena slouched in her seat, wondering how the topic had shifted from the dedication to her and Cort. Her face grew hot from the embarrassment of having her love life on full display.

"Dad, Mum's right. The American is the first guy who's ever made Nena disobey Tribe directives." Elin had a glint in her eye, enjoying Nena's death stare through the computer screen. Their parents didn't need more reminding, especially their father.

Noble grimaced. "Which is exactly why she should forget him. If a person can cause you to break rules, you should have no part of them."

"Fu—"

Their parents' heads snapped toward Elin as if on a string.

"Bollocks," she corrected carefully. "If it wasn't for Cort redirecting the police, they would have continued sniffing around the case until they uncovered who attacked him and took Georgia that night, which could have eventually traced back to the Tribe."

Elin was careful not to say who that attacker had been. They tried not to speak his name often. It was a pain neither sister cared to be reminded of, yet it was also one of the most prominent things in both their minds. Elin's growing belly was a constant reminder that Oliver— Ofori—would remain with them the rest of their lives.

Their father snorted and rolled his eyes, returning to his newspaper.

Nena took advantage of the lull. "Don't worry about me and Cort, Mum. I am fine with how things are." She gave a tight smile, hoping it was enough to dissuade any worries her mother might have about her. "I have to be."

"Bullshit," Elin muttered.

"Elin."

"No, Mum, let's be real." Elin directed her next words at Nena. "This is the first wanker you've shown even an inkling of interest in. Yeah, he's pissed, but you two had something genuine. That's worth trying to see if there's another chance. At least try to see. At least you have someone to try and see with."

Elin could have slapped Nena, and the feeling would have been the same.

"Hey now," Mum said sharply, at the same time Dad said, "That'll be enough of that, Elin. You're being unfair, and we won't have it. Understand?"

For a second, Nena questioned if Elin's words had been meant the way Nena and their parents had received them. But the anger that flashed in Elin's eyes was confirmation—while the man Nena loved was alive and well, the man Elin loved, the father of her child, was not. And Nena was the reason why.

Nena didn't answer. There was nothing to say when it was the truth. Instead, she focused on something beyond the screen, a bird that had settled on one of the trees dotting her backyard. Today Nena's idyllic oasis provided no comfort for her. Even though Elin understood why Nena had killed Ofori, that it had been his life or hers, it didn't make his loss any less devastating to Elin, because she'd loved him.

Just as quickly as she'd launched her passive-aggressive comment, Elin became chagrined and embarrassed for not keeping her feelings in check. Aloud she said, "Don't mind me. Pregnancy and all."

It wasn't just the pregnancy, but Nena would accept the excuse just the same. There would be a time when she and Elin would have to sort the whole Oliver-Ofori thing out. They would both have to come to terms with what had been done and determine how they'd move on, if they could. Nena hoped beyond hope all would eventually be well, that her actions weren't what would break the unbreakable bond she and Elin had shared since the moment Delphine had brought Nena into their home sixteen years ago.

Nena prayed that by killing her brother, she hadn't lost her sister as well.

10

Nena tugged at the plum-colored tuxedo Elin called couture. It hugged her body more than she preferred. "What if there's work I need to do?" she'd protested while Elin had played dress-up.

Elin had raised an eyebrow. "At a dinner party? Our mission is to smooth things over, not dispatch anyone. Make nice and ensure everyone comes to next month's Council meeting with an open and courteous mind."

Nena eyed the mediumish crowd from the hotel patio, wondering if she could slip away without being noticed. Witt was there and could talk up any of the stateside Council members or their emissaries. Having been with the Tribe long enough to be trusted implicitly by all the Council members, Noble most of all, Witt was more than just the head of Dispatch and Network operations.

"It's not so bad, yeah?" Elin asked after pulling herself away from the pockets of guests to join her. She looked even more beautiful than usual in her one-shouldered powder-pink gown, its fabric swirling around her as she moved.

"Why go to all this trouble to smooth things over ahead of the full Council meeting in Ghana next month? What's there to smooth?" Nena grumbled. "Paul is dead."

"And deservedly so."

"End of story."

Elin groaned. "You sound like Dad."

"And you like Mum," Nena returned. "You two are trying to appease whoever might have been supporting him, when what we really need to do is root them out. But have you considered that one of them could be behind the missing supplies?"

"Okay, Noble Knight the second." Elin shook her head. "We aren't going to root anyone out by pissing everyone off. You know, more flies with honey than vinegar and all that. Besides, I'm not ready to get Dad all worked up about it until I know more. You know more than anyone we are about facts, not conjecture."

Nena reined in her irritation. Maybe Elin was right. Mum was right. This get-together was supposed to allay hurt feelings, not the opposite. She pointed at Elin's dress.

"Pink? You'll have everyone assuming you're having a girl."

"Which is exactly what I want them to think. Last thing we need is anyone fixating on a male Knight heir that they want to kill for some archaic *boys are a bigger threat* ideology. They don't realize girls rule the world." She cracked a smile.

Nena found herself following suit. "At least in this one they do."

"In *every* one, we do." Elin took a step back, giving her younger sister a once-over. "You look so gorgeous, Nena. I wish you'd—"

"There are some guests trying to get your attention." Nena motioned toward the room inside, where a Council member based mainly out of New York was waving at them to join him. Three unfamiliar men milled around him, each holding a short glass of liquor as the waitstaff bustled about with silver trays laden with hors d'oeuvres and flutes of champagne.

"Duty calls," Elin said, sweeping up her dress in a hand so she wouldn't trip over its hem. "Councilman Badu has been wanting me to meet some people. You know, ever since Dad told the Council the

Tribe would be going partially public in the next year or so, everyone's been champing at the bit."

Nena knew this, had heard their parents discussing whether it was time for the Tribe to go public and make a full announcement of who they were and what their place was in the business world. But that was Elin's lane. The business. Nena wanted her business to be Dispatch. Only that. To handle the missions and make sure things behind the scenes were running as they were supposed to.

Still, she asked because Elin was giving her that raised-brow look that said, *Your turn.* "Champing. How so?"

"I get why Dad wants to take it slowly and pick and choose who invests with us. Who we partner with. We can't just let all sorts close to what we've established here. He doesn't want to go full public where we can't fully vet who puts their money into our ventures. Some members want that. Like Badu there and some others. The White guy there is a representative of some company that deals in precious stones. Diamonds."

Nena's jaw clenched. "Western companies mining diamonds in Africa. A tale as old as time. We aren't possibly considering doing business with a company that exploits—"

Elin's weighty look warned her that she was getting too loud. "Of course not. We smile and nod and feign interest like Dad said. And when he gives the word, we politely say no." Elin started off, waving her empty hand in the air while the other held firmly on to her dress. "Be less suspicious, little sis."

Nena didn't know how not to be.

She dropped her head to rub between her brows, eyes closed and running through a mission sequence she wanted to try with the team. She didn't notice she was no longer alone until she felt a presence beside her. Her eyes snapped open, and she spun, hand curling into a fist should whoever was there end up being a foe.

"Ma'am, are you okay?" The woman's eyes betrayed her surprise as she blinked rapidly and held out the silver tray of champagne flutes and a water bottle as if to ward off evil. Or—Nena glanced down at her fist—an unprovoked attack. She uncurled her fingers, letting them hang at her side.

The gold-plated name badge read *Mariam*. The woman was taller than Nena, with a deep ebony hue, like Nena's. Her long, dark ponytail, pulled firmly back and cinched at the nape of her neck, swung from how she'd drawn back. "Ma'am?"

"Yes?" Nena forced her face to take on a reassuring demeanor. She looked beyond Mariam, ensuring Elin had made it to Councilman Badu and his friends. She was currently laughing at some unfunny joke she was likely being told.

"Water?" Mariam said, holding out the bottle. Nena eyed it and Mariam. "Apologies, ma'am. I shouldn't have assumed. It's just you haven't had anything else all evening and . . ."

Nena's eyes narrowed, and reflex again made her hand curl. She forced herself to ratchet down her intensity. Mariam was only doing her job and being kind.

"Thank you." Nena accepted the proffered water. "Observant in the midst of all these guests."

Mariam shrugged. "It's my job to know what the guests may want before they want it."

"Yeah, I know a little bit about observing others." Although Nena's observations were not to give anyone what they needed before they knew it. Hers were for a whole other set of particular skills. "At any rate, thank you for being so attentive, Mariam. These gatherings are not my thing."

"But you're a Knight!" Mariam blurted. "Everyone back home knows the Knights and the Tribe. You are like royalty."

Nena ignored the last part. Royalty was the last thing she wanted to be.

"And home is?"

"Mali." Her tone changed, giving the answer with a firmness that hadn't been there before. As if Nena would recognize something in her one-word answer. And she did.

Nena said, "I come from a small village. You have it wrong if you think this has always been my life."

Mariam nodded. "It seems that way," she said softly, as if seeing Nena through new lenses. "Me too. A small village. My brother, my ma, and I lived simple and happy. He took care of us because it was only us." She swallowed. "It's just me and my ma now."

Nena liked the way the darkness obscured their faces so neither of them had to see what the other's might betray. Mariam didn't have to say what Nena already knew, that her brother was no more. Yet Nena asked anyway.

Mariam's face tightened as she prepared her answer, and Nena's regret was immediate. She should have chosen silence. If this woman started to cry here, Elin would be pissed.

"Not sure what really happened. They say killed in combat. Missing in action, I guess, is what they would call it. All I know is that one week he didn't phone. A week became two. Then a month. Then six. Now . . . it's been maybe thirteen years? Give or take. Time gets fuzzy when you're busy scrimping to take care of a sick mother."

Something simmered beneath the surface of Mariam's demeanor. She looked resolute, yes, but there was an anger there.

Nena recognized that anger, evolved from loss and pain. Emotions she knew all too well.

"Having someone taken from you," Mariam said. "Ever experienced something like that?"

A time or two. "It never leaves you." Nena thought she answered in her head, but the twitch of Mariam's shoulder, as if someone had poked her, betrayed that she'd heard clearly.

"It does not," Mariam agreed. And in a blink, she was back to business.

"Nena." It was Witt, his voice carrying over the din of casual chatter spilling out onto the veranda. The liquor made the guests more jovial.

Mariam gave Nena a critical once-over. "Looks good on you." She waggled a finger up and down, causing Nena to look down at her plum-colored getup.

Mariam was already steps away before Nena could say goodbye or thank you, stopping to offer beverages to a group of guests. Witt came up next to Nena.

"A word?"

Nena straightened her jacket. Her push blades, tucked in tight at her sides, comforted her. But she reminded herself again that she wasn't on a mission for Dispatch tonight. There was a reason Noble wanted Elin, Witt, and her there playing nice with stakeholders who would hopefully vote the Knight way when the time arose. One of those potential voters could be a snake, and despite Elin's words, Noble needed to know what might be coming, conjecture or not.

11

Everyone in Nena's world held a special place. There was something about each that endeared them to her. She found that in all their differences, the things that made them individually special collectively helped her to feel whole, provided what she'd lost and regained with her found family. But out of all of them—the fierce motherly love from Delphine, the unquestionable devotion and protection from Elin, the sweet innocence and reminder of self from Georgia, the hijinks and antics from Keigel, the promise of a future with love in it from Cort—it was Noble, her father, whose special something held Nena together like glue. His soul was like hers. The loss he'd suffered. The intense need to protect those around him by any means necessary, even if it meant having to be the bad guy—which he was often, in his chosen profession. It was Noble who'd picked her up, dusted her off, and given her purpose again.

And it was Noble who understood more than anyone else why the method by which Nena carried out her purpose was also a release of the damnable guilt she felt for having survived the atrocities Paul had committed in N'nkakuwe. For having survived the Compound. For having survived the man who'd taken her from the Compound . . . when so many unnamed others had not. And it was Noble's steady resolve to allow Nena to be who she was going to be, no changes, just honing and fine-tuning so that when Nena had to do whatever she had to do, she did it with skill and came out a survivor, again and again.

That was what made this conversation difficult for Nena. That she'd have to tell him her suspicions about what was going on in the Tribe again. Tell him that the dream he had, the empire he'd cultivated and grown with his blood, sweat, and tenacity, still had a ways to go. That someone he'd allowed within was working against the Tribe.

She needed to tell him, as Keigel had sagely reminded her, that not all skin folk were kinfolk.

Her troubled expression relaxed when the image of her dad dropped into focus. There was Noble Knight, ever his regal self, dark russet colored, with wide, dark-brown eyes that could be kind one moment and ferocious the next as he decreed that someone had only limited time left to live.

He was smiling at her, his closely trimmed beard checkered with salt that matched the edges of his short sideburns. He looked as if he hadn't just spoken to her the day before, asking after her and even after Keigel, who he liked to call "the American boy." What was funny was that Keigel liked the moniker. He wore it proudly and swore, "Papa Knight only calls me that because he knows I'm good people."

Her dad did think Keigel was good people, trusting Nena's judgment about who she brought into the Tribe's orbit. But he could never know what Keigel called him. That would be their little secret.

"How are things, Dad?" she asked, shifting in her chair as she sat in her backyard.

"Things here are fine," he said.

His face was a little too close to the screen. It was an age thing, she thought, and ironic because a man who held as much power as Noble still didn't know how to position his webcam a respectable distance from his face and often searched around to unmute himself after already speaking a full minute despite all the pantomimes attempting to alert him that no one could hear him.

"You are well?" Dad asked, his eyebrows furrowing as he studied her through the screen, reading her every facial feature. He knew when she withheld. He knew when she was being untruthful, so with him, she tried not to be.

She gave a single nod.

"Witt tells me all went well at the dinner party."

She smirked. "Yes, we stuck to the script."

He ignored that. "And you have the dispatch coming up in Kenya. I thought we agreed you'd take it easy."

"We agreed we both would take it easy." She tapped her chest, giving him a pointed look.

He raised his eyebrows innocently. "What? The pacemaker?"

"Mm-hmm."

It was a new addition; his heart had been weakened when Paul had poisoned him. Paul's lasting effects on her father were the gifts no one wanted at one of those white elephant holiday-party exchanges.

"I have been taking it easy. All I do is grumble and grouse about how lazy people are being."

She looked away. They both knew he did a lot more than just grumble and grouse. Managing all the personalities of the Council and of his family was enough to make anyone's pacemaker go off.

"I'm old, Nena. It's you I worry about. A lot has happened, and you need some time to deal with it."

"I've had time. And I'm dealing." It wasn't entirely a lie. But it was what it was. She settled the laptop on the small table she'd pulled in front of her and leaned forward, elbows on knees.

"I think things are getting back on track," her father said. "We had the near catastrophe with Paul, but you routed him out in time, yes? You kept the Tribe from falling into his hands."

Only to be pilfered by someone else's. How was she to tell him what Elin suspected?

"Dad," she began softly. She swallowed, not wanting to broach a subject that was potentially devastating. "It might not be completely over."

The energy shifted, crackling like static cling. "Come again?"

"Elin found some discrepancies in the finances," she said, bracing herself for a potential blowup. The Tribe was Noble's first child.

"Are you telling me someone is stealing?" His voice rose a notch. "Is this what you are saying? From the Tribe?"

With each word, his carefully cultivated British accent turned more Senegalese, thickening with his native tongue as it did every time he let emotion overcome the unflappable business persona he preferred to present. Any act against the Tribe was a personal affront to him. It was why Nena and Elin tried so valiantly to be the buffers when things and people did not live up to his standards. When it came to the Tribe and its goal of One Africa, Noble Knight was an idealist, a dreamer. He was always chasing that dream, and he could not handle setbacks to it in any other way than emotionally.

The Tribe was Noble Knight's kryptonite.

"Possibly, Dad, but please try to remain calm, okay?" She tapped her chest again, reminding him of the electronic device in his chest, regulating his rhythms. "I'm just giving you a heads-up. Letting you know there is something Elin is figuring out about these transactions."

"Tell me?" He was a shaken soda can ready to explode as soon as the tab was pulled.

She expelled a breath slowly so she could think of how to say it. Finally, she decided to just rip it off like a Band-Aid.

"There have been deliveries to several villages that are unaccounted for. Orders were made. It looks as if the supplies were sent. But there has been no confirmation from the villages of receipt."

"Where have the supplies gone?"

She shrugged. "That's what Elin is trying to find out."

"So someone has been robbing our trucks? Attacking the villages?" This came out in a bellow.

She shook her head. "It's more likely there were no actual supplies purchased. No drops made because there were no supplies to drop. At least that's how Elin explained it to me."

She stared down at her hands, hating that she was the bearer of bad news but knowing her father would rather know than not.

Noble paced the floor, hands on his waist, his open jacket revealing the vest beneath it, as he worked through the new information. He was remarkably reserved, aside from his earlier display of emotion. Nena waited.

"Who is it?"

"We don't know yet."

"What do they want?"

"We don't know that either."

He turned to her. "Then what do you know?"

"At least the people haven't been stolen from directly."

His anger flashed. "But any money taken is money stolen from the people. It was money meant for the people."

He was right.

"But Nena," he said, his frustration peeking through. "What am I supposed to do with this? I can't go to the Council and give them half information. I can't yell *fire* when there are no visible flames."

What if Elin had been right about not worrying their father with conjecture? No—Nena had to say something. She wouldn't hide information anymore.

"But there is smoke."

He stopped his pacing, his hand to his chin as he worked through what he'd just learned. "What are you telling me, child? Truly?"

"I'm telling you to be prepared, Dad. I'm saying it could be an outside attack from someone who's infiltrated our systems. But it also could be internal."

He made a *pfft* sound, dismissing her with a hand and looking as if she'd insulted his honor.

"There is no way. If there is theft, then it is from outside factions, because there is no way anyone within the Tribe would steal from her. We all made an oath, a pledge, to the African Tribal Council, to the advancement of the African people and the diaspora. We pledge this, Nena." His eyes begged her to take back her words. To not tell him his Tribe was diseased. "We swear on our nationality, our family, our blood. We are a *tribe*. Who would dishonor that?"

She had no answer. Her dad was still for a long time. So long Nena thought her screen had frozen. It hadn't. Her father was a statue, lost in his thoughts. His anger was simmering. She could see it just below his brooding demeanor—the rage that someone would dare.

"The audacity of them," he growled. "The fucking audacity."

She didn't let her surprise show. Rarely had she heard her father curse. He thought it was unrefined, and while Nena didn't think it unrefined, just thought it betrayed more emotion than she deigned to share, she, too, shied away from it, leaving it to Elin and Keigel, who made cursing sound like a sport. When she tried, it came out clumsy.

"Elin must find me who did this, Nena."

"Yes, Dad."

He was back at the screen now, staring intently, the static of energy becoming lightning. "And then you know what to do. I don't even care why. I only want to end them entirely because no one steals from the Tribe."

She nodded once.

"No one steals from Africa again."

She nodded again. "Sir."

She didn't want to send her father into an utter spiral, but she was thinking of the lessons she'd learned from the actions of people who'd once been called *brother* . . .

If Dad allowed himself to consider it, if he wasn't so blinded by his ideology, he'd remember where earlier threats had come from, that while Paul had been caught and eliminated, and grumblings from anyone who'd blindly thought him an ally quelled, someone had packaged Paul like a gift and presented him to the Tribe. Nena had tried saying as much from the moment Paul had sat at her sister's dinner table. Who was behind Paul? Not the Gabonese people, who he had also misled, but someone already inside.

"We cannot be seen as weak, Nena," Noble was saying. His once-kind eyes were a mix of troubled and sad. They held anger and the slightest speck of fear. "We cannot allow anyone to think we cannot protect and sustain the Tribe's interests and its goals. No one should think they can get to us, can intercept us. Do you understand what I'm saying to you?"

"I do," she affirmed.

"Above all, I do not want anyone—not Council members, not Tribe members, not the countries in our organizations or the people of Africa, and not the world—none of them should think we cannot keep Africans safe or that Africa is not strong and a real contender."

She understood. It was about more than just rooting out a few embezzlers.

"Soon, Nena, we will open ourselves to the world. Show them the African Tribal Council as a force in the business and philanthropic world. We will solidify our legacy and our place in this world. It's imperative we are above reproach. No fractures, no conflicts transpiring within the Tribe. We must come out, truly, as One Africa because once we go public with our ventures, there will be plenty from the outside who will try to bring us down and more who will want a piece of what we have to offer. They're already sniffing around. That American mining business, for example. The one you met at the dinner."

Noble's point was clear. The Tribe had worked within the shadows, had worked to become the new fabric of a new society for Africa. And if they weren't vigilant, that very fabric might be torn right out from under them.

Nena had no intention of letting it ever get to that.

12

Goon used to call the physical act of killing people *wet work*. Matter of fact, it was a term widely used on both sides of the law and in between. Witt had hated whenever Goon used the term. Witt thought the term was offensive, demeaning even, because the Dispatch teams didn't just kill unceremoniously. They did so by Council decree. It wasn't a joke or a cool word. It was their job. Nena understood Witt's meaning, and while Witt might have thought Goon played around too much and took what they did lightly, Nena knew Goon believed in what they did as much as any of them.

Goon had been the first friend Nena had had when she'd begun training all those years ago after she'd first joined the Tribe. He'd been like a big brother to her. Schooling her on the ins and outs of the team and of Witt. Goon was the levity they all needed—as big as a house, all muscle, but as gentle as a lamb. Not a day went by when Goon wasn't in Nena's thoughts. It was the thing about loss and trauma. Years might smooth out their rough edges, but their ghost effects remained, just outside the peripheral vision, waiting to haunt again.

So Goon came to mind as Nena sat outside in the dark, watching her mark's shadow pacing back and forth in his apartment. Because this wasn't a dispatch. This was wet work.

Three days were what it had taken for Nena to decide to take out the mark and determine the best time to dispatch him. She'd memorized the basic floor plan of the garden-style apartment complex. If she was right, he'd be leaving his apartment momentarily to rendezvous with his crew, check on his corners, make sure all were doing as they should.

She really should have been at home making last-minute preparations for tomorrow's mission, the one to General Konate's outpost in Kenya. It was a mission that had everyone on edge, for some reason. Was in a location that they hadn't been to before, and intel on places like this was always changing, thus making it hard to nail down a routine the team could bank on. The general was not a creature of habit. He was too nervous, always on the move, thinking—and rightfully so—that someone was out to get him. But he was who the Tribe wanted dispatched.

But now wasn't the time for Nena to be thinking about the general or the fact that Alpha would likely try to be a cowboy or that Sierra might freeze when she was needed the most. Nena needed to concentrate on the mission at hand, because even if it was a small job, it would require all her ability. There was no room for errors.

Nena would dispatch the target swiftly tonight. That was the only reprieve she'd give him for all the trouble he'd caused. He should thank her because she could do so much worse. She almost wished he'd try something just so she could.

The lights went out in his apartment. She slipped out of the driver's seat, closing the door softly. She surveilled the parking lot again. It was empty, except for her, at ten at night. She had parked behind his car, blocking him in, and popped her trunk. She briefly thought of the comment Elin had made about her uniform—all black—and decided it was smart. Black did hide the bloodstains. She might get some on her tonight.

Being suited up in all black worked well for her as she hid in the shadows, listening to her mark's sneakered feet *tap tap, tap tap* down the steps. If the scenario running through her mind played out correctly, he'd—

"What the hell is this?" He walked from beneath the apartment building's awning and realized his car was going nowhere.

"What the fuck?" His voice became higher, and he passed his white Charger, walking toward the weathered Corolla that Nena had lifted from an impound lot. He stopped just short of the passenger-side door and looked around the deserted parking lot. He could see no one. "What. The. Fuck!"

He was at a loss as to what to do. There was no one around. Call a tow truck? And pay for the car to be removed? There would be paperwork, and he was not a paperwork kind of guy. Call one of his boys? How long would they take to get there? He had places to be, and this motherfucking car was eating up his time. He was so easily read. And from beneath the balaclava Nena wore because one never knew what cameras were around, she watched him have a bit of a temper tantrum, throwing his arms up and down in frustration.

He was on the move again, pulling the Corolla's passenger-door handle. Locked.

"Shit."

He rounded the front of the car, peered in the driver's side window with his hands cupping his face to block the reflection of the streetlights. He saw the keys in the ignition. Tried the handle. Locked.

"Are you fucking kidding me?" he muttered. Nena had left the keys in to tease him. Make him angry. Take him off his guard, just a bit. It had worked. If he weren't so despicable, he'd be downright comedic.

By now, she was moving out of the shadows, inching toward the cars.

He tried the rear passenger door on the driver's side. Locked. Then he moved to the back of the car, in the exact scenario Nena had orchestrated in her mind. She appreciated when marks followed the script.

He was in front of the open trunk. Peering in while muttering a string of curse words. He put a hand in, likely looking for a crowbar or a jack to break a window. Instead, he noticed the plastic covering the floor and snatched his hand back toward his chest as if he'd been burned.

"What the hell!" he squealed.

He pulled out his phone. Maybe thinking now was the time for some backup. His own version of 911. Maybe he was getting that inexplicable tingle prey got when a predator was nearly upon them. When someone was watching. He took a step backward, away from the yawning black trunk. How many times had he relegated someone to the same fate that was about to befall him? A body in the trunk.

"Whose fucking car is this?" he asked the night air.

"Mine," she said right behind him, then stepped around him, so close they practically touched. "Hello there, Trek."

He attempted to spin around and go for his piece at the same time, like he was in some *Lethal Weapon* movie, but she was too quick for him and had him disarmed and twisted in her grip, his arm angled painfully behind him and his body bent nearly backward, looking up at her.

She plunged her blade deep through the soft skin beneath his chin. His body spasmed. His eyes were as round as jumbo marbles as he seized. His brain losing its function. His body following suit. She moved his head over, hovering over the trunk so his blood could drip there. They were in a weird dance, a reverse dip. She laid his upper torso in the trunk, pushed it in quickly, then folded his legs in behind him. She took a second to put her gloved finger to his neck and found no pulse. But to make sure her kill was good, she pulled her blade out and plunged it once into his chest, where the rib cage connected, at an angle that hit the already-ceased-beating heart.

She dropped his gun into the trunk with him. Wrapped the plastic quickly so the pooling blood wouldn't slip and slide onto the carpet.

She wiped her gloves on a towel she'd stuck in there for this very job and closed the trunk. Then she peered around before checking her watch. Not bad on time. It had felt like hours, but from the moment he'd appeared until now was only five minutes. Not too bad. Not the best either. She'd let him play around looking through the car too long.

Her go bag was on the floor of the passenger seat. With the key fob, she unlocked the door and got into the Corolla with its rusted parts and faded paint. She did a quick sweep around the area, looking for anyone who might have been watching. If they had, it was of no consequence. She'd obscured her face well enough with her balaclava.

She turned the key in the ignition. Tonight, her wet work dictated she'd be serving as her own cleaner.

13

The truck holding the team bumped along the road heading to the outpost's coordinates, driven by a local contact enlisted to transport them to and from the mission.

In exact replication of their earlier practice runs, the team snaked in sync, one behind another, on approach to the outer perimeter of the compound. Their goal was to locate and dispatch their target and the ragtag bunch of people he called his soldiers. They'd perform a check for any intel Network could use to trace the general's political and financial backers, then rendezvous with their transport. The driver would take them to the private airfield they'd flown into. If all went well, the team would be in and out without detection by Kenyan authorities. They would be long gone by the time the corpses at General Konate's outpost were found.

Donned in full gear with guns at the ready, they swept the perimeter through the murky green of their night vision visors: ahead of them, to the sides, and behind for any signs of movement—any indication that the team had been spotted. It was nearly 2:00 a.m., and the area was devoid of any human sound, save the soft toe steps Nena and the others made as they approached. Nature surrounded them with the eerie howls of hyenas and jackals who foraged the treeless terrain, searching for their night meal.

The outpost was bare bones, unlike what General Konate was likely used to. Not when he was on the run from several governments and couldn't afford any luxuries while he waited for his supporters to ferry him away from this place, re-up him with the supplies and funds he'd need to try again elsewhere . . . with this same country . . . with a new country. It didn't matter. The general enjoyed spreading unrest wherever he went, until something finally stuck.

Several small low-lying buildings dotted the grounds, with a dirt road running through the center and smaller trails splintering off to the left and right between the buildings. A smattering of jeeps, trucks, and cars sat parked between the structures.

Six thick, towering light posts cast a haze of white light over the compact area, which now resembled a small village rather than a collection of military domiciles. Through a covering of tall brush and bushes, the team surveilled the area, looking for signs of movement and waiting for their eye in the sky, Network, to give them a count of how many warm bodies there were and who was moving or not.

"You are a go," Network confirmed through the comm devices integrated into their visored headgear; their helmets and neck gaiters together prevented anyone from knowing anything about them, even their race or likely their gender either. "Twenty signatures by our count."

Nena signaled the others to move in, and like the well-trained team they were, they followed her command in perfect synchronization—the six of them, one behind another, automatic rifles drawn and engaged. Nena, team lead, always first, followed by Alpha, Kilo, Sierra, Charlie, and Yankee bringing up rear.

As they made their way farther in, they moved, paused, held, taking cover behind piles of disturbed rocks and stones, cement walls, an old, rusted tanker truck that was no longer in commission. They wove between lines of strung-up laundry: boxer briefs and socks, shirts and camo pants and T-shirts. As they reached the edge of the closest building, Nena signaled them to turn off their night vision, leaving their clear visors on. The outpost was lit well enough.

Consistent with Intel's report, the general's guard duty appeared light; only a few men, Nena counted, about what was to be expected with a skeleton crew of soldiers.

Armed subjects. Not friendlies. Nena raised her hand in signal, and after a quick succession of silent shots, the guards were down. The team continued, finding no others on duty, no moving heat signals Network could detect outside the buildings. Network cleared them to proceed with the plan. Divide and conquer.

As they'd done so many times during their dry runs at the Miami training facility, they moved into the middle of the outpost, clearing each object large enough to hide a person. Up and down, up and down, their muzzles went. This was a compound of men, and with men came women to keep their beds warm. The team had to ensure they didn't take out anyone who wasn't a target.

Once in the heart of the place, they fractured into teams of two, each pair headed to their assigned building. Carry out their objective, collect any intel, regroup. Nena with Alpha, Sierra with Kilo, Charlie with Yankee. Alpha flashed both hands: ten minutes to do what they needed and return here. In and out.

Nena and Alpha went to the building farthest toward the back, which Intel had predetermined was the location of the general's sleeping quarters. Confirmation came again back to back, letting each paired team know how many bodies were in the buildings. Nena and Alpha had two glowing heat signals. They stood on either side of the door and waited a beat before opening it and rushing in. It was indeed the general's room. His uniform was hanging on a wire hanger in the corner. Jazz music played softly in the background. It was warm in the room. Very warm, which could be because the single window was closed, preventing the cooler night air from making its way in.

The table held automatic rifles, two laptops, a handgun, and two small glasses, one empty, the other with a small amount of clear liquid in it. Next to them, a partially consumed bottle of Maker's Mark. A figure was lying in the bed, and at the desk sat another person, a man in a tank top, briefs, and socks. Alpha moved to the bed, while Echo went for the man bent over the desk, having fallen asleep atop papers and binders. His balding head rested on his arms.

Nena aimed her gun at his head, moving in closer, preparing to ID him before she made her kill shot. Alpha was at the bed, bending over the figure, a woman whose hair spilled over the top of the covers. As Nena neared the man, she felt the temperature increasing, confusing her. She wasn't sure if it was her imagination or not.

Alpha pulled back the covers at the same moment Nena prodded the sleeping man's shoulder with the tip of her gun. His arm fell away, and she noticed the dark pool of liquid beneath his head. Across the room Alpha yelped, then cursed.

"She's dead. One in the chest," he said. "There's a heating element around her."

"A what?" Nena asked, prying her eyes from the dark pool to look at Alpha and the body of the dead woman. A rectangular heating pad was wrapped around her and an extension cord plugged into the wall socket.

Network said, "Repeat? Confirm subject is down?"

Nena looked down at the man, moving him so she could see his face more clearly. He was not the general. And he was very dead. She bent over, finding the space heater beneath the desk that was giving off the heat signal they'd mistaken for his.

"A trap," she muttered.

"What?" Alpha asked. "Echo, what the hell is this?"

They were to use names as little as possible in case there was a breach in their comms. But in moments like this, she couldn't fault him.

The comms sounded patchy, heavy static playing tag with the Network operative's voice at the other end saying, "Repeat? Repeat?"

"A trap," she said urgently, her breath catching as she backed away from the dead man. "Fall back," she said into her comms, hoping her team was reading her. "Repeat. Fall back. Someone knows we're here."

All hell broke loose. Outside the room, there was a crack and then a thundering boom that sent vibrations through the ground. Nena heard her team through comms, asking what was going on—screaming that the people in their buildings were all dead. Gunfire erupted around the outpost. Men were shouting, and Nena spun on her heels, drawing her rifle back up when a man in camo pants and a soccer T-shirt ran into the open doorway, gun in hand, and started firing.

She threw herself out of the line of fire. Hoped Alpha had had a chance to do the same. She twisted up, aimed, and fired off a shot, taking the man out. They had to get out of the room. In there, they were sitting ducks.

"Move," she commanded, getting to her feet and heading toward the doorway.

Alpha was in lockstep, steadily repeating, "What the fuck? What the fuck?"

She needed him to be quiet. She had to think. Figure out a way to get the team out of there.

"We're under fire. I repeat, we're under fire. Need an opening or an extraction."

She could hear nothing but garbled response on the other side of her comms. She needed to get outside, where the reception would be clearer.

Alpha was already shooting through the door, clearing the way for their exit. She grabbed his back and followed him out into the blessedly cool night air, but that did nothing to calm her. The team was engaged in heavy fire. The once-sleepy outpost was alive with soldiers; the general's supposed skeleton crew seemed pretty meaty. The firepower they showered on Nena and Alpha kept the pair on the defense.

They took cover around the corner of the building. The rest of the team was nowhere to be seen. Nena still heard them through comms, under siege, trying to get out. Kilo screamed. And then she could hear him no more.

"Kilo's hit. He's down," Sierra yelled, her voice near panic. "I-I don't think . . . he's dead."

Nena wasn't about to go out like this, tricked and taking cover from gunfire. Somehow their mission had been compromised. The general had had warning they were coming and had been waiting for them. She needed to get her team out. She'd already failed, and now losing Kilo . . . Nena didn't have the words.

From what she could tell, enemy fire was coming from above. She wasn't sure what the explosion was, but it had sounded farther away.

"What do we do, boss?" Alpha asked.

Nena tapped her visor. The protective covering retracted so she could see the scene for what it was. Commotion was all around them. The general's men running about, engaging in fire with the rest of the team. Sierra weeping into her comms and seemingly unable to continue with her job.

"Blast your way out," she said. "Get it together," she added to Sierra. "Get it together and get to the rendezvous. We'll meet you all there. Clear a path for yourselves."

One by one, the team confirmed. Nena pushed out the thought that one of their own had not. That was done now, and there would be time to grieve later.

Alpha was watching her, his eyes alight with adrenaline. "We're doing this?"

She nodded. "We are."

She pulled her explosives from her utility pockets and activated them. Alpha followed suit, and they tossed them one by one up and over the tops of the buildings, hearing them land, hearing the men yell warnings, hearing the men scream when the explosives went off. And with the explosions, Alpha and Nena were on their feet and on the run.

"Network, we need a way out of here. Is the area clear? How many do you see? We need backup." Nena ran through the list of needs that weren't being met. She heard nothing in response over the roar of explosions as she kept her head low. *Get to rendezvous. Get out of here.*

She led the way with Alpha at her back. Picking off the men they came across. Before her ammo could run out, she ejected the magazine, inserted another, and took a calm breath to ease her nerves so she could focus and aim properly. She turned, aimed, fired. Did it again. And again, clearing their pathway at the front while Alpha kept their rear protected.

Charlie and Yankee were ahead of them and to the left, moving toward their designated location, away from the hub of the outpost where they'd entered. *Good,* Nena thought. *They're close.* And Sierra? Where was she? Nena couldn't see through the smoke and fire. The small, confined area between the buildings served as a perfect receptacle, containing it all so it was impossible to see through.

There was a sudden flash. A bang right in the location where Charlie was running, the explosion going off beside him. Nena yelled; she knew she did. She couldn't help it as she watched two more of her team sail into the air and come down hard, their bodies twisted, burned. Unmoving. Gone.

Alpha waved her off. "Go. I'll cover."

"No," Nena said. "Not leaving unless we go together."

"Sierra is pinned down back there. There's no way she's getting to the truck by herself. You'll need to help her. I'll cover you both."

Nena quickly ran through other scenarios. Finding no better option, she begrudgingly agreed. Sierra needed her. Alpha would follow.

"Right behind me, right?"

Alpha nodded, sliding her a cocky grin. "This is the last time I'll ever be behind you again."

Nena didn't know whether to laugh or punch him. It was absolutely the wrong time for him to be throwing shade over leadership, but right now his shade was welcome.

Alpha reloaded his rifle and began laying down fire as Nena made a run for their rendezvous location and had her first glimpse at what had caused the first explosion they'd heard. Their transport, the truck that was supposed to carry them away from here, was burning up ahead, taken out by a rocket launcher, and the driver with it. They were trapped.

Sierra was pinned under heavy fire ahead of Nena. Luckily not nearly as paralyzed with fear as she'd been over comms moments ago. Sierra was picking off combatants with a cool determination Nena was proud of.

"Network." There was urgency in Nena's voice, a wavering trickle of fear that as wrong as all this had gone, it was getting more wrong by the minute. "Our transport is gone. Repeat. Transport is gone by enemy fire. Is relief coming?"

Nena chanced a look over her shoulder at Alpha, trying to pinpoint his location and gauge which combatants were the most threat to him. In that moment, she saw him rise to his knees, his rifle pointed and firing beyond her, clearing the way. His visor was retracted. But he missed one or two, and beneath the white light of one of those towering lamps, a bullet found its mark. With the first hit to Alpha's chest, Nena stopped breathing. His shoulder flew back from the force of the second bullet slamming into him. And again.

She turned to run back to him. But it was as if the world were devoid of sound. None in her ear from her comms, none in the chaos all around her. There was nothing.

Nothing but the piercing scream of the RPG as it streaked over her head toward where Alpha was now sitting on his haunches, listing heavily to his side against the tanker where they'd been taking cover before he'd told her to run. His rifle slipped to the ground, his life oozing out of him as he grinned at her through bloodied lips.

"No," Nena breathed, unsure if she said it aloud or if it was only her thoughts.

The impact of the missile hitting the tanker was so intense it lifted Nena off her feet. She sailed backward into the air. Seeing nothing but Alpha's cocky grin and then a bright orangey-red ball of flaming inferno. Hearing nothing but the echo of his last words to her over and over in her ear.

Last time I'll ever be behind you again.

14

It took a long moment for Nena to come to her senses as she rolled on the ground trying to get her bearings. She thought she heard her name. Thought someone was screaming at her to get up. To come on. She might even be dead after an explosion like that. As dead as Alpha was. And Kilo. And Charlie. And Yankee. Her whole team.

Sierra was still alive. And if Nena could believe what she was hearing, it was Sierra's voice calling her name. Telling her to get moving. Nena did as she was told.

The moment her boots hit dirt, she was off and running for cover. And time no longer stood still; the action resumed, the general's men firing upon her again. There were only two of them now, two of Nena's Dispatch team, and rapid shots over her head as she tried to remember to duck low. Her people, her team, had fallen. Alpha . . .

"Network, do you read?"

She couldn't think about Alpha now. Not about the way he'd been there one moment and gone the next. The spot where he'd stayed so she could get free now nothing but burning oil and dirt.

It was Sierra who snapped Nena to. Said they had to get out of there. Said she couldn't get any response from Network.

Network?

Bullets whizzed past them, so close Nena could feel the disturbance of air as they missed her. She ducked as a window in the building next to her shattered, its shards raining down on her, smacking against her helmet. She shielded her eyes, turning her head so the helmet took most of the hits that then fell onto the Kevlar vest wrapped around her chest. That was supposed to protect her too. Hadn't helped Alpha one bit.

"Network. Do. You. Read?" Nena called again. It was difficult to keep her voice calm. But she had to for Sierra, wanting her to maintain the same energy she had and not revert to the fear and panic she'd displayed earlier. Nena swallowed down the rising bile at the nothingness in her ear. She couldn't even hear Sierra clearly; Sierra sounded like she was in a bottle. But Sierra was supposed to be coming through her earpiece, and she was supposed to sound as if she were right there in the helmet with Nena. The earpiece was dead.

Network. "Request extraction," Nena said, trying again.

Sierra tapped her shoulder. Pointed at a pickup truck, old, full of holes, and well past its expiration date. Sierra put two fingers up, pointed to Nena and then to herself and then to the truck. Nena strained to hear above the bullets, above the combatants calling to each other to fan out and find and kill them.

"Cover me," Sierra said. "I can start it if it's not just decor."

Nena nodded. She pulled her rifle nose up and heaved herself onto her knees so she could sweep around the corner of the building. They'd have to be quick if they were making a run for the truck. The moment Nena laid fire on whoever awaited them around that corner, Sierra had to run like the devil was on her ass. Then Nena would have to take fire to give Sierra a chance to start the engine. If it could be started.

Nena counted off, gave the signal for Sierra to move, and let loose her fire. She saw enemies hiding behind various buildings and automobiles and aiming for them. Nena returned fire, then loaded another magazine. She checked for Sierra, noting her teammate had made it to the truck and had managed to get the door open. She was pressed against the machine, shooting so Nena could run the few yards across the open space between the building's sanctuary and the truck.

Nena ran.

"What's going on?" Sierra yelled when Nena had finally made it to her through the plumes of dust that bloomed like tiny little napalm clouds whenever a bullet with her name on it hit the ground instead.

Hot metal pinged metal, bullets thudded against brick, and wood splintered. Nena saw Charlie, one of his arms hanging limply at his side, trying to make a break toward them and the truck, and for a moment, he was the best sight in the world.

She held up a hand for him to wait where he was until they got the truck started. But he panicked, maybe thinking they'd leave without him. He ran for them, approaching on her left as another burst of rapid fire ripped through the air. Charlie's body jerked as each bullet made contact. He was down, for real this time. Unmoving in the dirt. Nena pounded a fist on the truck in rage and anguish, letting Sierra know to work faster. The truck was old and sputtering, taking a minute to get its momentum going.

Nena pulled another explosive from the pack strapped to her thigh, activated it, and launched it in the direction of the gunfire. It exploded on impact, offering a brief respite.

Sierra was half in, half out of the driver's seat of the truck, rummaging below at the wiring, yelling at Nena that they had to get out of there.

"Network, do you read?" Nena couldn't understand it. Why weren't they answering? Where was their eye in the sky? Where was air support, which should have sent missiles the moment they'd started taking fire from the general's men? Where was Recovery to take them out of there? There was nothing.

Heat from the exploded tanker added to the already-sweltering air. This outpost full of ex-military had somehow known Nena's team was coming, had been lying in wait for them. But how?

Where. Was. Network?

Above the din of the fire's roar, the lull in the gunshots, and Sierra muttering to herself as she attempted to hot-wire the truck to drive them to safety, the high-pitched squeal of feedback. Nena's eyes rose to the speaker at the top of the nearest light post. A click, and then someone—a man—spoke.

"Is this on correctly? It is? They can hear me?" More feedback. He cleared his throat. "I am General Konate. The Tribe sent a team to find me. I hear you were supposed to be the very best. And yet you lie beneath the rubble of my wrath. Let your deaths be proof of my power, and let your commanders know that their so-called Tribe failed in this and will fail in all things."

The general began laughing, a giddy, chortling noise like a thousand knives stabbing Nena with her own failure. She'd been too arrogant, thinking she knew all, thinking this mission would be a success like all the others. She hadn't considered . . . this.

"Screw his noise." Sierra broke in through Nena's thoughts, correctly reading her eyes. "We're getting out of here, understand?"

Nena nodded, swallowing hard. Someone had jammed their frequency. It was the only way Network, the most reliable resource they had, could be immobilized. "I think I nearly got it. There are sparks," Sierra grunted.

How would the general have the capabilities advanced enough to intercept and take down communications at the level of Network?

Miraculously, the truck coughed, sputtering to life. Sierra twisted off the wires, then climbed into the seat, keeping low against the intermittent incoming fire.

Sierra said, "Maybe we'll catch a signal farther out."

She pounded the outside of the driver's side door twice, gunning the sputtering engine. Nena hauled herself into the bed of the truck, lying down flat. She wanted to be able to see what was coming from behind. Keep the road clear so Sierra could drive them through. She peeked over the rim, saw combatants running toward them through the thick plumes of smoke, orange sparks from their gun barrels flashing.

The truck lurched and began to roll, starting off slow before gaining momentum. Shots rang out, forcing Nena to dive down in the truck bed for cover. She pulled her last two explosive packs and launched them into the abyss behind them. Flashes of white and orange erupted from the darkness as each pack exploded, adding to the fire from the burning tanker. She fished out another round, pushed it into her rifle, and shot blindly into the curtain of acrid black smoke and flames. She thought she heard engines behind them and braced herself for an envoy chasing them.

Nena remained in position, continuing to lay down fire at whatever was still behind them, anything to give her and Sierra the slightest chance at getting away. She chucked her mag and loaded another. With no more rounds for the automatic left, Nena tossed her rifle to the side. It clattered against the metal lining of the bed. She pulled out her sidearms and kept firing, hoping it would be enough.

Nena and Sierra rolled past the ruined and burning remains of the truck that had driven them there, Sierra slowing as they passed, and Nena got a good look at the wreckage and the burning remains of the driver who'd helped them get there. Then they rode into a darkness where no extraction awaited. No relief. No support. They were all alone.

Nena's last try into her comms was weak, with no belief behind her words. "Network, do you read?"

No Cleaners. No air support.

No Network.

Because Network had gone dark.

15

To say Network was in chaos was an understatement. The last of Nena's team touched back down into Miami International after spending hours debriefing at the nearest Network safe house, glad to be back to whatever semblance of normalcy they could have after losing the rest of their team.

"In a horror movie, we'd be considered the final girls." It was Sierra's bad attempt at a joke. "Think Stephen King would be interested?"

Nena humored her with a half grimace and an even briefer nod.

"Wrong kind of horror," she answered, trying her best to erase images of Alpha's body slumping when he'd been hit and then, adding insult to injury, hit again in the RPG explosion.

Sierra spied Witt waiting for them beyond their exit from the terminal and slowed her steps. Her face became guarded, and she moved as if she dreaded taking another step.

"What is it?" Nena said.

"Do you think they made it back home yet? The rest of the team?"

It was customary, just as with the military, to never leave one of their own behind if they could avoid it. When she and Sierra had made it back to the airfield, to the plane waiting to take them out of the country, there were already reinforcements on the ground and on their way to the outpost—the relief Nena had desperately called for during the mission. All in vain.

When Network finally came back online, Nena and Sierra were well out of danger with none of the general's people following. Network came in like a rush in their earpieces, calling for updates, calling their names. Receiving nothing in return but the life signals of the last two standing as they finally blinked back on in their systems. As the cacophony sounded in their comms, the two ignored it all. For several minutes, they ignored the endless streams of questions, feeling stranded, confused, and not a little bit lost at being left in the dark.

Only when Witt's voice finally came through the comms like a brilliant ray of sunlight in a black hole abyss did Nena snap out of her morose silent treatment. "Echo, do you read? What is your status?"

"The mission was compromised and failed. Lost four."

She listened to the pause that followed as her words traveled through the airwaves and settled on the shoulders of everyone listening in.

"Understood." Classic Witt. Business as usual, with no room for emotion, for grief, for anything else. "Come on in."

Nena wanted to hit something. Blame someone for what had happened to her team.

The relief teams, a day late and a dollar short, had been heading out as Sierra and Nena had arrived at the airstrip, with promises to retrieve Nena's fallen team members and return them home. The "team" was now a duo, and what was Nena supposed to do with one other member besides herself? Did she even want another team? Not to mention, What would Dad and the Tribe do with her? A failed team leader.

And now, Sierra and Nena walked side by side down the terminal to catch their rides. Ahead of them, yards away, stood Witt, who'd timed his arrival from London to meet them. His appearance was as haggard as she felt.

Nena gave him a wary look, understanding Witt's reason for being in Miami. To drill her more about what had happened at the outpost, about why General Konate had gotten away.

Sierra asked, "What happens to us now?"

"What do you mean? We go home."

She shook her head. "I mean with the team. With the Tribe." She whispered this part. "Will there be an inquest or something? Will we be retired?" She whispered that ominous word too. It even gave Nena pause.

She wanted to lie. "I don't know. Never happened like this before." Her shoulders gave a slight shrug.

Sierra broke out into a coarse laugh that sounded more like a bark. "Ha! Uh, you think?"

They were nearly to Witt, who studied them from beneath intense eyebrows and pursed lips with endless questions lurking behind them.

"Do you know their names?" Sierra said.

"What?" Came out sharper than she'd intended, but the question had startled her.

"The guys. We always go by our team names. Even when we're off duty and bowling, we still go by those names."

"It's how we were introduced to one another. That's not unusual."

Sierra stopped short of Witt, who remained at his post, taking their cues that they wanted to speak privately. She prodded the floor with the toe of her black-and-tan New Balances. Her short copper-honey ringlets bounced as her eyes bobbed from the floor to Nena's face. Nena was uneasy with where Sierra was going, not wanting to think about the team any deeper than she already was.

"I feel so guilty right about now," Sierra said, her eyes beginning to well up. "These guys died beside me, and I don't even know their names. What kind of teammate am I? Does the Tribe know? Do you?" Sierra's eyes were beseeching. "Do you know mine?"

"I don't know their names." First lie. Nena said it without missing a beat, without blinking.

Except Nena did know their names. Charlie was Daniel. Yankee was Lewis. Kilo was Richard. Alpha was Albert. A name he'd hated, Nena was sure. And Sierra . . . Sierra was—

"Jesus Christ," Sierra said.

Nena paused. No. That wasn't it.

Sierra's eyes flashed in anger and hurt. "My name is Jessica. Since you didn't care to know our names. Know mine. And I know yours, Nena." She shook her head, disgusted. "Guess we all have to since you're a Knight and all and we're just peons to your family and the Tribe."

Wasn't true. Sierra's words cut away at Nena's center, but Nena didn't respond. This was Sie—Jessica's anger talking. Her grief. She couldn't believe Nena really did care for them beyond the missions. After all, Nena had done nothing except bowl a couple of rounds to show her team she saw them as more than people to dispatch with.

"Sie—"

"Jessica." She said it with accusation, with anger and hurt. Looked at Nena as if the veil of illusion was pulled back and she could see Nena and their employer for what they truly were. The way she was looking at Nena cut through all Nena's bravado, down to her core. For the first time Nena felt guilty at how easy it was for her and the Tribe to move on, to see people's deaths as a problem needing to be remedied or, as in the case of her and Sierra's fallen comrades, collateral damage. Par for the course.

Sierra glowered at her, then walked off, deflecting Witt's incoming words with a hand held up to his face as he attempted to stop her, because more debriefing and all. Not today. Not for Sierra.

"Let her go," Nena said, watching her last team member retreating. She wanted to go after Sierra, tell her she'd always known their names and would never forget them, that her team was more than just that. They were family, warts and all. But she didn't.

Because at the end of the day, Nena was still Echo. And Echo knew work came first, which meant finding answers to what had happened to Network. How had the general known they were coming? The two had to be connected.

And that connection meant there was a mole inside the Tribe.

16

Nena took in the scene as she was tackled by a fifteen-year-old who had more strength stuffed into that little body than Nena had remembered. She blinked, unsure if her eyes were deceiving her. Cort was at a table by the glass doors leading to the balcony, papers strewed all over as he pored over them. Elin, grinning triumphantly at Nena, stood behind him. Her hands were on her hips, and her smile was knowing.

Gently, Nena extricated herself from Georgia, but not before taking a deep inhale of the coconut-shea scent of her hair. Nena knew that scent. She'd gone to the beauty store to buy it for Georgia and was happy Georgia was still using it.

Maybe Elin knew Nena needed this reprieve. A week after what had happened in Kenya, after losing her team, Nena was still reeling. This was the first time she'd really left her home and not spent every waking moment going through the events over and over, trying to figure out where they'd gone wrong. What had happened to their intel? What had happened to Network? Witt couldn't provide answers, and after meeting her and Sierra at the airport, after grilling them about what had occurred, he'd flown back to Europe to continue his investigation.

At least the bodies of her team had been retrieved from the deserted outpost, a battlefield of dead—both the general's people and Nena's. Retrieving their bodies was the only consolation she had. She'd made sure directives were given to send them home and to make sure their families would never want for anything again. Not that any amount of money could replace their lives. It was Alpha's death that haunted her the most—not just the knowledge that his body had been burned beyond recognition, with only his tags to identify him, but that he was the reason she and Sierra had escaped.

She pulled Georgia away from her so she could take a good look at her. Turned her head this way and that. Didn't see any injuries. The girl didn't look scared. The exact opposite. She was beaming at Nena, and before Nena knew it, she was beaming back. But for now, she needed to know what was going on, and Georgia's mouth was running a mile a minute.

"I'm so happy to see you! I've got so much to tell you. Why haven't you answered any of my text messages?" Georgia winked at Nena, then lifted an eyebrow before sliding a look to her dad. "It's rude, you know. Even for an adult. Even for a—" She glanced over her shoulder at her dad, saw he was pointing out something to Elin, and leaned in close to Nena to whisper, "For a wudini."

Georgia pronounced the Ghanaian word like it rhymed with Houdini when it most certainly did not.

She leaned back, as if satisfied, as if only the two of them shared this little secret.

"Your hair looks good. You've been doing what I taught you?" Nena twirled her finger into one of Georgia's loose curls. It glistened and looked hydrated. A frisson of pride snaked through Nena's belly and made her chest swell with love for Georgia Baxter.

"Yep, I keep at it," Georgia answered. "Do you think you and Dad can be cool again?"

Nena foraged her thoughts for a satisfactory answer. "I, um . . . well, you know. Your dad and I are taking space from each other."

Georgia flipped her hand. "He's like a straight arrow. He needed a little time to get used to what we do."

"We?" Nena repeated, entirely puzzled.

Georgia didn't answer, nodding. She mouthed, *We,* with a glint in her eye.

This was weird, like a scene out of *The Twilight Zone*, but Nena opted to let it go. There were more important things to figure out. Like what the Baxters were doing here talking it up with Elin as if they were all the best of friends. Nena shook her head to ward off the weirdness. She suggested Georgia see if Elin had anything good to eat in the kitchen. Georgia shrugged and separated herself from Nena; Georgia was an expert at disappearing when she received the *grown-ups want to talk* signal.

"What's going on?" Nena asked, preparing herself for the other shoe to drop. "Has something else happened?" She gestured to Cort but spoke to Elin. "Were they threatened?"

"We're fine," Cort said. She couldn't bring herself to meet his gaze. "I'll let your sister fill you in on why we're here and her bright idea."

Elin smiled innocently. "So I appreciated the heads-up right before your"—she cast a guarded look at Cort—"last trip that you'd spoken to Dad. I still think we should have waited till we had concrete proof, but whatever. I get it."

"He needed to know," Nena answered.

"He did." Elin sniffed. "But now that he's aware, we need concrete proof before he can make any recommendations to the Council."

Cort watched them with a curiosity Nena found unnerving. She wondered if his cop intuition or his lawyer's penchant for legalese was firing on all cylinders behind those watchful eyes. The elephant in the room was so big she was incapable of ignoring it. Yet still, she tried to focus on what her sister was saying.

Elin said, "Since we don't know who to trust, I figured we needed an outside source. One who is unaffiliated with the Tribe, can be totally objective, and knows how to follow the money trail." She spread her hands with a wide smile as if saying *ta-da*. "Who else but your guy Cort to save the day! Genius, innit?"

"But he's with law enforcement," Nena said. Her glance in Cort's direction was cautious. Six months ago, when she'd decided to spare his life and disobey her Dispatch orders, his affiliations hadn't bothered her much. Or when she'd allowed herself to be smitten by him and his daughter and the notion of being a part of their Baxter life.

Nena hadn't cared anything about law enforcement then, and she only brought it up now in a feeble attempt to hide the relief on her face. To keep at bay the joy she felt realizing that Cort, despite the hurt and betrayal with which he'd looked at her from his hospital bed the night he'd told her they were over, was here now.

Cort cleared his throat. "Not anymore," he said. "I've been gone from the federal attorney's office for a while now." He rubbed his hand over his head of small curls. He still looked the same, the kind of brown eyes that made Nena want to take a dip in them. He slipped his hands into the pockets of his jogger pants, which were fitted enough to emphasize his athletic frame beneath them. "After losing my ex-partner, Mack, and all that's happened with us . . ."

He looked as uncomfortable as Nena felt, and Elin was eating it up.

"While I still have reservations," Cort continued, eyes holding Nena's, "you saved my daughter from a madman. And you saved me. I owe you."

"I was there, too, you know," Elin chimed in. "At your flat. *I* called the authorities to take you to hospital and stayed there with you until my sister came." She pointed at herself repeatedly.

Elin ignored their groans.

"Fine," Cort said. "I owe you too."

Elin beamed at Nena, her face saying *I told you so.*

"Right," Nena answered, slowly. "I put you in danger. And now Elin has brought you right back in." She glowered at her doe-eyed sister, who was rubbing her belly as if that would ease Nena's growing ire.

"Don't be dramatic." Elin produced a rectangular slip of paper, waving it in the air like a flag in front of them. "Anyway, I'm paying Cort for his services. It's a check for a nice sum that sets you and your kid up for life, brother."

Cort backed away from it, his hands in the air. "Call this pro bono."

Elin snorted. "Pro bono is the last thing we need."

"Well, I don't want any part of whatever kind of money that is."

Elin rolled her eyes so hard Nena was positive she'd suffered eye strain. "Now you're trying to be insulting, mate. The money's legit."

"I didn't know people still wrote checks," Nena murmured, glancing to make sure Georgia hadn't sneaked back in from the kitchen. The girl had a way of materializing like a ninja in places where she did not belong.

"It's ceremonial," Elin returned.

"Ceremonial or not, I'm not taking it."

Elin trained her brown eyes on Cort. Nena watched as the jovial Elin melted away. Cort didn't stand a chance now. "Doesn't matter whether you take this check or not—the funds have already been transferred into your account. Like I said, the check was ceremonial. So should there suddenly be a change of heart . . ."

There would be a trail linking Cort to them. Ashamed and embarrassed at her sister's behavior, Nena said, "Elin."

"You're blackmailing me." Even irate, Cortland Baxter was one hell of a good-looking man.

Elin countered, "You're being overdramatic."

Cort fumbled with his phone, pawing at the screen to pull up his bank app. He stared disbelievingly at the new thousands now flooding his account.

"There's more money, but I'm not trying to raise red flags with large-sum deposits," Elin explained as if all were well and they were merely conducting regular business. "And it's not blackmail. It's a retainer for your new private practice. We're your first clients."

"Bringing Cort in is dangerous," Nena protested. "The missing shipments, what happened in Kenya, what happened to Network—if all of these events are connected, it means someone's coming after the Tribe. I don't want Cort and Georgia around it."

"What are the chances of someone launching a full-on attack at us like that?" Elin said, repeating a debate they'd had more than once since the disastrous dispatch last week. "Cort is the perfect outside person to look into the financials. The accounting discrepancies could be someone low level or even just someone hacking in and stealing. That general still has connections in high places—and us taking out his bookkeeper, it probably put him on guard. Let's not overreact; let's get evidence." Elin grinned. "Cort's going to save the day, isn't he?"

Cort and Nena's only response was to stare.

Elin used that as her cue that they were on board. "Now, you two, sort yourselves out. So we can get back to the business of tracking these accounts."

Elin gave one last meaningful stare at Nena before lifting the hem of her rainbow-colored caftan and sweeping out of the room like some regal African queen, chin held high, leaving Nena alone with Cort wondering how to begin sorting any of their mess out.

17

Cort looked down at his hands, folded over the balcony railing of Elin's condo. Beside him, Nena waited for him to speak his piece, gripping the railings herself. She didn't trust her sister not to eavesdrop inside. The balcony provided more privacy.

"Sometimes it feels like we take two steps forward and then a giant leap backward," he finally began, running a hand over his hair. "Finding out what you do and about your family . . ."

"Is what? A giant leap backward? My family?" Nena knew she was nitpicking at Cort's words, cutting him off instead of allowing him to complete his thought. She knew what he was trying to get at, that the wudini part was the leap backward, not her family per se, yet him bringing her family into the point he was attempting to make needled her.

He must have realized how he had come across. "What? No!" he said quickly, his face shocked and horrified, which was calming to Nena. Meant there was still something to reason with. "Your job. The dispatching. That's the giant leap backward."

She took a breath, using his clarification to guide what she said next.

"What am I doing but trying to make the world a better place for my people by removing those who have caused them harm and only served as obstacles to progress and their advancement?"

Though he looked ready to say something, no response came.

"Is it wrong to want better?" she asked, gaining steam. "You've been looking through some of the Tribe's business. You can see all the humanitarian ventures our foundations are involved in. We are working on building a training academy to teach skill sets to people who can't attend university. We are trying to make it so African people have no need to rely on anyone but themselves and the riches their countries provide. In those reports you've been looking at with Elin, you can see what we purchase for the people. People, Cort—not governments or facilities that funnel supplies elsewhere. Those are the opportunities my job clears the path for. Without what I do, those things wouldn't happen as they currently do."

He was rubbing the top of his head. Nena knew his tell, what he did when situations were overwhelming or stressful. "Nena, your world is unlike any others."

She scoffed, "You would be surprised."

"I don't know if I can do it . . . ," he said softly.

She waited for him to continue, holding the balcony railing tightly in her grip.

"Dispense your brand of justice," he finished, giving her a look of both determination and shame.

She snorted. "You don't have to dispense anything." She put some space between them. Movement from the other side of the sliding glass doors drew her attention, and there was Georgia, waving at them from inside. She was grinning widely, euphoric that her dad and Nena were finally in the same space together. And talking.

She returned her attention to Cort, who was waiting for her to continue. "My brand of justice," she intoned. "The brand of justice you speak of, the Tribe's, is not for your judgment, to be honest, Cort." She used her hand to gesture between the two of them. "You and I have had this discussion before. Remember? The first night I came to your house to eat spaghetti with you and Georgia. We spoke of different systems of justice. Of black and white and shades of gray. Is mine wrong because it's different from what you have practiced here? If you lived abroad, if you had stayed in Haiti, would your 'brand of justice' be different and therefore okay? Is your definition of justice determined by where you live? Or by who you are and what your belief system is?"

His mouth dropped, then closed. He hadn't thought of it that way.

"I won't purport to know what it's like to be a Black man in America, but I know what it's like to be a Black woman. An immigrant, a Black Ghanaian in a world outside of my country? I know the injustices of this country well. I've seen what those in power do, how they wield their power and resources to—I don't know—exert control and elicit fear. I watch the news reports of Black and Brown people dying at the hands of police and how very few of those killings find justice. People should just wait for the court system, which is already stacked against them and will inevitably fail them when it's needed the most? Where's the justice in that?"

She shook her head, disgusted. "I believe your system is flawed, highly so, but I don't judge it. It is misused and imbalanced, constructed to serve only a select group of people, and we know who they are. They most certainly don't look like you or me." She raised an eyebrow to put a period on her point. "When other brands of justice pop up to even out that imbalance just a smidge, shouldn't you be relieved? Shouldn't you be like, *Finally, justice is served?*"

"You're talking vigilante justice, Nena," Cort said. Frustration coated his every word as he implored her to understand. But she understood perfectly well. Understood more than he ever would because her world was expansive and his was a protected microcosm. But she couldn't fault him for the world in which he lived. It was all he knew. She only wished he would allow himself to see more than what he's known.

He continued. "We discussed that at the spaghetti dinner too. Just because you think something is unfair doesn't mean your way is the right way to handle it."

"It may not be the right way all the time. May be the *only* way. Sometimes, Cort, justice is *just us*. And that is what the Tribe does."

She hoped this was the final time they'd have to have this conversation. Hoped they could be done with it and move on . . . together. Apart. But a conclusion in which they would no longer be at an impasse.

Nena believed in the Tribe's mission. Yes, Paul—an evil man—had infiltrated the Council. Yes, there were bad players in the bunch. But that was where she came in, with Elin and Witt and Network, to root them out. Yes, there would always be imperfection, but what in this world was perfect? Certainly not any government Cort spoke of. She needed him to understand that.

Her hand lifted, and she yearned to touch him as she used to. She wanted to feel the warmth of his smooth cheek against the palm of her hand. To trail her fingertips along the edges of his beard or the fresh fade on the back of his head. She wanted him to hold her and lie to her that the deaths of four of her people weren't her fault. She didn't touch him, stopping herself just before she made contact. Her fingers curled into a fist. If she touched him, her resolve to stand firm in her words would crumble. And that couldn't happen. Because she was a woman of her word and her words were her actions. And her actions for the Tribe would never falter. This was fact.

She whispered, "Let me know what you've decided."

They stood side by side, each consumed by their own thoughts until Nena's phone began ringing, intruding upon the serenity of the balcony and the beauty of Miami. She ignored the phone at first. Knowing it was work. Not caring what they wanted. More questions she had no answers to. And no answers to the questions she had about what had happened to their comms last week.

The phone refused to be ignored. Its incessant ringing continued despite Nena pressing the side button to shut it up. It would only start back up again.

Cort said, "Don't you want to get that? Could be work."

She considered him a long while, wondering if he was being facetious or not. Elin appeared at the door, her face tight and grim. Nena believed in folktales and stories of things that went bump in the night. In bad juju. That trouble came in threes.

One: the suspicious transactions.

Two: that Network had gone down during a critical mission, which had cost the lives of four of her team and the trust of the last remaining one.

And number three?

She didn't want to ask. But her job was to do so.

"What's happened?" she said. This was the first she and Cort had shared the same space in months. First time he was but an arm's reach away. She didn't want anything to shorten their time. Even if all they were doing was arguing about who had a right to exact justice and who didn't. Being near him and Georgia had been the infusion of life she'd needed.

She held her breath, already feeling the icy-cold touch of Echo sliding in as work came a-calling. *Time to get to work,* Echo was saying.

Elin, without preamble or a glance Cort's way, said, "You're needed home in London. There's been a hit."

18

Nena was on a plane and landing in London within twenty-four hours of learning that one of their many Network satellite stations had been hit. Witt was already in town to update her father on the Kenyan mission and the search for the general, who'd evaded his dispatch and was currently in the wind. It was dusk when Nena stopped in front of Witt on the walkway, looking as if he didn't feel the bite of cold beneath his wool overcoat and cashmere scarf. Security guards flooded the entire block, ensuring no one came in or out of the nondescript building that housed the substation. From the outside, it looked like every other storefront and home in the area. But inside, it looked like a mini version of an intelligence room at Interpol. However, this time, its three rooms were littered with gore. Some of the computers, those that hadn't been destroyed by bullets, were still on, eerie with the previous day's risks and assessments the team was scheduled to track.

Nena had left Cort without saying much more than goodbye. She'd only had time to run home and get her go bag, containing money, passport, and other various IDs. On her way to the airport, she'd made calls to ensure that security was doubled at Elin's. Her parents had doubled their security as well. She had no idea what they were all walking into.

First, Network had gone dark in the middle of a dispatch for no reason that their experts had been able to determine so far—a cyberattack was the most they could say. Now there'd been a physical attack, with bodies. It was becoming clearer that both attacks had been premeditated—and cold. Network members were the anonymous analysts, not the killers, not the decision makers. And they'd been taken out in their own house in a ruthless dispatch.

They were about to enter the building when Witt said, "Not in the history of the African Tribal Council has anyone ever dared such a thing, attacking us in our own home."

Nena considered her mentor. He seemed aged from when she'd last seen him. As he stood facing her, she noticed the deep circles beneath his eyes.

"Witt—"

He waved her off. "It's nothing. Stress. Lack of sleep. My focus is my dead people."

"Who do you think did it?"

"People who don't know better. A local gang stakes out the comings and goings of our operatives here and thought they had something worth selling. Our people are well trained, but someone must have gotten sloppy."

Nena wasn't buying it. "What about my team?"

"Malware, Nena. I didn't have a chance to tell you before . . . this. Tech found a virus that temporarily disabled our systems."

The news was so unexpected Nena took a step back. "You're saying four people died due to some computer virus? Come on."

Witt was unmoved. "People have been killed for less."

The wheels churned in her head, but she wasn't ready to share. Witt seemed to hear them anyway.

"No one would dare to go up against the weight of the Tribe, Nena." His eyes flashed from beneath his bushy brows.

"They've already dared. We're just too many steps behind."

She followed him into the building. Trace scents of gun oil and blood filled her nostrils, even through the narrow stairwell. Two guards were posted at the door, their guns ready but not displayed in case anyone passed by. This was a business district. It was closing time, and people were leaving their places of employment to head home.

She whispered, "What if this has to do with the suspicions I've had about who brought Paul into the Tribe, onto the Council?"

"They go from inserting Paul to killing their own? If you're talking about a Council member, why would they bite the hands that feed them? They rely on Network for personal protection in their countries and to keep them in power."

The Cleaners were already at work, shutting down the technology, bagging bodies for removal, spraying the areas splattered with blood. They would scrub this building clean. Nena stared at the corpses still strewed about as unceremoniously as they had been killed.

"All died of gunshots," Witt said as if hearing her thoughts. "Swift in and out."

"What did they take?"

"Nothing. No data breaches. No uploads or downloads. The other satellites have gone over everything with a fine-tooth comb."

She paused at the body of a young woman whose face was serene, as if she were merely asleep. There were only a few speckles of blood on her face to betray that things were not, in fact, serene. The young woman was cute, maybe early twenties, and now she was gone without having lived her life beyond school and here.

"There will be a ransom," Witt surmised, following Nena to the window. They looked out.

"But they haven't taken anything to ransom, and you say nothing's missing. No data, right? Network going dark. Now this," Nena said. "It doesn't feel like a ransom is what these people are after. It's like . . ." She couldn't put her thoughts into words.

He nodded slowly, his face a mask of dismay as he picked up where she had left off. "It's like they're trying to poke the bear. Take potshots at us. Each shot increasing the stakes."

"Yeah. And what if the stakes include a plot to overthrow the leadership?"

"But who?"

"That's what we need to find out." She thought for a moment. "Could we get Dad to cancel the dedication in Ghana? Have others do it in his stead?" The thought of him with a bull's-eye on his back like some target sickened her.

"He'd never go for it. He'd die before showing weakness."

She bit her inner lip, unable to look Witt in the eye for fear he'd see how scared and clueless she was about the next steps. "That's what I'm afraid of."

She was supposed to be the one who made things happen. She was the one who acted, but at this moment, she felt totally helpless.

A flicker of movement at the corner of her eye drew her attention, and her head snapped to it. Witt caught it as well. Nena spotted a lone figure—looked like a man—standing below at the corner, out of reach of the light of the lamp. He was watching them and didn't appear to be one of their security. Nena had no idea who he was. Only that he was someone who might hold some answers she needed.

She raced out of the office with Witt close on her heels, coming to the same conclusion about the man below. They thundered down the stairs and burst through the doors to the surprise of the guards.

"Sir," one of the guards called after them as Nena and Witt blew past.

Witt kept pace as best he could as Nena ran toward where the mysterious figure had fled. She could just make out his silhouette in the growing darkness as night swallowed them up. Her breath huffed as she increased her speed. Witt was still several paces behind her. She could hear his panting.

If it were any other time, she'd turn around and tease him for being an old man, make a remark about putting him out to pasture. And he'd return some brilliant comeback or that look of his that said he was

118

thinking of ways to kill you. But now was not the time for that. Now was the time for getting ahold of the running man and finding out what he knew in the most horrendous way she could think of.

Nena's hand slid to her back, her finger flicking the button latch that secured her piece in its holster on her hip. They ran, blocks blowing past them. She should stop, she thought. He was drawing her away, leading her into a probable ambush. She knew this like she knew her own name. And yet she followed him.

She pulled at the grip of the gun. She might be running into a trap, but at least she'd go out in a blaze of glory. She thought about taking a shot, but she couldn't risk hitting anyone else. He moved swiftly for the burly man that he was.

She held the barrel down toward the ground as she ran. The man turned a corner, and she was only paces behind him. Witt was . . . too far back. She didn't chance a look. She didn't hear his panting, just his faint footfalls, and guessed he was not too far behind.

"Nena, stop!" Witt called. "Wait for backup."

But she couldn't. She rounded the corner, breaking free of the maze of buildings and alleyways and into a wider section of road. But God, it was dark. She lifted the gun. Her finger sliding to the trigger. She saw the man just ahead of her and called at him to stop, knowing he wouldn't. If he was smart. But he did, and for the briefest second, she faltered, confused at his sudden change.

She felt the whoosh of air first before something hit her from behind. Stunned, she dropped heavily to her knees. She tasted blood, and her tongue was on fire from where she'd bitten down on it. She toppled forward, disoriented. Likely concussed, but like a quarterback she never let go of the gun. The impact made her shot go wild. Then a viselike grip grabbed her wrist and slammed it on the edge of the curbed street.

The pain was so surprising she yelled out.

"Let the Tribe know we're coming for them." The words came from in front of her—she knew, somehow, that it was the man she'd been chasing—but someone else was holding her down from behind. That someone else had hit her and twisted her wrist. She struggled beneath the weight.

"Think we should take her out now?" That came from the one pinning her down. His voice was light, whispery, reminding her of Gollum from *The Lord of the Rings*. Why in the world was she worried about fictional creatures when a real one was about to kill her in real life?

"No," the one she'd been chasing said. "We just needed her attention. Have I got your attention, YA?"

YA. The nickname was a gut punch. She jerked her head up to see who was calling her that relic of a name. Nena hadn't heard it since she was sixteen and training with her first Dispatch team. A name her only friend in the group had called her before he'd been retired. The man on top of her ground her head into the pavement so she couldn't get a good look at him, couldn't make sure he wasn't who, for the briefest moment, she had hoped he was.

"The old man's coming," the weird-sounding one said and lifted off her. She hoped Witt would do just that, hoped he would come for them all. With the weight suddenly gone, she sucked in a deep breath of air. Her vision was still skewed from the impact. Her wrist throbbed, and her tongue felt as if it had grown ten times its normal size.

Witt came around the corner. Before he could squeeze off a shot, one of the men fired in his direction.

She yelled, "No!" Panic rose at the thought he'd been hit. No one answered. There was nothing but the sound of the men's feet pounding as they ran away.

"Witt," she called out weakly at first. Then louder.

"I'm fine," he said, his volume increasing as he approached. "Two on foot. See if you can find them. Alive," he demanded into his comms.

His calloused, warm hands took ahold of her arms and pulled her to her unsteady feet.

"You're bleeding," Witt said, his fingers pushing and tugging her face roughly. She winced.

"I'm okay." The men hadn't intended to harm her. Not too much. "Just gave me a message."

She batted his hands away so she could stoop to retrieve her gun from the pavement. She refused to groan, though she wanted to on the way down and back up again. She'd be sore the next day.

"What was the message?"

The too-late-to-the-party security detail rolled up to assist, fanning out to look for any traces of the two men and giving Nena an excuse not to answer Witt's question. The two men were long gone. Or hiding until the Tribe cleared out. If they were found, Nena would be shocked, and right now she couldn't do any more shock. She just wanted to go to her parents' London home, sleep, and think tomorrow about what was looming.

19

Nena faced the two computer monitors in her home office as the emergency Council meeting got underway, staring at the small squares containing the Council members, her sister, Witt, and her father and mother. Delphine was always by her dad's side at meetings. She was Noble's better half, his voice of reason if he ever happened to go off script or couldn't rein in his emotions—a rarity, but one never knew with Noble Knight.

As the members' secure feeds came online one by one, they all sat in their boxes, like an episode of *Hollywood Squares*, waiting for the fingers to start pointing. Nena picked up her cell and began toggling between giving the meeting her attention and reading through messages from Georgia and Elin.

She tried to ignore the way her heart *thump-thump*ed whenever she thought of how she hadn't heard from Cort since their talk on the balcony. She couldn't focus on any of that right now because—her ears perked up—her father had begun speaking, and that was never boring.

"I know the time is late for some, early for others. I called this emergency meeting because of what happened first at the dispatch of General Konate and then the infiltration of a London Network satellite and the murder of our employees there. There is a serious assault being waged against the Tribe, one we cannot ignore, and I mean to uncover who is behind it."

"Ah, but was it not a robbery? How do we know it was an attack? No one would do such a thing."

Another Council member said, "But no one knows our Network locations except those of us within the Tribe. No one would infiltrate these premises to merely rob them. For all intents and purposes, locations look like a cell phone call center to the naked eye. Why would anyone seek them out unless it was to gain access to our intelligence?"

"Employees are not unarmed. They are not Dispatch, but they aren't careless enough not to have protection."

"But they are not Dispatch, as you noted, Councilman Clifford," Noble said. "They are regular people who work in cybertechnology. Weapons and defense are not what they do in their everyday lives. They may not carry."

"Well, that's ridiculous," Councilman Godwin bellowed. "The work they do dictates they should assume danger at all times. They should have been prepared. It was just a robbery gone wrong. We have things like this in Nigeria. It happens in every part of the world."

Councilwoman Felicity from South Africa asked, "But how would they even gain access to such a secured location? That is what worries me."

Godwin, sounding as if he'd solved all of the Tribe's problems, replied, "Someone could have followed one of them in." He dusted off his hands. "Simple."

"Through security?" another asked. "That makes no sense, Godwin."

"We don't know, is what I am saying. This never happens, so why, the first time it does, do we call it an attack and attach more substance to it than a simple invasion by bandits?"

Councilman Bartholomew interjected, "We should be focusing on expanding our enterprises. We have companies worldwide begging to utilize our shipping services, wanting access to the ports we control along the west coast of Africa, our ports in Europe, and even in the US.

We are making great strides internationally. Now is not the time to be mired in trivial things."

"The murders of Dispatch and Network team members are trivial?" Nena asked, unmuting herself. "The dispatch of the general didn't fail only because Network lost comms," she snapped. People had died. Nearly her whole team had died. And some of the Council wanted only to talk about money? "The target knew we were coming. They were ready for us. How does that happen?"

Godwin sucked his teeth, gesturing wildly at the screen. "Ah, but what is this? We let non–Council members speak at the table? This is procedure now?"

"Then consider me saying it," Elin interjected, her face glamorous even at midnight Miami time. Everyone else was five to eight hours ahead. "As stand-in representative for Gabon's seat, I concur that this is a grave problem. An egregious act has been perpetrated against the Tribe. Someone infiltrated one of our locations, endangering the Tribe as a whole, and we need to—"

Godwin had a right-hand Council member who always tag teamed with him. He did so again now. "Ah, but who elected you stand-in?" Bartholomew asked.

Elin's chin lifted as she stared coolly into her screen. "As the widow of Oliver Douglas, the only heir to his father, Lucien, who had been sworn in as a Council member before dying, I inherit his seat, territories, and holdings and am the rightful person to assume control."

Nena's insides knotted. She didn't need a reminder as to why Elin had to sit as a Council member.

"Convenient, yes? Taking out Konate as you did Lucien."

"Means what?" Dad growled, daring the shiny-headed man to say more. Noble's tone sharpened to levels Nena rarely heard, and their mother placed a calming hand on his shoulder, though her face was as stern as their father's.

Bartholomew said nothing, reconsidering his next words.

"My youngest also speaks for me," Noble confirmed, even though Godwin was correct and Nena had no business speaking out of turn at the meeting. She was there even though she was not on the Council and probably shouldn't be.

However, there were some perks the Knights had that others did not. And it caused ill will in that regard, sure. But what could they say? The Tribe had begun with the Knights, and everyone could tell the Knights were fair in all things—most of the time submitting to the will of the Council over Noble's own preferences.

"Calm, Bartholomew. Tread carefully before you say something you will regret," another Council member warned. "We know who that man really was and that his behavior was detrimental to the people in his country and to the Tribe's interests."

"We don't know that. Seems like a lot of fuss—"

A lot of fuss. Nena bristled at the words. People's lives were never *fuss.*

"—the man could have changed is all I am saying. Stop yelling at me!" Godwin complained during a chorus of objections.

Dad raised a hand for silence. "I mean to quell this subversive talk now because, Godwin, you speak of Lucien Douglas and compare his dispatch to Konate's. You think Lucien was dispatched for personal reasons, and you infer Konate was the same, though the entire Council voted, you included. But let it be known for the last time that Lucien Douglas and his ilk meant my family direct harm. And beyond that, he meant the Tribe and all she does harm. Whatever you are implying, whatever doubts any of you may have are incorrect. Ask outright, and I will answer. Lucien was both personal and business. There are members here who vouched for him. Bartholomew, I believe you to be one, yes?"

Bartholomew coughed. "I had no idea of his past. None whatsoever. I have said this over and over and have opened my finances and entire history for all of you to see that I was duped like everyone else."

"And we believe you," Noble answered. "Extend the same courtesy to me. Lucien Douglas is a closed issue. General Konate is not. When he is found, he will be dispatched as we decreed. Period. But we will not make baseless accusations or innuendos, and if anyone has something they want to say, say it plainly so we can address it, for this Council is to be without secrets."

A message came through on Nena's phone from Elin. Are you all right?

At the same time Nena had sent a message asking the same exact thing.

Nena smiled and sent a thumbs-up.

Elin wrote, These fuckers with their heads up their asses. G and B piss me the hell off.

Godwin said, "Fine. If we're speaking plainly. Am I not saying what everyone thinks? That it's interesting Lucien Douglas . . . Paul Frempong . . . whatever it is you claim his name was, was fast-tracked onto the Council, only for him and his son to be assassinated by a Knight. And then another Knight assumes his seat, inherits his holdings, which puts two Knights on the Council. Your interests can be pushed through easier with an extra guaranteed vote."

An uproar followed. Delphine jumped out of her seat, launching into a stream of Ewe that made Nena sit back to clutch pearls she wasn't wearing. Her mother's anger was so intense, her litany so sharp, the group fell silent. It was Noble's turn to place a calming hand on her arm, and she switched to English, the international speech.

"Godwin, you insult my children and my family. You know what that man did to my daughter's natural-born family and her village. You know he and his son tried to assassinate your High Council and then his daughter and some Americans, which could have been a catastrophe for the Tribe politically and with the authorities. Let's not think about what he would have destroyed had he been successful in all of his attempts."

She leaned in. "*I* sanctioned the dispatch while at my husband's bedside, while he was incapacitated and fighting for his life. If you think for a moment that some wrong was done, then I must question why you, Godwin, and anyone else feels that way. Perhaps you are the one who got him in. Perhaps you are the one who hired the hit on a Network location or infiltrated the cybersystems with the intention of killing my daughter during a dispatch, in which she risks her life each time she goes out there while you sit in your gilded homes and eat like kings and queens. Do not ever forget this family, the Knight family, serves each of you and all of Africa. We sacrifice, and have sacrificed, for you. And we never ask you to do the same. We never doubt your intent. We trust you have a clear heart. Let us hope we are correct. And let it never be forgotten what we Knights do for you."

But what she really meant was, *Never forget who runs this here.*

Delphine resumed her seat, her mouth set firmly as her stare challenged anyone to say otherwise.

Elin texted: Think Mum's a bit put off?

Put off weren't the words for what Delphine was. Nena tried to keep her face straight. She might have been muted, but she was on camera, and someone was always watching. How Elin could crack jokes in such a heated moment was beyond her, but Nena was grateful for it.

Witt said, "Esteemed High Council, if I may?" He continued when Dad nodded. "Evidence does point to the hit on our Network office being premeditated. We are looking into the events at the Kenyan outpost during General Konate's dispatch. Our focus must be on ensuring safety for all of you as we complete the investigation. Ensuring Network remains secure and impenetrable. And locating the person or persons responsible for the sabotage. Those are imminent dangers, and with the dedication for the women's and children's medical center and the charity dinner set to occur in Ghana shortly, it is of utmost importance that we take care of this matter. I propose we halt all Dispatch operations for the time being. We need to tighten our procedures and focus on self-protection for now. Continue with business and all other legitimate ventures. Pause everything else for now. Until we know more."

Elin hadn't mentioned the odd money transactions. It was something the Knights had agreed to keep to themselves for the time being, so as not to alert the culprit. If there was one in the Tribe's fold.

The Council voted and agreed. Unanimously.

"Yes, the charity dinner for the medical center," a member agreed. "Noble, we are with you, one hundred percent. Let us focus now on this dinner, which celebrates one of our biggest achievements in Africa. Thank you, Witt, and when you know more about the hit, please keep us informed. Yes?"

Witt nodded. "I will. Thank you, ma'am."

The Council moved on, with most members relieved to pivot to a more palatable subject. Nena just kept studying their faces, wondering which one of them she'd need to take care of because they'd sold out the Tribe.

20

There had been no word from Cort since Nena had given him her ultimatum while Elin had given him the blackmail check. Not that Nena'd had much time to think about whether he'd call, let alone what answer he'd give her about their future. Yea or nay. She'd been consumed with trying to figure out the incident at the London satellite office and what had happened during the Kenyan dispatch. She'd been calming her father down after the volatile Council meeting where everyone had come down on her family's head like never before.

Morale was at an all-time low with the Knights. The last thing any of them wanted was for others to question their motives or to think them incapable of leading the Tribe where it was destined to go. This trip to Ghana would be pivotal in more ways than one. After all that had transpired in these few weeks, the impending trip didn't bring about the nervous excitement she'd initially felt, but being able to experience Keigel's first trip to the lands of his ancestors was worth the worry she had about whatever situation she might be roping him into.

She and Keigel were on their way to Miami International in the Mercedes Sprinter van that Elin had called for them. It blew Keigel's mind. Not because he wasn't used to riding in style. The man loved his fast cars and old-model rides. He liked his bikes (because every able-bodied—and not—guy seemed to have one in the lovely state of

Florida). But Keigel especially liked the idea of a car being called for him, not to mention how the driver had taken his suitcases, called him *sir* in front of his soldiers, and loaded him up in the car like he was the Migos or some other rap group.

"I'll be back, fam," he'd yelled at them from the steps into the auto. "Hold shit down, a'ight?"

He'd laughed, given them a two-finger salute before climbing the rest of the way into the van.

"I could get used to this shit," Keigel said, pulling a chilled bottle of beer from the refrigerator as the driver pulled away from the curb. The rest of his crew spilled into the street, watching them leave.

Across from him, Nena casually looked his way, assessing him as he got himself "good and comfortable" (his words). She inclined her head toward the rear window of the van.

"They'll be good? First time you're leaving them for a couple weeks."

"They'll be fine. They know how shit should go down in the hood. They know how to conduct business, and they know to contact me if anything goes left."

"On WhatsApp."

Keigel scowled. "Yeah, Nena, I know what's up. And I know WhatsApp, okay? We good."

She held up her hands deferentially. "I know you are. My apologies. It's like a parent leaving their kid at school for the first time, 'nnit?"

"Lil bit," he conceded, allowing unease to slip through his cool demeanor. "But even in my absence, I know my fam will be good because they always fam first."

Keigel's words couldn't be truer because they were words Nena lived by herself.

———

Miami International was especially busy so close to the Christmas holiday, and Nena's shoulders were tight. Traveling always made her this way, even when she traveled for missions. It was the process of going and coming, she surmised. The act of getting somewhere and settling into whatever needed to be done. She was focused on ensuring Keigel got through TSA without incident. His documents were perfect. She'd seen to that herself when she'd had Network get them together.

They made it through just fine, and Nena's next immediate worry was if Elin was at the gate and waiting. Elin lived by her own rules, but she—like their father—was a stickler for time. Only, on the way to the airport, Elin hadn't responded to Nena's text messages or answered her call. For someone in Elin's position—and condition—it was worrying when she couldn't be reached. Nena planned to let her know as soon as she set her eyes on her sister.

Plans, however, were never meant to be carried out, because just as Keigel and Nena rounded the corner with their gate number in view, Nena heard a familiar girlish squeal and the rapid approach of sneakers. It took her a second to recognize Georgia's halo of hair flowing behind her as she ran straight into Nena's arms. The force behind Georgia's run nearly toppled Nena backward. Nena held the girl tightly, inhaled her shea-butter-and-argan-oil-infused hair. Her hands slid up to Georgia's shoulders, pushing her away slightly, looking at her to make sure she wasn't imagining that Georgia was really there.

"Keig!" Georgia grinned up at him, giving dap to the fist he held out. "Have you missed me?"

"That's what I was just 'bout to ask you," he answered through an easy grin. "What are you doing here?"

"That's what I was just 'bout to ask you," she returned, leading them toward where Elin was seated facing the windows over the tarmac, watching planes filter in and out.

Elin wiggled her fingers at them as she continued her phone conversation. Nena was barely paying attention, because Cort was standing behind Elin's chair, where he'd stopped to watch his daughter sprint for them when she'd spotted them first.

Sound and the steady flow of people coming and going past them fell away. Even Georgia's excited ramblings about the last trip she'd made to Haiti and how she was soooooooo excited to be going to Ghana and all her friends would be soooooo envious of her.

Nena took a real good look because even though she'd just seen him last week, it was like something had changed about him; there was still some apprehension, but he was smiling at her with his eyebrow raised in that way he did that said the world might be a dumpster fire, but things were all right with them.

They met halfway, and he took her hand, much to her surprise, leading her away from the other three, plus four of their security who stood nearby, trying to look inconspicuous but failing miserably. Nena liked the rough feel of Cort's hand against hers. She liked how warm it was and how it held on to her tightly. She liked the feeling of not having to be as on guard as she always was, either for work or just because being a Black woman moving around in this world meant staying on guard twenty-four seven.

"You never called" were her first words. She didn't know why. It sounded kind of weak and needy, and she didn't quite like that. But it was too late to recall the words, and she wasn't going to clean it up and make it worse.

"I had to think."

She could appreciate his answer, and she appreciated more that he didn't lob blame back on her, saying she hadn't called either. She remembered liking that trait about him. He never what-abouted.

"And did you?" she asked when they'd stopped and were facing each other. The sun glinted in his eyes, making the hazel seem more luminescent. She could easily get lost in them.

He slipped his hands into the back pockets of his tapered brown cargo pants. "With Peach's help." He glanced over at his daughter, in animated conversation with Keigel while Elin pretended she wasn't soaking it all up and likely taking notes for her own use later.

"Yeah, I think so." He squinted as he thought of his next words while Nena patiently waited.

"It's not cool how Elin did me with the whole blackmail check. It was unnecessarily over the top. I would have helped you all regardless. It's not like I'm with the DA's office anymore, so there's no conflict there. But more than that, I owe you and your family for saving Peach's life. And for mine as well."

"Even though we were the cause of your trouble? Me? I was the cause of it."

His shoulders lifted and fell. "I mean, yeah, you were. But you didn't send that dude after us like that. You can't help what people do. Who knows better than an ex-cop and ex–assistant district attorney who's had his life threatened a time or two." He scratched his head. "Or three."

She half snorted, nodding that she could relate. Who hadn't been threatened?

He scratched below his nose, more serious now. "I owe you all. But more than that, I want to see what you all are about too. Georgia and I had a talk about what you do, and she was like, 'Dad, you're law, and you think justice is one way, the way this system says it should be. But think about all the wrongfully accused Black people or the Black people murdered for living while Black.' I'm not trying to get all political or self-righteous right now, but she's right in a way."

"She is," Nena agreed. "But my family are not vigilantes."

Cort held a finger up for emphasis. "Not in the least. But I think Georgia's meaning was, I was thinking too black and white, by a book that doesn't really mete out justice fairly in this country. The number of cases I've come across that are heavily weighted against people of color. Immigration cases. How can I say the justice system I've worked in for twenty years is right when men like Keigel go to prison for lesser offenses than men who own big corporations and aren't Black?" He shook his head. "I'm parroting back a lot of what you said to me the other day. But knowing how Georgia sees the world in shades of gray . . . she understands that sometimes things need to be done that aren't what we're used to, but that doesn't make them wrong."

"Just different."

He broke into a grin, and before she knew it, Nena was smiling back at him. She pulled her face into seriousness.

"Sometimes things have to be done for the greater good." Cort raised a warning hand. "But to a degree, okay? I'm not saying I totally agree. I'm saying I understand better, and I commend anyone who is fighting to make the world a better place for a group of people who were given the world's ass to kiss for far too long."

She frowned, trying to under—

"Never mind that," Cort interrupted, reading the look on her face. He stepped closer, so close they were touching. Her breasts against his chest. The sensation was both exhilarating and unnerving. She wanted to step back and take a breath. But she didn't want to break this moment either. She didn't want to move from this spot, looking into Cort's eyes and inhaling his cologne—a new scent she'd never smelled on him before but found really intoxicating. What did that even mean?

The thoughts swirling through her mind were ridiculous and . . . just ridiculous. But they were a welcome change from the dark, death-filled thoughts that had been muddying her mind for months now. It was as if the storm clouds had parted and sunlight were peeking through in beams people claimed were rays from heaven. God, she was being so melodramatic. So not like *her*.

"We're playing it by ear then?" she asked. "Is that what you're saying here? Because Ghana is too far for playing anything by ear. You get on that plane, you're in for a penny, in for a pound."

He was perplexed. "How do you know that idiom, but you don't know 'give someone your ass to kiss'?"

She pulled a face. "It's British." Obviously.

He chuckled, saying nothing more.

"But seriously, I need you to understand that there can't be quibbling if you get on that plane, Cort. Before, I didn't tell you the extent of my family's reach, what we do, how we live. It can all be overwhelming. Believe me, I know that above all. I'm not sorry for doing the things I did. I tried with everything I had to protect you and Georgia and shield you from any fallout from my actions with our organization. I am sorry you were hurt in the process. And I'm devastated that Georgia had to even breathe the same air as that man. And I regret any decisions which caused you harm."

Cort raised a finger, touching the side of her face, stroking it so softly it tickled. "For someone who speaks so little, you sure can talk too much," he told her.

She gaped at him, relishing in the way he kept touching her.

"I understand it all, Nena. I don't know if the decisions I make are the right ones in the long run. But I can't deny my daughter, or myself, someone who has brought a light back into Peach's eyes. A light I thought died with her mother. Above all, I realized that for me, life without you in it is one I can't imagine."

Nena's chest expanded triple time, feeling as if it would burst open. She was sure he could feel how hard her heart thumped. She had an inexplicable urge for them to be alone. For what? Just the thought of it filled her with a giddiness she'd laugh at if she read it in a book. Come on, really? Could Nena even go there? With Cort? Was she really considering doing the thing she'd never done before of her own volition and never wanted to? He moved his hand away. Their proximity was the intimacy Nena had craved for so long but could never put a name to.

She was caught in the everything of him. In the way Cort was looking down at her, with his head dipping, and lower still, coming just a hair's width from her until their noses practically touched. He hovered in midair, waiting for her permission because he knew that about her, about the demons that plagued her.

And Nena wanted to. So very much. More than she ever had before. The way he bit his bottom lip, sucked it in as if to keep himself from kissing her, was . . . God, what was the word? Why couldn't she articulate this feeling as well as she could shoot a sniper gun with a crosshair trigger with nearly 100 percent accuracy from miles and miles away?

Cort looked at her with longing and . . . hunger. And the look didn't repulse her, didn't make her run and hide in abject terror at what was to come. Nena didn't want to shrink back. She wanted to step forward, to grab ahold of Cort, pull him to her, and never let him go.

But they were not alone. They were in the middle of thousands of people. With Georgia looking on, and Keigel, and Elin sitting there like the cat who ate the canary and the *told you so* cocky grin that was probably on her insufferable face.

Nena wanted to. She really did. But here and now. In front of everyone. The sudden bout of shyness undercut her, freezing her in place.

Cort's warm eyes looking down at her held not a speck of disappointment or annoyance as he forced himself to pull his body back, away from her. She searched for it on his face. He still had his lips tucked inside his mouth, keeping himself from saying more, or keeping himself from grabbing and kissing her. Which Nena kind of wanted. A little bit. She found the space he'd once occupied cooler in his absence and herself disappointed that their moment had ended.

Not *ended*, his eyes promised, glinting with mischief. He leaned in quickly and said, "When we're alone." And grinned at her.

She grinned back, nodding. In Cort's eyes, Nena saw nothing but infinite promises of what was to come. Didn't have to be right now. But later. Like, when they didn't have an audience watching to see how the tension between them would play itself out. Promises of more to come.

No, not now.

But later.

21

The next morning found the weary travelers rested and at the food-laden breakfast table in the sunny breakfast nook off the kitchen. It had a spectacular view; all the rooms at the back of the posh mountain estate had various views of treetops sloping down the terrain, so full they were like green cotton balls, except the palm trees, whose leaves were too spiky to be compared to anything soft.

The house girl, Patience, Nena had met at market during her solo sojourn home several months prior. She'd taken a liking to the baby-faced young lady and found herself agreeing to Patience's offer to help her around the house during Nena's stay and whenever Nena was in Ghana. Patience took classes at the University of Ghana and was studying to be a nurse. "Not a doctor?" Nena had asked, curiously.

"Not for me," Patience had replied after an easy laugh. "Nurses are the ones who get to care for and comfort the patients after the doctors break bad news. I like to be the good cop."

Nena found her utterly endearing. "And the doctors are bad cop?"

Patience had nodded. And from there, their friendship was forged. Soon after, Patience traveled to Nena's rental on the cliffs several days a week to cook and clean, earning more American dollars than she could have imagined. It was Nena's intention to make sure Patience's school fees were fully funded. That she was too proud to take a handout—so

Nena had gathered from the first moments they'd begun conversing—didn't mean Nena couldn't pay her an obscene salary to ensure Patience wouldn't have to take loans or, worse, stop attending school altogether.

During their stay for the holidays—Christmas, Boxing Day, and New Year's, as well as the two weeks after that the Knights would stay on for the charity dinner and groundbreaking dedication—Patience would stay in housing in a nearby town, making the short commute up the winding roadway daily in the car Nena had set up to retrieve and return her home. The only people staying in the Knights' rented house were the Baxters, Keigel, and the family, to ensure privacy. The guards, on continuous rotation in and out of the premises, also stayed in a rented house nearby.

Though the flights and layover into Ghana had been draining, and the drive from the airport up Aburi Mountain to the house had felt like it would never end, the group was fairly bright eyed and excited and anxious to be together under one roof. Nena looked around the glass-and-chrome table—at Elin talking about how she planned to lounge the day away poolside out back, and Keigel commenting that he'd never thought any place could be hotter than Miami, and Cort poring over an Accra newspaper, his eyebrows furrowed in deep concentration, and Georgia thanking Patience for the waffles just placed before her along with a bowl of whipped cream—and had to take a breath, bewildered at what life had become. She'd never imagined being back in Ghana like this. To be honest, she'd never imagined being back in Ghana ever, let alone happily and with some of the most important people in her life.

The immense thought consumed her, and she didn't hear Elin calling her name.

"Nena, you've got that brooding look about you again. Have some breakfast? Maybe some tea? Lighten you up, yeah?" Elin suggested, popping a piece of mango in her mouth. "Perhaps some candied dough like the girl there?" Her eyebrows waggled in Georgia's direction.

Georgia was unfazed, not taking her eyes from her plate. "You're hatin' because you can't have it. Doctor's orders and all that."

Elin's eyes bulged. "You little eavesdropper! Your dad never taught you to mind your manners and not listen in on private conversations?"

"You had them on speakerphone. I can't help I heard that you've been eating too much junk." Georgia gave an innocent smile as she cut into her mound of breakfast sugar with a knife dripping with syrup. "Earbuds . . . are a thing people use."

It was true. Elin had been eating way more trash food than she should have been. She shot Georgia a dirty look, pointing her fork prongs, sans melon pieces, at the young girl. "Why, you cheeky little sh—"

"Elin," Nena intoned, already envisioning where this was going and not wanting the ridiculous back-and-forth to go any further.

At the same time, Cort intervened. "That's enough, Peach," he said, cutting her off as Georgia's mouth readied a retort likely to send an already-temperamental Elin into an uproar.

He turned down the corner of the newspaper, issuing a firm look at his daughter for emphasis. "You already know how I feel about being disrespectful. And being nosy. Nothing changes even on vacation."

Georgia's lips twisted in a pout. "Yes, Dad. Sorry, Elin."

Elin nodded, though her face said something totally different. A few seconds later she was pushing a small plate of strawberries across the table toward Georgia.

"Suggest you take it." Nena gestured toward Elin's peace offering. They didn't need any strife on their first full day of holiday, or bad feelings to make living together like living in a prison. It wasn't how Nena wanted any of the people she cared about to spend their time together in the country she was eager to show them.

Nena added, "My sister enjoys food too much to ever voluntarily part with it. This is huge."

Elin scowled at her. "Are you calling me greedy?"

"Well, she ain't calling you Mother Teresa, that's for damn sure," Keigel chimed in, ducking the blueberry Elin chucked at him. It narrowly missed Nena's nose as it careened past.

"But doesn't whipped cream go on ice cream?" Nena asked. She grimaced as she stared at the melting white goop slathering Georgia's waffles next to Elin's peace-offering strawberries. "On desserts?"

"Apparently everything is dessert to Americans," Elin retorted.

"You can get it at IHOP," Keigel said. "All sorts of toppings besides whipped cream. Chocolate chips, you name it."

Nena was disgusted. It all sounded like a waste of a perfectly good breakfast.

"I'm fond of International House of Pancakes," she added. "I used to frequent it quite a bit when we first moved to the States."

Keigel said, "Yeah, *I-HOP*."

She pursed her lips, realization kicking in. IHOP. For some reason, that they were both the same had never dawned on Nena. "And all this time you let me continue to say it wrong?"

Keigel snickered. "I just didn't have the heart to correct you."

She narrowed her eyes, unamused that she was the butt of the joke at the table and everyone was laughing at her.

"Even I knew they were both the same," Elin said, adding insult to injury. She'd never eaten at an Inter—at an IHOP—in her life. "Buck up, love—a little dusting of imperfection looks rather good on you." She offered a satisfied smile before redirecting her attention to her plate.

They were joined by Noble Knight's booming voice as he and Delphine entered the room. "Anything good happening in Accra today?" They looked more refreshed than anyone sitting at the table, having arrived a day earlier to allow jet lag more time to wear off. Delphine went around the table giving everyone kisses on both cheeks, then sat in the chair next to Nena that Noble pulled out for her. Keigel and Cort were already out of their seats when she entered, and they retook theirs once Noble took his.

Noble pointed to the paper. "How goes it, chale?"

Cort's face contorted while he worked out what to do next. Elin snickered, while Keigel shook his head.

"Let it go, bruh. Charlie, Cort, all starts with *C*. He's close," Keigel whispered loudly. Elin shared an amused look with Nena and burst out laughing.

"Dad's not calling you Charlie," Nena said, wondering, not for the first time since this whole breakfast had started, whose bright idea it had been to bring them all together under one roof. She fought to keep from fleeing to the sanctuary of her room.

Dad gave them each a quizzical look. "But who is this Charlie? I thought his name was Cort."

"*Chale* is slang," Nena explained. "For *bruh* or *man*."

Cort had been worried the entire plane ride about how he'd be received by Nena's parents, her father especially, and when he heard Nena's explanation, his shoulders dropped in visible relief.

"Sir, I have no idea what's going on in this newspaper even though it's in English," Cort said, answering Noble's original question. He passed the paper to Noble's outstretched hand.

Elin said, "Then why bother reading it when you don't know the politics or anything they're talking about?"

"Gotta know what's going on wherever you lay your head," Cort replied, pulling the whipped cream away from Georgia as she reached to scoop a third helping onto one tiny sliver of waffle. "That's what my grandma taught me."

Noble opened the paper. "You are well taught." He took a sip of his tea and began reading. "Perhaps later I will explain to you what is going on in Ghana. Yes? And then when you read tomorrow, it will be with understanding."

Nena leaned forward at the same moment Elin did, both sharing a look that said: *Whose dad is this?*

22

"Can I get a round of applause?" Elin announced, breezing into the sunroom, which spanned the length of the back of the house. It led out into an open oasis of exotically treed backyard and a lagoon-like swimming pool, which Georgia was currently exploring under the watchful eye of security and house staff. Her yelps of joy could be heard through the couple of windows that were open. Cort had a Ghanaian newspaper spread out on the table in front of him, as he continued to study the politics and culture of a world new to him.

Occasionally, his light-brown eyes would rise, scan the horizon for his daughter to ensure she was safe. They'd find her and be satisfied before returning to the paper. And occasionally, he'd touch Nena, who sat next to him. Maybe her knee. Or her arm to ask about something he'd read. Maybe her elbow as he leaned in to whisper how much he loved it here, how relaxed she seemed in her element, in her country.

She would half smile, nod, agree with him, all the while her mind churning as she worked to figure out how best to keep them all safe. Was the entire family being essentially holed up in this mountain fortress the safest for them? If someone wanted to take them all out, eliminate the entire family, they could do so. All they needed was an army assault. Or a rocket launcher. All they needed was an opportunity. And it was already proved that Network was not impenetrable or without folly. Clearly, Network—even though they had eyes in the sky and round-the-clock surveillance of the mountain—could be intercepted. Shut down. It had already happened. Despite her smiles and humoring Cort's exclamations and musings, Nena's mind churned with what could happen and how to prevent whatever it was from happening to the people she loved.

"Are you paying attention? I said, a round of applause, please!" Elin tried again when no one paid her any mind. Their parents were resting in their room, or maybe on a walk in the woods. Keigel was flirting with Patience, who he'd had his eye on since they'd arrived.

Elin plopped down next to Keigel, shooing away the girl, who scampered off quickly.

"Hey!" Keigel was dismayed, watching all his sweet-talking hard work succumb to fear of Elin's ire and a dismissal from well-paid employment. "I was just about to get her number."

"What number? She lives in town. Walk your ass over there if you're so hot to get some ass." Elin dropped a stack of papers on top of Cort's newspaper.

"Elin, come on," Nena chastised.

Cort's face crumpled at the disturbance, and quietly, he plucked his newspaper from beneath Elin's stack. It was endearing and something Noble would do. Rather than argue, just quietly continue about his business. Nena suppressed the urge to reach her hand out and touch—

"My bad," Elin said, "but when I give you my updates, you'll understand my excitement." With a flourish, as if revealing a huge trophy, she pointed to the stack of papers. "Cort and I have been working, and there are definitely a series of well-hidden transactions that align with the supply purchases."

"The purchases that never made it to their destinations," Cort clarified.

"Because there weren't any purchases. The invoices were dummied to look authentic. Our businesses have so many transactions coming in and out, so many purchases funding the various ventures we are involved with, and so many supply invoices slated for goodwill drops that it would be relatively easy to slip some fake ones through."

Elin held up a finger with nails filed to a point, lacquered a creamy tan, a tiny sparkling diamond in each center.

"Everybody knows I don't play with money."

"You chased off my girl to tell us that?" Keigel scoured the area for Patience, becoming visibly upset when she was nowhere to be found. "Damn."

"But we've now confirmed no one was stealing supplies. This was purely to embezzle money. You didn't know that."

He gave a half-hearted shrug, more interested in where his crush had run off to.

"From my experience if people go through the work of funneling money to places and masking it to look like purchases, that means they're trying to hide where they're sending the money," Cort said.

Elin clapped happily. "The square's got it."

"Elin," Nena warned.

"Okay, okay. Cort is correct. Why are they siphoning money from the Tribe? Why not make the purchases and resell for a higher price?"

Keigel said, "Because it's not about making a quick buck selling back the same supplies. That happens a lot on the streets. You lift someone's product and sell it back to them at double, triple the price. This ain't that, though."

Elin, her eyes shining as if she already knew the answer, asked, "Then what?"

"Intimidation," Nena said.

"Intimidate who? For what?" Elin's eyes went around the table.

Nena fell silent, her mind going a mile a minute. If only the theft was for what Keigel had said, flipping product.

"For ransom?" Cort asked.

Keigel pulled a face. "Ransom for what? They're not holding supplies hostage. There are no supplies to return, and who the hell would return money they stole?"

"This is corporate ransom," Cort explained. "Think about what happens when the companies we hear about on the news get hacked. The beef industry. The pipeline. Why did those companies pay up?"

"Okay, okay." Understanding beginning to dawn on Keigel. "I feel you. So that they'll stop and leave the company alone."

"Classic power move," Elin confirmed. "We are being ransomed."

Keigel hesitated, his lips pursing. "I . . . don't think that's a verb, baby girl."

Cort flipped through the pages Elin had dumped on his paper, his finger gliding down the highlighted rows of suspect transactions.

"Is it really ransom, though? Or just greedy-ass people who found a way to steal money without getting caught?" Keigel asked. "Could be just that."

It was a fantastic question. Made no sense to ask for a ransom to stop when they could have kept siphoning money off without the Tribe ever missing any of the money—had it not been for eagle-eyed Elin. Elin didn't think twice about blowing wads of her own cash on her lifestyle, but when it came to the Tribe's money? She protected its interests, and money, at all costs.

Elin said, "As long as we stop them, it doesn't matter why. But I figure eventually they'll notify us and say some ostentatious figure like, *Give us five hundred million pounds, and we'll stop stealing your money and fucking up your Network.* Like Cort said, it's what the Russian hackers do all the time."

Nena wasn't buying that. Russian—or any—hackers didn't kill innocent people in cold blood. They stopped the flow of money. They didn't take lives. These acts against the Tribe were more than ransom. And the money was just one part of the bigger picture.

"No." Nena said it softly, but the other three heard her as clearly as if she'd yelled it. Their cross banter stopped, and they looked at her.

"It's not ransom they're after. Network going dark was to get our attention, a show of strength. The hit on the satellite office was an act of war and intimidation. It made the Council shut down all operations. It's making the Tribe turn on itself. Whoever is doing this is amassing a fortune," Nena summarized. "Which means we need to find out what they plan to do with it before they do whatever they intend to do."

23

After a morning going around in circles about who was gunning for the Tribe and why, Nena joined Keigel at the pool, sitting on the edge as he pulled himself up from the water and plopped down beside her, splashing her with cool droplets. She handed him a towel, then dipped her feet in the water next to his. It was quiet out here. Her parents and Georgia had gone to the market. Elin had gone to take a shower, and Cort was back at it, combing through the paperwork Elin had brought them, comparing names, dates, and locations to find a connection, the who behind the what.

"You good?" Keigel asked, squinting against the sun, droplets scattered over his body evaporating off his skin.

She was. "You know, Keigel, you often joke, but you are one of the wisest people I have ever known."

He colored slightly, opting to look everywhere but at her. "Then you need to get to know more people."

She stopped suddenly. "Don't do that," she said. "Don't block a compliment."

"Isn't that a bit hypocritical coming from you? Nena, you're the queen of downplaying yourself," he said dryly.

Nena was having more moments of introspection and oneness like these lately, with Elin, Cort, Georgia. Now with Keigel. Each opportunity to formulate individual relationships with the most important people in her life made her feel like she was finally getting these relationship things right. She was seeing growth and making the effort. At least that's what she was supposed to be doing according to Mum. She'd be so proud.

Keigel kicked his feet as they dangled in the clear blue pool. Even though they sat side by side, Nena could feel his eyes on her. She hoped he wouldn't make a big deal out of any of this. Wouldn't get too mushy.

"All right then. Rewind." He made a whirring sound. "Play that line again, boss."

"Seriously?"

He nudged her with his shoulder.

"Keig, you're one of the wisest people I've ever known."

His eyes widened. "You're just now realizing this, girl?" His eyes sparkled mischievously.

She shook her head ruefully. "You're something else."

"Only thing I can be," he boasted. "But seriously, my world got bigger when I met you and your family. Who would have thought I'd be here in Ghana during this time of return, in the place where a lot of it started for Black American folk like me?"

"How do you mean?"

"Descendants of enslaved people stolen from Africa. Being here puts things into perspective for me. I'm proud of where we came from and how far we've come. We've come a long way, Nena. We've been through so much and are still here."

"Thriving."

He nodded, pride radiating from him. "What we can do is limitless. I didn't think of that before. But now with the co-op I proposed, I started to, you know?"

She nodded.

"Never realized it. I love my world and my people. I love my family . . ."

He referred to the 102s, the crew he'd been born into, grown up in the ranks until he'd become the leader. They were his family, for whom he did everything. Like Nena would for hers. It was a common bond that only made them closer, Nena and Keigel, because they understood the lengths they'd go to for their family.

"It's no different here or in London, you know?" she said, enjoying the cool water on her feet. "I was listening to this discord between Black Americans and Black Londoners, or Africans, and I didn't understand why they all couldn't realize that Black people as a whole have been treated as less-than everywhere they are. They've been conditioned to believe they were second- or third-class citizens, to accept the privilege of others over their lack of as the norm."

"Or no citizen at all."

"Exactly. Sometimes I wonder if they all know we're in this fight together."

"That's why I proposed the co-op, you know? Because I wanted the heads in my city to realize we're in this fight together. Together we are strong, and we survive. Alone . . . the shit's harder." He looked around them, to the cultivated backyard and the miles and miles of lush mountain surrounding them. "Ultimately all our roads lead here, to this continent. To the islands. To all the places of our origins, wherever they may be. But all of our fight is the same. Oppression. We all fight for our equal piece of the pie."

She agreed. She didn't have to verbalize because Keigel was saying it all eloquently enough. "We all want to be seen in the places where we are," Nena said. "Sometimes you get those who don't see the grand scheme, only the right now. Like the Tribe. It's fighting itself . . ."

"Is that why Trek disappeared?"

She hadn't thought of the leader of the Flushes in weeks. Not since the night she'd left him to the gators in the Everglades. She and Keigel had never discussed him.

"Because he didn't see the grand scheme of the co-op?" he asked.

"He would have come after you, you know. Co-op or not. He wanted you gone."

Keigel nodded slowly, all traces of humor wiped from his expression. "I know."

"And he would have never let the co-op exist without trouble."

"Get that too. I would have done what had to be done."

"I don't doubt it, my friend."

Keigel smiled at that.

"But you would have given him too many chances."

He sneaked a look at her. "You got me sounding like your ol' man."

"Exactly. And sometimes neither you nor he knows when it's time to cut people off."

Keigel guffawed so loud birds took flight. "And so you dispatch them."

"And so I clear the way for you both to do what you do best. Lead."

Keigel couldn't answer. He was visibly moved and could only shake his head in wonder.

"How'd I get so lucky to have a friend like you, Nena?"

Uh-oh, here was the mushy part Nena wasn't prepared for. She hadn't meant to make him feel emotional. She was just stating fact. "Anyway, I am very happy you are here."

He bumped her arm with his. "Me too." He paused. "You think you can now call me Keig the Wise?"

She slipped her feet out of the water, pretending to think about his request. "No. No, I don't think so."

24

After leaving Keigel, Nena planned to take some time in her room. She needed to recharge. Living in a house with six other people, plus the people who managed the house, when she was used to living on her own was a lot for her. She loved everyone there, but she'd lose her mind if she didn't get a moment to herself to think.

However, isolation was not in the cards, because Elin was lying on the floor of her shower, the water spray cascading over the huge swell of her belly. Nena had found her like this as she'd walked past Elin's bedroom. The sounds coming from within put Nena on alert, and she rushed into the bedroom thinking someone had broken into the house.

She wasn't wearing her gun, not in the house with Georgia there. She took a quick assessment of the room, seeing nothing out of the ordinary. It was empty and quiet save for the shower running. And then Nena heard the sounds again. The ones that had made her rush in, blades ready to kill whoever was not supposed to be in there. Through the open door of the bathroom, she heard mewling, animalistic sounds.

At first, Nena thought someone was attacking Elin, that someone had scaled the walls and gotten past security. Or maybe Elin had gone into premature labor. It happened, and with all the traveling and running about Elin was doing, she was a doctor's worst nightmare.

It wasn't any of those scenarios. It was worse. Nena found Elin on the floor of the spacious shower, in a ball, crying. Seeing Elin like this was a shock, and Nena stood there a moment, unsure what to do. Should she leave? Did Elin require privacy? Did Elin need their mum, who was likely downstairs tending to whatever business she had for the day? Nena didn't want to leave Elin to find out, so she would have to be the one. She placed her blades on the countertop, then removed her shoes and socks.

She finally took the time to think about what could be wrong, and Nena realized she'd known the moment she'd seen Elin on the floor. There was nothing Mum would have been able to do about it. Nothing Nena could do, either, but sit with her sister and let Elin say whatever it was she needed to say. It had been long enough. And Nena had been waiting for this moment for six months.

"Elin."

Elin looked up, her face crumpled and puffy from the crying and the sauna the shower had made. Droplets of crystal-like water held on to her hair, which was now a beautiful black cape around her head and shoulders.

Nena said, "What can I do for you?"

"Why?" Elin asked, drawing the word out. "Why'd you have to do it? Why Oliver? He was *my* Oliver!"

Nena stepped into the shower, bending down to sit next to her sister, not caring that her clothes were getting soaked and her just-done hair would poof into a bouffant and she'd have to do it all over again. She stretched her arms out, pulling her older sister to her, folding Elin into the strength of her arms and the love Nena had for her. Their roles reversed, and Nena was now the comforter, soothing Elin in her moment of grief.

Her cries were on a scale ranging from soft sobs to full-out howls.

"Why?" she kept asking.

Nena wasn't sure if the question was rhetorical or not, but she took a guess and opted not to respond.

Elin's body was racked with grief, and Nena pulled her closer. The belly between them.

"He was good," she said. "He was good to me. God help me, I loved him . . ."

Nena remained silent. She just held her sister and allowed her unanswered questions to flow. She had no answers for Elin. She had no answers for herself. They had died with Paul and with Ofori earlier that year.

Nena couldn't fault Elin for thinking Ofori had been a good man. He *had* been good to Elin. She'd brought back the humanity that had long left him, just as she'd brought back the humanity that had deserted Nena the night she'd been stolen from her village. The Ofori—Oliver—Elin had known was sweet and gentle and had loved her and given her a legacy in his son.

Elin had held her grief in for as long as she could, had tried to soldier on for the family, for her duties, but most of all for Nena, because she knew what Nena had been through with Ofori and with Paul before Nena had ended up on the Knights' doorstep. Elin had held it all in until she could do it no more.

"It's okay," Nena whispered to Elin and to herself because now it was her turn to push past the memories of the night N'nkakuwe had burned. Of their fight to the death and how Ofori had still tried to kill Nena even after realizing that she was his sister.

Yet, in his final seconds of life, as he'd lain bleeding out from the knife wound, he'd been Oliver. He had asked for Elin. Asked Nena to tell Elin he loved her. In his final seconds, he had been the man he was supposed to have been, had Paul not relieved him of that choice.

"Why couldn't you let him live for me?" Elin's anguish was so visceral it was as if she were being stabbed with it. "Why'd you have to take him after I've given everything to you? Shared everything with you?"

And there it was. Nena closed her eyes. Her throat was so thick with emotion it hurt, and finally Nena released it.

Her tears mixed with the water from the shower as she listened to her sister vacillating between anguish and anger. Elin loved her; of that Nena had no doubt. But Elin had meant what she'd said. Anger did that to a person. Love did that to a person.

Nena had taken the man she loved.

"I can't do this," Elin said.

"You can."

"I can't be a mother."

"You already are."

"I can't do this by myself. I can't."

"You won't. I'm here. I am here, Elin, and I am sorry."

She was unbelievably, irreversibly sorry for the death of her brother. But she remained at war with herself over the love and hate she felt toward him. She waffled over forgiveness though she had forgiven him. It was the forgetting that was hard. Yes, that was it. The forgetting was what made it hard to remember that she had forgiven. Ofori had been the last of the Asyms along with her. The last male heir to their father's legacy. Nena had loved him in spite of what he'd nearly done and what he'd chosen to do afterward. Despite his cleaving to Paul and calling him father, the man who'd killed their father and burned their village.

All of that would always matter. She would always feel the violation, the betrayal, the heat of the flames and the sight of so many deaths of her people. But Nena would also remember the moment when Ofori had awoken and asked forgiveness and to be taken home. The moment when he'd become her brother, Ofori Asym, again.

So Nena didn't fault Elin for her accusations and her anger or that for just a second, she'd forgotten that they were sisters.

They stayed in that position, holding each other, until Elin's sobs subsided and she announced that she had to pee and didn't plan on doing it in the bloody shower, for which Nena was grateful. She'd do anything for Elin, but sitting in a puddle of urine-filled shower water was not ideal.

Later, when they were dry and dressed in fresh clothes, when their hair had bloomed into crowns of soft, thick coils in afros to rival Pam Grier's, Elin said, "Thank you," looking over Nena through red-rimmed eyes and a mask of shame.

"You don't ever have to thank me."

Elin held a hand to Nena's arm to stop Nena from moving about, stop Nena's efforts to distract from further sharing.

"I do. For letting me get all those negative vibes out, all of the vile feelings I've been suppressing. My head has always known you had to do it, that it was either you or him. My heart just needed more convincing."

Nena paused. Elin was usually not so deep or eloquent. Nena told her so.

"Shove off," Elin laughed. She grew serious. "Nena, my heart would have chosen you. Always. Despite what I said in the shower, okay? About the giving you everything and sharing everything. That was a bitch thing to say. And while I was mad that you killed Ofori, I don't regret that you came into my life and became my sister. Know that, okay?"

"Sure." Nena nodded. "Okay."

Elin wasn't done. "I know what you've been through, and I think Cort can help you with moving on from it. I think you can be happy with him if you allow yourself to."

The lump in Nena's throat wouldn't let her answer, so she managed a throaty acknowledgment and busied herself with arranging the hair supplies strewed across the table.

"You can be your own worst enemy, you know. You deny yourself all these things that will make you happy because you don't think you deserve them. But . . ." Elin leaned in to catch Nena's eye, as if discerning if Nena was listening. "Who deserves happiness more than you, Aninyeh?"

Elin caught sight of herself in the mirror then. "Bloody hell, look at me." She twisted around on the bench, facing the mirror. "Help me whip myself back into respectable shape, would you? So I don't scare off the Americans."

25

After a considerable amount of convincing and a final decision from Delphine Knight, Nena relented and took everyone on a grand tour of popular locations in her home country. It felt good not to worry about corruption or threats or all the other things that worried Nena at any given moment.

"Chill out for a change, dear," Mum instructed, placing a calming hand on Nena's arm. "Let people have a little bit of fun. You especially."

"Thank you, Mum," Elin interjected with faux relief. "I've been telling my sister to relax for years! Loosen up, I said. Have some se—"

"I am loose enough," Nena broke in with a biting glance at her chuckling sibling. "I have plenty of fun."

"Fun with humans, Mum means. Not shooting your guns or stabbing people or riding your motorbike or watching Netflix and all your other streaming services."

Nena was practically baring her teeth, appalled that Elin would come for her favorite pastimes. It felt like betrayal. Nena had half a mind to push back, if only their mother weren't standing there nodding in complete agreement.

"Go. Show them the Ghana they should know about. Don't mind your sister."

Against Nena's better judgment, because she was always thinking about security and the safety of everyone but herself, they'd already made plans, called for cars, and set a tentative itinerary cleared by security. There was no getting out of playing hostess, and begrudgingly, Nena quietly took up the rear, following everyone out of the house to the Mercedes Sprinter van that would carry them down the mountain to get a taste of what Ghana had to offer.

The first stop was Delphine's hometown of Elmina. "I grew up here," Delphine said to the group while holding Noble's hand. They stood at the corner of one of the bustling streets, trying to keep out of the way of the townspeople rushing by with carts of produce, hanging meats, or baskets of fish, heading to and from the market by the sea.

Delphine went back years to a time when none of them had existed to her yet. "My brother, Abraham, and me. We lived only a couple blocks away from the largest slave port in this country."

"Elmina Slave Port," Georgia whispered to Nena, enthralled by Delphine's recounting. She was astounded by the town she'd only read about in textbooks and the part it had played in the history of trading enslaved people. She moved closer to the older woman. What were history books when history was right beneath her feet?

"When I was a girl, my friends and I would walk to school, to market. We'd see the castle and port. Every day. There were always tourists just like you see, taking pictures and posing nice and fine. Someone's tourist attraction was my daily reminder of how lives were chained and forever changed. They went through the 'door of no return.' Isn't that horrible? The very thought of that name. It's absolutely terrifying. But it was a responsibility for me, you see? To respect the history here. To understand why so many people come. To learn."

"It's like living near plantations," Keigel said, understanding Delphine's meaning. He was the only American descendant of the enslaved Africans among them, so Elmina Castle felt different for him, held a different meaning for his history than the others'.

"I never imagined ever coming here. Never thought I'd see where my ancestors may have come from, a port they may have traveled through on their way to . . ." His voice hitched; a rare moment when he wasn't making a joke, the sheer weight of where he was overwhelming to him.

"Me and my crew sometimes talk about lost culture and how sometimes we feel we don't know where we come from or feel we don't have a history beyond being enslaved all those years back. We go back and forth about it. I tell 'em we do have history beyond what happened four hundred years ago. We may not know it, but it's there just the same."

"And you make new history and culture where you are," Elin added. "Me too, Keigel. Even though I'm first gen, my mum and dad didn't bring me back to their countries. All I know is London and what my parents have told me of Africa."

"Yeah, but at least you have a direct connection to here. Me and my crew, we don't have that. I mean, we know it's there hidden beneath years and years. But we don't have that direct link."

"That doesn't make your link any less significant," Delphine told him, putting her arm around his waist. He smiled down at her, bowing his long body toward her to lay his cheek on the crown of her head.

"Why didn't you ever bring Elin here?" Nena asked curiously. There was no accusation behind it but rather curiosity since Noble had always been so bent on African roots and the Tribe. Seemed he would have had Elin in Africa every year so she'd also know where she came from.

Noble furrowed his brows in deep thought. "You know, I cannot really say. Before you joined us, Del, Abraham, and I worked hard to get the Tribe off the ground. We wanted to be seen as equals to the White people we were trying to forge partnerships with, and it narrowed our focus."

"You interrupted my history," said Elin bluntly.

Noble hesitated. "Okay. But not because we were trying to hide anything."

"No, never that," Delphine continued. "Life just got away from us, and then we sent money to appease our guilt." She chuckled. "And when Nena came to us, chose us to be her family . . ."

Nena looked away, as was custom when any of her family became too sentimental. She definitely didn't need them getting weird now with the Baxters and Keigel watching. Not to mention security.

"We didn't think it was a good time to come back to Ghana until Nena was comfortable being back."

Nena could feel eyes burning holes through her. "Perhaps we should go to the castle and continue on," she said, glad for the sunglasses hiding her from the others.

Thankfully, they listened, and the temperature instantly felt degrees cooler. She didn't know how much sentiment she could stand, especially when she was the focus. It made her feel not in control.

Seeing the castle was a whole other experience. Though still annoyed by her parents, Nena couldn't deny the beauty and awe that was Elmina Castle. They walked through the stone structures, went in and out of the room used to contain the Africans before they were shipped to their final destinations, looked through portholes carved in stone that gazed out at the ocean, a crystal-bluish-green sparkling body of water that looked idealistic and pure and yet had been used for insidious purposes, holding countless souls of those who hadn't completed the crossing beneath its crashing waves.

Nena thought about those people who'd been forced to leave their lands centuries ago. Nearly seventeen years since it had happened to her.

It was while gazing through one of those nearly bleached-white portals that Nena made the decision. It was time she visited her own door of no return.

26

"Where are we going again?" Georgia asked as they bounced along the rock-filled, dusty one-lane road heading away from the coast, from where they had toured Elmina as Delphine had regaled them with stories of her childhood: helping her father ready his canoe for fishing with all the other fishermen, and how she'd loved getting into mischief at Benya Lagoon with her friends. Delphine had made them stop in the market so they could visit the food stands, just as she'd done when she was young. They'd enjoyed strips of smoked fish and beef, goat kebabs, Inca Kola and Kola Champagne, and other delectable treats until they could barely move.

They'd all relished Delphine's trip down memory lane. Elin most of all, who had never really seen this side of her mother before. Gone was the proper British woman with impeccable poise and mannerisms, and in her place was this youthful girl who was relaxed and as free as a bird. The Ghanaian part of her blended accent became more dominant, and her eyes shone with nostalgia and wistfulness Nena recognized as missing home.

That was something Nena and her parents could share. She knew all about missing home and what it meant to be back in the land where they used to walk, run, and play as children. When the world was more innocent and the only cares they'd had were their schooling and making sure chores were done in time to go to market and maybe pick up some sweets to carry them through the night.

Their caravan had moved along the coast, on the main road heading back toward Greater Accra and back to Aburi Mountain. The entire trip was long and tiresome, but it allowed those new to Africa (Keigel, Georgia, Cort, and Elin) to have a shortened tour of the Ghanaian world, only a slice of what all of Africa consisted of. And it allowed those previously gone and now returned (Delphine, Nena, and Noble) to remember a part of their life that reminded them why they did what they did.

"You see this?" Noble said, gazing out of the large van windows at the vibrant green fauna, contrasted against the orangey brown of the claylike road. "How beautiful is this land? How beautiful is this world? Can you see why we fight so hard for it? Even among ourselves to preserve her purity and innocence? This is why the Tribe works."

Nena sat in the row of seats behind her father, silently agreeing with him as his words traveled the length of the van, quieting the murmuring group so that they listened intently. Nena peered over at Cort. His face was a mixture of introspection and appreciation. She knew there was a *but* in that jumble of thoughts he was no doubt thinking.

"We've been given resources to give to others. We've been blessed with wealth, opportunities, chances so we can give the same to others. Is that wrong?"

But why the killing? Why the need for a Dispatch team? What Cort wanted to ask, really, truly, was why the need for *people like her?* She couldn't fault him for wanting to ask the question and also not wanting to sound judgmental. It was the final hump, his internal conflict; he just couldn't get over it.

"Those who seek to be wrenches stopping our wheel of progression. Those who are self-serving, warmongering, faithless to our cause. Those against their own people are the ones who will always need to be stopped. It is unfair to allow a few to impede the advancement of the many for their own personal gain and selfish reasons, you all understand?"

Noble answered Cort's unspoken question, rising from his seat, twisting around against Delphine's calls for him to remain seated on the bumpy road. He made eye contact with each of them, settling his darkened stormy eyes on Cort. He was speaking to the group, but his words were very much for the last holdout. The van was eerily quiet, save the rhythmic *thump-thump, thump-thump, thump-thump* of the wheels along the road.

Keigel was the first to break the silence. "That's what I'm always saying, Mr. K. I was just talking to Nena 'bout it a while back. Not all skin folk are kinfolk."

Elin's eye narrowed in confused irritation. "What does that even mean? Is that an American colloquialism?"

"A Black one, baby."

Noble clapped loudly once, a sound like a thunderclap, and broke out into a grin. "Exactly that! This situation with the attacks on the Tribe is exactly what I mean about wrenches trying to stop progress. They don't want everyone to succeed, only themselves. Why is that?"

To that, no one had an answer. If there was one, then there wouldn't be a need for the Dispatch team anymore.

To kill was not an easy thing, whether it was by defense or otherwise, if one had a heart and cared. There was a weight one carried with each life taken. Nena's shoulders often ached from the heaviness of it all. But . . . it was a weight she gladly carried because sometimes it had to be done.

Cort would refrain from asking his question because he'd promised to give the idea of the Tribe a real chance at his understanding and acceptance.

Part of the group's plan was to make stops at a sprinkling of towns and villages the Tribe had long been working closely with to support their needs—basically to ensure those towns and villages knew the Tribe was their ally.

Nena watched Cort as he sat on the other side of the van next to Georgia, who pointed out all the sites they passed on the jam-packed road like a little kid. Nena loved that for Georgia, how her face glowed at seeing things she'd only read about or watched on TV. Nena was happy to have Cort be a witness to just a small bit of the good the Tribe did for countries and towns like Elmina, Winneba (where they were about to stop), and a growing number of others.

She wanted him to see that they were more than the mob-like organization he believed them to be, despite the methods they used to achieve their goals. Maybe the visit would make it real for Cort. Real in a good way.

The caravan pulled to a stop in a little village on the outskirts of Winneba, and they all disembarked, stretching and taking in the vibrant colors and people walking with baskets and pots of newly dug yams, bushels of cassavas and green and ripe plantains, and nuts. Others whizzed by on bicycles and mopeds, two to a seat. Women dressed in traditional cloths tied tightly around their waists gave nods of hello as they passed. Men in Western wear or dashiki tops waved and came around, curious about the visitors.

"Why'd we stop here instead of in Winneba?" Georgia asked, carefully pronouncing the town's name. Since arriving, she'd been trying hard to learn Twi and not mispronounce anyone's or anything's name. Nena thought it was adorable.

"The driver tells us there's an outdooring happening," Nena answered, pointing to the procession of villagers filing into a large home carrying an assortment of goods and gifts.

"An outdooring," Delphine cooed. "I haven't been to one since we were teens. Remember, Noble? My uncle Harold's daughter's baby? You, me, and Abraham had to attend."

Noble scratched beneath his chin. "I remember, love. Abraham and I were so angry because we couldn't make a run for Singleton that night. It was nearly the end of us."

"What's an 'outdooring'?" Georgia asked, her eyes eagerly drinking in the scene. She practically buzzed with anticipation.

"It's a naming ceremony." Nena searched for what she wanted to say. "Kind of like a baptism and those sip-and-sees that southerners have, but for the baby's name."

Georgia's eyebrows wrinkled. "I don't get it."

"It's the first official introduction of a new baby and its name to the world."

Keigel joined them. "That's cool as hell. Did you have one?"

"I suppose I did." Nena half shrugged. "If I did, I would have been just a few months." She didn't remember the event, of course, but she did recall photos of herself in her mother's arms, surrounded by a crowd of elders she'd grow up with.

Another photo materialized in her memory then. It was of her mother's father, the chief before Nena's father had assumed the role, holding her as he gave the formal announcement. Her older brothers (Wisdom and Josiah, the twins) standing mischievously at the feet of their proud parents, and Ofori, barely two, nestled in their mother's arms—his face burrowed in her neck, either camera shy or over all the attention the newest Asym was getting.

The driver and her parents were already in animated conversation with the villagers, with Cort and Elin near the watching guards, quietly speaking among themselves. Every now and then, Cort would glance over at Nena, they'd make eye contact, and he'd smile and mouth something, asking if he needed to pull Georgia and her never-ending stream of questions and comments off Nena or some other poor adult. Nena would always decline the offer. Having Georgia around was always a pleasure, her chatter as well.

Delphine called to the waiting group. "The chief said we can join."

Prior to their stopping in this village, Nena hadn't thought much about outdoorings, much less all the preparation that went into them. African traditions were held on a much smaller scale abroad or not at all when they were in London or America. And realistically, her family was too involved in business to enjoy this part of the world they were working so hard to uphold. How had they allowed themselves to work so much that they missed out on the living part of life?

"It's a work-life balance that I see now that we need," Noble answered when Nena had sidled up beside him and taken his arm in a half hug, half squeeze. Her form of affection that sometimes overcame her in these moments of nostalgia. "You miss this as much as I."

She sighed. They were in procession with the villagers, approaching the chief's home, wearing swaths of fabric donated to them by a few of the village women and wrapped around various parts of their bodies so they could be a part of this time-honored African tradition.

"I don't know that I'd missed any of it, until I see it and remember."

He didn't answer. Instead, he squeezed her shoulder. Her father understood entirely.

"Perhaps we shouldn't let ourselves forget again? Perhaps this year of our return needs to be a reoccurring thing?"

"Hmm," she answered in agreement.

Nena sat with Cort and Georgia, watching as the new mother and father presented their squirming baby girl to the chief, who was garbed in full Ghanaian cloths of colors so bright and beautiful it was as if the sun shone through them.

Everything about this lively village reminded Nena of N'nkakuwe. Everything about every village or town she traveled through did this. But it didn't bring sadness anymore. She'd let the sadness of village memories go when she'd brought Ofori back home and visions of her dead family had compelled her to live. Now was not the time of old memories; now was the time to make new ones with her new family. And that family consisted of Georgia, Cort, and Keigel.

They watched on as the chief announced the name of the child and held her up like she was Simba from *The Lion King* (Georgia's observation, not Nena's—but it was an accurate comparison), and she was received by the room, nearly bursting with bodies, as a new member of society and God's child.

It was beautiful, and Nena felt stinging prickles behind her eyelids. She couldn't help herself, couldn't decide what it was that was making her emotional. But she went with the flow and didn't feel like dissecting it right now, because the good part came next. The party.

The music. The local musicians who played their Ghanaian beats to the crowd of attendees, who broke out in dance.

Nena, seated at one of the tables in the back of the brightly lit house as night came upon them, watched her group enjoying themselves, thinking, *This is what I can live for*. What did any of the tragedy and trauma she'd lived through before mean if she refused to allow herself to enjoy what her life had become now?

A hand was thrust in her face, and she blinked, trying to register why it had appeared in front of her.

"Come on," Cort was saying to her over the noise. His eyes glinted teasingly, as he knew Nena was not one for public displays. "Show me what you got."

"Sis, this man doesn't even know what he's asking." Elin shook her head. Of all the things Nena did not do for fun, dancing was the exception. Elin had caught her dancing in her room more than once. If it had a beat, Nena was moving to it.

"I know a little," Cort returned, reminding Nena that they'd danced once before. On their only official date. When she took his hand and stood, he whispered in her ear, "Let's show your sister what *we* can do."

He kissed her in the space just below her earlobe. The act sent a wave of pleasure through Nena, making her involuntarily shiver. She ventured a glance back at her sister as Cort led her into the throng of people. Elin looked back, a smirk spreading across her lips, daring Nena to make a comment.

Of course, Elin was witness to Nena's millisecond of loss of control. The shrewd woman missed nothing.

The energy of the party even got Noble out of his chair, dancing in the middle of the crowd with Delphine. The village chief, his wife next to them, a raised glass of Jameson in his hand. Noble had one, too, and the two leaders took a shot to the sounds of cheers and more music, before the DJ took the musical reins and started playing modernized afro beats. The younger generation displayed the carefully synchronized dance moves that they'd obviously spent hours perfecting so they could perform them to thunderous applause and cheers.

Nena didn't know how many songs she and Cort danced to. The music was an endless stream until, overhead, the skies broke, and fat droplets began to fall into the flickering flames of the torches that the villagers had lit for ambience.

Cort's hand slid down the length of her arm before cupping her hand in his. His head cocked to the side, indicating they should go. Nena's eyebrow quirked. What did he have up his sleeve? But she followed. He led them away from the crowd to the outskirts, where it was quieter and they had more privacy. She didn't question him, especially when Cort knew less about this place than she. She was enjoying this giddy feeling of only living in the moment.

They'd rounded the side of the chief's house when Cort stopped, and Nena nearly bumped into him. He turned, facing her, stepping into her. He held her on either side of her hips, placing his fingertips against her waist and guiding her backward, stepping into her so she had to step in reverse or lose her balance.

Cort backed Nena up against the stucco wall of the home. He didn't stop until he was nearly pressed against her. With their noses, their lips, just barely touching. She looked up at him and he down at her. The heat between them was building into a crescendo, each wanting to make the next move but holding back—just barely—as people passed by behind them.

Her chin lifted slightly as he tucked a piece of flyaway hair back into her style. His lips curved into a smile as he bent down closer, the tips of his lips parting.

She couldn't process further. Because he was kissing her.

The perfection of the moment swept her up into its embrace as he held her chin in one hand, the other flat against the wall beside her head, their bodies pressed together with a soundtrack of music they barely heard. It was a moment they both had been anticipating since Nena had seen Cort at the airport while the rest of the world watched on, or ignored them, whichever.

All that mattered now was that they were here together. The world could come crashing down, and Nena and Cort wouldn't care one bit. Because everything either of them needed was right here.

27

To say Noble Knight was a complicated man was an understatement. It took a lot to run an organization the size of the Tribe, with all the ways the Tribe moved—aboveboard, below, and in between—while managing his own family interests and negotiating the love lives of his daughters. He could be a difficult man when he wanted to be, could make life miserable for someone he disliked.

Noble had been nothing but polite with Cort, as Africans and Britons typically were, but there was always an undercurrent of something else. Long, watchful glances as if Cort were in a petri dish and Noble were on the lookout for fungal growth. Nena wasn't sure what to do about it. Couldn't really call her dad on doing his due diligence, she guessed. But she also didn't want to disavow Cort's feelings at having to constantly be in the hot seat, waiting for her father to blow, either. He must have been feeling as if he were in high school all over again.

"It's because Dad was a DA," Georgia surmised. Elin had dubbed Georgia "the Wise One," and Nena was finding it to be an accurate moniker. She and Georgia were walking the trails in the forest, having some time to themselves after a particularly testy situation at the house. Noble had nearly lost his temper when Council business had been brought up at the breakfast table and Delphine wouldn't let him excuse Cort. "That's why Mr. Noble doesn't trust him yet."

"And I'm sure your dad doesn't feel entirely comfortable around us, either, now knowing the full scope of what my family does," Nena replied, picking up a long piece of bamboo stalk that had snapped from the rest.

"True, but Dad said he'd get over it, and he is. I can tell. Your dad is older, and it takes old people longer to reacclimate." Georgia found her own bamboo stalk, picked it up, and began using it as a walking stick.

Never disappointed, Nena said, "Very intuitive of you." After another thought, she felt she needed to add, "You know, I'm not the baking-cookies-and-cupcakes type of person. I'm, like, not a mum. Mums don't do the work I do."

"Well, maybe not all moms have jobs like you, but I bet you're not the only assassin mom in the world. Plus, I don't want a cupcake-making mom anyway—though I do like cookies." Georgia grinned. "And I don't want any other kind of you than who you are, 'cause you're like a *mum* to me, in every way that counts."

28

Delphine Knight went all out for Christmas and Boxing Day. She worked side by side with the house staff to decorate the home on the cliffs with holiday decorations and had eagerly overseen the lines of packaged parcels streaming into the house by carrier vans. The whole house smelled of spiced meats, stews, baked goods—a spread that would be way more than the group of them could eat.

But Delphine would make sure the staff took whatever they wanted home and that security walking the perimeter outside would also be fed and taken care of. She knew they had to work—they had all worked during a holiday before—but it didn't lessen Delphine's motherly guilt that anyone was away from their family because of her.

When the group got downstairs, each awakened by Patience under Delphine's instructions, they were taken aback by the house's transformation into a winter wonderland that looked like it had come straight out of a Macy's or Harrods window display. Keigel's eyes were biggest of all because he wasn't accustomed to Delphine's eccentricities, although he was getting used to them.

Nena stood off to the side, letting everyone chatter and exclaim over the gifts Delphine and Noble had gotten for them. She didn't touch hers. She rarely did. Through the years, the Knights had learned to not overwhelm Nena with gifts she'd never find a practical use for. Nena found her satisfaction in always knowing what each person wanted the most. Cigars, pipes, or some sort of soccer paraphernalia from Dad's favorite teams, of which he had many. Mum liked books; she liked to lose herself in different worlds, she'd once told Nena as a teen, and Nena remembered that. Ever since then, she'd find a first edition of whatever her mother fancied that year, and she'd get it for her. Elin was the easiest of all. She liked to shop, but she hated to be shopped for. Thus Nena often gifted her shopping sprees. Elin could never have enough shopping sprees.

"Georgia, come sit next to me," Noble said above the low noise of rustling paper and opened boxes. "I've got one more thing for you."

Georgia's eyes shone. She'd already been bestowed a new MacBook, some money from Elin—to get her a better wardrobe, Elin had said—a camera, a multitude of multicolored bracelets from the bead kiosk in the market in Koforidua from Keigel, which she loved the most because they went with the beaded belt she'd asked Nena to tie around her waist when they'd visited the market a couple of days ago. With the rows of bracelets and the waist beads, Georgia was beginning to look more like she'd been born and raised here. Seeing the way her face lit up was the best gift Nena could have hoped for. Honestly, having all her favorite people here—even Witt, who rarely attended family events and would likely leave soon, had flown in that day—was a present Nena would have never even hoped for.

While Noble waited patiently for Georgia to pick her way across the minefield of discarded wrapping paper, boxes, and plastic wrappings, then sit next to him on the couch, Nena saw Cort watching warily from across the room. Nena could practically read his thoughts. He was already thinking about how he would unspoil his newly spoiled daughter. She hid her smile, knowing she'd probably hear about it later.

"What are you, sixteen?" Noble asked, scrutinizing Georgia through a narrowed eye.

"Not yet, sir, fifteen. I'll be sixteen in May."

"Well, that's okay, then," he said gruffly. "Never too early to have one of these."

He pulled out a silver key hook, and on it was a black key fob with a red emblem on it. The room fell to a hush as everyone waited. For Georgia's reaction. And then for Cort's. At first, there was none.

"What's that, Dad?" Elin asked. "Are those keys?"

"Is that for a car?" Keigel asked.

"What?" Elin looked at him, wide eyed. "An auto? You got her an auto?"

Inside, Nena was cringing. She didn't even want to look at Cort, who in her peripheral vision had jumped out of his seat.

"No. Wait," he said.

"For real?" Georgia asked, wide eyed and staring at the sparkling thing dangling from Noble's index finger. "Like for real, for real?"

He laughed. "Definitely not for fake."

"Mr. Knight—" Cort began, following the minefield path Georgia had taken moments before. "Wait a minute."

Delphine entered the room, taking in the sudden rush of activity, and said, "Oh, Noble dear, you really did it? I thought you were just joking when you mentioned it."

"What you get?" Keigel asked. "Is it a Porsche? A Tesla?"

"God, no," Cort groaned. "She can't have a car now. She's only fifteen."

"I have a permit," Georgia corrected.

"I'm not crazy," Noble said. "It's a Fiat. That's reasonable for a young lady."

"She's fifteen!" Cort exclaimed, taking the key from Georgia, who had irreverently taken it from Noble.

"Dad, come on. You can't get a kid an auto without asking her dad first," Elin protested. "Mum, tell him."

"I tried. You know your father."

"It's too much? You don't like it, Georgia? You can choose whatever you like if you don't like it."

"Get a Tesla." That was Keigel, making his way to the afternoon spread on the table.

"It's a Fiat! That's a reasonable car. Small, cute. Isn't it an American rite of passage or something?"

"It would have been nice if I could have held that rite of passage for her," Cort said through clenched teeth, as he waged tug-of-war with Georgia for the keys she did not want to relinquish. "Or had some say in the matter."

Elin snorted. "Oh, love, welcome to the family. No one gets a say with Noble Knight around."

Dad looked at Delphine as if he were being unfairly attacked. "Witt, can you believe this?"

"I'm just here for the food, sir." Witt crossed his leg at the knee and continued to read the newspaper.

Noble looked to Nena for safe harbor, but she was shaking her head, not upset, because Elin was right and she knew her father. She resigned herself to the fact that it wouldn't matter what any of them said, even Cort. Her dad was determined to give Georgia a car and be her favorite person.

"It's not often we have young ones around. In another month we'll have the baby too. What's a grandfather for if not for spoiling his grandkids?"

That was when Cort stopped midprotest. Nena remembered why she'd loved the Knights so ferociously that she'd give her life for them. Because family to them wasn't only from blood. Family was anyone for whom they cared.

Nena could have stayed there, content to watch her family all day, but her phone began vibrating with a call from an unknown number. Nena hesitated a moment, taking stock of the room and how everyone who mattered was in it with her.

The room barely noticed Nena excuse herself. Perhaps it was more intel about the satellite-station attack or specifics beyond speculation about what had happened in Kenya.

She'd just made it into the hall, was heading toward the back of the house, where the view was best to look out at the mountain, when she connected the call. The caller began speaking before Nena said anything.

"Wasn't sure you'd answer on your personal line." The voice was female and obscured—the caller attempting to disguise her voice from recognition.

The voice was also controlled, assured, and unhurried, as if the speaker had all the time in the world.

Nena's first instinct was to hang up. Her next was to launch a series of hot-air threats about how she'd find whoever was calling and end her life. All of that dramatic business. Instead, she decided to engage. The longer she kept the caller on, the easier it would be to discover clues to her identity—despite the voice manipulation. Nena had had her fill of coincidences even before the attack on Network. She had no doubt this call was somehow related to everything that had been going on.

"I don't get many calls."

"Then you need more friends, honey." The woman laughed, causing a jolt of irritation to zip through Nena. She hated to be laughed at. She swallowed it. She needed to catch this fly with honey.

"We can be friends, you and I," the woman said, her laughter trickling off.

"Friends don't kill innocent people."

"Hmmm." As if she were really pondering it. "Are there such things as innocents, wudini?"

Nena's skin prickled, her breath catching in her throat. Was the caller Ghanaian, to know the distinctly Twi term?

"Consider the irony of your words. How many innocents have you killed in the name of your Tribe, this one that sends you on missions to eliminate people they don't like?"

Nena remained silent, though the mention of dispatches was concerning. That was a part of the Tribe kept highly secret. Nena had to keep the caller talking, revealing anything Nena could use to uncover her identity.

What did the caller know about the Tribe? She had said *your tribe*, not *the*, which could mean she didn't feel herself a part of it. And yet she was very familiar with their inner workings.

Nena stopped in front of the floor-to-ceiling windows, looking out at the lush forestry of the mountain. She heard her mother's laughter ringing louder than everyone else's. All of them unaware of how close danger lurked.

Nena got straight to the point. "What do you want?"

"Your attention."

Nena rolled her eyes. She hated these cat-and-mouse conversations, a result of people who liked to talk because they enjoyed the sound of their annoying voices.

"Have I gotten it?"

"As if I have a choice? Tell me what you want and don't waste my time. You're an intelligent woman, so you know I'll find and do away with you. It's a thing I do."

The caller seemed unconcerned. "Finding and doing away with people? Like you did—who were those vile men—Attah Walrus and Kwabena? Like Paul? Like you did your brother? You found and did away with the entire lot."

Nena reeled. Her mind searched for how this woman could've known what had happened with Ofori. Who was she? A compatriot of Paul's? His lover or wife out to seek justice for his death? The caller pretended innocence, pretended to sound admirable when what she truly meant her words to be was a gut punch. And she'd succeeded.

"I bet you're wondering how I know so much. You would be surprised at how much about you I know. I have been studying you for so long, Aninyeh Asym. Wudini of many names. You are a case study, and I am your biggest fan."

"Yeah, well, I'm no Beyoncé," Nena deadpanned.

"I don't care what you did to those men," the woman continued. "I have no doubt they deserved it."

Those men. So not a lover. Not even a friend. Nena began pacing, the movement keeping her calm and thinking.

"One day we can discuss your brother. I find that to be interesting because he was a victim, too, was he not? He was a child, groomed by a sadistic asshole who removed every choice he had."

These ruminations were nothing new to Nena. She'd spent the last six months agonizing over her actions, questioning her choices—if she'd made the right ones, if she should have spared Ofori because of his circumstance, despite the fact he was trying to kill her and had nearly succeeded. He would have done it. He'd have taken the choice from her, and then he would have taken her life.

"Family is important, yes? You find value in them. You would do anything for them. You do for the Knights. You do . . ." The woman hesitated as if weighing whether she should or shouldn't proceed. She shouldn't.

She did. "You did for the Baxters."

Nena leaned against the wall to steady herself. She turned to find she was no longer alone in the atrium. Witt was there, his face awash in concern.

"Tell him you're okay, or I will shoot him dead where he stands."

Nena's head snapped around, and she stepped away from the window. She hadn't been thinking. Hadn't considered that if her phone was compromised, this house and everyone in it could be as well, and that she stood in direct shot of any good sniper who wanted to take her out.

Her stomach lurched to her throat. The caller was nearby, had been watching the entire time. Nena felt as if she were being stripped naked and bare, laid out for the world, for this woman who was laughing, *laughing at her*, to bear witness.

Nena held up a hand to Witt, mouthing she was fine, and stepped away from him, away from the window's view, to repeat her initial question. "What do you want?"

"The end to the Tribe as you know it."

The call ended.

Nena didn't bother sending security to check the grounds. The nameless caller—if she'd even been there to see Nena, if she hadn't just been making a guess—was already in the wind. Nena knew that because it was exactly what she would have done.

"What was it?" Witt finally asked when Nena returned to where he stood.

"The person behind it all," Nena replied grimly.

Witt startled. "What? Here? They called you?"

"Not *they*. *She*."

He was confounded, pulling out his own phone to slip into his role as Network lead. "What is it she wants?"

"All of us."

29

When Elin found Nena, she was on the balcony of her room, looking out onto the mountain just as she'd done as a young girl, at dawn and sunset, standing on the edge to look down at Aburi's valleys below her, watching as the beautiful terrain prepared for its rest at night. That was where Nena felt most serene, felt in tune with nature and what was wrong or right with the world: on the edge of it, looking down.

Elin said from behind, "What are you doing here? Everyone's downstairs having Christmas supper, which is where you should be."

Nena didn't turn around. "I'm screwing everything up."

"Screwing what up?"

"Everything, Elin," Nena whispered. She threw her hand out in a flourish that waved over the valley beyond. "All of this is on me, Elin, all of it. I've slipped up somehow. That woman called me. Me specifically. Not Dad. Not Witt. Me. This means she has an issue with *me*."

Elin sucked her teeth, sidling up beside Nena to look down at the sparkling pool below them and the black outlines of trees carving into the night sky. Only the moon cast a glow, illuminating the sparseness of the mountain. "You're speaking in riddles. And looking down at this height is giving me vertigo. Come on, let's join the family."

Nena reared on Elin, eyes flashing, beseeching her. "Don't you get it? Everything I try to put together becomes a failure. I wrapped the Baxters up in the mess with Paul. It's my fault because I didn't do my job."

Elin frowned. "So you should have killed Cort instead of Attah Walrus, as the Council originally decreed? You're saying you should have let Paul get away with manipulating all of us? Is that what you're trying to say? What state do you think we'd all be in right now if you'd carried out the original dispatch?"

Nena blanched. "What? No. I—" What was she trying to say?

"Georgia would be grieving her father and God knows where. You would be dead. No, no," Elin said when Nena attempted to argue. "You would no longer be in Dispatch. Paul would have seen to it. He'd have had you retired immediately. Dad would no longer be High Council, I bet you that. Our family would be in shambles because it would have been Paul's first course of business. We would have all posed too much of an immediate threat to him."

"No, I'm not saying any of that."

"Then what, Nena?"

"I'm saying my actions began this domino effect. Whoever is coming for the Tribe, for our family, does so because of me."

Elin cackled. "And you say I'm self-absorbed."

"What?"

"So you didn't kill the nerd; you killed the bad guy instead. And so what? You think killing the fat bloke caused some reject to take potshots at the Tribe all these months later? You don't think the Tribe has accumulated enemies all on its very own? Girl, please," Elin scoffed, shaking her head in annoyance. "The Tribe—Dad—has had enemies since before either of us were born. Dad makes decisions that piss people off all the time. It has nothing to do with you."

"And you're okay with blaming Dad like that?"

"Are you mad? Of course not. I want to kill whoever is causing this trouble and wants to harm my dad. But I know what Dad is, and you should too. He is no saint, Nena. Our dad is a man of contradictions."

Hadn't Nena said as much to Cort? Said her family toed the line of right and wrong, of justice and not, in the areas of gray. This was what she'd meant, which Elin had put so eloquently. The Knights were a family of contradictions.

And yet the guilt consuming Nena knew no bounds. It was changing her. She second-guessed herself and every decision made. She'd been doing it since the failed mission, since she'd lost her whole team, save one. And even that team member she'd left in the wind. Left Sierra to grieve their teammates and heal all by herself while Nena had gone to Ghana to be with her family, to be in Cort's arms, to forget her poor decisions.

Nena returned to the present. "What if all that's transpiring is retaliation for Paul?"

"The embezzling began before Paul's death," Elin said tiredly, taking a seat in a chair away from the balcony's railings. "We've tracked the thefts to a year before his name was even floated to the Council."

They stopped talking when they heard footsteps approaching and looked toward the bedroom to see their father crossing the plush carpeting.

"What is this? Your own party of two? Can your father join?" Noble asked, smiling until he looked properly at his girls and noted their expressions—one grim, the other over it all. Easy to guess who wore what. "What's happened now?"

"Nothing. Nena's playing martyr again," Elin deadpanned, drawing her feet up onto her seat.

Nena narrowed her eyes at her sister but noticed the slight smile playing at her father's lips. "Really, Dad?"

He shrugged. "Let me guess. It's all your fault. The attacks. The stealing."

"World hunger," Elin added.

"Okay," Nena muttered.

"Global warming," Noble offered.

Nena balled her fist at their jests. She didn't need any of this.

"The breakup of Destiny's Child. That's huge. Throw her to the wolves."

Noble asked, "Of who?"

"Beyoncé." Elin rolled her eyes.

He broke out in a grin. "Oh yes! I like that one."

"Are you two done winding me up?" Nena cut in curtly. "Because if so, you can both leave me be. It's all fun and games to you, but it's serious to me."

"Which is why we jest," Noble said, coming up beside Nena and throwing an arm around her to give her a squeeze. "Because you are your worst tormentor, dear girl, and the burden does not lie with you. None of what's transpired is because of you, and if no one blames you, then why are you blaming yourself?"

She opened her mouth to say, *Because it's true*, but the expression on her father's face made Nena think better of it.

"Who's doing what?" came their mother's voice. Nena's head dropped and she groaned. She'd never missed the isolation of her Miami home more than she did at this moment. Elin brought Delphine up to speed while Delphine sidled to Nena's other side so she was properly closed in with no way of escape. Nena wondered if the Baxters and Keigel would be next to bombard her.

"If it's anyone's fault, it's mine," Noble said.

"What'd I tell you?" Elin quipped from her seat, poking a finger at their father. She mouthed, *His fault*.

"Look what I have brought upon my family. I have worked over forty years building the Tribe and its wealth to provide for the three of you. Everything I do is for you." He touched Nena's cheek tenderly, a rarity because of her aversion to physical displays. Though sometimes her dad managed to get away with it. Like in this moment, breaking through her defenses and making tears spring to her eyes.

"Yet I still brought a wolf into the henhouse. I brought a pestilence into my legacy, and it has poisoned what I have made."

"No, Dad," Nena said.

He moved, placing himself in front of her so he could look her straight in the eyes, so she could see every emotion he had laid bare. "The greatest regret of my life, Nena, is that I failed you when I didn't ensure Paul was gone in the first place. When they said they couldn't locate his body, that he'd likely died with the rest of his people, or that if he was in hiding, one of his enemies would sell him out, I made the bounty on his head so high no one could ignore it. And still he survived all those years to swindle me. I gave him the keys to my house, let him into your life, and he nearly killed you."

"He almost killed you, too, Dad."

"And I would have died a thousand times over rather than to have him lay another finger on you. Or to have kidnapped that little girl down there." Noble took in a breath, wiped his eyes, but not before Nena saw the tears in them. "I will go to the grave with that regret and failure on my heart."

Nena couldn't look at any of them. She put her arms over the railing, bending over. Her forehead dropped onto them, and she bit down on her lip. Again, the Knights had rallied around her. Again, they'd saved her. But this time, it was from herself.

The emotions within her were too much to bottle. Too much to will away. Before she could stop it, a hard sob escaped. She felt the presence of her father beside her as he covered her with his arms. And then her mother on the other side. Nena's throat swelled, pulsated from trying not to cry. And she almost had it.

Almost.

Because when Elin sidled up to her with her belly resting against Nena's side, when Nena felt the baby kick through her sister hard, into her rib cage, everything Nena had bottled up inside of her was let loose.

Delphine leaned in, whispering into Nena's hair. "My love, never claim regret and failure that is not yours to bear. We all have done our part. We all have made mistakes. We, like everyone else, are a work in progress. But we are always your family."

The Knights, a family of contradictions, absolutely. But a family, nonetheless. One of immense love and loyalty. One who knew what Nena needed when she laid herself bare, and they gave it to her, always and freely with no conditions. Even the newest Knight not yet born.

30

The last leg of Nena's tour of . . . what—redemption? Forgiveness? Acceptance, perhaps—was about to occur, though Nena wasn't sure what to expect from it. Maybe it was time. Time to reconcile herself to what life was for her now. With whom she had become. She, Elin, Delphine, and Georgia were to travel by helicopter to the site.

The call from the unknown woman had left Nena unsettled. Had made her check and double-check security around the property. She hadn't slept well in the couple of days since, often waking in the middle of the night, armed, and walking the perimeter, checking the grounds, looking up at the trees for sniper blinds, checking the systems. And she was concerned for New Year's Eve, when they'd all leave for Accra and then split up, the Baxters and Keigel going back to the States, she and Elin going to Gabon to meet with the representatives there, and their parents making final preparations for the charity dinner to be held soon after.

Nena felt as if a heavy thundercloud loomed over their heads, about to split open and rain hell on them all, though she tried to hold her feelings at bay. She didn't want to ruin the rest of the vacation for the group. She didn't want Cort, Georgia, and Keigel leaving Ghana scarred with horrible memories, as had happened to her. She'd thought she had everyone fooled, but clearly not. Late the night before they were to travel to Kumasi and the Compound, Witt called to her from his poolside seat as she again cased the grounds and looked deep into the dark, dense woods that surrounded them, thinking of the poor choice in lodging she'd made.

"Nena, a word," Witt's disembodied voice said, drawing her from her calculations.

He was in one of the rattan chairs, the glowing blue pool water stretched before him with barely a ripple moving its surface.

"I don't know how we thought this location was secure enough. There are too many areas for someone to hide and attack. I should have asked for the family to be moved to a more secure location after the London hit." Nena's rapid speech showed her irritation as she approached her mentor, sliding her .45 in its back holster.

He studied her. "We can't think of everything. And the measures I put in place before you all arrived will hold."

"Risk assessments. Ensuring things are safe. Thinking ahead of the enemy *is* my job," she answered, still standing, a ball of tightly wound nervous energy. "You taught me that. You taught us all."

He adjusted in his seat. "Maybe I shouldn't have focused on those teachings."

His words made Nena drop heavily into a chair beside him. "What do you mean?"

"I mean maybe some focuses I have drilled into all of you were misdirected."

Nena didn't understand. She'd never heard Witt doubt anything he'd ever said or done. His standards were what all of Dispatch followed. And Dispatch carried out their missions unapologetically.

"Sir?" She didn't know where any of this was coming from. Or where any of it was going.

Witt crossed a leg over the other. "Nena, I am proud of you."

She pointed at herself.

"Regardless of what I've taught you and what the Council decrees, you have made decisions you knew were the right ones. With Cort—you didn't just follow through with the dispatch. You stood by your decision . . ." He trailed off. "Continue to do that." If Witt had more to say, he didn't.

There had been something rattling around in Nena's mind ever since she and Sierra had returned to Miami. "Sir, have you ever regretted a decision you made?"

For a long while, Witt didn't answer. Maybe she'd overstepped.

"I have." He left it at that. "Is there something you regret?"

She thought about it, wondering if her issue was even worth the mention. It felt kind of insignificant now that she'd brought it up. She shrugged and said it anyway. "Just something Sierra accused me of when we came home. She said I didn't care about my team as people. That I only knew their handles, not their names. That I didn't know them."

"Was she right?"

She shook her head. "I cared about them all."

"Good thing she's still alive for you to make amends." Witt paused. "For me, my amends must come another way." He looked out at the darkness warded off by the lights from the house. "Get some sleep, Nena. You've done all you can do for the night."

———

The helicopter landed in a small makeshift airfield not too far from the Compound grounds. Nena's silence held a large swath of unease and fear she wished she didn't have at seeing one of the places of her nightmares.

She'd struggled with the idea of going, wondered why she'd agreed to it. Why she'd even let Dad and Mum offer to build the medical center on grounds that held so much death—of humans, of innocence, of dreams. She wondered if anything could ever wash away the blood that had been spilled there. But then her thoughts drifted to their trip to her mother's town of Elmina. The historical site was practically a sanctuary, was revered—exalted—despite its dark history. Perhaps the same could be said of the Compound land once the medical center was built there.

Around the airfield was nothing but dirt terrain and sparse trees. A hardtop Mercedes G-Class, nearly the color of desert sand, awaited them, a man standing sentry at the driver's door. Another idled behind with four serious-looking guards seated inside. Nena reckoned they were armed to the hilt, as she'd requested, just in case any bandits or other issues arose during their journey. There was probably more security than Nena needed, and she wished they could travel with a lower profile than they were, but with the others here, she couldn't be too safe.

As the rest of her entourage was helped out of the helicopter, Nena met up with the waiting man, who would run lead on their drive to the Compound. In the few moments she'd been out of the helicopter, Nena already felt the back of her navy blue T-shirt sticking to her skin. The sun was ferocious on her head, and she used her hand to shield her sunglasses-covered eyes from the blazing sun.

"Thank you for accompanying us," Nena said. The other three security guards spilled out of the auto. Nena was glad to see a woman included in the detail; there were so few of them in Dispatch and security as it was. She acknowledged the woman, inclining her head, and the guard, from behind her sunglasses, replied with a solitary wave.

Nena asked, "Anything come up?"

"Nothing," the lead replied. "We've already scouted the location, and all is clear. There's a town near it, but it's small, and the people are farming people. The area is completely abandoned."

"How long is the drive there?"

"Maybe thirty minutes, if that. There's a town another fifteen or twenty minutes beyond that."

Nena nodded, taking in the information. Town. She didn't remember much about a town nearby. If there had been one, she wouldn't have known. They'd arrived and left the Compound in covered trucks. Ferried away and cloaked in darkness that the outside world either didn't know or didn't care about. She might have heard whisperings of a little town, but it had all seemed like a hopeless wish. She hadn't bothered with fancies of running away from Paul and his men.

The thirty-minute drive felt shorter than Nena had anticipated, and by the time they arrived, by the time she caught sight of the remnants of the Compound's guard towers, her stomach was in knots, and her hands gripped the handles of the door. She barely heard the hushed questions and conversations occurring among the other occupants of the automobile.

Her breath held as they approached the high towers, now aged and run down, leaning to the point that it looked as if they would tumble over any moment.

"Are you okay, dear?" Her mother's familiar voice broke through the haze of awe and trepidation like a lighthouse guiding her wayward ship back to shore. The Jeep was freezing, yet Nena had broken out in a sweat. "Should we stop? We don't have to continue further."

"She's right, sis—you don't have to do this," Elin added. For the first time, Georgia was completely silent.

Nena didn't look at them. "I'm fine. Proceed." As if she were on a mission and speaking with her team. She corrected herself. "Let's go on."

They did, slowly, as her mother instructed, following a road that was now crumbled and beaten. The wire fencing had been torn down. The front gates were gone, and Nena saw them lying on the ground, in the same place they had been thrown when the Tribe had burst through them so many years ago.

The two Jeeps stopped just inside the fence. Nena opened her door, no longer hesitating. She had to see what it all looked like now, had to see if she'd feel anything like what she'd felt when she'd first arrived. It was like she was fourteen all over again, and while her eyes saw the few buildings left standing, blackened lumps of wood and metal corrugated slats that had served as the roofs, her mind saw the area as she had seen it when she'd first stepped off the truck.

The bull's-eye layout of the grounds. Paul's housing at the front. The guard towers were no longer leaning but upright and newly erected, with two guards, rifles in hand, walking their little balconies, leering down at the captives, with itchy fingers eager to shoot anyone who even thought of fleeing.

There were many faces of different hues, boys and girls, young and older, peeking out the cutouts that served as windows in the buildings, watching the new captures filing out of the trucks and directed to sit in the dirt of the square, the middle of the bull's-eye. They all shared the same hollow-eyed, distant look of people who were in shock, but those who had been here awhile wore a glint of relief on their faces. Relief that perhaps these new kids—for that was what they all were, kids—would occupy the guards' time and that maybe, just maybe, the others would be left alone for a little while. They had been right. They'd been wrong too.

Nena remembered all of this. She licked her dry lips and fought down the urge to vomit. She turned and could see Paul leaving his house, securing his belt through his pants loops, tucking his gun in the back. She saw herself, frail, shivering, lost among many who looked, and most assuredly felt, like her.

Her family hung back, giving her space. Everyone gave her space— the security detail had fanned out and was making sure there wasn't any danger lurking about, no one hiding in the cut to try to rob them, no wayward scavenger animal preparing to attack them.

Nena walked the perimeter, looking all around her. She didn't need the actual buildings there for her to see the Compound as it had been. There was the medic dormitory where Essence had nursed her back to health with hot, light soup after Nena had spent days in the Hot Box. *The Hot Box.*

Nena turned on her heel and charged through what used to be the Compound's front gates. No more stalling. She moved across the bull's-eye's center, where all the captives had been corralled, forced to listen to or watch whatever horrific lessons Paul had wanted to teach, and past the back row of buildings where the guards had been housed, where the guards had pulled their victims after making their nightly selections. It took Nena longer to find where she thought the Hot Boxes had once stood, those small, cramped tombs that had sent many an inhabitant either to their death or to insanity. Nena had been sent nearly to both.

The night she'd been sent to the box, with the blood of the guard who'd assaulted her still in her mouth, she'd barely been awake. She'd been beaten into submission because she was surely going to fight to her death right there and then. She had refused to allow anyone to denigrate her father's name in her presence. To do that meant death. It would have meant death for the guard that night had they not removed her from him—though at least his ear had come with her. Later, in a different tomb, Robach the Frenchman had certainly paid the death price for what he'd said.

She shook her head to clear it. The box, yes. It was difficult to remember how she'd gotten into the box that night. She couldn't remember how she'd gotten out of the box either. But she'd seen plenty of others sent to their fates. She'd been made to dig graves for those who hadn't made it. Made it through their time in the Hot Box or through their time at the Compound, period.

That had been Nena's job while she was there. To bury those who'd died under the most peculiar of circumstances. She'd seen it all. Death by consumption. Death by gunshots. Death by beating. Death by asphyxiation from high temperatures in the box. Death by disease. Death by suicide. Death by merely giving up all hope.

"And when that happened, when deaths occurred, here is where I would bury them—where me and those tasked with me would take shovels, and under the watch of the guards in the south towers and the ones on the ground, we'd dig ditch after ditch." Nena was talking now. Somehow, a group had formed around her. Her family and even the security detail, though on alert, were enthralled by what she was saying.

Nena hadn't realized she'd begun to speak out loud. The conversation, the retelling of what she'd endured here, had been in her head all this time—or so she'd thought, but as she glanced up, startled by the pairs of eyes staring at her, open mouthed, uncomfortable, in shock at her firsthand report, she realized that they had all heard every word of memories she hadn't even told her own sister before.

But she continued. Because the release of these memories—no, nightmares—was cathartic and seemed to be absolving her of the guilt she'd been feeling for surviving all of this.

"There would be two of us. One to grab the feet and one the hands because the guards would pile the bodies there." She pointed with one of her long fingers, her mind seeing the mound of dead waiting for burial. "The guards would yell at us to hurry, would make threats, but we knew they didn't mean them because they wouldn't want to have to dig more graves either.

"Plus, they were already in trouble with Paul for so many of us dying. Dead meant no sale. No sale meant no money. But it took a lot to get a sale together. He had to vet the buyers, make sure they weren't the authorities in disguise and that they had the financial backing they said they did. Paul would sell to people and to rebels of different regions and countries. There were those of us who were sold to become soldiers and were not even ten yet. Paul had no limit on what he was capable of and where he'd send us."

She stopped herself, glancing warily at Georgia, who unknowingly clung to Elin, and Elin to her. If Nena had had a mind to, she would have snapped a picture with her camera because this was a sight that wasn't usually seen, the two of them glomming on to one another, both of them captive in the inescapable clutches of Nena's retelling.

"That is what I was tasked to do. Dig the graves, put them in. Sometimes more than one in a grave. Fill the hole. And when the guards weren't paying much attention, I'd offer a little prayer, a few words for the dead, wishing them well. Wishing them a good journey home. Telling them they didn't have to suffer anymore, that they were better off than we were." She sighed. "Being dead felt like it was better than the existence we were forced to suffer through."

None of the men would hold her eye contact, ashamed for whatever reason. Probably thinking of the many times they'd thoughtlessly objectified women, and now they stood on land where men had gone beyond mere objectification.

It was then that Nena noticed the single female guard wiping at moisture trailing from beneath the lenses of her glasses and onto her cheeks. When she caught Nena looking at her, she turned away abruptly and walked back toward the Jeeps. Her long, straightened brown hair billowing in the hot, dry wind. Her actions moved Nena. This stranger, this person who killed as she did, for the Tribe, and had lived through whatever it was that had brought her to this moment where they were here together, was crying. For her.

31

Am I really doing this? Nena studied herself in the full-length mirror in the hotel room. Last time she'd done this much fretting over an outfit, she'd been preparing for her first date with Cort. Was she really done up in a strappy metallic mesh mini-wrap-dress number that was way too short? And about to don heels she likened to torture? She turned her body this way and that, hating the fact that she was going to spend the night done up like Elin's own personal Black Barbie.

"If I can't look the way I want, then it must be you," Elin said matter-of-factly as she lay across Nena's bed watching her sister hold the garment up like it was an alien. It was. Nena faced her, wrapped tightly in the white terry cloth robe gifted by the hotel.

"But it's silver." Nena's voice was whiny and high pitched, like something Georgia would say to Cort during one of her teen moments. "Like a Christmas ornament. And it's tiny."

Elin was unmoved, staring dispassionately at her sister. "It's actually pewter and silver. Yes, it's a mini. That's the point. It's fabulous, and you're fabulous in it."

Nena's lips twisted in disagreement. "It's too short."

Elin groaned, closing her eyes as if to stop herself from wringing Nena's neck with the sharpened talons she called nails. "Nena, dear, sis.

You know I love you, right? You have legs for days and days. Show the fucking things off once in a while. It won't kill ya."

With some maneuvering, Elin got herself up to a sitting position. She held her hands out, her fingers wiggling in silent demand. Begrudgingly, Nena took Elin's outstretched hands and gently pulled her up to standing. Elin was covered in a matching robe and fluffy slippers—the kind people had started wearing outside the bedroom more these days, which Nena could not understand. If someone was chasing them, there was no way they were getting away in those things. But that was neither here nor there.

Nena watched Elin move toward the door, on her way to her own room to finish getting dressed. She'd only paused to bring Nena the dress and heels.

"Must I?" Nena asked again, begging her sister with eyes promising to do anything in the world that Elin wanted. "It's a club. Trousers are permittable."

"It's Bloom, and not on New Year's Eve, love." Elin winked at her as she closed the door behind her. "See you down in a few."

Nena didn't want to admit it, but when she finally made her way to the lobby to meet Cort . . . the way his mouth literally dropped made her heart flutter. She put an instinctive hand to her midsection. Then ran the other nervously down the length of dress. Her hand didn't have far to go, but she wanted to make sure it wasn't riding up higher than it already had been. But also, the way Cort was staring at her made her suddenly shy, with the feeling like he was seeing her for the first time.

Keigel whistled but smartly kept any further comments to himself. He had his hands full with Elin anyway, who was wearing her own rather short dress, but hers was a white shimmery number with long sleeves that ballooned at the cuffs.

Why couldn't I wear long sleeves? Nena thought, not a little jealous.

Nena's eyes traveled to Elin's feet, where she wore—Nena shook her head—a fancier pair of fluffy bedroom slippers, white long-haired furry contraptions that Nena was sure would trip her up and be filthy before the night's end. But she wasn't going to tell Elin anything. They'd all learned that lesson. The woman was eight months in, and no one was eager to be on her bad side.

Cort slipped his hand around Nena's waist, and for a moment she froze, worried he'd feel the pencil-thin blade she tucked into the dress's inner lining at her waist because, well, never leave home without one. He leaned in, his mouth against her ear.

"You look amazing."

She shivered. The cold from the air-conditioning in the lobby. Him. Both. Probably him. "Thank you," she said, her voice low.

"Shall we get started on your last night in Ghana for a while?" Elin asked like some grand master, her hand sweeping in a flourish as the front doors of the hotel opened as if on command. "Our chariot awaits."

It was an even-fancier version of the same Sprinter vans they'd traversed all of Ghana in, and Nena was happy to see that security at a high-end club like this was tight, her added security making it tighter. It gave her a bit more confidence to enjoy the night.

The van took them to Troas Street, where Bloom Bar was located. It was one of the most popular night spots in Accra, a favorite of both the natives and the visitors. The lines wrapped around the corner, and the thumping bass, a mix of Ghanaian, reggae, dancehall, hiplife, and highlife—hip-hop and R & B with a Ghanaian flare—pulsated from the building, audible long before they could see it.

Elin and Keigel were relieved at finally being able to do what they called "grown folks' business." No offense to the parents and teen back at home. Nena and Cort, wrapped in their own world of just two, took a more mellow approach.

The two weeks had been good to them, had allowed them to be in their own element. Had given them an opportunity to relax and enjoy the other's company. And had let Nena seriously toy with the idea of taking things further than she'd thought possible. Unbeknownst to Cort and even Elin, with whom Nena shared just about everything, Nena was thinking tonight would be the night for her and Cort. It was both a terrifying and titillating thought.

They got into the club without a wait, bypassing all those in the line who craned their necks to see what famous person was visiting tonight. They saw Keigel, and whispers began running rampant that he was one of the Migos or Future, maybe that American footballer—Marshawn Lynch—because, *the locs, yes? Looks like him.* Probably nothing Keigel hadn't heard before . . . and liked.

"Yoooo," Keigel commented with wide eyes as his hand fisted to his mouth and he took in the lavish club scene, the string of lights, upscale seating, and beautiful decor. His eyes rounded at the streams of beautiful Ghanaian women moving past him, smiling flirtatiously, with coy offers of bringing in the New Year with him. "Miami clubs ain't got nothin' on this place!" Keigel was in heaven.

Nena didn't blame him. Accra was a beautiful city and Bloom a mere speck of the beauty and advancement that Ghana had to offer. This was what Noble meant when he said the world underestimated what Ghana was capable of. The nightclub wasn't just filled with locals; *everyone* was there. There were celebrities from Ghana and other countries as well. There were plenty of White people from all over. Ghana always had White people who had long ago come to colonize with religion and whatever else they believed Africans needed saving for. And well, they'd never left.

It was fine. They were welcome now, Nena supposed. At the moment she didn't care.

She wondered how often she'd have been visiting this spot if she'd been living here all her life. She didn't let the thought last, because what did it matter, the what-ifs and how-oftens? The fact was that Nena was here now. In her city. In her country with—she glanced over at Cort, looking so charming in his all-black attire that Nena wondered if she was bold enough to suggest he take her back to the hotel. Her hand flew to her neck at the obscene thought. She was not herself tonight.

They sprawled on one of the half-circle blue-and-green couches, against a sleek cherrywood-slatted wall that curved up and into an overhang above them, like a pergola. Huge industrial fans swirled lazily, blowing cool air on the crowd milling around the tables and the pockets of dancers. Nena was determined to enjoy herself. To forget that there were people stealing from the Tribe, that she and Elin would be back to work with their trip to Gabon the following day. That Cort, Georgia, and Keigel would be returning to the States.

She felt a nudge against her arm and found Elin grinning at her lasciviously. Nena gave her a confused look, and Elin arched an eyebrow, twisted her lip, and looked down, then slowly back up again. Nena followed where Elin's gaze had been. Cort's arm was drooped around her lower half, his hand resting against the exposed flesh of her thigh, massaging it lightly with his fingers. She hadn't even noticed, and she was trained to notice everything. It had all felt so natural.

Her eyes wide like saucers, Nena met Elin's satisfied ones.

"That's the point of a mini," Elin said, the smugness rolling off her as she raised her hand daintily and said, as if her words were purely sugar, "Drinks, please."

———

Nena and Cort barely made it back to the hotel and to Nena's room before their bodies smashed together so tightly it was as if they were one. She could still feel the pulse from the dance floor as their lips devoured one another, seeking the other out as if they were lost in a house of mirrors, surrounded by multiple versions of themselves but unable to find each other.

Nena's arms wrapped around Cort's neck. Then slid down his muscled arms, feeling, truly exploring him for the first time. She was against the wall now, his body pressed to hers, still kissing, tasting, licking her neck, and leaving a lake of fire in his wake wherever he touched her. He was so gentle, and yet it was she who wanted it rougher. Harder. She'd been thinking of this moment, this very one, for weeks—since the moment she'd seen him waiting for her at the airport. No, she had been waiting for this for months. Since their first date walking on the beach. No. The first night she'd laid eyes on him. She'd known.

She moaned. Something deep and guttural as he sucked at her neck. Her hands circled his shoulder blades, dipped lower to his torso, to the sides and how his body curved into that V, that perfect V that she'd heard her sister bemoan missing so much but had never herself given much thought to.

He pulled away from her, ever so slightly, his hand cupping her face, and in the moonlight of the darkened room he looked at her. Gone was the quiet, studious, ever-thoughtful Cortland Baxter. In his place was some Haitian Adonis with dark, smoldering eyes that seemed like they'd catch fire at any moment. The kind of look ripped-bodice romance books talked about. Like he was some duke about to ravage his duchess. She, Nena, was the duchess. Who would have thought?

No one right now, because he was kissing her again. Her fingers worked at the buckle of his belt, fumbling with the hidden latch. Damn fancy name-brand things. She nearly laughed, a vision of herself as some clumsy teen boy outsmarted by a girl's bra.

She got it undone with no help from Cort, because he was busy hoisting her up by the waist. Her legs wrapped around his hips, her toes kicking her heels off. The room was silent save the sounds of months of slow-burning tension building between them, culminating in this one moment.

Below her, near her very essence, she could feel his rise. She could feel him. The part of Cort she'd always been curious about, like some naive little schoolgirl. It was the part of him least known, yet the part she'd been wanting the most to meet—she thought.

They sat on the bed, her on top of him. The straps of her dress—that itty-bitty pewter mesh number—had slipped well below her shoulders.

She had no idea how it would feel. She soon learned it felt amazing. Was this what intimacy, true intimacy, felt like? What sex would feel like? She could barely help herself, grasping his head with her hand and pulling him toward her chest, wanting more of this wonderful feeling.

But it wasn't all she wanted. She wanted him. She was sure of it. She wanted to feel every bit of what she'd never really known, not the way she should have. What she'd been denied and denying herself. She pushed him back against the bed, resuming her exploration of him. She explored the length of his body while he gave her all the time to do whatever she wanted. In his eyes, she could read how much Cort yearned for her, how much desire he locked away to give her time to adjust and be comfortable. She loved him for that, and it only served to increase her hunger for him.

When she didn't stop him, he continued downward, until—

Nena gasped. And she . . . she couldn't sort out all the feelings. She'd have to sort all of them out later. She felt her body relaxing, riding the waves—

Cunt.

The word slapped her hard, and she jumped as if stuck with the hidden blade Cort had found when removing her dress. The one he'd chuckled over and tossed to the side along with her dress.

He paused, looked up, thinking he'd hurt her. She told him he hadn't. He continued, and she closed her eyes, breathing out like meditation.

Bitch.

Whore.

In the voice of the soldier from the Compound. Of Robach, the Frenchman. Their faces flashed behind her closed eyelids. Too close. Her eyes flew open to release them from her proximity. The shock of them, even in memory, was too much to take.

The ferocity with which the names assailed her was debilitating. Her body tightened, going into automatic lockdown, and Cort—she felt him climb up onto the bed beside her, barely touching her, saying only a gentle "Hey." Her hands clutched the sides of the bedsheets in a death grip. Her teeth clamped down. Her eyes stared beyond him, not seeing this moment where they were—in her *after*. She could only see her *before* . . . all of her *before*s.

He knew without Nena having to say anything. She was grateful for that. If only she could lean into him, relieved because Cort just got it. Got her. But Nena couldn't. Aninyeh wouldn't let her. Both Nena's body and her mind were betraying her, and she could not turn to him for comfort. She could not tell him apart from all the others. She was a woman split in two: Nena the adult, who wanted to be with this man entirely as they should be. Aninyeh the child, who knew of nothing but pain and misery at the hands of men.

Nena, with her years of training, could not overpower Aninyeh, whose strength and endurance in survival outmatched, outweighed, out-everythinged Nena's.

She fought against the swirl of memory. Against the snatches of herself in this very position and in pain, crying out. Begging for them to stop. Begging for her life to end. She could feel the hot, damp packed dirt as Paul's soldiers held her down. Held down her wrists.

Bitch. Stop.

Whore. Please.

Take her.

Souris . . .

She did not know it, but she'd been speaking, begging out loud. Burning-hot tears were slipping down her face. Her eyes, not seeing but *seeing* too much. *Remembering.* Too. Much.

Ghostly echoes of pain pierced through her pelvis, through her abdomen, so deep it drove Nena upright. Her screams chasing her. Cort had just enough time to jump off the bed before she slammed her head into his, thinking he was one of the others.

Aninyeh told her to kill him. As she had gutted Robach. As she had bitten off a hunk of the soldier's ear.

She bolted, the streak of her but a shadow in the moonlit room. Cort called after her, rustling behind her in an attempt to catch up to her. But she was too quick, and that was purposeful. Because had she not moved when she had, had she not removed herself from his proximity, she would surely have hurt him.

Because she could do that now as she'd been unable to before, back when she'd been Aninyeh.

The *before* her felt betrayed that the *after* her even considered giving of herself in *that* way. Even if it was to Cort, who had never hurt her, never given her a reason to doubt him. Cort, who had shown her nothing but love and deep consideration. But Aninyeh didn't care. She only knew that Nena was betraying her, in Nena's enjoyment of him, in Nena's want of him, in Nena's intention to go through it and put all of their past—Aninyeh's past of fear and tumult and pain—behind her. No, Aninyeh was thinking, she could not let this be. Not ever.

And there was nothing Nena could do to stop her.

Nena shut the bathroom door behind her, locked it, inhaled deep breaths to beat down the suffocating, stifling pressure rising up in her chest. Her body trembled. Her skin broke out in gooseflesh. All because of the internal war between that girl Aninyeh and this woman Nena.

She took more breaths, placing a hand on either side of the white porcelain sink. On the other side of the door, she heard a soft knock and the gentle call of her name.

"Talk to me, please," Cort said, his voice muffled. "Tell me how I can help you?"

She closed her eyes, willing herself to be calm. Be still.

"Stay with me, baby," his faraway voice said. "Stay present. Stay here."

She tried to use his voice as a guide, leading her back home, leading her back to that bed to finish what she'd very much wanted to start.

She did not move. Her feet wouldn't listen. Her body wouldn't follow. Because however could she face Cort again? How could he want her? After this? How long would he stand by her before he tired of her inability to do as she desperately wanted to do? And she wouldn't blame him for deciding to leave. Not one bit.

Finally, after what seemed like eons had passed, she chanced a look into the mirror. Gathered enough courage to see who was looking back. And she saw the both of them. The child. The woman. The younger. The older. The haunted. The hunter. Side by side, two halves of the same being. The girl was satisfied, a haughty glint of satisfaction in her eye. The woman was hopeless, wide eyed, and pleading to be set free of her, of Aninyeh.

You will never be free of me, the girl said.

Because I am the survivor.

It was true. Nena would never rid herself of Aninyeh. And she would never want to. But she would learn—no, they both must learn—to coexist. And that meant coming to terms with how things needed to be, for the both of them to survive. And thrive.

She slipped back into the dark bedroom. She was no longer naked, now wearing the bathrobe she'd hung behind the door earlier. Cort wasn't waiting for her at the door. She wouldn't be surprised if he'd left. If he flew off tomorrow when it was time for him to return to the States. And never saw her again.

He was lying in the bed.

She let out a long breath, having held it in anticipation of seeing him gone. He wasn't asleep. He didn't speak. He was bare chested, but when she'd walked to the bed, slipped in, and pulled up the sheet to cover herself to her neck, she saw he'd put his pants back on.

He lay still beside her. The weight of what had happened so heavy it might smash them both. She bit her bottom lip, staring at the nightstand, at the clock with the bright-green figures giving her its time. She swallowed, waiting for the questions to come, for the barrage of accusation and disgust. For the inevitable *this won't work*.

Instead, she felt him slide closer toward her body. He left a space between them.

He asked, "Can I just hold you?"

She paused, weighing the words. Asking, *Can he just hold us?* But the girl in the mirror was gone.

So Nena answered for them.

Cort slid closer, slipped one arm beneath her and the other over her, enveloping her in the cocoon of him. She nestled within his comfort, his protection, as he quieted all the demons that had driven her away. The tears followed, sorrowful, embarrassing, hot tears she couldn't stop and didn't want to. Her shoulders rocked with the force of them.

He held her until she finally fell asleep.

32

Nena, Elin, and Witt arrived by private charter at Léon-Mba International Airport nearly five hours after separating from the Baxters and Keigel at Kotoka International in Accra early that morning. Their plan was to meet with the Gabonese reps, where Elin would discuss how one of them might assume the Council seat, before turning back around to return to the airport and their jet. The flight and the preparation for their upcoming meeting were a perfect distraction from last night, which Elin wisely knew not to ask about, and it kept Nena from feeling the absence of her American family.

Though the coastal country, located on the western side of Central Africa, was gorgeous even as Nena had gazed down upon it from the air, neither sister wanted to stay longer than they needed, opting to return home that same day in order to finalize the preparations for the charity dinner next week. It would be a long day, they agreed, but better to be home than in a country among new associates they weren't quite sure about yet.

"It really is beautiful," Elin commented, staring out of the window of their car. And while Nena was glad for the security detail Witt had brought with them—a cadre of nine in a convoy of three SUVs, four guards in cars one and three, the driver and Witt in theirs—her caution wasn't abated. She didn't know this place—not the layout, not the streets. The city was densely populated, which wasn't unusual for her—after all, she lived in Miami and London—but still. It was the not knowing that gave Nena an unease she couldn't quite place.

"Perhaps we should have held off on the meeting until after the dinner? Give me and Network some time to find more intel on them?" Nena asked, not for the first time.

"I can't put off the meeting any longer. Yes, I'm technically still grieving my husband, but this is business, and they're eager to continue what Oliver and his father started."

Nena tried to keep herself steady at how effortlessly Elin spoke of Paul and her brother Ofori—Oliver.

"I suppose," Nena replied. Witt sat across from them with his legs crossed at the knee, reading a newspaper. What was it with the men and newspapers? Couldn't they scroll for news on their phones like everyone else? "What do you think, Witt? About the meeting?"

They were supposed to be meeting down in the business district, at one of the high-rise businesses owned by the reps.

Witt's eyes remained on the paper, his tone flat. "I think you're worrying for nothing," he said. "I think the Gabonese want the seat at the table and the Tribe wants the oil connections they have."

It was one of the selling points Paul—alias Lucien—had used to secure his seat at the Council table. Gabon received most of its money from the oil industry, and before that from logging. The majority of their country was rain forest, and while the Tribe wouldn't go for destroying rain forest by cutting down the trees, they did want a piece of the action. Wood went a long way in building safe and stable homes throughout Africa. Oil-lined pockets were needed to purchase cut logs and replant forests. Gabon could be advantageous for the Tribe and vice versa.

So there it was. Nena was effectively hushed and subsequently forced to quell the gnawing in her belly that she didn't . . . what?

Elin considered Nena, taking a moment from her phone calls and internet swipes to acknowledge Nena's concern. "I understand your worries, sis. We'll go meet briefly as a show of good faith. We'll calm them down and let them know we're not trying to take over whatever setup they have here. And then we'll beg off all the wonderful food I know they want to throw at me. I hear their seafood and pizza are fabulous here. I'm intrigued."

"Are the two together?" Nena asked, temporarily distracted. How everything reverted to food with Elin was beyond her. And how Nena allowed herself to be distracted like a cat with its toy ball was equally perplexing.

Wit added, "We'll have the guards keep extra vigilant, Nena. I trust your instincts, and I'm only here to ensure Elin doesn't scare them away."

Elin put a hand to her chest, her face drawing into a pout. "You wound me, dear Witt. And here I thought you had not a funny bone in your body."

"It's the old age."

Elin's laughter rang through the car. Nena cracked a wry smile and eased into her seat a bit more. They were right. This was a trip of goodwill. To get the Gabonese fully on their side.

"Welcome!" Charles Bekale greeted as Nena, Elin, and Witt entered the executive suite at the Radisson with three of their security guards. The rest of their detail remained positioned outside the door and downstairs at the front of the hotel.

The round, bald man, who reminded Nena of an overly joyful uncle, gave Elin a peck on both cheeks and then attempted to do the same for Nena until he saw her death glare and retracted his lips. He offered her a nod and semideep bow, which she acknowledged with a head incline. He and Witt shook hands, clapping one another on the back.

Charles turned to his partner, a gangly man with a scarred face indicating which Gabonese tribe he was from. "Do you think these girls know French? Or shall I speak English?" he asked in French.

"The Knights," Nena interjected in effortless French, "will speak whatever makes you comfortable."

Charles couldn't mask his surprise, and neither could his partner, James.

"Of course," Charles replied, switching to English, the global fallback for communication. "My greatest apologies for the assumption." He spread his arm over the lavish display of foods, including the seafood Elin had mentioned. However, no pizza, Nena observed. Elin hid her disappointment well. There were others in the room. Charles's wife. An accountant. Another rep who worked with James and Charles in their investment business.

At the table, Elin got down to business, on Nena's same page and not wanting to stay longer than necessary. The Gabonese were polite. Pleasant even, but still they were unknown and thrown in with Nena and Elin under the most unusual of circumstances. Their point person, the man they'd chosen to represent their interests in the Tribe, was dead. And so was his son. And before them was the son's sudden wife, whom they'd never met.

"You can see why we'd be wary of the circumstances of Lucien's and Oliver's deaths. So untimely."

"Rarely is death ever a planned thing," Elin commented easily.

Nena and Witt remained straight faced. Dispatch was proof that death could very well be a planned thing. But they kept their mouths shut.

Charles nodded. "Of course. But Lucien was our man, you understand? We had been working with him on business dealings for years prior to his coming to us with this Tribe membership."

"Of course, we'd heard of the African Tribal Council," James interjected, his voice much deeper than Nena had anticipated. He was the calm one to Charles's overtly jovial nature. "Who hasn't heard of your organization in Africa. This organization that wants to rebuild Africa from within."

"But Africa was never destroyed," Elin countered.

"No, of course not. Overlooked, maybe," James pivoted agreeably. "Your prospectus is solid, steadily gaining. The countries who align with you see profit; their people in the outskirts get supplies and support. Who doesn't want that? I was just telling Charles this the other day. Lucien or not, this is the business that Gabon needs."

Witt said, "The Tribe also feels that Gabon has a lot to offer. The companies and associates you represent can do a world of good within the Tribe, which is only a group of businesses combined to form one large conglomerate that can be international, an umbrella for all the various interests that our members have."

"Right," Elin picked up, animated. Business was her wheelhouse. Nena wondered if she'd be rude to leave and walk the premises with the guards downstairs. They really didn't need her here. Charles and James seemed innocuous enough, if a bit too eager to get within the fold.

"The Tribe doesn't dictate what you should or shouldn't deal in, except if it's inhumane. We do not tolerate that. No human trafficking. No sweatshops. Nothing that debases other people."

Both men shook their heads. No, of course not, they swore. They would never.

Nena's face ticced. And yet, they'd fallen in with a man who'd done everything they'd just said they wouldn't. They'd funded a man who was the epitome of one who debased others. She really should leave before she said something.

"We're in agreement, then," James said. "Wonderful!"

Charles held up a hand as if telling his partner to slow his roll. "Cousin, wait," he said soberly. "There is still the matter of your family."

Elin pointed to herself. "Our family?" she asked, only a slightly raised eyebrow indicating her confusion. "The Knights? Or the Tribe?"

"Your family," Charles confirmed. He rested his elbows on the glossy conference table, leaning forward as he looked Elin directly in her eyes. Her right hand, the hand Nena could see, was balled up, the fingers working against one another to prevent Elin from rubbing her stomach, from reminding the men that they were speaking to a woman with whom they normally would not. Nena was both saddened that Elin had to go to such lengths to not give any man reason to doubt her power and legitimately in awe of Elin's resolve.

"Your family is extremely powerful. Your father sits as High Council. He created the Tribe. Nothing moves in the Tribe without a Knight involved."

Not true. Someone was currently stealing funds, had infiltrated Network and assassinated innocent tech workers, and nary a Knight had anything to do with it. There were things going on within the Tribe that the Knights knew nothing about. The thought was terrifying.

Elin waited a beat. "What are you getting at, Charles?"

Charles's eyebrow twitched at being referred to by his name. No doubt he was used to people only calling him *sir* or *mister*.

James said, "He means no harm. We are fine. Right, Charles? We discussed this."

"But I'd like to hear from Elin here and her compatriots."

Nena tensed. This was why she hadn't wanted to come. Why she'd been feeling uneasy. Because they were in Charles's territory, and even though he looked like a bumbling simple uncle, he was about to cross a line he couldn't take back.

"How do we know your family isn't trying to acquire our assets for your own gain?" Charles continued, taking a giant step over the line. "How can we be sure you didn't have the Douglases killed to inherit all they've amassed? To have access to our resources and money? You sit in Lucien's chair."

There it was. Said plain for all to hear. James swallowed, his large Adam's apple bobbing behind the thin skin of his throat. The room, despite all the people within it, was deathly quiet. Behind her, Nena could feel the shift of their guards, tensing as she was, preparing to make a move if needed. Witt sat ramrod straight, his mouth drawn into a firm line of properly shared anger. But Elin, the hot-tempered one, the sister with the short fuse who was lightning fast with a comeback, merely sat in her chair. Rubbing her thumb over the knuckles of the fingers of her balled-up hand, studying Charles as he unabashedly did the same to her.

Nena scooted forward in her chair. "This isn't what we came here for. Not to be accused. Do remember that Lucien, and you, came to us, to the Tribe? Before that, we knew nothing about you."

Elin held up a hand. "It's fine."

Nena blinked at their role reversal, at Elin being the voice of reason while Nena was prepared to cross the table and slit Charles's insinuating throat.

"It's really not." Nena refused to back down, squaring her shoulders. She'd allow people to say a lot, but she wouldn't allow anyone to denigrate her family's name. Not after all they'd done and continued to do.

"But it is," Elin said calmly, still watching Charles. "What you need to hear, Charles, and understand is that my sister is correct. You approached us, not the other way around. But I understand your worry. We will not take over your business. We will not edge you out, if that is your concern. We seek partnership, not takeover. And the deaths of my husband and father-in-law were not of our doing."

The first lie Elin had said since the start of the meeting.

"Their deaths were a surprise and have had a great impact on my family, as they have for you." Not a lie, but not what the Gabonese were thinking either.

"I am carrying the Douglas heir, and my family would have never harmed its father."

Nena had a sudden urge to scratch an itch that had made its presence known on her cheek.

"I loved Oliver Douglas," Elin said. "If you are hesitant to believe anything, believe that most of all. He and I loved one another, and I believed we'd have a life together."

Elin's words carried weight. The silence stretched out among them, connecting them in this moment of shared loss. She touched her belly then, her hand on a slow crawl from one end to the other, highlighting the expanse of it. For Charles to see. For all of them. She allowed a touch of her true feelings to show.

Witt, who had the pleasure of sitting between Nena and Elin, stretched out his fingers, a direct signal to Nena to cool it. She didn't need him to remind her. Not after Elin had opened herself to a man who was wholly undeserving.

James cleared his throat, turning to his cousin with a look that read, *See what you've done?* Charles glanced away in shame, knowing his show of force had made him look like the bully he was.

"Ms. Knight," he began, "I am sorry for my insensitivity and lack of decorum. I never should have—"

Elin waved him away. "Forgiven, especially if now we can proceed and I can propose my plans for when the Council seat is transferred to one of you."

Nena hoped it would be James. He was definitely the more sensible of the two.

Both men were nodding. The silent accountant too. The wife was fluttering around the room ensuring the refreshments were still refreshed.

"Of course." Charles fell over himself to respond, relieved it seemed as if there would be no hard feelings. Little did he know Elin had a memory like an elephant when it came to people who got on her bad side. And Charles had taken up residence there.

She considered him a beat too long, making him squirm uncomfortably. Then she broke out into a brilliant smile, which was sunlight burning away the gloom of the conversation.

She said, "I heard Gabon has the best pizza. Please tell me you have some here?"

33

Nena and Witt walked out of the hotel with two of their guards in tow, heading toward the curb where their three SUVs and their drivers waited on the street. Elin was still upstairs with four of their security, wrapping up the meeting before she came down to join Nena and Witt.

It had crept up on her, and Nena was beginning to realize she rather liked the business side of things. Liked the shift from the boots-on-the-ground mentality of conducting missions and taking out targets assigned to her without consideration of who they were or why they were on the kill list.

The low grumble of motorcycles pulled her attention from thoughts of where she wanted to be. Sounded like two, maybe three, high-powered bikes, coasting down the street at a speed considerably lower than the posted speed limit. Witt and Nena approached their waiting SUV, second in the line of three. There was a trio of bikes, each with two riders on it, all in black. Her nerves tingled, ticking toward high alert. The lead bike revved its engine, increasing its speed, and the bikes rode past, obscured as they passed the parked SUVs, then reappeared toward the end of the street, where they idled.

"That's interesting," Witt muttered under his breath.

The first SUV exploded in a fireball so intense it was lifted inches into the air. It crashed back down in a ball of orange flames and black plumes of smoke. The shock wave threw Nena and Witt backward and to the ground.

Gunfire erupted immediately. Pedestrians—innocents—began dropping. Nena and Witt scrambled to their knees and took cover behind a large potted plant. Nena pulled her gun free from her ankle holster and checked that it was fully loaded. Beside her, Witt did the same. Around them, people were screaming. The two guards who'd been with Witt and Nena returned fire, as did the drivers in the remaining SUVs. But they were taking more hits from the onslaught of fire surrounding them than they were landing.

Nena and Witt knew the procedure in a scenario like this. They'd practiced it over and over during training. They twisted around either side of the planter, firing.

Her clip nearly out, Nena released it, pulled out a full one, pushed it into locking position, and started up again.

Pop. Pop. Pop. Pop. She laid down fire, suppressing their attackers' ability to return, her breathing slow and steady. She spotted, aimed, fired. Spotted. Aimed. Fired. Again. Again. Re-up. Again, all the while advancing toward the remaining two SUVs. Witt followed suit. Calling commands in his comms for the guards to keep Elin upstairs.

Nena's concentration fractured. Elin. What if she was locked in with people who meant to take her? She looked over her shoulder at Witt, about to tell him her thoughts. That they needed to ensure Elin was with friendlies. But a high whizzing snagged her attention, and before she could utter a word, the world exploded in a ball of heat and light and battlefield screams.

Nena and Witt tried to shield themselves but to no avail. They were lifted off their feet, slammed against their car, the only protection they had against the barrage from the street.

The incessant wails from activated car alarms screamed. Behind them, the hotel's fire alarm replied. The few police and hotel security still alive were dazed and gathering their wits. Bystanders attempted to hide behind cars or make a run for the hotel's front lobby, only to be mowed down by cross fire.

This wasn't a dispatch, or the assailants would have stormed the hotel. This was meant to terrorize. Or to extract someone. Nena hoped the four guards they'd left with Elin were enough to protect her. But what if the Gabonese were involved? What if her sister was in trouble up there with Nena unable to get to her?

Smoke from the blaze made it hard to tell where bystanders ended and assailants began. The two guards who'd accompanied them were down. The driver from the third SUV was out of the vehicle and firing around the bumper.

She wanted to go back for Elin but wasn't sure there was enough cover. The attackers would know what she looked like, had intel on her to maybe pick her out and then pick her off as she made a run for the building.

"I need to go back," she said, reaching for another clip at her ankle. She fired into the street at the bikers, who had ridden up farther and were laying out bullets, clearing the path for their extraction team inside to come out with Elin. Nena couldn't let that happen.

Through the haze of smoke and fire, a black van pulled up, stopping her. She'd used the same type of vans for her own extractions. Her stomach dropped to her feet. Acid took up residence in her throat.

"Don't. It's . . . too much. Too much fire," Witt huffed, calling into his comms for whatever backup Network could scramble up nearby. No one had imagined anyone would be so bold as to attack the children of the Tribe's High Council—certainly not with this large a force. Even Witt's unflappably calm demeanor, always the eye in Nena's storm, was flapping. Its trickle-down effect made her anxious and unsure of her own next steps.

Witt said, "We don't know how many are left or what they're waiting for. It's like they're trying to keep us down." A line of sweat beaded his brow, and his eyes read worry.

"The guards could be coming down with Elin." She had to protect her sister, the baby inside of her. "Anything could happen to the baby," Nena argued.

On the other side of the car Nena and Witt sheltered behind, an army of footsteps was approaching, and fast. The doors of the black van slid open as they prepared to whisk Elin into it, hold her for ransom . . . or worse. Nena couldn't think of that now.

"I'll go first," Witt said. Before she could protest that Elin was her sister, her responsibility, he was running into the smoke and firestorm toward the hotel.

Nena ducked as bullets whizzed over her head, off to her side. She saw one of the bikers round the front of a car, rifle raised. She fired. Her target went down. Crouched low, so she could see below the car she was using as her cover, she saw booted feet and shot at them, satisfied to hear the screams and watch their legs buckle as they fell into her line of sight on the other side of the vehicle.

She squeezed out more rounds. Head shots if she could because they were wearing vests. She hoped Witt made it to Elin, but if he didn't, she needed to get closer to the van so she could take out whoever escorted Elin down. Better position to save her from up close.

She saw more feet advancing. Heard the shrill of a rocket launcher as it screamed above and hit home, connecting with a nearby car and throwing the scene into more chaos. She took a chance and rolled under the car as the advancing feet rounded the car to kill her.

Beneath the car, she didn't think about the driver shot dead above her, the one burning in the truck in front, or the one who'd been firing behind them. Was he still in the game? Either way, she couldn't stay there. She slid over, toward the bodies she'd just shot. She pushed, moving them aside. The van, its yawning mouth open, ready to be fed with her sister, was there, and she refused to let that happen.

But hands were on her now, roughly pulling her from beneath the car. She saw Witt on his knees, a gun barrel trained to his forehead.

His arms raised in surrender. He was speaking, but she couldn't hear the words.

"No," she whispered, her stomach twisting, flashes of her father, Michael Asym, on his knees, hands tied and kneeling in front of Paul as Attah Walrus was about to take his head with his machete.

"What are you doing?" Witt asked now, always the authority, even in the face of a bullet. "You're making a grave mistake. This is not the way."

The masked man said, "Good thing you're not the big man here, mate. You don't give commands here."

Witt was a man of different talents than Michael Asym. He faked to the side, bringing his arm up in an outward sweep. His arm connected with the gun, and the man let off a shot in surprise, too near Witt's ear. Witt grimaced from the pain, but his foot shot out, hitting the man in his knee. He yelled out as Witt's hand went to his head as he tumbled over from the concussive effects of the shot going off too close.

Nena struggled against the people grabbing at her. They dragged her from beneath the car, kicking away the two bodies she'd killed. She couldn't make out anything about them, not even their race. One of the attackers punched her, the knuckles of his gloves covered in hard plastic. The impact nearly rendered her senseless. She tasted blood mixed with stomach acid. She'd be sick if they kept it up.

Would be dead before that.

She looked at Witt as another man with a gun advanced on him.

"No," she yelled out this time, breaking every protocol of combat. She wasn't Echo in this moment. She wasn't on a mission where emotions had no place. She needed to be, though, because with each sound she made, each word she uttered, they knew exactly how to hurt her, by hurting the people she cared for.

"Leave him! Let him and my sister be." Any second the attackers would burst out of the hotel with Elin between them.

"We got her."

She reared, bucking her body. Her world collapsing. They'd gotten Elin. They had her, and Nena hadn't been able to stop them. She'd failed at her most important duty, to protect her sister, to protect her nephew. She should have never left Elin alone up there. She should have swallowed her distaste for Charles and remained in the meeting to watch Elin scarf down whatever pizza they'd managed to get for her. Instead, she'd left her post. She'd been selfish. And now. She'd be losing her sister and her mentor.

"Let Elin go. You don't want the Tribe's wrath."

One of the men holding her laughed. "Ah, such a wise one," he said in a tone suggesting the opposite. "We are not here for her. We are here for you."

There was a sharp prick in her neck, the cool spread of something beneath her skin, replaced with sharp stinging that burned as the drug coursed through her veins. She turned her head as they pulled the syringe from her neck. She blinked. Long and slow. Then again. Longer and slower.

And a third time, but this blink Nena's eyes didn't reopen.

34

Nena wanted to die. The pain was diminishing as she came to, her senses sharpening, making her starkly aware of the blackness and stale smell of recirculating air in the dank, scratchy sack that covered her head. Beyond the sack, she knew whatever space she was in was dark; no light shone through the tiny holes in the fabric.

She was captured. Imprisoned. Again.

She struggled against her bindings, testing how much give they had. None. Ropes circled her wrists, coiled down her legs, wrapping around her ankles. Hog-tied with no way out. It was a fate she'd never believed she'd be in again. It was a nightmare that she had promised herself to never revisit.

The air in the bag lessened as Nena's breathing increased with each petrifying inhalation. Her mind was a fog of shadows and pain. *You're losing air,* she kept thinking. *It's going. Soon it'll be gone. And you, you will be dead.*

At first, she couldn't recall how she'd come to be in this situation. In the back of her throat, she could taste a medicinal flavor. Images of explosions and gunfire and motorcycles and people falling and Witt on his knees, a gun pointed at his forehead. Her stomach twisted, heaved, and she thought she'd be sick. Then not only would she lose air but she'd drown in her own vomit.

Maybe that was for the best. Anything was better than being imprisoned again. That she'd survived the Compound and Robach's basement cell was a fluke. That she'd spent all these years performing dispatches and never, *never*, been captured was a stroke of luck. Not talent. Not something she excelled at. Because if she were good at her job, if she had lived up to the promise she'd made herself as she'd fled Robach's quaint little house of horrors, she wouldn't be here, in this place, tied like a carcass, about to lose her mind.

Nena swallowed the scream climbing up her throat, tried to set aside fear to focus on what she knew. The man who'd laughed at her had said they'd come for her. Why her? What did they want from her? So maybe Elin was fine. Maybe she'd managed to make it to safety; maybe the guards and Witt . . . but no. Witt had been fighting with one of them when they'd taken her. She hadn't seen what had become of him. Surely they hadn't let him live. His demise, coupled with her capture, would cripple the Tribe's defenses. She had to assume Witt was dead.

She felt the beginnings of panic coming. Too many losses: her mentor, maybe her sister, her freedom. Nena was captured. Imprisoned. Again.

But this time, she wasn't a young girl anymore. She wasn't brave but helpless Aninyeh. She wasn't without resources and training. And while she was devoid of her blades and gun, she had her mind. And she needed to think. She needed to collect herself and be strategic. And she needed to accept whatever came next and deal with it as it did. And it started with getting this blazing thing off her head.

She jerked her head. The sack, she realized, was not cinched around her neck. It hung loose, and if she focused on this one thing, the removal of this thing, she'd have a minor victory. And she'd have air.

She moved her aching body, rolling until she came to a stop against a wall. Willing herself to be still enough, she rested her forehead against the wall and slid down. She did it again. And again, until inch by little inch the sack bunched up her neck, up her chin, over her mouth, allowing in a lungful of earthy air. Fueled by the fresher air, she kept working, training her focus solely on this feat and beating away the crippling fear that threatened to overtake her every step of the way. The cloth rose over her nose, and she took a deep inhale, confirming wherever she was was full of dirt. Like—her breathing seized—a hole. A coffin. She gulped.

No, she chided. *Be still. You're not done, girl. Remember your purpose and get the sack off.*

She went back to work on its removal, inching it up over her eyes. She kept them closed, not ready to see anything. Over her eyebrows. And then she was free of it. She used the wall to work her way up to an awkward half-sitting, half-lying position. Next, she'd turn her attention to the ropes. They were tight but not entirely unyielding. Interesting, because why allow her enough give to move at all? But first . . .

She opened her eyes, blinking. Disorientation made her think she hadn't opened her eyes at all. Her head twisted on her neck, but she could make nothing out. Even as her eyes grew accustomed to the dark, she could barely make out the shape of her body and the length of the small square room. She battled against the memories of past rooms and tight spaces wrestling each other to be the first to burst through into her mind and retract all the progress she'd made.

The little bit of work she'd done to remove the hood had exhausted her. And she was thirsty. Her mind, running rampant, siphoned every bit of energy from her. Her head pulsated with pain, and her body followed closely behind.

Something caught her attention as her eyes further adjusted to the dark. The outline of a door? But she couldn't hold on to the thought. Her mind was giving way to a grayish fog she knew meant she was slipping back into unconsciousness.

Her last thought, as she passed out from sheer exhaustion and the side effects of the drugs . . .

What comes next?

35

Nena was awake long before she saw the fleeting shadows finally stop in the sliver between the door and the dirt.

They were there for her.

First thought: *Finally.*

Because now things would happen, either for the good or the bad. Second thought . . . no, she couldn't think any second thoughts. Second thoughts would allow that minute dot of fear in, and it would swell and expand into an all-consuming, sanity-snatching void. She'd just barely gotten herself together. Had willed herself to stay awake until her eyes had accustomed themselves enough for her to get a better idea of her bearings.

She was in a small cell, maybe ten by ten. There was no toilet or sink. No windows or fresh air. No light. The temperature was too warm, but nothing she couldn't handle. The air had a dank quality, making her skin and clothing feel damp.

Using the bit of give in the ropes, she'd searched her entire body, holding out hope that maybe they'd missed her blades lodged in her belt. But when her fingers had grasped empty belt loops, that hope had left her. She didn't have the hunting knife she kept sheathed on her shoulder harness or the other side blade, but that was because she'd left

Yasmin Angoe

them on their chartered plane, because Elin had said it would look bad if she came in fully armed.

If Nena got out of this mess, no one would ever tell her again to be without her weapons.

But Nena, she rationalized, *you'd still be without your weapons right now.*

She sighed. What else was she right about? So she could rub it in Elin's face, and Witt's too. For being too trusting of people. If she saw Elin again. And Witt—she didn't want to think about him. She was relieved she hadn't been witness to his end as she had been to her first father's.

Whoever these people were had gotten their mark. Nena nearly laughed. She must have been going mad, because Aninyeh Asym—Nena Knight—Echo—wudini—could now add *mark* to the long list of names she'd been called throughout her life. The irony of it was too much for her.

When the metal door was pulled open, it made a grinding noise of rusted metal on rusted hinge. She dipped her head to the side, the light too bright and harsh and shocking for her eyes. She braced herself as two blurred beings rushed in toward her while one stood at the door, rifle trained on her in case she had any ideas. She could practically read the person's mind. Male, she guessed from his stance.

They pulled her up by the armpits, her bound hands rubbing painfully against the rope bindings. She was unsteady on her feet, couldn't get her footing quickly enough before one of them thumped her hard on the side of the head. It stunned her, her equilibrium off, and she staggered.

"Walk," he growled.

She did, held on either side by two guards, their rifles slung across their backs. The guard who'd been standing at the door walked behind them, his muzzle trained at her back. The hall was narrow, lengthy, and reminiscent of an old security fort or outpost. More packed-dirt ground. More cinder block walls. Doors positioned at alternating spaces on both sides of the hall. All closed so she couldn't see what was in them. Other prisoners? Outside?

Likely not. She licked her cracked lips with a dry tongue. She was dehydrated. Her throat was on fire. And the drugs had left her stomach with a queasy feeling. Nena didn't allow herself to think long about it, but they hadn't bothered covering her head. They weren't obscuring their faces, allowing her to see them. She knew what that meant.

This place had the feel of an underground bunker. Probably so it wasn't noticed by the authorities. Or the Tribe when they came looking. Because she knew her father. They were looking. Harsh industrial lights hung from the ceiling. At the end of the hall was a massive metal double door. She thought the doors were her destination, but instead of heading straight, they turned right and entered the last, smaller door.

The door opened into a wide room. Its walls were lined with computers in an advanced surveillance setup that looked very much, to Nena, like a mini Network. A well-muscled man, his back to her, faced the monitors.

The guards placed a metal chair in the middle of the room. They untied her hands from behind her back, then retied them to the sides of the chair, all while she kept her eyes on the man. Looked around the room while he wasn't watching, studying the way the file boxes were stacked. Spying a ventilator system through a crack between stacked boxes. The table was littered with knickknacks, paperwork, rounds of artillery, handheld radios, a map of schematics. She strained to see what was on the map—a building was all she could tell. She averted her eyes before anyone caught her looking.

The guards retreated into the recesses of the room. Nena flexed her fingers, her wrists. The ropes weren't too tight. But they weren't loose enough for her hands to slip out without a lot of pain either. Okay.

She resumed her study of the man, took in his dark shirt that looked more like a second skin on his bulky torso, tucked into black utility pants. A belt with attached holster, gun tucked in. Another holster stretched across his broad back, weapon nestled against his side. He looked no different in attire from the men holding her, but there was still an air of authority, a cocky essence about him as he kept his back to her, as if he were making her wait until he was good and ready to announce himself.

That was fine. She could play the waiting game. Just gave her more time to take in the room, remember their mannerisms. Like how the men were talking about what they'd have for dinner when this was done. They spoke English, two distinctly different African accents. She couldn't place the countries. Not Gabonese. Or Ghanaian. Not Nigerian either. They could be holding her anywhere.

She took another look at the six monitors, each of them flashing various areas of the grounds. A safe house of some kind. A compound. But again, where?

"Is she on her way?" the man asked without turning around. Nena's ears perked up; his voice sounded very familiar, too familiar. Her heart skipped a beat before she was able to calm herself. Ghosts, she thought, were haunting her.

"Soon come, sir."

More to the party with Nena as the guest of honor.

On screen were shots of the outside perimeter, the hall they'd just come from. And her dungeon, she surmised. It was empty, dark, and loathsome even from where she sat. At least, she assumed it was the room where she'd been kept. Why else would an empty room be on the monitor? And no other images of prisoners?

Because she was the only one in this place. And this place could be anywhere. The thoughts were chilling, too reminiscent of a time before when she'd been someone's captive. She shuttered herself, wiping her face of emotion, pushing any confusion and apprehension away. She locked them up tightly behind a door in her mind. More secure than the vaults at the London Exchange.

However, when the man spoke next, her blood froze completely. The shutters she'd sealed blew apart.

"Ropes not too tight, I hope?" he said in his easy drawl. Same voice from the hotel ambush. Same voice that had spoken to Witt. But now . . . the voice was clear of the helmet that had obscured it.

Nena straightened as if a rod had been rammed up her spine. Her nerves screamed red alert. Like hairs standing on end right before a lightning strike. It wasn't possible. And yet . . .

As if in slow motion, he faced her, wearing that slick smile of his, the one he showed when he knew he'd received the best time on a practice run or had taken out the most targets. He was the Cheshire cat, leering at Nena as if lording some huge victory over her.

Her subordinate, now her captor. Her supposed-to-be-dead subordinate.

36

"'Sup, Boss Lady." Alpha grinned at her. "Did you miss me?"

Nena's decision right then was that she preferred him dead. She gave him no response, though plenty were running through her mind. And they weren't pretty. They were a cacophony of strategizing and confusion and worry and fear and disorientation clashing against one another like waves against ragged moonlit rocks. The intensity with which her brain tried to compute Alpha's reemergence and her situation was deafening.

Behind Nena, sounds from the hall increased as the door opened and someone either left or entered. She heard the men behind her talking among themselves, and then a woman spoke. Nena couldn't place the voice, but she'd heard this person before.

"Is our guest well?"

Alpha's eyes left Nena's face, looking dismayed at the interruption. Thank God. She didn't think she could tolerate any more of his aggrandizement. His upper lip turned down into a pout like some petulant child.

Nena's curved up in a near smile. Behind her, two sets of footsteps approached.

Nena didn't bother turning to see who had spoken. She knew already it was the woman from the phone call, though her voice had been distorted. But the phone call wasn't where Nena recognized her from.

"Having someone taken from you. Ever experienced something like that?"

A time or two. *"It never leaves you."*

"It does not."

Same conversational tone—welcoming, even, which was weird considering the circumstances. Her companions didn't speak, but one of them walked slower than the other. Nena tried to focus on their steps, to gauge the distance from the door to where she now sat. Not too far, she gathered, though after the amount of time she'd spent in the cell, her perception of time was skewed.

Nena kept her eyes trained on the floor, not ready to make eye contact with anyone until she was sure hers would give them nothing back. She watched the woman come into view, the legs of the formfitting black pants she wore tucked into the low boots, steel toed and similar to ones Nena often wore on missions.

The second woman came from Nena's other side.

"Hey, Nena," she said, voice soft and almost apologetic.

Nena's head snapped up as she forgot the first woman entirely. She couldn't shutter her emotions. Couldn't help the shock at who had called her name.

Coming to stand beside Alpha was Sierra. Sierra, who Nena was positive she'd left back in Miami. Hadn't seen since the airport, when Sierra had dressed her down. Sierra standing next to Alpha, who Nena had seen take bullets and then die in an explosion. Doubts about everything she thought she knew assailed her. Doubts that made her question everything she thought she knew about her abilities—hell, about her judgment of character.

Her eyes volleyed from Alpha to Sierra and back to Alpha again.

"What is this?" Nena exhaled. She forgot about the woman watching her. Or the guards at her back. Forgot she was tied down to a chair and about to be killed. All she knew was the shock at seeing two people she'd worked alongside and trusted for years. One she'd grieved and blamed herself for his death. The other she'd regretted not doing enough for, blamed herself for running to Ghana instead of providing the support she knew Sierra had needed as she'd mourned the loss of the team.

Sierra was here. Nena finally looked at who'd accompanied her, though that surprise was dulled. Mariam, who had offered bottled water and conversation about lost family at the Miami dinner party. Both of them standing there with a reincarnated Alpha. And none of them bound to a chair as Nena was.

Nena's stare could drill holes in Sierra, but Sierra wouldn't return her gaze. "Sierra, what is this?"

Alpha answered instead. "The new Tribe. The Tribe as it should be."

She blanched, then snorted. "What are you saying? What *new Tribe*? Tribe as it *should* be? The Tribe is already as it should be."

Questions were screeching in her mind. How could Alpha have possibly pulled off his death, hidden all this time, and then taken her at the hotel? How could he have pulled double duty?

The answer was this: He couldn't have. He just wasn't that smart.

As she tried to reconcile what was happening and where this all was going, she kept seeing him grinning at her, looking like he could dance a jig. Traitorous bastard. Confusion and amazement were replaced by unadulterated anger that he'd had the nerve, the audacity, to put one over on her. And that he was standing in front of her, with his swollen chest, proud of his accomplishments, which couldn't have been his. Because . . . well . . . he just wasn't that smart!

Had the entire team turned on her and the Tribe? The team she'd genuinely grieved for, shed wasted tears for. Were they all traitors?

She tried to twist around in her seat. "So where are the rest of them? Are they here too? Have you *all* lost your minds?"

Sierra flopped against the tabletop, looking somberly at Nena. "No. Kilo, Yankee, Charlie, they're really dead. That happened."

Unable to help herself, to rein herself in, all the control Nena had spent years honing as her shield slipped through her fingers, dribbled on the floor into a complete mess. She said to Alpha, "And why aren't you dead? You should be."

"You'd like that, wouldn't you?" His eyes flashed. "I was too much competition for you anyway."

"Competition?" she spat. "Not in your wildest dreams were you ever close to my level—"

Nena's head snapped left as air exploded from her body. She tried to absorb the blow, screwing her eyes shut so tears of pain wouldn't spill and Alpha would think he'd done no damage. He had—her cheekbone could attest to that—but no real damage.

He'd always had a short fuse.

She spat a glob of blood onto the ground. Her teeth had cut the inside of her mouth. She breathed out, channeling the pulsating throb on the side of her face. Then she righted herself and looked up at him.

She said, "Is that it?"

He snarled, readying to hit her again, but Mariam—though she doubted now that it was the woman's real name—stopped him with a sharp rebuke.

"Alpha, cool it."

Nena's eyes traveled the length of her. She'd traded in her caterer's uniform. Her beverage tray had been replaced with a weapons holster, where the handles of two guns stared at Nena, saying hello.

Nena finally rested her gaze on the woman's face, on the deep-chestnut-brown complexion, full lips, upturned nose, and straight white teeth in a mouth currently smiling at Nena.

"Hello again," Mariam said.

Nena shook her head in disbelief, looking away.

Here, under the industrial lighting, Mariam's face held a semblance of familiarity that Nena couldn't quite place. She kept her head bowed, trying to knock the recollection from the recesses of her brain. When she finally spoke, it wasn't to Mariam.

"Why?" Nena asked Sierra.

The younger woman opened her mouth to speak, but again, Alpha's voice came out instead. "Because we run shit here. We're appreciated here."

"You felt underappreciated?" Nena would only look at Sierra, speak only to her.

Alpha didn't get the hint.

"The only people who are appreciated in your daddy's Tribe are the Knights. It's why they let you get away with all the shit you did. Killing that Council member. Yeah, we all know 'bout that," he said when Nena's eyes flickered to him, "even though you all tried covering it up. The Tribe decides who lives and dies, but we put in the work, the wet work, and don't get nearly the money those Council members get, that your daddy gets." Alpha spat. "That's bullshit."

"You don't get paid well? Hundreds of thousands of dollars? Nearly a million? If you can't manage your finances, then that sounds like a personal problem." Nena's refusal to look at Alpha must have irritated him. He crossed into her line of vision, blocking her view of Sierra, who still had yet to speak.

He bent to her eye level. "It's eating you up inside, isn't it? Me here and you bound up like a lassoed piggy?"

He bared his teeth, so close Nena could see the patches of individual coarse hairs scattered over his cheeks and chin.

"You think you're too good for us. Something special because Knight was tacked onto your name. They let you think you run the team, but it was me propping us all up every time."

Nena let out a deep sigh. She couldn't avoid having to finally deal with this child in the throes of a temper tantrum. She rolled her eyes until they met his. She leaned forward, just a little. "Are you done?"

"Fucking smart-ass bi—"

Nena closed her eyes, bracing herself for the strike she knew was coming. There was nothing. She opened her eyes to see Mariam holding a gun to Alpha's temple. His hands rose in the air in deference. His mouth forming a little O to match the *uh-oh* Nena read in his eyes.

"I think you are done, yes?" Mariam said, slowly pulling the Glock away. "Could you see about our other guest? Please. See him in?" She sounded sweet, as if she hadn't just held a gun to one of her own. But then again, maybe she knew that people who defected could never entirely be trusted.

Alpha left, but not before Nena read the resentment in his face. This woman was no more a leader in his eyes than she had been. And soon, he'd turn on her, try to take her position too. As soon as the opportunity presented itself.

"And while the boys are away . . ." Mariam grinned.

She pulled the chair in front of Nena, remaining at a distance. She might have been acting like she was a grand madam of the manor, but she wasn't obtuse. She knew who Nena was and what Nena was capable of.

"Any word yet?" Mariam asked.

"No," Sierra said.

She turned back to Nena, motioning at the door Alpha had gone through. "He tends to have a lot to say." She shrugged. "But he gets the job done."

And yet he's here, Nena wanted to say. She was full of questions she wouldn't ask.

Mariam pointed a polished fingernail in the air. "You're trying to figure out why I'd work with him, a misogynist and traitor? I mean, if he betrayed you, then what allegiance would he have to me? Never trust a cheater, right?"

Nena's eyes flickered once again to Sierra, now busy on the phone.

Mariam followed Nena's gaze. Her lips pursing. "What about her, you're thinking?" She shrugged. "Women always have deeper reasons for rescinding their loyalties."

Nena was still deciding if she should speak or if it was best to remain silent.

"You have that look," Mariam said, "like you're trying to place me. You want to know who I am"—she smirked, leaning so her elbow was on her knee and her chin in her hand—"and how I had the nerve to take you."

She wasn't wrong. Launching a direct attack on members of the Knight family, abducting Nena, took a lot of nerve. Grinning in Nena's face while talking about it was a death wish.

"My name is Mariam." She waited for Nena to connect the dots, but when she didn't, annoyance rippled over the woman's face, hardening the disarming smile that had been there only seconds ago.

Nena stared at her dispassionately; the hostess act was getting old, and Nena had no time for it. She was finding it more difficult to remain impassive. Would be nice if the woman would cut the games.

"Still no word?" Mariam asked.

"There's been no response from your contact," came Sierra's answer.

Mariam's teeth grazed her bottom lip. In her eyes, Nena saw doubt. Nena saw worry and concern. Nena saw insecurity. Then Nena saw those emotions get swallowed up like a bitter pill and washed away, returning her to her earlier disposition.

Mariam refocused. "I bet you're wondering why I approached you at that dinner."

Sierra didn't hide her confusion. So the party hadn't been part of the original plan. "You said you wouldn't make contact until Gabon."

"Plans change."

Nena barely listened. She only stared past Mariam at Sierra, who had joked that the two of them were "final girls" after the rest of the team had been killed. Nena's stomach twisted. She thought she might get sick from the realization that Alpha had been a part of the ambush, had gotten his teammates killed in cold blood. Sierra was not that great an actor, was she? So when had they pulled her in? Had she been at the satellite office, killing Network operatives?

The cell was looking better and better to Nena by the minute. She didn't want to breathe the same air as them.

Sierra wouldn't look at Nena. She looked everywhere but at Nena. Shame, anger, and confusion written all over her face.

Mariam leaned forward, placing her elbows on her knees. Her hands clasped together between them. "I wanted to meet you, Nena. Officially. And I admit I was a little anxious and maybe upped the pace of the plan."

Nena said nothing. *Interrogation.* Say nothing. Wait for anything she could use to her advantage.

"My benefactors had other ideas of how we'd bring you in. But I'm a little too impatient. It was something my brother always said would mess me up."

Brother. Though no one could tell, Nena's mind was racing to find a connection. *Use anything. Anything to your advantage.*

Mariam said, "I was at the Compound with you as part of your security detail. Do you recall?"

The female bodyguard. Of course. If only Nena had looked closer.

Mariam patted Nena's knee. "Don't beat yourself up for not recognizing me. Wig, sunglasses, a little distance . . . works wonders."

Nena sat back in her chair. "You were moved when I spoke. You were emotional."

"Even 'bad guys' have feelings." She air quoted as if sharing a private joke between them. "Because that's what you think I am, one of the bad guys. Except I'm not the bad guy of this story."

Tell that to the innocent people Mariam had killed at Network's satellite office or outside the hotel.

"Who are your benefactors? The Gabonese? Is it them you work for? Who on the Council has been funneling money to you and away from Africans who needed it?"

"What is she talking about?" Sierra asked, stepping forward.

"Where do you think the money funding all of this is coming from? From the Tribe." Nena looked at Sierra. "Should have done your research."

Mariam was smirking, but her eyebrow twitched. A tell. She hadn't wanted her team to know that part.

"Seems like your partner here doesn't keep you in the loop," Nena said. "You didn't know about her stalking me in Miami. Didn't know who's financing this whole operation. And I'm guessing the hotel was not on the agenda either."

Mariam was a statue; the only indication of life was the barely perceptible nerve twitch of her right eye. Sierra moved to her shoulder.

"You said we got the go-ahead to take her at the hotel instead of at the dedication per the original plan," Sierra reminded her new boss.

Mariam's stare could drill holes in Nena. Bullet holes. "You talk too much," she said, glowering.

Well, that was a first.

"Why am I here?" Nena countered.

"So I can better understand why my brother had to die because of you."

Revenge. Nena cocked her head to the side to keep herself from rolling her eyes. "If you know anything about me, then you know this business. At least I don't murder innocent people. The people you killed at the satellite office? The bystanders at the hotel?"

"Maybe you don't actually pull the trigger, but you still get innocent people killed."

The accusation made Nena's body rigid. She looked at Mariam, really looked at her familiar face, slowly connecting the dots. Pulling fragments from the recesses of her mind, from years ago. From a time when she'd made her first friend in her new world.

"Now." Mariam nodded affirmatively. "*Now*, you know me."

37

When Nena was sixteen, Goon was the one who'd looked out for her during the intense Dispatch training. He'd been like a big brother to her. Called her YA for *young adult*—which was what the men outside the satellite office had called Nena. Mariam must have told them to call her that. Nena remembered the times Goon had said she reminded him of his little sister, who was a couple of years older and about to enter uni. He'd saved enough money for her to go. He'd been taking care of her and their mother since he was young and had become the man of the house. But that little sister had never had a name. And when Goon had been retired, Nena had never given her a second thought.

Until now. How could Goon have thought they were similar? They were nothing alike.

All pretenses and impassiveness blown apart, Nena stared at Mariam. Same brown eyes. Similar mouth. Goon was in there, in the face staring back at her. She glanced at Sierra, who watched with as much interest as if she were watching paint dry.

"At the dinner, you spoke about your brother. You were talking about Goon."

Mariam sat back in her chair with an air of satisfaction. She crossed one leg over another, drumming her fingernails against her knees. "It never disappoints, you know. That look one gets in their eyes when they are hit with the big realization." Her arm lifted, and she balled her fingers, then burst them out like an explosion.

"I didn't kill Goon." She hadn't. She'd been eaten up with guilt when she'd realized he'd been retired and that retirement meant death because of one slipup. Because he'd been hungry and left his post.

"I am aware." Mariam furrowed her eyebrows. "I thought we covered that part?" She turned to Sierra. "Right?"

Sierra shrugged. She didn't care. "I guess."

"See?" Mariam smiled. "Covered."

Nena said nothing.

"However," Mariam continued, holding up a hand. "Your father did."

Noble Knight had ordered Goon's retirement, his death, for leaving his post, which had messed up the mission and nearly gotten Nena killed. Her father had been angry. The first she'd seen him so. And Witt had carried out the retirement at his command. Nena thought back to the hotel and when she'd seen Witt on his knees, a gun muzzle at his forehead. If this was Mariam's revenge, then Witt was as dead as Nena was soon to be.

Nena took a brief moment to collect herself and release the hope she'd been holding on to. Hope that drained out of her like air from a tire that had run over a nail. There was none after Mariam had ambushed Nena's team, murdered Network members, and mowed down any bystander in Gabon to get at Nena and, in turn, get to Nena's father.

"You think killing me is an eye for an eye for Goon?"

"For Marcel, you mean?" Mariam's forehead wrinkled. "Did he choose that nickname? Goon? It's horrid, but I guess my brother always fancied himself a gangster. However, our mother and I knew him as Marcel." She grew serious. "And no. It's not enough to take a daughter, because even his daughters aren't what your father loves the most."

She had no idea where the woman was going with this. Had Mariam been on Nena's team, she'd have been trained to say less.

"The Tribe," Mariam said. "Alpha was actually right about one thing. He said your Dispatch team did all the wet work while the leaders of the Tribe reaped all the benefits. What's the fairness in that?"

"You know nothing of the Tribe," Nena said hotly, glaring at Sierra, who should have known better. "Sierra should have told you. We were paid exorbitantly for our duties. Have you seen where she lives?"

Mariam laughed. "I have. Nice, isn't it? But where does your father live? And for doing what? And when he sends you and your team out on missions—he and the other twelve Council members who sit at the table where no one else can come—what have they done to be able to live in luxurious homes with private jets like the ones you charter? Deciding what countries are blessed with the Tribe's help and which are not? My country, by the way, Mali, is not."

That wasn't true, and the Tribe was working their way through establishing those diplomacies. It wasn't as easy as Mariam was making it out to be. "You have a convoluted way of thinking. You diminish all the good the Tribe does."

"I don't give a fuck about their goodwill or what they do for Africa."

Nena was speechless.

"I don't even give a fuck if they never help Mali at all." She leaped out of her chair, a ball of unspent energy, and began pacing the room. She stopped, facing Nena. "I only care about what was done to my brother. What was taken from me. And how to get it back."

"Goon is dead and gone. There's no getting him back."

"Of course not. But I can take what killed him and make it my own."

"You keep speaking in riddles."

"Pay for play." Sierra spoke up suddenly. "That's what she's getting at. That's what Alpha was talking about and why I'm here. Tired of feeling underappreciated."

Nena was confused. "What is that? I mean, I know what pay for play means, but that's not the Tribe's way. If we must kill, it is for a purpose. For the betterment of the African people."

"And what do the African people give you in return?" Mariam said. "Do they thank you for the kills you make in their name? I think not. They don't know who the hell you are."

Sierra nodded. "Right, they only know the rich-ass Council. They only know your dad."

Mariam looked at Sierra as if saying, *Bless your heart.* "Why should the people who do the most, Network operators, Dispatch teams, the Housekeepers—"

"Cleaners," Sierra corrected.

Mariam tapped the side of her head. "Yes! I always get them confused. These factions within the Tribe doing all the work and only getting a pittance compared to what the Council gets. They make all the decisions and do the least. You're told where to go, who to kill, and you do it and get paid and rinse and repeat. Foot soldiers. Like the military. You have no say. You don't get to determine if you want to take the job or not. You just do. You don't get to set an auction and go with the highest bidder. You don't get to set your rates. You don't get to go kill for someone else, should you choose. And if you say no or you fail? Death. *Retirement.* What kind of life is that? One of no choice. Betterment of Africans, you say?"

Sierra was more animated now than she'd been since she'd entered the room. "That's the spiel that got me, to be honest. Like, I want to work for myself."

"As mercenaries with no allegiance. No tribe to be a part of," Nena clarified. "That's what you're talking about here, yes? Hired thugs who go to the highest bidder. No honor. No ideals. Selling yourselves."

"On our terms, though."

"Your brother would have never been a part of this."

Mariam's eyes flashed murder. "The fuck would you know? You know nothing of who my brother truly was."

Nena couldn't respond. It was true.

She attempted to reason with Sierra. "There's no honor in this, Sierra. We are teammates."

"There's no honor among thieves," Sierra replied.

"I'm not a thief."

Mariam snorted. "There's no honor among the rich thieves that own you."

"Be careful," Nena warned. It didn't matter that she was tied down. Mariam was going places she had better not.

Goon's sister put her hands up in surrender. "There are Council members who think like me, Nena. So you should know that this is happening. A takeover. The Tribe will be a tribe of mercenaries. We'll sell our wares to the highest bidder and offer protection to those who can afford it. My benefactors, whatever they choose to do with the business ventures and the philanthropy, blah, blah, blah, I couldn't care less." Her eyes gleamed with dreams of grandeur. "I just want to dismantle the house that Noble built, in my brother's honor. And when I kill your father, it'll be with Marcel's name written all over it. Once he is dethroned . . ."

She paused to study Nena's face for reaction. Finding none, she continued. "The proverbial shit will hit the fan. My benefactors can take over and set things to rights."

It all made sense how everything happening with the Tribe had led to this. Embezzling to fund Mariam and her band of mercenaries to launch an attack from within. Turning supposedly loyal Dispatch members—how many of them were there? The betrayal must go all the way up, nearly to the very top. A traitor—traitors—sitting at the side of her father, within killing distance. For how long?

"What about the people? Don't you care about their welfare? That's what the Tribe works toward. To ensure everyone eats. Everyone. That takes time, Mariam."

"I know who will best butter my bread. I don't care to make everyone eat. I only care if I eat. And I learned that from your dear old daddy when he killed my brother and neglected to see about my brother's family. I had to find a way for me and my mother to eat. And if it's aligning myself with the people who ruined my family, then so be it."

"Whoever approached you will only turn on you in the end."

Mariam grinned. "They've trained you to expect that, your precious Tribe. But what if I prove you wrong? It doesn't have to be this way. Join us. You don't have to die."

The door opened again, and Mariam broke out into a smile. "There he is! Welcome, General Konate. Man of the hour."

38

Nena wasn't surprised. She'd expected anyone to come parading into the room. She half expected Paul to rise from the dead as Alpha had. The general here? Of course he was.

"Is that her?" the general asked. "The one the Tribe sent to assassinate me?"

He entered her line of vision, clad in green fatigues and dusty combat boots. His belly strained against the buttons of his shirt and over the poor belt losing its battle to hold up his pants. He wore a black beret and worked a toothpick around in his mouth. His beady eyes peered down at Nena, and all she did was look back at him with not a care about him.

He waggled a finger at her. "I have plans for this wretch. I will use her as an example to the Tribe, to the people, so they know my power." He reached a grubby hand out to touch Nena's face. She jerked back. An image of one of the guards at the Compound flashing in her eyes. The door opened, Alpha rejoining them.

"Thank you for delivering her to me," he continued, working the toothpick around his voluminous mouth. He reminded Nena of two-thirds a snowman. Round head atop a rounder middle. No neck.

Nena's eyes flickered to Mariam. She wouldn't show that a trickle of fear was working its way through. She didn't like the sound of the general. Didn't like the way he leered at her, like he had more in mind for her than the example he claimed he was going to make. Nena was all too familiar with *that* look. It was the *only* look that was the stuff of her nightmares.

Mariam was studying Nena intently through all of this. Alpha paced the floor behind them, antsy for them to move on, while Sierra watched, her eyes jumping from face to face.

Mariam, her voice full of curiosity, asked, "General, what makes you think she's for you?"

"What do you mean? She is the one who led the assault against me. By rights she is mine to do away with."

Alpha snorted. "By rights. What the fuck are we in, the Middle Ages?"

"Control your man, eh?" the general told Mariam. "The two of them were also with her. If not for you, I would call for their heads as well. Infidels. Now come. Call for my chopper and let me take her to my destination. This dungeon of a place offends me."

Sierra said, "Mariam?"

Mariam smiled patiently. "General, I don't think our agreement was for you to take Nena anywhere."

Nena didn't know which side to root for. She had a better chance of survival with the general. There was little chance he could overtake her in combat. But he was vile and disgusting, and she'd rather take on Mariam and the traitors over him any day.

"Are you mad, girl? I decide the agreements here." He bent so he was eye level with Nena, sneering at her through yellowed eyes. "She tried to kill me. Shot up my safe house. I own her."

The gunshot was deafening in the enclosed room, but there was no comparison to watching General Konate's face explode in front of her. Nena, who'd seen horrors one would find difficult to imagine, had not expected this. She reacted as the spray of blood and brain matter doused her face and front. Her eyes closed and her lips squeezed tightly, shocked but intuitive enough to not want the general's blood in her mouth.

"What the hell?" Sierra squeaked.

Mariam waited as Nena blinked blood away from her eyes, attempting to see through hazy, blurred red vision. The muzzle of Mariam's gun still pointed to where the back of the general's head had once been.

"Ferdinand, grab a towel for our guest, and then remove him, please?"

The summoned guard shoved a rough piece of cloth at Nena, nudging her with it.

"Her hands are tied," Mariam said in a deliberate tone. "Clean her face for her. And be nice."

Sierra shifted from one foot to the other, a hand at her mouth. "What did you save him for at his outpost only to kill him here?" She stepped over the general's body as a second guard grabbed his feet and began to tug at them.

"He was merely a means to an end. A way to throw off the Tribe. And then he became a gift for Nena here." Mariam winked at Nena. "You're welcome."

The general wasn't a small man. The guard was half his size and struggling, tugging at his feet and making no progress. Ferdinand wasn't happy either. He dragged the roughly spun fabric, which felt more like a scouring pad, over Nena's face, pushing her head this way and that.

"Be gentle, Ferdinand." Mariam's tone drove home her message. If someone as important as the general was so easily dispatchable, Ferdinand wouldn't warrant a second thought.

Ferdinand's touch became as gentle as a lamb, and he finished cleaning Nena as best he could.

Mariam turned to Alpha. "Check on the helicopter?"

Alpha left. When Ferdinand was done with Nena, he joined his struggling partner, each taking one of the general's feet. Nena tried to ignore the large smear of blood and gore marking their trail.

Instead, she concentrated on preparation. Preparing herself for what would inevitably come when Mariam delivered her final ultimatum and Nena would have to give her decision. Nena needed to prepare herself for how this would inevitably end.

Badly.

39

Mariam gestured to Nena. "You've been through some shit." She pointed to her chest. "I've been through some shit. We can get into some shit together." She smiled, looking so much like Goon. "We're not so different, you and I. We loved our brothers."

Nena met her eyes. "I killed mine."

Mariam's mouth dropped open. When she'd recovered, she gave a short laugh. "My brother took a liking to you, Nena. I can see why. Help me take the Tribe down. Join me and help me avenge my brother and your family against the people who looked the other way and let the man who slaughtered your village live for all those years."

Well, when she put it that way, the offer was nearly tempting. The irony of it.

She'd been in this same exact place months ago. Once upon a time, Nena had been Mariam. It was only half a year ago when she'd had no other thought than to kill the men who'd murdered her family and done irreversible damage to her. How could she fault Goon's sister, as maniacal as she sounded, for wanting revenge against the people who'd ordered her brother's death?

And yet . . .

Her and Mariam's stories were not the same. Not their methods. Not the outcomes they desired. Nena had only wanted three men. Mariam wanted to burn everything down.

"I'll only ask once," Mariam said, softly.

Nena's eyes rose to meet Mariam's. Then she lifted her chin. Her response firm and resolute.

Mariam's face twitched as if she was disappointed at Nena's rejection. She'd thought she could turn Nena. She'd thought herself so convincing, as she'd convinced Alpha and Sierra and whomever else to follow her.

Her heel tapped rapidly at the ground. Her tic. She was at a crossroads and wasn't quite sure how next to proceed. She'd jumped the gun by taking Nena—she'd admitted as much earlier. Now Mariam had to deal with her. And there was only one way to do that.

The door to the room opened, and Alpha filled the doorway. The other two guards flanked him.

"Copter's ready," he said.

Mariam confirmed. Then said, "Do what you need to do here. Then clear out."

Sierra said, "And me?"

"You two will join me in Accra. I'll need to handle Noble myself to ensure he is eliminated."

"But that wasn't—"

Mariam silenced Sierra with another murderous glare as Alpha began to undo Nena's bindings.

"If he can't be bothered to call, then the show goes on without him."

Nena thought of the contact Sierra had been trying to reach earlier.

"We shouldn't have taken her," Alpha grumbled, looping Nena's ropes through a metal ring protruding from the ceiling. "I told you it was a bad idea."

"I make the decisions now," Mariam said. "Take it or leave it. But if you leave it, you go the way of the general."

No one had to look at the thick line of blood marking the floor to know what she meant.

She and Nena regarded each other again, two sides of the same coin. "I think in another world, we would have been friends," Mariam mused. As if she didn't like what was coming next but was resigned that it had to be done.

Nena's eyes shifted to the console of monitors as she listened to Mariam and the guards walk out of the room. The door wasn't yet shut the entire way, and Nena could hear the three sets of footsteps receding, but not for long. Marching up steps, unlatching a door. The doors Nena had spotted when they were bringing her here. The way out.

Now it was just the three of them. Nena gazed at her ex-teammates, people she would have died for. And now, people she'd have to kill.

She told Sierra just that while Alpha tightened the rope in the ceiling ring until the toes of her boots barely touched the ground.

In response, Alpha embedded a stone fist into her belly. She doubled over in pain, couldn't breathe. Threw up bile.

He walked over to the table and came back holding something. "Been waiting a long-ass time for this."

The sudden electrical spasm from the cattle prod made Nena temporarily lose her wits. The current brought only searing pain, and a scream erupted from her lips. Her eyes watered, blurring the image of the grinning and pissed-off face before her until she could see it no longer.

Then darkness swallowed her whole.

40

Alone. In the dark. Nena opened her eyes. Was she dreaming? Probably not. Hallucinating? Probably. She'd been slipping in and out of consciousness, seeing Robach's grinning face as he force-fed her lo mein; Atta Walrus's machete as it dragged across the ground toward her to lop her head off. Saw her severed head with strings of noodles trailing from it.

She begged the ghosts to go away.

Not real. Not real, she kept telling herself.

But what was real? The shock of pain as it worsened? The line between wakefulness and sleep, between reality and dreams? She kept her eyes closed. Fought through the urge to scream in pain. To lash out at Alpha, who was pummeling her, switching between the cattle prod and his fists. Sierra in the background telling him to get on with it, sounding bored.

Bored.

Nena's saving grace? Alpha's cell phone ringing just as he was about to zap her again. Her arms shook from the strain of her body weight pulling on the rope from which she was suspended.

"Mariam?" Alpha said. "Yeah, we're wrapping up now."

Nena heard Sierra sucking her teeth. Alpha wasn't wrapping anything up. He was playing with his food. Nena opened an eye, then the other when she saw their backs were to her. Sweat slicked her face, ran down her whole body. She was cold. She was hot. The wetness made the ropes cut into her already-raw wrists.

Her fingers worked the knots, and she used the blood seeping from her wrists to ease them, but it was taking too long to undo them. Alpha must have been something like a Boy Scout or sailor with these knots.

Her next idea was to pull up. The building was old. There was no telling how long the round hook had been embedded in the ceiling, and if she could get herself up there, she could brace herself and try to pull it out.

She had to move quick, before their call ended. She wrapped her fingers around the hanging rope and pulled. It wasn't like climbing a rope; she had nothing to grip with her shoes. She imagined a pull-up bar. That was what she was doing, and she lifted herself, pulling her knees up to her chest.

She pulled again, inching up the rope while Alpha and Sierra argued over the call, the directives Mariam had given them, then the cattle prod that Sierra had snatched from Alpha's possession, brandishing it.

Nena's fingers touched the metal ring. It was rusted, which was good. Rust meant old, and old meant she could pull it free. Working as quickly as she could, Nena grasped the ring, pulling her legs up and planting her feet against the flat of the ceiling like some acrobat she was not. Her body screamed for her to stop, straining from the effort. The blood was rushing to her head. Now the rope had plenty of slack. She wrapped it around her wrist and arm, hooked her hands through the metal hoop, bracing her feet, readying to pull the ring before her strength gave out.

This was nothing compared to what Alpha would do if she didn't get free and get out.

She pulled, tugged with what strength she had. At first the ring didn't give. But she fought it, twisted it, and then it relinquished its hold and gave up the ghost, coming free along with pieces of the ceiling. And then Nena was falling. Alpha and Sierra froze in twin silence when they turned to see her crashing to the floor. The impact knocked the wind out of her. But she was amped up on adrenaline and the even-stronger will to not die by their hands.

Get up. Nena did.

Her leg lashed out, catching Sierra and upending her. The cattle prod clattered to the floor from Sierra's hand, skittering out of reach. With Sierra at her level, Nena kicked out, connecting with her face. Sierra let out an *oomph*, stunned. For now. But Alpha was on Nena.

He grabbed her by the leg and upper torso, hefting her like he was deadlifting her. He took off and launched her like a shot put. She soared through the air before crashing into the boxes and cabinets. They toppled over her.

He grabbed her feet and pulled her toward him from under the rubble. Her vision was a haze of red from the blood coursing from her split scalp. She clawed at him. He punched her side, in her already-sensitive ribs, and she could practically hear the crunch of breaking bone.

She rolled onto her side, using all her force to kick his knee and bring him down. When he buckled, coming down to the floor, he grabbed her, and she reached up, clapping him on both sides of his head around his ears, as if he were a pair of cymbals.

Sierra was stirring and would soon regain sense enough to attack. Nena couldn't take them on at the same time. And Alpha was still so strong. She wouldn't get him with brute force. She had to go for the soft spots. His throat. His chin. Didn't work.

She felt his weight lift off, and it looked like he was going to body-slam her. She moved, scrambling to get some space between them, to get to the cattle prod, which had spun out of their grasp. Her fingers gripped it, pulling it to her while he punched her back from behind. The pain nearly ended her. She inched her finger to the switch, and as he raised his arm again to land a final blow, Nena twisted around and jammed the electrode to his chest.

Alpha growled, his teeth biting down on his tongue as bolts of electricity coursed through him, long and unrelenting. He was a petrified tree, hovering in midair above her, his spit flying onto her face, his hand clawed and suspended as if by an invisible rope.

She let go and pushed him. He fell onto his side and writhed on the floor. Sierra was up now, fumbling with her utility belt, her nose gushing blood. She was woozy but steadily coming to and reaching for a long, serrated knife. Nena had to act quickly. She tugged free Alpha's sidearm and aimed.

Sierra's eyes widened, her hand drawing back from her knife, trying to ward the gun away. "Wait. Lemme explain, okay, Nena?"

"It's Echo."

With Alpha beside her, Nena pumped two shots into Sierra, watching her fall.

She switched her attention back on Alpha, pumped one into his chest as he reached out for her and another into his forehead, putting him down. This time for good.

41

Nena only gave herself a second's rest before crawling to the console. She wasn't sure how many of Mariam's people were left. Wasn't sure who'd heard the shots from outside the room. She was on borrowed time, and she needed to get out of this place now.

She wiped at the blood dripping down her face. She could barricade herself in here, or she could get out. If she was going to engage anyone else, it would be out in the open, not where they could pin her in. She went to the door, gun pointed and ready, and listened. She heard nothing and cracked open the door. A bullet slammed into it, and she stuck her hand out, firing to give herself cover. She hit something because she heard a yell.

It took only a moment's thought before she went for it, launching herself into the hallway. She shot out the lamp above her, darkening her location. She fired at Ferdinand as he came through the double doors that she knew were her out. She aimed, fired, brought him down.

She checked her gun for the number of rounds she had left. Not many. No time to go back and get another mag. She had to move. She crossed over Ferdinand, who was gurgling blood. She couldn't find his gun, but she pulled out a knife. She looked down at him, stuck the gun in her waistband, and used the knife to finish him. Then she went through those doors.

The courtyard was bathed in dim yellowed lighting that barely warded off the night. It was overrun with weeds and brush. The low-lying structure from which she'd emerged was crumbling. The helicopter Mariam had mentioned could be heard off in the distance, and she wasn't sure if it was coming closer or not. She wasn't sure about Mariam, but her people had to have heard the shots. Nena didn't know their numbers, but they'd be coming for her, and there would be too many for her knife and a gun without a full load. She had to go.

She kept low, taking refuge against the pockmarked walls, using the building for cover as she rounded corners. She was thankful for the shoddy lighting. Whatever money Mariam was being paid, it wasn't enough. Time to move.

Her brain Rolodexed through her training, stopping at Escape and Evasion, then filing through all she'd learned. She would not engage. There were too many of them, too few of her. There was a narrow clearing between the dilapidated building—which, now that her eyes had adjusted to the lighting, seemed to be a partially underground bunker surrounded by other low-lying structures—and the tree line ahead of her. But it was still a dicey crossing to make with a helicopter above—closer now, she'd determined—and the throng of mercenaries now coming out from those smaller structures. She didn't have to guess why: Word was spreading that she'd escaped and killed some of their own. They'd want blood because of it. But they owed her because Sierra and Alpha had been hers first.

And now? She was on her own. The only one on her team left.

To the tree line. She couldn't get distracted. Couldn't stop to think about everything that'd happened. She wasn't even sure what day it was, how long she'd been gone, if Witt and Elin were . . . *No. Stop it.* Now was not the time. Evasion rules stated to stay focused. Stay alive. Find cover.

To the tree line, Nena. Run.

She heard them shouting orders to spread out and find her. The high grass concealed her, as did the dark clothes she wore. *Small favors,* she thought as she left her hiding place. If she got shot, she didn't care. But she was going to run and keep running until she made it to the tree line. There, she'd be enshrouded in the darkness jungle could afford her. And then maybe she could think about what else she was supposed to do.

She couldn't risk using the gun now, not if she wanted to keep her location unknown. So she used the knife when she came across one of the men alone, emerging from the latrines bewildered at the chaos around the camp. She sank the blade in his neck and left him spurting like a sprinkler when she pulled it back out.

If she escaped this alive, Elin could never again talk about her choice of clothing color. Her clothes made her a chameleon, blending her into the shadows until she'd crossed the clearing and reached the trees—and whatever was out there waiting for her.

Behind her, torches—flashlights—bobbed in the darkness, like oversize lightning bugs. Again, she heard the mercenaries shouting commands. She heard engines gunning and revving and sounding closer and closer no matter how fast she ran. They were on her trail. They were coming for her. And she told herself:

Run.

42

The dark forms of men with rifles were visible against the night sky. Helicopter searchlights raked the brush and the brambles and the tops of the baobab trees toward Nena. She threw herself back against the dark foliage, wincing as sharp sticks and broken branches stabbed at her. Small, slithering, scaly, hard, multilegged things scuttled under her hands. She forced herself not to scream. The bugs took her back to *that* time. When she was fourteen. Beneath the tree. In her village when what felt like thousands of insects had wormed their way beneath her prone body—

No. She forced her mind to push away those images. She'd had enough of them. Enough of remembering the times before life had begun to make sense once again. She needed to remain in the present. *Before* no longer mattered. Only now did.

Crouching on all fours, she had to figure a way out of her situation. She'd made it out of the bunker. She had no idea where she was, if she was still in Gabon or in some other country or continent. They had to be relatively close to Ghana to exact whatever kind of revenge Mariam was planning against the Tribe and her father. It would take too much time, waste too many resources, to go far away only to have to travel back in again.

Okay, she was still in Africa. Still, could be any country, and in the near pitch blackness, there was no telling which. Whether the country was an ally of the Tribe or not. But she was near the sea. Nena could smell the salt in the air and could feel the mix of sand and dirt with her fingers.

She had nothing she could use to call for help. Why hadn't she used Alpha's phone when she'd had the chance? *Because I was scared,* she wasn't afraid to admit. Because she'd been too terrified to remain in that claustrophobic, horrible place for one second longer. She had cut and run. Hadn't planned. Hadn't assessed. Hadn't thought things through. Like a newbie. Like some brand-new trainee who knew no better.

She needed to recall her Escape and Evasion training. She'd done the escape part, right? So now she needed to avoid recapture and evade her pursuers, the men she could hear shouting around her and thrashing through the same woods she was hiding in. What Nena needed to do was keep moving. Create distance between her and the encampment. Use the darkness, because once morning came, she'd lose her cover and they'd spot her in a heartbeat. They needed only to wait her out until the sun rose. Time was on their side, not hers.

With a quick breath, Nena forged ahead, shaking the creepy-crawlies from her hands. She could hear engines in the distance and assumed there was a road not too far away. A road to one side, the sea at the other. She tried to parallel the sound of the traffic, careful to remain in the dense undergrowth. She figured she was making good time, tempering her will to move quickly with the knowledge that quick movement made too much noise.

She kept her head low, dodging the hanging vines that wrapped around her neck like a noose. She tripped over roots protruding from the ground, her toe catching a particularly thick one. The pain shot through her foot with such intensity that her teeth slammed down hard onto her tongue—and then she heard the helicopter overhead.

Briefly, she wondered if Mariam had implanted a tracking device on her while she was unconscious. Likely not. They hadn't anticipated she'd make a run for it, much less escape. Mariam had expected Nena to either join her ranks or die in captivity.

Searchlights crisscrossed the ground, and shouts rang out, echoing against the tree trunks in a cacophony of languages. Snatches of some she recognized. Most she did not. But she could tell that they were pissed at her for making them work longer. On edge about the consequences if they didn't return with her dead or alive.

She kept moving. She was exhausted, running purely on adrenaline and anxiety. Her body was beginning to betray her, trying to succumb to the injuries it had sustained . . . the trauma from the car explosion, the pummeling to beat her into submission, the fighting her way out against opponents who had shared in her own training. She was so focused on just trying to stay on her feet that her head smacked full force into a low overhanging branch, like right out of a comedy. Only it was far from funny. It hurt!

She was down in an instant. Stunned. Lost in a swirl of consciousness and not. The breath knocked loose from her wouldn't return. She was not in control of her body, couldn't even comprehend if she'd made any noise or not. She lay there, dazed, for how long, she wasn't quite sure. She blinked repeatedly, trying to clear her mind, trying to take stock, once again, of her surroundings. Where was she? What had she been doing a moment ago? What was her mission?

There was warmth, starting with a trickle but moving into a flow, coursing down her face. She thought, *Sweat*, but when she touched it harder than she'd intended, she winced from the sharp pain and her fingers came away slick with liquid thicker than water. Blood.

She tried to move, but even for someone as trained and conditioned as she, it was too hard. Her body betrayed every wish she made, forcing her to listen to it and stop for a moment—several moments, for however long it took for her to feel in control again, to continue some sort of path to freedom.

She did manage to tug herself beneath huge palm fronds and other plants to conceal herself should anyone pass by and to stop them from trampling over her. Snatches of conversation wafted in and out of her hearing—something about triangulating the area so they could pin her in their net. Reprimand for there being no heat-seeking devices to give them an idea of her location. Wait until light, they said. They'd be able to see her then. She couldn't hide then. All were true.

She tenderly touched the large gash at her hairline. She could lie there forever. Die right there. At least her death wouldn't be at the hands of her enemies. Had she survived all her monsters just to die smashed and broken in the jungle?

Her eyes stung with hot tears, and she shut them tightly, refusing to cry. She wouldn't, couldn't do it. It would be the end of her. It would mean she'd given up. But as she sucked in the sob welling in her, she felt warm splatters on her face and thought, *Yet something else of my body to betray me.* But the splatters were coming from above, dropping all over her face, her neck. The steady beats of it hit the plants and trees around her, lightly at first, then steadily increasing until it became a deluge of water. A storm.

The water was like an infusion of life. She brushed away the leaves, opened her mouth, allowing the rain to pour in, to wash her bruised and broken body. She luxuriated in it for a while and enjoyed the serenity of feeling like she was in the most untouched place on earth. But her ears picked up a sound that wasn't nature talking. It was the helicopter, circling back overhead, the beam of its spotlight sweeping over her. A memory of when she and Cort had been at the club in Accra, dancing beneath the disco lights in paradise, flashed in front of her.

Cort. Would they go after him next once they'd finished her off? Or would Mariam keep her alive to watch them kill Cort, then Georgia, her family, and maybe even Keigel? Would they repeat history and force her to watch as everything was taken from her all over again?

She should have protected the Baxters better. Should have stayed away from them as she'd originally intended, listened to Cort's initial request, and not let herself get wrapped up in rom-com dreams of happy endings.

Or maybe not. Another thought came to mind. Maybe she could really be like Dad and keep the Baxters close, as Dad did Mum and Elin. She could protect the Baxters—all of them—if she were with them. She'd be there when her nephew was born, her only blood relative in this world. To be there for that birth, to protect the ones she loved, it meant Nena had to live. The realization renewed her energy, but only slightly. And her mind began to clear. Thoughts, calculations, and planning began to replace the mental anguish and self-doubt she'd been wallowing in.

She exhaled slowly, begrudgingly retreating into the hold of her protective plant, and stayed there until the rotating blades of the helicopter and the calls of the search teams abated.

Slowly she rose to a sitting position, glad the sounds of rain continued to mask her movement. She hurt. There was no doubt about that. She steeled herself against the pain, regulated her breathing, gritted her teeth, and slid upward, through the floppy leaves, until she was entirely upright. She remained against the tree, letting it serve as her crutch until she felt her body would listen to her.

And then she started to move again.

43

Nena shuffled to the first dwelling she could see. Mariam's men could already be there waiting for her, but she didn't care. She tried, best as she could, to look for any movement, anyone waiting for her.

It was too dark to make out more than distended shapes. The warm breeze carried only the slight odor of livestock. Just a few steps more. She had to make it. To at least try to send word to her people that she was still alive, that they should be even more careful because Mariam and her people were coming for them, for Noble.

The déjà vu was debilitating, and all Nena wanted was to lie down and die right there. She was so very tired.

She made it to the door, lunging at it. Slapping it weakly in hopes that someone would hear. It had to be late, an evil hour, and who knew if anyone would answer a knock at the door during the witching hours, the way most African superstitions were set up. But beyond the door she heard scuffling, a low murmur of voices.

"Please," she whispered. Then louder. Her throat was raw. She was in desperate need of water. "Please."

She slumped to the ground and was leaning against the door when it finally cracked open. And wider when whoever was behind it felt her weight against the wood.

She didn't understand what they were saying, but it was a child, a boy, maybe, hard to tell with his voice. Heard a woman behind him. Nena felt two sets of hands grip her around each arm and begin to pull. She winced, tried her hardest not to call out, but as they pulled her onto a mat on the floor, the pain was too much to deny, to breathe through this time. She saw nothing but white hot. Then darkness.

Nena came to when something cold was pressed to her face. She started, ready to defend herself. The boy and his mother jumped back. When she saw they meant no harm, she relaxed, holding up an arm to say sorry and that she was safe. She didn't have a lot of time. She had to warn her family before Mariam's people found her and finished what they'd started. She had to maybe leave this home so that its occupants wouldn't be collateral damage.

"Please," she said through lips so cracked the slightest movement made them crack some more.

She rattled through all her languages in delirium—Twi, Ga, Ewe. Wait. No, she wasn't in Ghana. French, maybe? The moderate bit of Spanish she'd learned. Then she stopped. Nothing.

Finally, Nena asked, "English?"

The woman nodded, coming closer. Not woman. Girl. Teens, maybe seventeen. Was hard to tell.

"Phone. Do you have a phone?"

"Yes, ma. What are you doing here? Where are you coming from?" asked the boy. He was younger, maybe twelve. "Are you one of them? The soldiers?"

Nena shook her head. "Abeg. I need to get a message through."

They shared a look, the boy and girl, making a silent agreement between the two of them.

"Fast. Fast," the boy said. "They will come looking for you."

While he said that, his sister broke away into the darkness and returned with a smartphone, its screen casting a bluish glow. Barely able to concentrate, Nena gritted her teeth through the pain.

"WhatsApp." Her throat felt like it was filled with jagged rocks.

Through the fog of her mind, she recalled the emergency number.

Was hard to concentrate. Nena's fingers weren't listening, and she couldn't connect the numbers floating in her mind with body parts that would tap the digits in. The boy said he was going back out to check she hadn't left any trail outside. The girl took the phone from Nena's bent hands.

"Tell me."

And in a halting whisper Nena did, giving up the phone number. She'd undergone torture and never given up intel. All it took for her to give up the goods was a simple ask from an innocent child. *Tell me.* And then her ID number, personalized for her so when in danger, if she was without comms, she could use it and Network would come running. *If* Network hadn't gone dark again. If Mariam and her benefactor hadn't already made their next move.

"I need to go," she said. "Before they find you with me."

The girl shook her head. "No, ma, they will kill you. You stay. Someone is asking to verify location."

Nena wanted to throw something. She had no idea where she was. "I don't—I don't know." She felt useless, as if all her years of training had been beaten out of her. Perhaps they had, because she'd remembered nothing but to run and hide in the forest until her pursuers went away.

Before Nena could figure out her bearings or say to triangulate her location, which they were hopefully already doing, the girl was typing. Her thumbs flying across the lit phone in such a flurry they made Nena dizzy.

The door opened and they both jumped. Nena struggled to prepare for combat, to attempt to protect the girl. Her body barely followed direction, only managing to sit upright and hold out weak hands that would make absolutely no impact on assailants.

"Is my brother," the girl said.

Once upon a time, she'd had a brother. She had had three. But they were all gone now. And maybe now, she could finally join them and her father.

"We need to conceal her. In case they come." Sounded like the boy.

"No. No," she said with more bluster than she could back up. She'd leave once she caught her breath and wasn't seeing sideways. She wouldn't put these children in harm's way. Not for her. "Thank you for your kindness, but I'll go."

It was as if they didn't hear her. "Under the bed for now. Put Mama's baskets around it to hide her."

Then they were already tugging at her again, ripping open wounds just barely clotted together. The pain this time was hot coals raking against her body. She was no match for the sibling duo. Alpha, the forest, and the elements had had their way with her. And rather than scream out in the agony pressing against the back of her split lip, she buried her mouth in her shoulder as the boy tugged her arms over her head and the girl picked up her feet as they rolled her under the bed.

Nena had every intention of leaving them be, giving them a chance at survival instead of imminent death if Mariam's people discovered her.

Had every intention.

Until her eyes rolled up in the back of her head and blackness swept over her, enveloping her in its soothing arms and rendering Nena incapable of *intending* much of anything anymore.

44

It was blinding white light coming through her closed lids that brought Nena back to consciousness, but she kept them closed for seconds longer, afraid of what she'd see on the other side. She remembered all of it, the two heads hovering above her, small and smaller—a girl and her brother—as she lay on the floor of their home, under a bed. They had saved her life. Then the heat of unconsciousness had swept her away.

But now where was she? Who had found her? Nena wasn't too proud to admit she was afraid to look and see if she was in a safe place, if she was back in captivity, if she was—and she hoped she was—with the children who'd found her, aided her.

If she was back at the bunker, she couldn't feel any immediate pain. Perhaps that would come once they realized she was awake. Perhaps she'd be chained up again, swinging in the air, while Alpha pummeled her as if she were a sandbag. No—Alpha was dead. And Sierra—Jessica . . . Nena didn't want to think about her. What if Nena was still in the tiny home with the thatched roofing, with the kids, but they were dead beside her? Had their innocence been snuffed out because of her, while she still lived? Nena would never forgive herself.

Open your eyes, Nena, she bargained with herself. *Let's just get on with it.* Because drawing out the inevitable was more torture than the actual act. No, that was a lie. There was nothing worse than the actual act of torture. Nothing.

Slowly, Nena opened her eyes, squinting against the intense natural light until her eyes adjusted well enough for her to determine she was in a room. White room. In a bed with railings. Beneath covers. She heard machines bleeping a steady rhythm. A TV hovered in the air across from her. It was bolted to the wall and was playing a movie.

Nena watched the screen to see if she could recognize which. An old-time favorite, *Jurassic Park* with Jeff Goldblum. She liked him a lot. The volume was too low to distinguish the words, but she knew what they were saying. Not by heart, but well enough. It was one of her favorite movie franchises. One she could watch over and over and never tire of. But this moment was not the time to delve into hungry dinosaurs and screaming scientists.

Nena looked around. No phone. No chains hanging from the ceiling of dank dirt-smelling rooms. Hospital room. Okay. Monitors. She looked at her arms. Bandaged. One was in a sling. She wiggled her fingers, and though they were sore, they moved. Heartbeat gauge over her pointer finger. Blood pressure cuff over her left arm, currently constricting her arm as it took its reading. She didn't like it, but the fact that the pressure didn't bring on bouts of pain was a welcome relief. An IV line attached to the back of her free hand. And a door leading out into a hall. Through the window in the door, she could see people passing back and forth. Her anxiety dialed down a couple of notches. Hospital meant safety. She was safe.

———

Nena woke up facing the door to the pristine room she was in. She watched the people moving in the hall. Then she turned away, squinting against the sunlight shining through the blinds. And saw him. His forehead rested on his forearm, face down as he slept sitting in a chair at her bedside. She saw the long strands of carefully grown locs that reached nearly to his hip. And how he used a few outside strands to bind the rest at the nape of his tattooed neck like a scrunchie. She knew that head. And the arms serving as its pillow, adorned with more intricately detailed works of art.

Keigel. She exhaled, relief flowing through her. Her friend. That he was here when she awoke closed her throat around the lump that immediately formed in it. She was touched beyond measure. She lifted her hand from her lap, flexing her fingers as she moved her hand toward him. She paused, hovering just above his head, then laid her hand atop Keigel's crown and let out a deep, cleansing breath.

He stirred beneath her touch, and she pulled her hand back as his head lifted up and he blinked sleep away from his eyes. They widened when he realized she was awake and watching him.

"Hey, girl," he said through a smile, stretching his long body in the chair. He looked around, looked her over. "You good? You need anything? Let me call the doctor."

She waved her hand at him. "No." She paused for a breath, finding even that word hard to get out because her throat was so sore. "How are you here? You should be home." She'd left him and Georgia and Cort at the airport in Accra to fly back to the States. They were supposed to be home, far away from Mariam's reach.

"Well, I'm here. What are you gonna do about it?" Keigel showed her all his teeth. "And no, Cort and the kid are back home in the MIA. Though that dude was about to fight the hell out of me to get back here. Lemme tell ya." He shook his head ruefully. "I mean, we were on layover in Germany when we got word about the hit at the hotel in Gabon and that you were taken—"

Elin! And Witt! How had she been so stupid to have not asked after them. To have not even thought about their well-being in all this time.

"Don't even think about it." Keigel seemingly read her mind. "Focus on you right now. They're fine. Elin had Fort Knox–level security round her the entire time. And Witt . . ."

Nena's heart seized.

". . . well, that old-ass geezer takes a lickin' and keeps on tickin'," Keigel finished, pleased with himself. He leaned over the bedside table to pour a cup of water from the pitcher sitting there. He held the cup out to her, but not before plopping a white straw in it so she could take a sip. He was pushy, refusing to continue until she did as she was told. The cool water felt like both fire and ice going down.

"I should let the doctors know you're awake. And the fam."

"Don't," she said. "Tell me what happened first."

"Anyway, we're waiting in Germany, right? And a call comes in talkin' 'bout the hotel hit, and you've been captured. And immediately me and Cort are at the flight desk tryin' to see about flights back. We standing at the desk, right? And I look back at Georgia, who looks like she's about to fucking lose her shit! Because all we know is some gang of motherfuckers worked Witt over and took you. I'm like, 'Yo, what about home slice? She can't go back there with all this popping off. She needs to go home.' And lil homey's like, 'Nah, fuck that, Keig, I ain't leavin'.'"

Nena gave him a dubious look.

Keigel held his hands up. "Okay, okay, maybe she didn't do all the cussin', but she was like, she's going back to find you. So Cort's tellin' her no. And I'm tellin' him he can't go either. Somebody's gotta take lil homey home to make sure she's safe. Lil homey's like, 'Um, excuse me, I'm grown. I can take myself home.' And me and Cort look at her like, 'Seriously?' Cort wasn't tryin' to hear me out. He was hell bent on coming back here to find you."

Nena's mouth twitched, enjoying both Keigel's animated storytelling and that they had all tried to get back to her.

"So finally I was like, 'Dawg, look. Real talk, you can't go back. You got the kid, and she can't go back home without you. Who gonna watch her? You don't even know how long you'll be gone. And you know how crazy these motherfuckers are. You can't have no target on your back with lil homey here.' Then I told him he's like the first gentleman and shit. Like Kamala's old man. He gotta be home to batten down the hatches and keep the home fires burning and shit."

"You're a fountain of clichés, Keigel," she croaked, fighting against the urge to laugh—though she rarely if ever did—because she knew Keigel's retelling was no embellishment. He'd really had the audacity to tell Cort he was basically a house husband.

Keigel looked reflective. "I'm pretty sure I pissed Cort off then, because he reminded my ass right then that he had been a cop, was in the military, came from Haiti, and Haitians ain't soft, so don't try to play him like that. He said I had him all the way fucked up and he was gonna see about his lady—that's you, by the way."

Nena inclined her head.

Keigel's hands raised in surrender. "I was like, 'My bad, dawg, I didn't mean it like that!' I mean, he had my voice going all high and shit 'cause he gave me the low-eyebrow look. You know he got them bushy-ass eyebrows, right? I think he be linin' them up, 'cause they too perfect. Not a hair out of order. But anyway, when he gets all pissed off, they get all close together, all furrowed and shit, and you feel your balls drop because you know you about to be in *trouble* trouble." Keigel thought about it. "Well, you ain't got any balls, but your lady balls."

"Lady balls?"

He looked at her as if she was falling behind. "Yes, Nena, your lady balls. Those badass lady balls you got that allow you to Houdini your way out of shit anytime motherfuckers try to hem you up and snag your ass."

After three years, Nena was pretty good at deciphering Keigel talk when he was in his excited state. His words came a mile a minute, his body animated, and every possible Black catchphrase made its grand appearance. Keigel was the best storyteller. He'd have given the elders in N'nkakuwe a run for their money.

Keigel gave her a cool assessment with one eye slightly squinted. "I might just call you Houdini from now on, real talk. Because how you make your way out, how you survive time after time . . . that's like superhero shit, Nena. Real talk." His voice broke, causing Nena's head to snap up. Keigel looked away, not wanting her to see emotion overtaking him. His voice lowered, his speech slowed, and gone was the entertainingly playful demeanor of just seconds ago.

"In a minute I'm gonna get the doctor to look you over; then I'm gonna call the fam and tell them you're awake and good. You *are* good, right?"

She nodded.

He rubbed at his eyes in the way guys did when they didn't want anyone to know they were upset or near tears. "We were so scared, Nena. We thought . . ." He licked his lips, sliding his eyes over to meet hers. "I convinced Cort to take Georgia home. He needed to be there for her. He needed to stay alive for her. And I swore to him I'd come back and would not leave your side, ever, until I got you back to Miami and to them. I ain't breakin' that promise. You feel me?"

She nodded, feeling heat building behind her eyes, willing them not to betray her. He'd said she was Houdini, like superhero shit. Crying wasn't her thing. At least it hadn't been. How did she tell Keigel that she wasn't the only superhero and that she felt the same way about him?

"Unlike last time when you ran into that house to take down Paul all Bruce Willis *Die Hard*–style, you don't get to go in alone." His hand swooped the length of his torso. "'Cause you got me."

"So you're Bruce Willis now?"

Keigel started laughing. "Oh, to be sure."

45

Nena closed her laptop, her hand resting on top of it as if leaving it there for a second longer would keep her connected to the Baxters. It had been good to see Cort and Georgia, across the world and in the warm safety of their Miami living room, where she'd made Cort promise to remain. He'd wanted to return to Ghana, to be with her once she was out of hospital. But who would stay back with Georgia? And he surely couldn't bring her back here when Mariam was still out there, preparing to strike at any moment.

Nena needed Cort and Georgia far removed, away from Mariam's fury at Nena's rejection, at her apathy for Mariam's pain. Nena needed Mariam to forget about the Baxters entirely. Nena forced her aching, throbbing, banged-up body out of bed, wishing she could remain in it and not be made to do what she knew she had to do. She welcomed the agony of moving her limbs if it meant her loved ones would be safe. That her family could be protected. So that the legacy of the Tribe could be made whole again. So that all the blood, sweat, and tears that had been poured into this crazy idea of Noble's wouldn't be in vain.

Nena's once-creamy-dark complexion was now mottled shades of angry crimson, deep violet, and midnight black, with gashes that would heal into lighter-colored scars all about her arms and legs, as well as bandaging around her ribs. She couldn't hide all of that, but once showered and as presentable as she could get herself, she slipped on a pair of loosely fitting wide-legged linen pants and a white tee. She considered the blue-and-white sling strewed on the bed. Should she wear it or not? Maybe not. She had to condition herself to be without it, to move without its restriction. She took another longing look at the bed. It called to her, begged her to return to it. In all her life Nena hadn't wanted to lie down as much as she wanted to right now. It was the first time she'd thought about giving up, about retiring herself.

That was a lie. She'd nearly given up when Mariam's people had been beating her; when they'd locked her in that room, she'd nearly given up. But once again, she'd made her way out, hadn't she? Nena the survivor? Nena, the one with multiple lives, it seemed. When she'd tasted freedom again as she'd burst through the door of the bunker and hobbled her way through the wild while Mariam's guards had tried to hunt her down like some animal, Nena had recalled she'd had the same feeling when she ran from the Frenchman's house of horrors. Her lot in life was not to give up. It was not to lie down and die. It was to face her fate on her feet. It was to meet her end trying. And that was what Nena would always do, in agony or not.

Her family—Keigel included, because he was family now after staying by her side during her brief stint in hospital rather than returning to the States—was congregated in the living room of the rented house on Aburi. They were spread throughout the spacious room with Elin at the helm, standing in front of their parents, Keigel, and Witt—her color-coded spreadsheets up and on screen again.

When Witt saw Nena for the first time, he looked aged and as if the world weighed on his shoulders. It had only been a few days, and yet along with the series of cuts adorning his face, the scrapes alongside his neck and chin, and the purpling bruises beneath his skin, even his hair seemed changed. It used to be a mix of salt and pepper but was now more of the former. His eyes were the worst of all. As if the light in them had been extinguished.

"Lighten up, big man," Noble said boisterously. "Look how well you've taught my child. She lives because of your training. Celebrate that."

Witt was nodding, taking in Nena's injuries. He looked devastated.

Nena whispered to him as their meeting began. "I'm okay. It looks worse than it feels," she lied. "Are you okay?"

She thought she saw his eyes glisten in that moment, causing her to give him a deeper look.

"I'm well."

"It was Cort who helped me figure this out," Elin was saying as Nena found her seat. Delphine, seated on the long couch next to Noble, spied her younger daughter and mouthed hello. Nena waved back.

"It was the both of us, to be honest," came Cort's disembodied voice. "Teamwork."

"Makes the bloody dream work," Elin finished, flashing an overly generous smile. It wasn't directed toward working with Cort but rather about the grim nature of the topic for which they'd had to team up.

Nena surveyed the room, locating the computer screen where Cort was video chatting with them. She chuckled. In their chat moments ago, he hadn't mentioned he'd be logging back on a second later to talk business. It was surreal. Every time Cort joined them for Tribe talk felt otherworldly because Cort's job had always been on the opposite end of the spectrum from Nena's. How they'd gotten to this point, she wasn't sure. But she was glad for it.

"What's the deal?" Keigel asked after taking a long sip from the drink he held in his hand. His locs swayed from beneath the Miami Heat hat he wore as he studied the monitor.

"Well," Elin began, "Cort, could you pull up the cross-references on the transactions and accounts?" While they waited, Nena watched as the screen changed from the multiple rows of nonsensical numbers to another page of highlighted rows of dollar amounts. The new windows, side by side, first displayed a list of numbers, dates, times, and locations. And then a series of what looked like phone numbers.

"All right, what you see here are the transactions Cort and I have flagged. These transactions go back several years. From even before Paul came on board."

Noble visibly stiffened at the mention of Paul. Nena's eyes floated to him, saw her mother move her hand to rub light circles into his back, and then she quickly turned her attention to the big screen again, slightly embarrassed at observing the intimacy between her parents, even though she'd been audience to them before. As far as African couples and parents went, Mr. and Mrs. Knight were not afraid of public displays of moderate affection.

"We speculated that Paul was either flying solo or was in league with someone within the Tribe to get him in so he could continue his shady dealings on a broader scale or try to take over or whatever the case may be. But these transactions prove that something was going on well before he came into the picture."

"There was a case similar to this that I worked on," Cort interjected. "A stateside organized-crime family. And we found that the person we thought was the new kid on the block set to take over the family was really a prop. Smoke and mirrors."

Noble looked questioningly at Delphine, then back to Elin, though his question was directed at Cort. "Means what?"

"Means maybe Paul was a plan B, Dad," Elin replied. "He was smoke and mirrors just as Cort said, and whoever set him up to be the big baddie, so to speak, was already siphoning money and planning a coup."

"A what?" Noble jumped out of his seat.

Nena wished Elin had been more tactful.

"A coup suggests rebellion, Elin, dear." Delphine spoke up in her melodic voice of reason that almost always felt like balm on a sunburn. "What would anyone within the Tribe be rebelling about? Everyone with the organization is involved of their own accord."

"Exactly." Noble paced the floor. "We hold no one here against their will. A rebellion for what?"

Keigel raised his hand as if he were in primary school, but he didn't wait to be called on. "Oh, they do this all the time back home, just like my boy Cort said. In other gangs, families, organizations, if people go against you, it's either because you're oppressing them or they want to further their own interest and think they can run things better in their own way."

Noble slowly turned to face Keigel. "Run things better? Run what? We vote on everything."

But they didn't. It was the High Council who had the final say, who was the deciding factor if votes were tied. It was Noble who had predetermined what the Tribe's goals would be when he built it and who ensured their mission permeated every move the Tribe made.

Keigel shrugged, not intimidated in the least by the way the powerful man glared at him. Keigel was a powerful man in his own right. He was a leader of men, so he knew. And Nena knew he could make Noble understand. "Mr. Knight, I may be a small fish in a big pond with my fam back home. But when your soldiers or your right-hand folks don't feel like they're eatin' in the way they want, then they'll put in folk who will get them eatin' in the way they want. Or at least they'll try to."

Keigel stood up, his lanky body towering over Noble's shorter, stockier one. Nena's breath caught when Keigel placed a hand on Noble's shoulder, patting it affably. Elin's expression looked as if Keigel had stepped in dog refuse. Delphine's hand flew halfway to her chest to clutch her nonexistent pearls before she remembered herself and forced her hand back down.

Nena was relieved her mother tamped down her surprise because Noble took cues from her, and if she didn't look put out at Keigel's easygoing nature, then Noble wouldn't take it as him being too familiar. The Knights were a loving family, but they were still very reserved by American standards.

"Everyone in the Tribe eats, Keigel," Noble said, all stature aside. He was speaking to Keigel as an equal. "It's the utmost priority of the Tribe. It's the foundation on which I built it, for everyone from the lowest level on the totem pole to the High Council to be valued. To eat."

Keigel shrugged. "Sometimes it's not enough for some people. Those are the ones who will burn the whole Tribe down—and worst thing is that they won't care if they burn it as long as they're profiting from it. They'll never care who eats and who starves. Real talk. You know why?"

Noble told him to continue.

"Because not all skin folk are kinfolk, know what I mean?" Keigel gave the older man a knowing look, one with a life's worth of experience and understanding. In that moment, Keigel looked older than his twenty-six years. He glanced around. "Anyway, I'm 'bout to get me a drink. Anyone want anything while I'm up?"

They didn't. The room remained quiet while Keigel sauntered off to refill his glass and find a snack or the house girl. One of them. Or both.

Noble sagged, the burden settling heavily upon his shoulders. Nena felt for him. She hurt with him. But she also needed her dad to buck up and fight this one out, hurt feelings aside.

He sat back down, quietly, next to Delphine, prompting Elin with a hand. "Go on."

Elin said, "We traced phone numbers through a maze that eventually connected to these transactions. It was hard because the transactions cycled twice to make detection difficult. But our analysts found two phone numbers that are repeated and associated with offshore accounts.

We can't find who owns those accounts, but we did find that after a whole lot of routing and rerouting, the funds deposit into a single account, also offshore. The owner, also unknown."

"Doesn't matter the name of that owner," Nena finally said from her seat in the back. "It's Mariam's account. Whoever those phone numbers belong to have been paying her to turn our Dispatch members to her side. She's had them feeding her intel. Whoever owns those numbers likely fed her intel as well so she'd be able to ambush my team and the Network satellite and snatch me in Gabon."

Elin said, "I agree. They're using Mariam to amass a sizable group of people, soldiers, whatever you want to call them, loyal to her cause. That's what Nena saw at the bunker."

"And make the Tribe a for-profit mercenary organization," Cort finished.

"That part," Elin concurred. "Why start something brand new when you can take over something already established, put a new coat of paint on it, and present it nice and shiny for whoever needs it to pay for the new Tribe's protective services?"

Elin and Keigel were on a metaphorical roll this morning.

"We find this Mariam, then. That will stop the 'coup.'" Her dad used air quotes for that final word, refusing to give it any more power over him.

"But it didn't stop when I took out Paul and Ofori," Nena replied. "It kept going, probably harder than it had before. We need the people those numbers belong to."

Keigel returned with a glass pitcher of a pinkish juice and a platter of freshly cut fruit. "There was a note on the counter to bring this. Kitchen was empty."

Elin had sent everyone away to ensure their privacy. Keigel set the refreshments on the table and took his seat after helping himself to some of both.

"Those numbers could belong to anyone," Delphine said. "And if we called them now, no one would pick up. It would only alert them, and they'd flee."

"We can't reach out to them until the night they plan to attack."

Cort said, "Which could be any day."

"In two days," Nena said. "At the charity dinner."

Noble nodded. "She's right. It's the most opportune time. The time they can come after me, show how ineffective the old Tribe is and that this new regime will deliver the protection everyone wants. For a cost, of course."

"Of course," Keigel chimed in, raising his glass to Noble.

"What are you saying, Noble?" Delphine asked, anxiety lacing her tone.

He didn't respond. He didn't have to.

"Noble, no. You can't! If they're going to attack the dinner, then we won't have the dinner!"

"And run, Delphine? Hide? You would have me hide from my people? Hide from thieves and usurpers and those who think only of financial gain and not the good of our people? Fuck that!"

The room was dead silent. Noble's curse, one he never said because to curse was to show emotion, reverberated in the light-colored, tropical room. Noble wasn't hiding. Not his emotion. Not himself.

"The dinner will proceed as planned. Elin and Cort will do what they have to do to uncover who owns the phones. Nena and Witt will secure the perimeter as best as possible with whatever team members we can trust to get this woman when she strikes."

"Strikes you, you mean," Delphine said angrily, "because that's what she's coming to do. That's what they're paying her to do. To kill you, Noble."

"Let them try."

Never had words resounded so much within Nena as they did at that moment. She had always believed in her dad, had always thought he was the most honorable, bravest man she knew. In this moment, Noble Knight proved it to be true.

"I won't run. They won't chase me off. If it's my time, my end comes on my feet."

Had she not thought these exact words earlier as she'd struggled to dress herself over the bandages holding her together? That her father spoke these now meant something.

"Perhaps we can make it so it only *seems* as if Dad has been killed. I mean, before Mariam tries to take him out. He can channel his inner Denzel," Elin suggested.

"I do like Denzel Washington. Met him once. Great fellow. Down to earth too," Noble quipped.

Keigel's hand rose again, breaking the spell of the moment. "How do we uncover the Council members who own these numbers? Call them up during the dinner and say, *What's up, dawg?*"

Elin's eyes sparkled as she looked at him. "Why not do just that? We call the numbers when they're all there and see who rings or checks for messages. They could do it thinking Mariam's confirming her job's done."

Keigel held up his hands in protest. "Oh, but wait, waaaiiiit a damn minute. I was just joking about calling during the dinner. You can't just call up numbers during a dinner. Whose phone is gonna be set to ringer in this day and age?"

"Keigel, we're talking about a bunch of people sixty and over. Which of them won't have their phones set to ringer?"

"Then how would you tell those from the other ten whose phones could also ring? Or what if someone's dentist calls at the same time? Now we think that person's trying to commit mutiny, when it's really that they need a root canal. Now we're killing up innocent people instead of helping them get new teeth."

"Okay."

"Shooting 'em in their faces when they likely just need braces."

"We got it, Keigel."

"Labeling them as killers when they really just need fillers! Stabbing them in their ears when they only need veneers."

"Enough. Your point is made," Elin yelled.

Keigel had lightened the atmosphere considerably, and Delphine was more relaxed now than she'd been a moment ago, on the verge of a breakdown at the thought of her husband putting himself out there. She loved the Tribe, but not nearly as much as she loved Noble.

"Can we get back to the issue at hand?" Nena asked, thinking of how glorious a nap would be. Cort had rung off, having to tend to Georgia and not wanting her to overhear any of what was being said. "How do we uncover who owns those phones?"

Witt said, "Utilize our resources with Network. I'll get one of our people to dial in and work under the cover of darkness. That means we don't go to the Council with this operation."

"You're talking like a remote hack?" Keigel asked. "I can dig it. What kind?"

"Hell if we know," Elin groused. "Who do I look like, Best Buy's Geek Squad?"

"They're actually pretty damn good," Keigel said. "See, there was this one time—"

"We get it, Keigel, please!"

Elin looked as if she wanted to strangle him, while Nena could hug him—if she were into hugging. Keigel was the perfect source of the much-needed levity her way-too-serious family lacked, even if his joking was lame and relentless at times.

Nena added, "At any rate, we only have to make them think Dad's been taken out. Then you can call an emergency meeting, Elin, because Mum will be too broken up. They'll all be there to vote to put in place an interim High Council. We can have the phones ring then. Doesn't matter if someone else's phone rings at that moment," she added when Keigel's mouth opened, readying to bring up the dentist again, "because we'll have them all in one location and we can search the phones that ring for the ones whose numbers match the numbers we have on file."

Her parents were nodding, though Noble looked grim. And Delphine looked cautiously optimistic that maybe she wouldn't have to sacrifice her husband to the Tribe any more than she already had their entire marriage. But Nena could recognize the terror underlying Delphine's cautious optimism. Because Delphine was a realist, like Nena. She knew that there was no way Noble would survive that night without a scratch.

Elin agreed with Nena. Nena could practically see the scene playing and replaying in her mind, like a film roll. Keigel was talking to her about dead zones and infiltrating phone towers, to which Elin replied that they needed to keep things simple. Sometimes, simplicity was the best measure.

Nena would be doing the same thing as Elin, playing the film roll, imagining the best scenario to not get their father killed. But that was what it would take, wouldn't it? Mariam would have to get to her dad, but Nena would have to get to Mariam first. And was she ready? How could she be when she was as beat up and incapacitated as she currently was?

The rogue Council members would relax. They'd receive simultaneous messages or calls, whatever Elin and Witt would have Network do, confirming the mission was complete. Mariam would send her message, confirming her job was done. She'd likely want the pleasure of retiring Noble as he'd done her brother. It was Mariam's ultimate goal.

And when she came for Noble, Nena would be ready—bandaged, broken, not 100 percent—but ready. And she'd give everything she had to send Mariam to the same place as Goon.

Retirement.

However, this was real life, and Nena had learned long, long ago that life didn't ever quite work out the way people wanted it to.

46

The venue was packed, practically bursting at the seams with the who's who of Ghana and abroad vying to get the attention of the Knight family, to beg the ear of Noble to pitch their latest ventures and charities, local and global. The scene was a security nightmare, but there was little Nena and Witt could do, especially when they weren't entirely sure who was on whose payroll. But they managed as best as they could using comms they'd purchased from a contact around town to set up a second, private channel since they weren't sure how compromised Network was.

Nena directed Keigel to keep close to her sister. Noble had several guards surrounding him, but just in case, Nena wanted someone she knew she could personally trust guarding her sister's back. Because Elin and the baby inside of her were the blood heirs to Noble's throne (didn't matter what Noble said about blood and found family; it was what the world would see, and Nena was just fine with that), should the plan go awry.

Likely, it would.

Nena had taken as much ibuprofen with codeine as the doctor allowed her to take without it slowing her down too much. She just needed something to knock the edge off the way her breath caught if she jerked when she should have eased, jolted when she should have remained still, breathed when she should have held it in.

She moved slower tonight. She wore at best a pleasant expression so people thought she was in an amenable mood and not on the job. Directing them to the assigned seating Delphine had been so meticulous about arranging and then rearranging a day ago to ensure that all of Witt's most trusted Dispatch people were placed in locations where they could keep an eye out for anything suspicious and an eye on everyone—suspicious or not.

Witt had even gotten some Network members on location, wanting the people who knew tech the best to be nearby to scramble phone and radio frequencies when needed, to ensure that radio contact was limited to Nena, Witt, and their people and make sure Mariam and hers couldn't infiltrate their comms. For the first time since Nena had been under Witt's tutelage, for the first time since she'd made the Tribe and the Knights her family, she felt like the underdog, unprepared and worried that when this night ended, she'd be without a father . . . she could be without an entire family. Again.

She walked the premises, playing the role of the youngest Knight daughter. She was uncomfortable in the evening attire she'd worn. It wasn't a dress, but close enough. She'd managed to get her mother and sister to agree to a combo that didn't involve a dress but had some sort of skirt train at the back, a look she'd seen in a movie some time back.

Nena was okay with this look, actually, though she'd never admit it openly to Elin or their mother. She'd even allowed Keigel to take a pic of her.

"You know I gotta get one for my boy Cort," he'd said earlier, before they'd left for the charity dinner venue, as he'd walked by her open doorway and stopped as if he'd slammed into an invisible wall. "This is the second time I've seen you dressed up, and I forgot to take a pic on New Year's for the fam back home. I gotta show them."

"Stop." Heat flushed her face.

"You look rather regal yourself," she said when he'd handed back her phone to her after taking her photo. She meant it, studying the tuxedo he wore with the green, black, and gold cummerbund that matched the round wooden beads and necklace he always wore.

He raised his eyebrows, looking at her pointedly until she did what he said and sent the picture to Cort. He responded almost immediately, a sweating emoji that warmed her. When she looked up from her screen, Keigel was watching her. Warmth spread through her cheeks.

Keigel was grinning. "Yeah, that's what I thought. I know what up. He appreciates that stuff. They don't call me Dr. Love for nothing."

"Absolutely no one calls you Dr. Love, Keigel."

His smile was both brilliant and lecherous at the same time. "The ladies do all the damn time."

She had dismissed his silliness then with a smile as she'd agreed to take a selfie with Keigel so he could send that to Georgia and probably Cort too. And she dismissed it now as she checked closed doors and tried to single out people who did not look like they were enjoying themselves or were pretending like they were enjoying their jobs at the venue.

"Kitchen and services rooms are clear," Nena said into the air.

"Copy," Witt replied.

At the same time Keigel answered, "Over and out." He said it so gleefully, like a kid who had just been given his first spycraft set.

"'Copy' is fine," Witt said with a sigh.

"My fault," Keigel said.

Nena could imagine him shrugging. He was out of sight, with Elin and their parents, who were preparing to make their entrance toward the front of the room. From there, Noble would take the podium and begin to speak, while Elin and Delphine sat at their table. If Nena knew Mariam, his speech was when she'd strike. And it would be here. Nowhere else. Nena doubted there were many of Mariam's people here anyway. And Mariam wouldn't want to risk making her operation too big. She'd want it small, intimate. With little chance of screwups and even less chance of someone on her team betraying her plans.

It was an idea that had gone round and round between Nena and Witt. If Mariam would go big or go small. In the end, Nena's rationale had won out.

Nena walked the span of the main dining room's open space. Above it were vaulted glass ceilings painted with ornate images of various African landscapes: the Sahara, jungles, beaches, mountains, animals indigenous to their lands. She allowed herself a second or two to appreciate how truly beautiful the ceiling was, the beauty of this building, and the beauty that was Africa. Nena understood perfectly why Delphine had chosen this venue, built on the outskirts of Accra and nestled in the center of a maze of curvy roadways with lush botanical gardens in between them and sheer cliffs that dropped off into cavernous ditches. The landscape reminded Nena of an ice cream swirl.

"Good thing about the grounds," Witt had observed as they'd been driving up the winding roadway earlier, "is that it lessens the possibility for a quick getaway. There's no way one can maneuver these turns at fast speeds and not go over one of the sides. Single lane in and out. A plus, for us."

Bottles us in too, Nena thought, if they were the ones who had to quickly get her family away to safety and from this den of enemies.

She was in a corner at the front of the room, facing the audience seated at covered round tables. The room was filled to capacity as they all eagerly awaited her father. The tables behind the podium were where her family would be seated. Keigel would join them because Mum had insisted he be there, not as Elin's guard like Nena had made him promise to be but as family and an honored guest.

There was a round of applause, and Nena saw the side doors opening and her father walking in. He was waving at the crowd, now on their feet and clothed in a mix of authentic Ghanaian dress and Western formal wear. Mixed in were dignitaries, politicians, business CEOs, charity leaders, and chieftains of towns, tribes, and villages from all over. The chieftains still played an integral part in Ghana's politics, often serving as advisory council to the government on things related to Ghana's advancement and to their specific homes. And intermingled with all these well-wishers and good people were the two traitors who sought to destroy the house that Noble Knight had built.

The band began to play as Noble walked with the Ghanaian president by his side. Behind them came their wives, then Elin with Keigel. They waved. Even Keigel. And Nena hoped he hadn't forgotten his number one duty while basking in the limelight of Ghana's elite.

The crowd broke out in robust cheers and claps, finally settling once the VIP group were seated. The president was readying to make his introductions, then turn the podium over to Noble. Nena tensed. Only minutes before Noble would say his piece. When Mariam would maybe make her move. Maybe.

It would make more of a splash if she took him out while he spoke of unity, of raising Africa to the prominence she'd been denied for far too long, of being safe from outside factions, of Africans putting African people first for a change. Africa didn't need the world, Noble would say; the world needed Africa.

Mariam wouldn't be able to resist pulling the trigger just when he said he'd make Africans safe. It would be an ironic act for the world but poetic justice for herself, killing this great man when he promised safety. It would thrust Africans into a terrified spin and doubt about the Tribe's power and ability. How could the African Tribal Council protect anyone if they couldn't even protect Noble Knight?

The president was clearing his throat and Nena was preparing to make her rounds again when she saw something on one of the balconies, a ripple of shadowy movement that looked like there had been a tear in the fabric of time across from where she stood. It didn't make sense. No one had warped through a wormhole in front of Nena's eyes or anything, but there had been something.

Her head automatically wanted to home in on the peculiarity and confirm what she'd seen—or that her eyes were playing tricks on her.

But to do that would be to alert whoever was watching her, giving away her next moves, or at the least serve to remind them to be extra cautious. Nena didn't want to give them anything.

"And their youngest daughter, Nena Knight," the president was saying. She forced a gracious smile to her face when the president called her name, lifted a hand in hello to the audience, then ducked away from the front of the room, walking briskly but not as if there was a problem.

"She's the shy one of the family, apparently," the president joked, receiving a smattering of laughter.

Nena gritted her teeth. *Shy* was not the word for what she was about to do. But she had no time to worry about what anyone thought about her right now. Her singular goal was to get to that balcony where she'd seen the wormhole, or whatever, before her dad began speaking.

47

Once out of everyone's line of vision, Nena quickened her pace, vacillating between power walking and quick jogs. She ignored the elevator. Would take too much time. And looked at the winding stairs leading to the second floor. She took a breath, a fleeting thought about the number of stairs and how her body was already threatening to peter out. But the break in applause signaling the end of the president's speech pushed away any trepidation Nena felt that she was not in tip-top shape.

She used her recall from her position downstairs and from the building schematics she and Witt had pored over since the day her mother had informed them that this would be the charity dinner's venue. She knew exactly which balcony directly faced the podium. The sound of her father's voice reverberated through the speakers, bounced against the walls.

"Good evening, my Ghanaian friends and friends who have come from all over," Noble began.

Quietly, Nena twisted the handle, pushing the door open wide enough to slip into the rear of the balcony. She swept the space. At first glance anyone might have missed it. The balcony was large enough to hold several rows of seating that could be moved as needed, and that was what caught Nena's attention. The space between the chairs in the first two rows was larger than the rest. It could be by chance. But then again maybe not.

Nena inched toward the sniper's blind. She knew Mariam was readying herself, calibrating and recalibrating her rifle. Setting her father in its crosshairs and waiting fastidiously for the moment she'd take her shot.

"When I was a young boy in Senegal, I had little. Yeah? It is not an unusual story for us here. Am I right? I grew up watching Westerners come to our country and make profits that our people should have been making. And then when my family sent me to London, I learned that there was a world out there for the taking. I learned there was space enough for Africans to find their rightful place by the side of any first-world country.

"I thought, How dare anyone classify a country as first or third? Who are they to tell us where we stand? Who are we to allow it? To not raise our voice, put our foot down, and say no. I have just as much right—no, more right—to make profit, to thrive, to be comfortable off the fruits of my lands, than any foreigner who comes on our soil, claims ownership of our God-given rights, and then tries to make us ask them for what rightfully belongs to us. The only way we can make ourselves strong, make ourselves contenders, make ourselves be seen in a world that doesn't want to see us or people like us is if we are unified. Through One Africa."

The roar of applause was deafening, and by now Nena was nearly at the blind. Could see the backs of Mariam's legs as she lay in a prone position. Nena reached to pull one of her blades from its sheath, hidden between her pants and the skirt, as she advanced between the rows of red velvet chairs.

Noble was nearing the pinnacle of his speech; she knew the lines well, had overheard him rehearsing it in his office just days before. It hadn't been finished then. He'd said he liked to go off the cuff, and already the speech he was giving was not the same as what she'd heard earlier. But she knew he was almost done. Because he didn't like to prolong the speeches and use up time intended for revelry. Noble valued people's time too much. He was unlike many men in his position, encompassing compassion with a savvy business sense. When he said what he did was for the people, he truly meant it with every decision he made.

Her hand curved around the blade's handle and pulled it out. But she hadn't thought about the length of the skirt's train or the fabric and how it swished louder than expected as it rubbed against the chairs in the narrow space. Just like her bad decision to not bring a gun, opting for stealth. Kill Mariam quietly, with no one the wiser. She'd considered a silencer. But what if she'd shot just as Mariam's finger was on the trigger and the shot made her finger jerk? This wasn't like the training targets back in the Miami warehouse. Nena wouldn't take chances when it came to her father.

The swish of the dress sounded like a bullhorn, and the long skirt caught around her heeled feet. The heels, ones she'd worn before on missions and knew well, betrayed her, snagging on the hem of the skirt and ripping the fabric. She nearly stumbled before catching and righting herself.

Any other time, the mark would not have heard her above the booming voice of her father. But even James Bond made mistakes a time or two. Zigged when he should have zagged.

Nena was off her game tonight. Not at 100 percent. The stakes for this mission were much too high. They were intensely personal. And this mark was no ordinary mark. This one was a killer, like Nena. On a mission, like Nena. One who might not have Nena's experience or repertoire but had her drive. Had stakes just as high and wanted Noble Knight dead just as much as Nena wanted him alive.

Mariam's head jerked at the sound, but she didn't turn. It didn't matter who was behind her, because she had only one goal.

"And above all we must protect ourselves. This is the African Tribal Council's mission: to be the protector, the defender of all Africans."

Nena flung herself on Mariam just as the bullet left. It was a crack splintering through Noble's words. A gasp arose and glass shattered and someone screamed an earsplitting scream. It was a scream Nena knew. One of utter shock at the sight of someone they cared about being hurt. She knew it to be her mother's. And a scream like that, followed by a chorus of others, meant that Mariam had hit her target.

Pandemonium broke out below. There was screaming, but Nena couldn't make out who anymore or why. Because she was fighting for her life. Mariam pulled the gun from where it was propped up and swung it at Nena's head. It connected, and there was a flash in Nena's eyes as her head, already concussed from her previous encounters, took another hit.

Nena didn't let up; she swung at Mariam, her fist connecting with the woman's side, where her liver was. Nena scrambled to get to her knees and gain leverage over the writhing woman, but she couldn't get purchase. Her skirt was slippery. Her pants were too. And Mariam was at her full strength and mad as hell.

She kneed Nena in the ribs. Nena couldn't help it; she gasped. The breath sucked down into her windpipe, down into her gut, and wouldn't come back up. Her eyes blurred with tears. Mariam grabbed Nena's injured arm and squeezed. It was as if she knew exactly where all of Nena's hurts were and trained her attacks solely on those spots. Why couldn't she find new places to pick at? *That's right—there are none.* There was no inch on Nena that wasn't bruised, battered, or bloody.

Nena fought through the pain. They rolled against the chairs, toppling them over. Nena grabbed the leg of one, pulled it toward her, and lunged it at Mariam, who took half the hit and parried it away. But in the parry, she lost her grip on the rifle, and it toppled over the edge of the balcony. Nena flipped over, attempting to crawl away and give herself some space to gather herself and launch a different attack, but Mariam was on her, at her knees, pulling her backward. She tried to find her knife, clawed at her lower back for the remaining blade. The one she'd had in her hand earlier was long gone. She didn't know where or when.

Nena elbowed Mariam in the face, heard the grunt of the connection hitting home. Mariam released her hold, and Nena quickly crawled away. She grabbed onto a toppled chair, pulling herself up on shaky legs. Nena slipped out of her heels. Her hand curved around one of them, holding the heel outward as her new blade. She gripped it tighter.

"Nena."

There was a disturbance of air behind her, too close, and Nena turned to face Mariam. Nena's second blade was in the woman's hand, and Nena knew. This was it. Nena would be killed by her own knife. The irony.

Mariam raised the knife and swiped down in an arc. Nena stepped back, twisting away so it caught the back of her skirt and tore the fabric. Then she returned in a fluid sweep with the heel in hand, pointy part out and ready to impale. Mariam leaned back, surprised. The sharp heel scraped down the side of her body, not tearing, not impaling, not doing much of anything. It only served to irritate Mariam, and she grunted her annoyance.

Nena needed something with more power. She grabbed a broken chair leg and swung it like a bat, bringing it down on Mariam's weaponed hand. The blade dropped. Using both hands, Nena swung the chair leg up and around, like she was taking a golf swing. It caught Mariam in the stomach. She doubled over, clutching at it.

Nena didn't have even a second to take a breath as she charged for Mariam again, wanting close contact rather than fighting from afar, where there was room for the woman to pick up more weapons to use against her. Mariam caught Nena, her arms wrapping around Nena's torso as they toppled back to the floor, crashing onto more chairs.

The fall had to hurt. It hurt Nena, and she was on top. She could barely breathe. Her head felt as if it were splitting in two. Again, she scrambled to get to her knees and straddle Mariam atop the splintered chairs. She wrapped her hand around Mariam's neck and began to squeeze.

Mariam's eyes bulged. Her hands flew to Nena's, batting at them to release her. She curled her hands and clawed at Nena's injured arms, and without Nena's consent, her fingers betrayed her, disengaging from Mariam's neck. Mariam slammed a hand into the side of Nena's face and bucked Nena off her.

Nena thudded to the floor, dazed. Mariam was next to her, coughing, favoring the wrist that Nena had injured when she'd hit it, but she was better off than Nena was faring. Mariam stood. Looked down at Nena still trying to get her bearings, to shake the ringing out of her head. Mariam pulled her leg back and let it fly right into Nena's midsection. Into her ribs again. Nena made some muted sound, a cross between a groan and a cry. She couldn't roll into a ball fast enough before Mariam was kicking her again.

And again. This time in the back, the steel-toed boot hitting her in the spine.

Nena was positive Mariam was going to kick her to death as she lay on the floor with the woman grunting and snarling above her. Beneath the rubble of broken chairs and Mariam's equipment, Nena spied the handle of the blade she'd hit out of Mariam's hand. Needed to get the woman off her, away from her, to hit her, anything to make the kicking stop. Mariam brought her foot back, readying to kick again, but Nena kicked out first, pushing her into the typhoon of broken furniture they'd created.

Nena reached for the blade handle, the one she'd seen beneath the rubble, and pulled it to her, cradling it in her hand. Through a series of short breaths, she rolled herself to her knees, braced against the pain piercing her midsection, and got to unsteady feet. In front of her

Mariam was back on her feet and about to charge, her nostrils flaring, her mane of hair billowing around her, her fingers bent into claws, then into fists as she readied herself to finish Nena off. Nena did the same. The knife in her grip.

Mariam looked down, saw it, pausing to recalibrate. She was lunging when Nena parried, hitting her on the chin. Soft spot. Mariam bit down hard on her tongue, releasing her breath in a whoosh when it was knocked out of her. That and a mouthful of blood.

Nena was what stood between Mariam and the door, and Mariam knew she was not getting past Nena or the knife she held. But behind Nena, the door burst open, and suddenly they were no longer alone. Venue security pushed through the narrow door, flooding the balcony in a chorus of exclamations and commands to stop and put their hands up.

Mariam's hands were already up—but not empty. She spied a speaker amplifier and pulled it from its perch, chucking it at them. Nena's arms flew up, bracing for more pain. She quarter-turned to protect her head and allow her shoulder to absorb the impact. The amplifier hit her and whoever was behind her.

Mariam used the distraction to break into a run, pushing through security as if she were on some football field, the American kind, and rushing through a herd of players from the other team, trying to score a touchdown.

Nena tried to stop her, swiped at her with the blade as she rushed past, but Mariam shoved her into the clumsy group and got past. Nena relieved one of the guards of his sidearm and took off after her.

There wasn't enough space. The hall wasn't cleared. People were crossing and crisscrossing Nena's line of vision. She squinted through the slivers of spaces in between the moving bodies, trying to aim, fire, and hit her target before Mariam made it to the stairs.

Too many scurrying people. Too much screaming and chaos, making it hard for Nena to think. And the pain didn't help. She aimed the gun in the air, firing to clear the path. More screams, but this time the path cleared just enough for Nena to aim and fire again at Mariam's retreating back. But a blur of black and white bumped into Nena, sending her shot wild. Mariam ducked as the bullet sailed way over her head and the heads of everyone else, embedding itself in the burgundy-colored walls. Plaster rained down on Mariam, and she faltered at the first step, partly turning to chance a look behind her. The two made eye contact, and Nena advanced, not willing to take another shot with so many variables around her.

Mariam hesitated, and in her brief look Nena could tell she wanted the fight Nena would inevitably bring to her. But a gun superseded kicks, knives, and chair legs in any fight. And Mariam had always been good at math.

It was as if an argument raged within her. Her desire to stay and finish it, her certainty she could match and overpower Nena. Mariam was hurt, but Nena was hurt worse. And Nena's aim was off. She'd been moving slower all night, though she tried to pretend she was not.

At the end, Mariam's good sense won. She turned and flew down the carpeted steps, two at a time, her movements stiffened from the aftereffects of her balcony fight, pushing people out of her way, using their bodies as roadblocks to buy her time. The building was chaos when she reached the foot of the staircase, with guests and waitstaff blurring into a mass of bodies in gowns and suits. Security was locking the entrances down, trying to contain whoever had assassinated Noble Knight.

Mariam was already through the front doors before Nena started moving again. There was no time to think. No time to check if her father was okay or if the frenzied snatches of conversation she caught were true—that he was lying dead in the ballroom. If he was dead, she had all the more reason to make Mariam pay.

She heard a shot ahead of her. More screams. Yells for people to get out of the way.

Nena flew out the main doors, finding one of her security down on the other side. The holster of his sidearm empty and a hole in his chest. She looked up to see Mariam making a run, a hitch in her step, toward the valet stand deserted by the people who'd been working it an hour ago. Nena scanned for Witt, hoped he was with her dad and family. The venue grounds were filling with bewildered guests and guards trying to wrangle them. Mariam fired rounds into the air, making them clear her path. Creating chaos upon chaos to aid her getaway.

She turned, seeing Nena too close behind, and took a shot. But Nena was ready, easily ducking its trajectory. She returned fire, and when she heard Mariam cry out and saw her right leg buckle, Nena knew her shot was good. Mariam reached a sedan waiting in the drive, slamming into it hard. Her hand on the door handle of the passenger side.

Nena was almost there when she heard him.

"Nena! Don't!"

Somehow Keigel had followed her pursuit, was practically in lockstep with her, coming in at an angle as if he meant to intercept her as she advanced on Mariam's car, his tuxedo jacket flapping in the wind behind him. A stone of worry suddenly sat in her chest. She gave a quick shake of her head, hoping he'd get her silent message to back off. Her eyes slid to Mariam, who had the door open now. Her driver ready to move. But Mariam was no longer in a hurry. She favored her bleeding leg and made eye contact with Nena, a victorious smile playing on her lips. And Nena knew what Mariam meant to do next.

Nena slowed, changing course to head Keigel off while aiming her own weapon—she wasn't even sure how many rounds were left, hadn't counted what she'd fired, hadn't checked the gun that wasn't hers—at Mariam's head.

Time slowed, as if it took hours for Mariam to point that gun—not at Nena, as Mariam should have, but past Nena's shoulder—and fire.

48

"Brother. For brother. For brother," Mariam said, hanging half out of the passenger-side window, her arm lowering as the car began to pull away.

Nena reached Keigel as his body was falling to the ground. She had barely enough time to break his fall, throwing her hands out to catch him in the nick of time before his head made impact with the ground. His weight crushed her injured arm, but she barely felt it, thinking only of her unconscious friend who'd said he'd never leave her side, that he was in it with her. Nena called his name. Keigel couldn't hear. His eyes were closed, and his breathing was shallow. The white of his shirt blooming with the dark-crimson spread of his blood.

Keigel had taken a hit that should have been Nena's. But Mariam had purposefully used him as the distraction she needed to get away. What was he even doing out here? He'd promised her he'd stay by Elin's side and protect her—

"Nena," Witt called, a dark car pulling alongside her as she sat on the ground, half of Keigel's body cradled in her arms as if he were a baby.

"Keigel," she moaned. As if that would be enough to wake him.

"Nena."

She didn't—couldn't—leave Keigel, not as she had her father and brothers before. She didn't care what happened to anyone anymore.

"Are you not a wudini? Then act like it," Witt said sharply. "And do your job."

It was the second wind Nena needed. The reminder that she *was* the wudini and her work didn't end here.

Worry later. Work now. Feet pounded behind her. People to tend to Keigel, to watch over Elin and their mum. She wasn't even sure if her dad was okay or not. But she knew her work was not done.

There were hands on her shoulder. Someone calling for a doctor. Someone saying they needed to get her to hospital. She shrugged them off, gently placing Keigel's still body against the warmed earth. She used her hands to help push her to her feet. She turned to the person closest to her.

"You don't leave him alone for one moment," she commanded. "Make sure help comes."

"Yes, ma'am." It was a bellhop or server—someone in a crisp white uniform, nodding at her, his arms already reaching for Keigel's body.

She straightened, running to the door of the waiting car. Witt's foot was on the gas and the car moving before she got the door closed.

"I am going to fucking kill that bitch." Nena felt damn good saying it.

———

The sight of Keigel unconscious and bleeding out as Nena cradled him was all she could think about as shots rang from Mariam's gun. They pinged against the car, hitting the windshield, the back of the side mirror, the hood and grille as Witt swerved to deflect them. Nena flinched each time a bullet made contact, but the fear of being hit didn't stop her from reaching out her window and firing the remaining rounds at the weaving car as it raced ahead of Nena and Witt's car, going way too fast along the curvy two-lane road. Mariam shimmied back into the car.

"I'm out," Nena called to Witt, into the wind beating against her face.

"Where's the extra clip?"

"Not my gun."

She stuck her hand back in the car, leaving it there until Witt placed a fresh clip in it.

"There's nowhere she can hide now, Nena," he said. "We should turn back. We need to get things in order there, have Network locate her and dispatch her then."

Nena wouldn't turn back around now. Not with Mariam like a noose hanging over their heads. If they gave up the chase now, Mariam would be a ghost, forever haunting them, always elusive.

"Get us closer, Witt. We can't lose her."

"I'm the one who taught you how to give chase, remember? And there is a curve around here somewhere. It's bloody dark as hell."

There were no streetlamps to light their way, only their high beams bouncing off the terrain, kicking up dust. No moonlight to even help them discern road from the massive rocks out of which it had been carved. No sound except the two cars speeding faster than they should down a winding, narrow road with barely any shoulder on either side. Witt didn't dare try to move alongside the first car, knowing that if an approaching car appeared, they'd be done for. They'd drop straight off the cliff into a mass of brush and trees.

Witt might have had caution on his mind, but there'd been too many missed opportunities, and Nena couldn't let this be another. She drowned out the noise of the cars, squinted against the wind throwing grit in her eyes, and tried to get a better bead on her target in front of her. She fired off a series of shots, hitting the back window, the bumper, and then finally hearing a loud bang, like a big balloon exploding.

Mariam's car careened out of control and did a semispin as the driver fought to get it back. The back tire had exploded into pieces, and the smell of singed rubber permeated the air. Witt pressed the brakes carefully so they wouldn't spin out themselves and drove past the out-of-control car.

Nena threw herself inside, avoiding flying debris. They both watched in the rearview as brake lights flashed, heard the remaining three wheels and one rim squeal in protest and spin wildly over the loose dirt, which acted more like a sheet of ice, and saw Mariam's car cut a sharp left before dropping over the edge of the cliff and disappearing into the nothingness of the savanna-like terrain below.

There was no explosion when Mariam's car hit the ground, not like on TV. The cliff wasn't that high up. Just the sickening, heavy crunch of metal compacting on itself. Headlights bounced in the sky like spotlight beams from a nightclub. And then silence, like a thick quilt, settled over them. Witt pulled the car to a stop near the edge, and he and Nena got out.

They looked down at the wreckage, at the thicket of baobab trees whose branches had been sheared off by the car on its way down. The car rested upright at the base of a trunk. That was the most of what they could see from their height.

Witt moved first to begin the climb down. They didn't have to say a word, both knowing that in this line of work, there were no assumptions. A mission was never complete until the kill was confirmed.

49

The driver was dead. They found him ejected from the car. His eyes open, forever frozen in shock and fear. Mariam was grunting, using one arm to pull herself along the ground from the opened passenger side of the wrecked car. The other arm hung limply and at the wrong angle, trailing behind her. She was bloodied, badly hurt—maybe even fatally so. But she was still very much alive.

Mariam stopped when she noticed them. She stuck her good arm beneath her, pulling her gun, and pointed it at them. Her arm wobbled as if the weight of the gun was too heavy. She had barely any energy to keep it up long enough to get off a good shot. She aimed first at Nena. Then she shifted to Witt, who stood just behind Nena. Mariam's shoulder visibly sagged, the fight oozing out of her with her blood.

"Traitor," she coughed, her hand dropping, kicking up a plume of dirt. "You betrayed my brother, Marcel, and you betrayed me."

Of all the things Nena was, she wasn't that. "I betrayed no one."

"Who says . . . I'm talking . . . to you?"

The woman was out of her mind. Nena attributed her behavior to the last moments of a madwoman. "You are the one who dishonored your brother," Nena said. "Look to yourself."

Mariam spat a thick wad of bloody phlegm. "And maybe you should look deeper in your own house, honey. Think you know so much. How would I know where and when to hit? How would I know where to kill your Network operatives? Who could have told me that, hmm?"

The words were caustic, burning a hole through Nena as if they were droplets of acid, tunneling in deep until a sick and terrifying realization began to take hold. Understanding was a Mack truck mowing her over, reversing, then coming at her again. Nena moved as if underwater, turning to face the barrel of another gun, aimed not at Mariam.

At her.

"Witt?" Nena wasn't able to believe what she was seeing. She didn't want to entertain that what Mariam alluded to was true, even though her mentor was pointing a gun at her chest. Her mind could not compute what she was seeing with her own eyes.

Behind her, Mariam tittered. And then she coughed, something phlegmy. She was going to die, and it freed Mariam to enjoy the trauma she was inflicting on Nena. This was her last hurrah after all.

"You had one job," Witt growled, not at Nena but the broken woman on the ground. "And you screwed it up royally. You deviated from the plan."

"Your way no longer suited me, boss," Mariam said.

Boss. Like Nena would teasingly call him because the moniker annoyed him the most. Nena looked at him, then at Mariam. The woman was lying. Had to be because if Witt was Mariam's employer, as he was Nena's, it would be a betrayal worse than death, and Nena had already been through one of those. She wasn't sure if she was strong enough to go through another.

"Witt?"

He said nothing.

It was a singular ask, one curated after sixteen years of training and endurance, of mentoring and trust. Witt was family. He was as much family to Nena as her sister and parents, as the family she'd lost in N'nkakuwe. Witt had raised her as much as any of her parents had.

Taught her how to keep surviving. If not for Noble, Witt could have been a father to her. But even the ones Nena held the closest could betray her. Who could she trust if she couldn't trust family? The wound the realization made opened and grew, becoming a cavernous, festering maw Nena wasn't sure would ever close.

She tried to rationalize. "You couldn't have," she said. "You couldn't have betrayed . . ."

He scoffed. "Betrayed what? The family who took you in and made you one of them? Gave you all of this?" His free hand circled in the air. "Everyone believes the Knights are always righteous. That they could never betray. But they can, Nena. They ask for loyalty and do not return it."

Mariam's gritty laugh came from behind them. "The Lord giveth and the Lord taketh away. Or the Knights, I guess. I don't know."

"But why?" Nena's voice broke because boiling-hot rage was filling her, threatening to erupt like the volcano she was. "You are family, Witt. You are *my* family."

Nena hadn't thought there could be greater hurt than what she'd felt when Ofori had tried to kill her after learning she was his sister. This hurt more than that. At least with her brother, she knew he'd been twisted and manipulated by a vile man. At least with Ofori, he'd been her *before*. But with Witt, there was nothing but the present. There was nothing but her *after*.

Witt offered a tepid shrug, unable to speak for the emotion taking over. The hard demeanor that had defined him all these years, which he'd had seconds ago, one like a shark on the hunt, was cracking. His hand wavered, and the gun dropped from her face. It was still ready to fire, but now the urge seemed to have lessened.

Witt was conflicted, shifting from cool suppression to genuine sadness. His eyes implored Nena to understand. They shone in the darkness, and she saw him debating. She saw his regret.

"What will you do now, boss?" Mariam jeered. "Now that your most prized possession knows what you've done?"

"What have you done?" Nena forced herself to ask. Did she really want to know? Need to know? She already knew enough.

Witt hesitated, just barely. "You would not understand, Nena."

"Then make me."

He shook his head, disgusted. Broken. "I only wanted to right the cancer within the Tribe, to correct Noble's mistake and his impetuous decisions that are not for the good of the group. He leads with emotion, and he does not listen to logic. Your father is a great businessman and a poor soldier. When he gave the command to retire Goon, there was no honor in that. Goon was a good soldier. He was a good member of the Tribe. When it comes to his own people—to those who matter, like Goon—Noble treats them as expendable. But when it comes to people who might make the Tribe bigger and better, people who never give any of us Africans the time of day were it not for our bank accounts and stock options, your father can't do enough. He always wants to make friends with the wrong kind of people. We don't have time for friends. We have only ourselves, and history has proved there are people who would rather we be enslaved and indebted to them than be their equals. It's only a matter of time before it happens. So we get respect by force and by dollar."

Witt continued. "Noble turned away from his own values for the Tribe and the true vision of a One Africa. And what about the people who make that idea possible?"

Behind them, Mariam tutted disapprovingly, as if she was both disappointed and done with the whole thing. She wrangled herself to look Nena in her eyes, her look telling Nena all she needed to know. Mariam despised her. Nena doubted Mariam had ever truly meant for them to team up when she'd invited Nena to join their version of the Tribe. Mariam had only been curious about the girl who had taken her brother away. The girl in the gilded cage. The golden princess.

Witt snapped, "Is that why you blew up the plan? You were never supposed to take Nena hostage. You were never supposed to put either of them in danger."

"I didn't know you'd be there," Mariam said. "And I thought it would increase the panic if one of the sisters was abducted. Everyone would have taken us seriously."

"It was only supposed to be Noble."

"Yeah . . . well . . ."

"We would have turned the Tribe. Through the fear that it was already imploding, we could have turned it. I would have put you and your people in place, if only you had followed my instructions and not been so stupid."

He punctuated his words with the muzzle of his gun. Then he swung it in Mariam's direction.

"Please do it." She offered a bloody grin.

His finger moved to the trigger. His hand trembling. Then Witt yelled. It was loud and pained and full of rage and so much sadness and even more regret because there was only one way this thing was going to end.

Mariam mimicked him mockingly. "Spare me your sudden angst. You came to me, remember? You offered me the Tribe on a platter. Trained me up so I could be just as good as your golden girl here. And now, like her daddy did to my brother, you want to toss me out like trash. Like you did to my brother. Do it then," she said.

"Do it!" she screamed at him. "Do it, you lying bastard. Kill me because you have used me enough for your own purposes. I am done with you all."

He couldn't, wouldn't. Because Witt knew he was no more of the Tribe.

Nena took a chance then, backing away from Witt and toward Mariam. It was enough.

Mariam scoffed, "You people are ridiculous."

She moved her focus to Nena. Her eyes held no fear. No remorse. Nothing but righteous indignation and deep hatred for Nena. "You think you're some kind of he—"

A bullet in the middle of Mariam's face punctuated her thought.

The sound cracked the night's calm, the echo ricocheting off the canyons, causing a flutter of winged night animals to take flight. Mariam's head fell to the dirt with a thud. Beneath the deadweight, the ground began to darken with the steady trickle of blood.

Nena's gun hand fell to her side. Witt could shoot her in the back, and she wouldn't care. She'd had enough of that woman.

Witt said, "What is wrong with obtaining real pay from the highest bidder? And if Westerners and all the other continents wanted our resources, they could pay heftily for it too. I just needed someone to finance it and Mariam to begin building our mercenaries. Then the Tribe would be a true force to reckon with."

"The only thing you did was trade one ideology for another." She had turned to face him. "The thing about it, Witt, was that you are absolutely right."

Witt raised his brows, blinking back his surprise.

She continued. "You are right that the people who work for the Tribe should be as protected as those we help. You're right that Dispatch gives the ultimate sacrifice and never gets their true respect. We're feared, yes. But respected, no."

"Then you see," he breathed, his relief shining through.

"But," she said, "the way in which you set out to get Dispatch the respect and protection was wrong. You sacrificed many lives for something you could have just talked to my father about."

"Bah—you don't think I have tried?"

"Then you could have talked to me. You could have always talked to me. You sacrificed my team. You sacrificed Network operatives. How is that better than what my dad did to Goon? How have you honored your soldier?"

Her words hit him harder than any bullet could. He was bowled over from the pain of them, breathing rapidly—in and out—in a panic attack.

326

And then just as it had come upon him, Witt became serene. He nodded. Acceptance filling his face. "Then do what you must, Nena." Carefully, slowly, he held the gun muzzle up to show he meant no harm. He switched on the safety and let his hand drop to his side. His fingers released the weapon, and it fell into the dirt at his feet.

She pulled up to her full height. Indecision raked her. He looked at her expectantly, his eyes telling her to make her choice.

"This is the same decision I had to make for Goon," Witt said softly. "But I did my job."

As Nena had to do hers. Witt had trained her to mete out punishment as the Tribe decreed. There was no Tribe here, no Council. There was only Nena. Again. But this time, she wasn't in a place of revenge or self-defense. She was truly in the position, as a leader, to decide whether Witt lived or died. What kind of leader would she be? One who killed Witt for his beliefs? For becoming disillusioned when he thought her father had no loyalty to his people?

But then Nena thought of all the people who'd died in Witt's quest for righteousness and absolution. She thought of all the people he'd betrayed. Not just her. But Yankee, Charlie, Kilo. The operatives in Network's satellite office. The security detail who'd died during the attack at the Gabonese hotel. Or Keigel, who could be alive or dead as far as Nena knew.

If this all came out and the Tribe learned what Witt had done, it would destroy everything her father had worked for. It would destroy all the trust they'd been working to build. It would show the Westerners and other major players that the African Tribal Council couldn't take care of its own house and was therefore not worthy to join their ranks.

"For what it's worth, Nena," Witt said, "I am sorry."

But what if they went back to the dinner? No one would know but her and Witt. Those Council members would know, those in league with him. And to let them live would mean she was in league with them as well. They'd have something over her head. They'd have the tool with which to undo the Knights. Betrayal. Then she'd be no better than them. A liar and a traitor.

"It's worth everything," she answered.

Nena didn't think she had it in her to kill Witt as she'd killed her brother, to have his death on her conscience, always feeling guilty, always repenting and hating herself for having not afforded Ofori the benefit of the doubt that maybe he could change.

Though deep down she knew Ofori would have never changed. He'd been too far gone. Just as she knew now that Witt was too far gone. Had done too much.

Witt made the decision for her, giving her the briefest of nods. She saw his resolve and acceptance at what they both knew must be done.

"Do not carry this with you," he said. "And know, Nena, that the small part I played in who you have become is one of the greatest achievements of my career. It has been my honor to teach you. To be your mentor and work with you. To have been your friend."

"Not friend." She ignored the way her knees quivered. "Family."

Her throat was so raw it hurt more than what she suffered from her fight with Mariam.

Her eyes blurred, and she could barely see. Witt became nothing but a dark blotch in her vision. Her finger found the trigger of her gun. She sucked in a deep breath and then another while using her other hand to wipe furiously at the tears that betrayed her.

Witt was still watching with eyes that held every apology imaginable. Then Nena shot him.

As she watched him fall, one and only one wretched sob escaped. It was as if she were back in Paul's mansion, gazing over her brother's body after she'd killed him.

Nena walked over to the crumpled car and the assassin who'd marked her, checking Mariam's pockets until she found her cell phone. She moved on to the dead driver and tugged off his jacket, giving him one final appraisal. She'd leave those two for the Cleaners. Or the night scavengers. Whichever came first.

She took the jacket to Witt, each of her steps becoming heavier, like she was walking to her doom. She lingered by his side, knelt over his body, and touched the blossomed stain on his white shirt where she had shot him in the heart.

"You are retired," she whispered, touching his cheek. Then she laid the jacket over his face, the only way she could honor Witt in this moment.

Nena took his gun.

And began to make her way toward the rocky cliff they'd come down, her and Witt together, as they'd always been. Mentor and mentee. Now it was just her.

At the base of the cliff, Mariam's words stopped her.

You think you're some kind of . . . Nena completed Mariam's thought. *Hero.*

She cast a final look at Mariam. Then a longer one at Witt's covered body.

"In this story, there are no heroes."

50

The grounds were in chaos when Nena arrived, pulling off to the side of the road and walking as best she could up the curved drive to the front doors, where many Tribe security had suddenly converged. Sitting in the car during the ten-minute drive had already begun to tighten her muscles and opened a doorway to let the pain of her injuries flow right on in. She suppressed the urge to groan. To lie down on the pavement and just close her eyes for a moment. She forced herself on. She still had work to do.

When she reached the first line of security, they knew who she was. There was their lead, anxiously awaiting her arrival. He looked over her shoulder, expecting Witt to be behind her. She said nothing to him except to ask for his phone. With it, she made the call she'd never thought she'd have to make. She placed a call for the Cleaners, wherever they seemed to materialize from, to pick up three. One precious cargo to be held for special processing. The other two, the usual. The leader of the detail overheard her conversation, his eyes rounding as he began to comprehend her words. He looked away, then down. He'd been wearing a hat. One advertising his favorite soccer team from his country. He took it off, wringing it between his hands.

"What is your name?"

He met her eyes, and the wetness in his melted her, just a little. "Samson."

"We work now. We grieve later, Samson."

He nodded, pulling his shoulders back and standing at attention, ready to work.

"The American?" she asked, her voice affectless, sounding alien even to her. "The one who was with my family. What is his condition?"

Samson followed her as she entered the building. It was loud with people wandering all over, confused, afraid because they weren't allowed to leave. "They took him inside to triage. His condition is unknown."

"And my father?"

"I'm not sure, ma'am. Your sister and mum are sequestered with him in a secure room in the building. The remaining Council members are confined in the boardroom, where they are . . ." He trailed off.

She raised an eyebrow for him to go on, though she already had an idea of what was happening behind closed doors.

His voice lowered a register, the words coming out as if they pained him to say. "They're voting in your father's replacement."

Her eyes narrowed as she located the double doors to the boardroom. "Even though no one knows if he lives or not?" They were nearing those doors now.

"Shall I take you to your family?"

Nena wanted very much to see them and make sure her father was well. She yearned to check on Keigel, too, but there were more pressing issues. There was still work to be done. Seeing to the Council, who'd been left to their own devices with no Noble or Delphine to keep them in line. And the ones who'd consorted with Mariam would be awaiting confirmation of Noble Knight's death before transferring the rest of her money to her offshore accounts. At least according to the text messages on Mariam's phone. Nena had scrolled through it while sitting in the car, trying not to think about who she'd left at the bottom of the cliff and the explanation she'd give for why he was there.

She studied the guests, the security milling in and out, wondering if any of Mariam's people were mixed in with the lot. Likely not. There'd been no need of her soldiers tonight. Only Witt to get Mariam inside and Mariam to take Noble out. They'd learn soon enough that their leader was dead. Then they'd scatter to the winds until maybe Nena found them, one day.

Nena said, "Let the guests leave and let the authorities enter when they arrive. We'll tell them the truth. There was an assassination attempt. And there were several casualties as a result." She paused. "Thank you, Samson."

"And the perpetrator?"

She didn't answer. She was already entering the boardroom. She steeled herself to face everyone and answer how she'd come to return alone.

———

The room was in commotion when Nena slipped in. Council members were congregated around the rectangular table, and at its head, Councilmen Godwin and Bartholomew were heavily engaged in their speeches to the nine remaining members—nine because Elin was with their father and Noble made thirteen as the High Council, the tiebreaker.

Nena said nothing, quietly closing the doors behind her so she wouldn't disturb their discussion, so she could make her assessments now that they believed her father to be incapacitated again.

"We should wait," Councilwoman Felicity said, interrupting the back-and-forth between Godwin and Bartholomew. "We do not need to change leadership now. There is too much commotion."

"Which is exactly why we need to do it now," Godwin argued. "The Tribe must continue. It is what Noble would have wanted."

"You speak as if you know his fate already. You speak as if you want High Council," Felicity answered, looking at the hook-nosed man shrewdly. "Be careful what you wish for, Godwin."

"It is bad juju to assume a man is dead before we hear word," another member said. Nena couldn't recall her name now, but she'd always been kind when they'd spoken. She had gentle eyes. That was what Mum would say.

"Good thing we deal in business and not superstition," Godwin quipped.

They returned to the matter at hand, arguing back and forth, their voices rising into a crescendo as they argued next steps and who would assume leadership.

"Should be Elin, by right." Nena spoke up, pushing herself off the wall she'd been leaning against. The room quieted. "Elin is a Knight. She's on the Council. She's not incapacitated."

Godwin glowered at her. "The killer. Isn't there someone to go dispatch?" He spoke as if she were beneath him, and maybe she was, but she advanced on him anyway, determined to be heard, to finish out what they'd planned in order to uncover who was complicit.

"Elin is with child," Bartholomew announced. "She's probably having the baby now."

"Doesn't make her incapable of leading."

"Well, she's not here, so we proceed with the vote. I nominate myself," Godwin said.

"I think Councilwoman Felicity would do well," another member quietly suggested, ignoring the glowering stares and angry rumblings of the male members. The idea of a woman, any woman, assuming High Council was incomprehensible to a group of men so firmly entrenched in misogynistic societal beliefs.

"You can't change leadership until you know for sure my father is dead," Nena reminded them. "Those are Tribe rules. You can't change them just because you feel like it. And there is also my mother, who can lead in his stead, as she did when he was in hospital from the poisoning."

Godwin said through gritted teeth, "We are the Council, girl, not you. You are not permitted to speak on Council matters. And for all we know, your family is compromised. With multiple attempts on each of your lives—save your mother's, God bless her—you all are marked people. Cursed."

He narrowed his eyes at her. "And you're not even a Knight by blood. You're some little urchin they found on the street and brought home like a pet. And you run their errands like one too."

She straightened. Her fingers itching for her blades, to put one between his eyes.

"You have no business here, girl." He focused on the rest of the group; Nena was no longer worth his time or effort. She was an underling. An employee. Even if her name was Knight.

"We proceed because if we don't, if we continue to let the Tribe go without leadership, there will be chaos. Our business partners will lose faith in us. The communities we help will be in disarray. We open all the channels of goodwill we've established to be overrun with rebels and criminals. We must have stability. Our very existence, our legacy, depends on it. We must show the world this minor disruption does not diminish us, because that is what the world wants to see, our doubters— they want to see the African Tribal Council fail. They want to see these Africans who reach too far scurry back into the bushes like good little bush people. We are not that."

It was a good speech, Nena had to admit. The last bit especially. Godwin told no lies there. The Tribe would have a spotlight beaming down on them. The world would wait for them to fail so it could steal back all the Tribe had worked and fought tirelessly to reclaim. But it was time for Nena to make her own decree. From Mariam's phone, she opened the text chain and typed her message.

Godwin's phone buzzed in his pocket, and he reached for it, pulling out his burner in front of everyone, thinking no one was the wiser. The audacity. Nena watched as he read the message, a wide smile spreading on his face. He moved differently now, more assuredly, knowing his greatest competition was removed.

He responded while the others continued their discussion without him, and his message returned in seconds. **Very good. Will deposit funds shortly. Stand by.**

The phone was a bomb in Nena's hands, and if she could kill Godwin dead this very moment, she would. But she needed to let this play out.

Godwin's speech had done what he'd intended. It had pushed the remaining holdouts, the ones on the threshold of trying to decide if they should move forward and vote in a new High Council or if they should wait, as Tribe laws dictated, for confirmation that Noble was dead or that Elin or Delphine would decline to assume his position.

The applause when Godwin was voted in was tepid, more boisterous from his man Bartholomew, but that was to be expected. Godwin motioned for everyone to be seated, and when they'd finally settled, he prepared to give his acceptance speech. He'd probably practiced reciting it over and over in his mirror's reflection. Nena watched as Councilwoman Felicity and the other members sat uneasily, concern evident on their faces about what this meant for the Tribe now.

"What we do is for our people," Godwin drilled in. "We put the Tribe first, always, even though we grieve for Noble and we pray for his family. It is what Noble would have wanted. He is who we honor by continuing in his absence. And with new leadership in place, I will continue Noble's legacy to make the Tribe strong and feared."

Fear was never what Noble had wanted.

"We will prosper under a new plan," Godwin said. "We will ensure we are properly compensated for what we do for Africans."

Felicity turned to her neighbor. "Ah, but what does that mean? Properly compensated?" The response she received was a shrug.

"Our protection. Our resources. Our holdings must come with stipulations for us to survive and thrive like Noble has always wanted."

"What is this 'stipulations' and 'properly compensated'?" a member asked. He was older than her father, hair snow white, cane at his side.

Felicity tutted. "What is this nonsense you speak of, Godwin? You are only High Council not five minutes, and you speak of change that sounds like—what is it I'm thinking of? Help me."

"Pay for play," Noble said from behind them. "That is what our good brother Godwin is getting at."

As Nena had done, the rest of her family had slipped in without being noticed by the Council. They'd come in through a side door, Noble first, followed by Delphine and Elin. Nena nearly took a step toward her family. The relief she felt at seeing them, alive and okay, was overwhelming. Her father's arm was bandaged and in a sling. Her sister held a laptop. Her mother stood between them, always the strength from which the family drew theirs.

The room was in an uproar at seeing Noble alive. Everyone began speaking at once, with no one understanding anything. The Adam's apple in Godwin's throat moved up and down as he stared at Noble and understood that his time as High Council had ended as quickly as he had been voted in. His plan, the one he'd thought perfectly executed, was dissolving right in front of him.

As quickly as the shock had hit him, Godwin was spinning a new story, shedding another layer like the snake he was.

"God is good, Noble, you live! Praise be to him! This is wonderful," Godwin began, taking on a salesman's tone. "The Council voted me in so I could ensure things kept running until you and the family were able to assume the role. I was merely reaffirming the Tribe's key mission. We are so blessed that you are returned."

Noble feigned surprise, moving away from his wife's side. Nena moved up as well, her eyes roving from person to person, always going back to Godwin. To Bartholomew. She remained on high alert. She pulled out Mariam's phone.

"I've returned?" Noble said. "I never left. Though you would have wished it so."

Godwin tried to smile, inching away from the table. "Not so, Noble. Did the bullet penetrate your head as well? I am your man."

"And yet you have conspired to usurp my authority. To take my seat. To embezzle from the Tribe and sabotage it."

Again, the Council members began grumbling, asking for explanations. Their confusion was distracting, and it was what Godwin hoped for so he could talk his way out.

"This is ridiculous. I was one of the first Council members on the Tribe. Just after Mr. Epsom there." He pointed at the snow-haired man with the cane. "Is he conspiring against you too? Are you mad?"

"No, Godwin, only you conspire. Only you funded the plot to turn the Tribe into one of mercenaries. Only you have been paying the assassin who was to kill me and put in her people to help you take over."

Godwin was emphatically shaking his head. He looked to the other Council members as if Noble had lost his mind, as if they'd known him all this time and couldn't possibly believe Noble's claims.

"Not so. I have been your biggest advocate."

Lies. They all knew it. Wasn't Godwin the one who, at the emergency meeting, had claimed the Knights were taking people out for their own personal gain?

Godwin said, "It hurts me that you speak of me this way when I have given you no reason to doubt my loyalty."

Elin stepped forward, laptop in hand, and placed it on the table. "Financials. Dummy corporations and transactions that lead to you, Godwin. You've been embezzling funds from the Tribe and funneling them to a group of mercenaries headed by the woman who tried to kill my dad."

Godwin blustered. "Foolishness. Those corporations, the money you speak of could be anyone's."

"And you've just confirmed my dad's kill and your payment through text with the assassin."

Nena tossed Mariam's phone onto the table. It slid halfway toward the middle. Godwin looked at it, confused, and then as if a bomb were about to explode in his face. One of the Council members reached for it, using a finger to slide it toward them, peeking at the messages Nena referred to.

Felicity leaned over to look, and then her eyes lifted to Godwin. "Explain this, Godwin."

"A text proves nothing."

"Then let us see your phone. That one there in your hand that you just used," Felicity said.

Beside him, Bartholomew said, "Is this true, Godwin? Have you been conspiring against the Tribe?"

Godwin stared at the shorter man incredulously. "What?"

But Bartholomew didn't listen. Instead, he rushed at Godwin, the move surprising Godwin enough that Bartholomew was able to wrestle the phone from his hands. He brandished it above his head.

"She is correct. The message is here as she says," Bartholomew announced eagerly, while Godwin stood beside him in abject surprise and confusion.

"Now wait—" Godwin blustered. He lunged at Bartholomew.

However, his attack stopped before it had a chance to begin because Nena fired a round, hitting Bartholomew in the head. He crumpled to the floor against a chorus of screams. One down.

Godwin looked at her. "Wait a minute. It wasn't me. It wasn't my idea. It was W—"

A bullet in his head silenced him too.

"Dear God, child, they are Council members. We don't dispatch Council without decree!" Felicity said as they all looked to Nena, horrified at what she'd done, at the consequences she'd doled out without the Council's sanction.

"It is my father's decree," Nena answered calmly, lowering her arm. If only they knew. Tonight, she was handing out decrees left and right. These people really didn't want to try her.

She removed the clip, unchambered the next round, and dropped the gun on the table.

"I need a moment to think," she told her father. He touched her cheek and held her gaze. He tried to read what was behind her eyes, and when she offered him nothing further, he released her.

For now, the revelation that Witt had orchestrated all of this—the man who, above all, like Noble, was supposed to be beyond reproach—was known only to her.

If that information had been uttered here, it would indeed have toppled the house that Noble built forever.

51

A week after the charity dinner and the women's and children's center groundbreaking ceremony that had followed, Nena was holding a
swaddled little baby boy in the same Miami hospital that had cared for
Noble when Paul had poisoned him. She was sitting in a chair, looking
down at the boy, who looked back with one eye. The other was closed.
He held one of her fingers with all five of his little ones. And he caused
a peace within her that Nena hadn't known could exist.

She regulated her breathing to keep from getting emotional. The
last months had been a roller coaster of emotions that she wasn't sure
she'd fully dealt with. There had been so much death, so much betrayal,
so much pain and loss. The greatest loss was Witt.

The guilt of what Witt had done—why he'd felt driven to do it—
was a heavy burden on Noble. He couldn't comprehend how he'd had
no inkling of Witt's deception. He felt like a fool to have put his complete trust in Witt. To have believed him to be like a brother.

Noble hadn't missed anything. And he was right to feel for Witt as
he did. Witt's expertise had been in deception and evasion. Witt had
been Network. And now . . . Nena supposed . . . *she* was Network.

But right now, in this moment, Nena was celebrating new life. And
that new life was her nephew Michael Asym Knight's. Nena breathed
in the scent of him. It was all she could do whenever she thought of his

name. The name she had been born with. The name of the grandfather who little Asym, because that's what Nena would call him, would never know. Elin had honored Nena by continuing the legacy of the Asyms through her son, unifying Nena's *before* and her *after*. Binding Nena to the Knights forever by blood.

It was the greatest gift anyone could ever give Nena, she thought as she sniffed his newborn smell. She could sit in this uncomfortable hospital chair forever and hold this boy. He made the uncomfortable piece of furniture feel less so. He even made it easier to tolerate Elin's whining. She was not the best patient, and Nena was sure the nurses couldn't wait to discharge her.

Delphine and Noble were arguing with Elin about who would be allowed to stay at the condo with her. About purchasing a house because the condo, with its twenty-four thousand plus square feet, was still too small for their grandson. First-world problems, Nena thought. But she didn't fault them one bit. After all they'd been through and were now still going through to ensure there were no other defectors on the Council and in the Tribe, Nena's parents were allowed a couple of first-world problems.

And Elin should already know there was no getting rid of Delphine with the baby here. At least Noble had to return to work and prepare for the Tribe's next endeavors, the potential announcement of making the African Tribal Council's IPO public, and solidifying their place as stakeholders in the world.

But Delphine was all for Elin. She was an African parent, after all, and when African parents became grandparents, their children would be lucky if they didn't live with them for the entire first year. Whether or not Elin wanted to believe it, Delphine would now be a Miami resident. Indefinitely. Nena kind of liked it, but she wasn't going to share that with Elin anytime soon.

"Nena," Elin called from the bed. "You have no thoughts? Tell Mum you and me can handle the baby and she can get on."

Nena only smiled and buried her nose in the nape of the seven-pound, fourteen-ounce Asym, who she'd moved onto her chest to sleep peacefully. Even Asym knew to stay out of the fray.

"Uh-uh. We're just hanging out over here. Carry on, on your own."

Elin glared at her. "Traitor."

Yes. Nena absolutely was. Happily, in this case.

But eventually she left her bickering family, taking the elevator down a couple of floors to where Keigel was preparing for his discharge after his own stint in hospital. Her family had seen to it he was transferred here from abroad because Keigel was now family to them too.

Nena had been visiting every day, and when Elin had gone into labor (which had gone so fast she hadn't gotten the good drugs she'd been looking forward to her entire pregnancy), Nena had suddenly had three reasons to stay at the hospital.

She knocked on the open hospital door. "Ready?"

Keigel had Nena beat in the bandages department, having taken a bullet to the chest. They were lucky a doctor had been on the premises the night of the dinner and had been able to stabilize him until the medics could arrive. The infection he'd developed afterward, which had prolonged his care, had been worrisome. But Keigel had survived that, too, and was now ready to get home to their neighborhood and see his crew, whom he'd been missing for longer than any of them had expected.

"They won't let me leave walking," he groused, gesturing to the wheelchair and the attendant standing beside it.

"Them's the rules," Nena joked.

Keigel jerked. "Babies do wonders for you, girl. I think you told a damn joke."

She shrugged. Asym did have a little to do with it. Or maybe it was the knowledge that once she dropped Keigel off at home, she planned to head straight to the Baxters'—and to Cort.

343

"Do you mind . . . ?" she asked the attendant when Keigel had settled himself in the chair, his duffel bag on his lap, along with a plastic hospital bag carrying the huge plastic water jug and slip-proof socks Keigel refused to leave without. He'd even managed to snag an extra pair.

"Elin and lil man doing okay?" Keigel asked when Nena began wheeling him toward the door. It was a little hard; she herself was still healing from the injuries she'd suffered, but she wasn't going to let that prevent her from being by Keigel's side as he'd been for her.

"They are perfect," Nena answered. "You'll help me bring them home day after tomorrow?"

"No doubt." The moment Elin had gotten the all clear, Keigel had asked to Zoom in with her and Asym. More Asym than Elin, to be honest. Delphine had told Elin to get used to no longer being the center of attention. Nena didn't know how well Elin would take to that.

"What we about to get into?" Keigel asked when they were on the freeway heading toward their neck of the woods. "I know you about to get me some lemon-pepper wings because it's been a hot minute since we had some. You know that's just what the doctor ordered."

Nena flicked on her signal light, indicating they were about to get off the ramp. "Pretty sure the doctor said you needed to lay off salt and that your cholesterol was too high."

Keigel waved her off. "That's complete bullshit. The man has something against wings. I'm not sure what it is, but he should lose his license for saying such horrible things. Plus his job was to treat an infection, not check my fuckin' cholesterol." He gave her a hopeful look. "We're hitting the spot, right? Wings?"

Of course they did. Nena loaded him down. They'd deal with his cholesterol tomorrow. Tonight they'd celebrate making it home safe and mostly intact. They'd been through a lot. They had gotten even closer than Nena had believed possible. And she'd found a brother for life.

Nena sneaked frequent looks at Keigel while he entertained his crew with stories about Ghana's hottest club, the market where he and Georgia had experienced the best of Ghanaian cuisine, and of course the shoot-out at the charity dinner. She'd been wrong to think there were no heroes when Keigel was very much one.

Jury was still out on her.

When he was settled, Nena made Keigel promise he'd take his medication and would not leave to drive through his territories. She kept from him that a letter had appeared in her mailbox that day, addressed to her, in Witt's handwriting. Of course Witt would opt for old school and not electronic. However, Nena wasn't ready for what was in it or ready to think about Witt right now.

"At least wait until tomorrow to check on things," Nena offered, to which Keigel unhappily agreed. She tucked thoughts of Witt's looming letter in a compartment deep inside and locked it.

With Keigel taken care of, her parents at their hotel, and Elin and baby Asym safe in the hospital with security around, it was time for Nena to put herself first. Something she had held off on since returning home. It was late, nearly ten, by the time she rolled onto the Baxters' street. She slowed her Audi just before reaching their driveway and let her car idle for a few moments.

She took several cleansing breaths, trying to regulate her rapid heartbeats. She wasn't going to lie; she was nervous. But she was excited as well . . . she thought. She'd already second-guessed herself all day, and her nerves only triplicated as the time drew near. She hadn't even told Cort she was coming over just in case something came up or she changed her mind.

More than a couple of times, Nena considered turning the car around and going home. Cort would be none the wiser. But in Ghana, Nena had decided that she would make a change, that she needed to make some changes to move forward, to grow. She shifted into drive and pulled forward, turning to park behind his car, the electric-blue SS winking at her in the moonlight as if it knew why she was there.

She pulled her overnight bag from her car's trunk and faced the front door of the house. Her thumbs grazed the tips of her fingers, her nervous tic, as she battled a bout of insecurity and doubt. The second-guessing again. She refused to repeat her and Cort's night at the hotel room.

She pushed through, marching up the three steps of his porch and to the door, where she rang the doorbell. Her chest was tight with rising panic and the idea that there was no going back. She should have called. She hated when people dropped in on her unexpectedly. It was a firm rule for her. And yet here she was, doing the thing that annoyed her the most. But if she hadn't, if she had told him she planned to come, she wouldn't have. She would have made excuses.

When Cort opened the door, she would not leave. She would not back out. She'd have to go forth. And if she was going to run, if she was going to bow out and hide, now would be the time, before he—

The door opened.

Cort stood on the other side of it. The first reaction was always telling, and his was surprise, pleasant surprise. Happy surprise that she was there. He was smiling at her, genuinely happy. There was nothing in his eyes but joy. And that joy began to melt away the anxiety and insecurity and abject fear that had been driving Nena whenever they neared intimacy.

Something else washed over her in its place. Something warm and not a little excited. She took in his sweats with no shirt to hide the healing scar from when he'd been shot earlier that year, and rippling abs Nena remembered so very well.

It was her turn to bite her bottom lip, suck it in to keep herself from saying something stupid when the only word screaming over and over in her mind was *damn!*

"Is Georgia in bed?" was the first thing she asked, even before Cort could speak. It came out breathy and low. Didn't sound like her, which was surprising and not unpleasant. It renewed the courage she'd thought nonexistent.

Cort was slow to get her meaning. He blinked. Blinked again and once more. Then his head jerked back, and a slow smile crept over his face. He stood there, studying her studying him, a silent question from him to her being asked. A silent response from her to him being given.

"Yeah." The word hung in the air. "She's asleep."

His smile was infused with something more. Became hungry and hot as hell. He stepped from the door, extending his hand beyond the threshold.

Nena took his hand in hers. Then stepped through the doorway into Cort's home, with not an anxious thought or worry within her. Only something just as hot and hungry as the way Cort was looking at her. He pulled her to him, until their bodies connected and there was nothing separating them but clothing. Their lips were practically touching, their noses nuzzling, the heat between them rising as Cort took a step with Nena toward his bedroom.

Letting the front door close behind them.

ACKNOWLEDGMENTS

To my Tribe, who continue to amaze me with their own achievements . . . my family: kids, husband, mom, siblings, in-laws, and close friends, thank you for continuing to hold me down and lift me up when I think I may fall. The kids and my husband have been especially giving and understanding of their time with me, especially when deadlines loom. I'm going to work on doing better with time management.

Thank you to Melissa Edwards, my agent and friend. You already know how I feel about you, which is love and admiration always.

To Paula Benson, who I met at my first meeting of the Palmetto chapter of Sisters in Crime. Paula has become such a close friend. She's an amazing writer, and I can't wait for you to read her first novel soon. I am blessed to have her as a true friend.

My amazing editor, Megha Parekh, who trusts my process and my ideas. She champions Nena Knight and me at every turn.

To Caitlin Alexander, my developmental editor, who catches the plot holes and helps me bury the literary bodies (there are no real ones, okay?!?!). And the rest of the Thomas & Mercer team: Grace Doyle, executive director, for always being the best cheerleader. Her emails and tweets are everything! Rachael Herbert, my production manager, and Riam Griswold, my copyeditor extraordinaire. Riam's worked with me on both books and is a rock star with catching stuff I've completely forgotten I wrote. Thanks for keeping me and all of this story straight! And to Alicia Lea, who proofread, catching my flubs, and everyone else on the production team who helped get this book into tip-top shape, I appreciate you!

Thanks to the publicity duo Megan Beatie and Brittany Russell, who landed me great interviews, allowing me to meet even more great people for the book launch.

And to the entire Amazon Publishing marketing team, who got Nena on a billboard in Times Square for New Year's Eve, blowing my mind. Andrew George and Sarah Shaw (client relations), whose promos, commercials, and ads put Nena out there in ways I never expected.

To my writing friends, critique partners, chat groups, and organizations where I have forged friendships I hope last a lifetime in Crime Writers of Color and Sisters in Crime. You all keep me rolling and learning in these hard publishing streets. I am your biggest fan, real talk.

I must correct a mistake I came across after the first book had been published. I realized I had misspelled a name, so I must make amends to S. A. Cosby, who graciously said it was okay. It's not. Thank you, Shawn, for being cool as hell.

Thanks to Calvernetta and Randy Brown, my go-tos for weapon and law enforcement talk, and to Deirdre Edwards, who excitedly talks martial arts with me and explains all the moves I wish I could do, so I give them to Nena.

When *Her Name Is Knight* was published, I had no idea how it would be received. I knew I loved Nena's story, and people on my team whom I expected to say good things loved it too. But I never dreamed my Ghanaian girl who loves lemon-pepper wings and, yes, happens to kill for a living but has an unfathomable love for family would ever get the kind of love she's received.

I put my heart and mind out there for everyone and am so thankful to all the podcasters, journalists, bloggers, bookstagrammers, magazines, and media for your coverage and for being so welcoming to Nena and me, for getting what her story is about.

Thanks to all the readers who chose to read my book. To the book clubs for the talks and deep dives that make me, and my Black characters, feel seen and valued.

To the independent bookstores and owners who put my book on their shelves and who support and highlight authors, especially authors of color. You all are the realest!

And . . . if I didn't have a chance to mention you here, I haven't forgotten you in my heart. Thank YOU!

—Yasmin

ABOUT THE AUTHOR

Photo © 2021 Rodney Williams, Creative Images Photography

Yasmin Angoe is the author of *Her Name Is Knight* and a first-generation Ghanaian American currently residing in South Carolina with her family. She's served in education for nearly twenty years and works as a developmental editor. Yasmin received the 2020 Eleanor Taylor Bland Crime Fiction Writers of Color Award from Sisters in Crime, of which she is a member. She is also a proud member of numerous crime, mystery, and thriller organizations like Crime Writers of Color and International Thriller Writers. You can find her at https://yasminangoe.com, on Twitter at @yasawriter, and on Instagram at @author_yas.